Thunder O Dragon

Dragon Fires Rising

Book 3

MARC SECCHIA

Copyright © 2021 Marc Secchia

All rights reserved. This book or any portion thereof may not be reproduced or used in any manner whatsoever without the express written permission of the publisher and author except for the use of brief quotations in a book review.

www.marcsecchia.com

Cover Art By:

www.bookcoverzone.com

Interior Dragon Images:

www.freepik.com

ISBN: 9798540013130

THUNDER O DRAGON

"My rage shakes the portals of fate."

CONTENTS

	Map of Solixambria	vii
1	Thundersong	1
2	Scaring Kings	13
3	Having a Ball	28
4	Dragon Chef	43
5	Migration	59
6	Second Migration	74
7	Cultural Surprise	88
8	Hamirythe	106
9	Warrior Power	120
10	To the Mountains	133
11	Breakdown	146
12	Terror Effect	159
13	Great Grinder	176
14	Taking the Camp	191
15	Flying Sprint	204
16	Oddly Pleasing	220
17	Ignita's Roar	233

THUNDER O DRAGON

18	In a Flap	250
19	Into the Fire	265
20	Snoozing off to War	280
21	Beneath the Desert	296
22	Sands Arise	313
23	Siege	327
24	Night Terrors	340
25	Quicksand	356
26	Water Sniffer	371
27	What a Plot	384
28	War Host	402
29	Zapped	417
30	Together, We Rise	433
31	Epilogue	449
	About the Author	461

THUNDER O DRAGON

MAP OF SOLIXAMBRIA

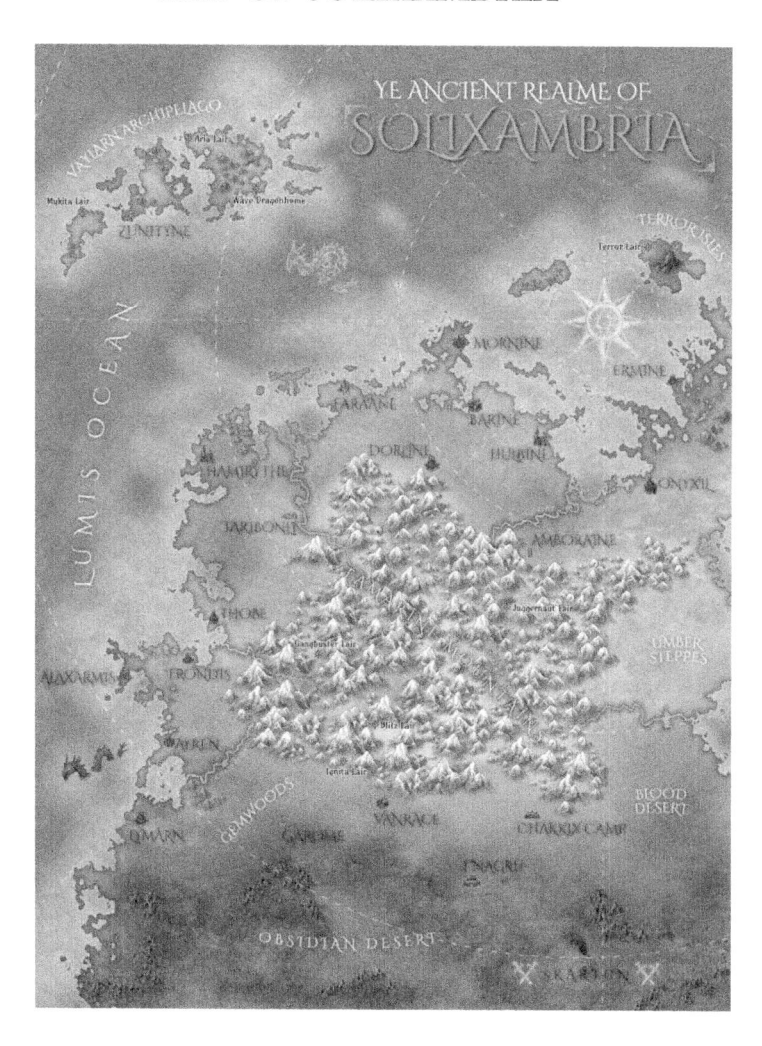

CHAPTER 1

THUNDERSONG

DRAGONS DID NOT APPRECIATE being called small. Nor puny. Most noble fire-breathers would be enraged, wounded and depressed to field sobriquets such as tiny or diminutive. Not so much his Princess. She was tiny, in truth. Knee-high to a grasshopper. Aria Seaspray? Also petite, but lethal in ways so innumerable, even an attempt at counting said ways was likely to end in a fatality.

For his part, he had always been the overlarge, over-awkward relative lurking at the back of the lair.

Aye, smallness was relative, but … tiddler?

Tiddler?

A Dragon did not know whether to be insulted or fall over laughing.

"Thunder-minnow," he grumbled to himself. "Storm-tiddler. Gargantuan white guppy paddling in puddles, never mind the actual ocean. Aye, how the mighty paws have shrunk in the proverbial wash – good morning, Princess."

By way of greeting, she kicked him firmly in the lower lip.

"Ouch?" he growled.

"Good morning to you too, *Thunder*song."

One could only be dazzled by such sweet brutality.

What were friends for?

"I know," he groused. "Vast paws to – ouch! Woke up with a nasty scale rash this morning, did we? Ouch again. Alright, alright! Enough of the conversational punctuation with your foot. What is this?"

She smiled the smile of a cobra eyeing up a mouse.

"Understood," he purred, wondering how under the suns it was possible for a diminutive morsel of a black Princess to make a Dragon feel like scuttling back into his lair, tucking his tail in behind him and not emerging from hibernation for a hundred years.

"Do you?" she inquired archly.

"Do I what?"

"Understand."

He eyeballed her doubtfully. Devious creatures, females. Complex, contrary and cunning. Like smelling a posy of gorgeous blossoms only to discover that they pricked like a porcupine with a severe case of haemorrhoids.

"Of course I understand," he lied heartily.

The Princess of T'nagru, who went by the title of the Black Rose of the Desert and attracted adoration from Human males like nectar attracted bees, could produce a sceptical frown to out-glower a passing thunderhead. Right now, that little crease between her brows threatened gale-force winds, accompanied by hailstones the size of her clenched fists, and widespread environmental devastation.

Hint given, hint taken.

He said, "I'm sorry. Was I projecting again?"

"Merely pouring the contents of a cesspit into my ear," she said pithily.

"I apologise."

After a moment, a tiny dark hand moved to stroke his muzzle, near his left eye. That was a bit of a reach for a four-foot-eight waif – concentrated royalty, one might suggest – but she managed, scrunching her bare toes into the perfect white beach sand meantime.

"My friend, we need to have a talk about your self-talk," she said. "It's clear to me that no-one and no creature is harder on you than you are on yourself."

"Benefits of our telepathic connection?"

"Aye. Dragon, I *hear* your thoughts. Often. And before you stalk off in a steaming huff, thinking it isn't pretty or nice in there, I appreciate that you get the very best of me, too." Her wry sarcasm made him grin briefly. "Shall we make a deal?"

"Snap out of it or my lip gets another bruise?"

"Every time."

"What about when you start, Princess?"

Her left eyebrow twitched perilously. "Aye?"

"I'll have King Azerim nibble your lip."

"*Dragon!*"

"Just a minute ago, someone was trying to convince me that I'm actually a Thundersong," he grinned, deciding that the morn had just taken a turn for the better. After all, even the most thunderous tiddlers must meet certain stereotypes by paddling in life's shallows. "Sounds like quite the beast, that Dragon."

"Habit." With a wink, she added, "Your namesake's right behind you."

"Stop tugging my wings. No Dragon that humungous could possibly –"

"SNEAK UP ON YOU?"

"Aargh!" He very nearly leaped out of his sparkling new white hide with its dramatic golden brown scale detail. "How do you do that?"

MWAA-HAAA-HARRRGGH!! Evidently, his great-grandsire could do sneaky plus an evil-Dragon laugh with the best of them – with a flavour of waves booming on rocks, to be fair, probably causing the local fishermen to imagine a squall must be brewing.

Indeed, he now knew exactly where his predilection for wicked laughter came from. It ran in the bloodline, like song.

THUNDER O DRAGON

The Songs were his Sea Dragon pod, the equivalent of a Tamarine Dragon Clan. They were all now very much awake, thanks to his great-grandsire's hijinks. His Dragon hearts flip-flopped like a quintet of beached fish as he gazed about the beach, situated on the very north-easternmost tip of the Vaylarn Archipelago. The fine, crystalline, white sands were awash in white Sea Dragons. Family. Dragons who looked like him! Best of all – could it be just the day before yesterday – he had met his dam, Sirensong, for the first time in twenty years.

Well was it said, an egg knew its dam. Stolen in a treacherous plot by his real sire, Blaze the Devastator, he had been raised as one of the Tamarine Mountains Dragons, rather than according to his oceanic heritage. Even now, despite the overwhelming thrill of joy, an echo of grief still prickled along his spine as he regarded his dam's half-unlidded eye. She had slept the night right alongside him.

She said that this was her right and joy. He understood the fierce, motherly possessiveness in her tone as she made the assertion.

A beauty, Sirensong. What an unbelievable privilege to meet his dam, at last, and to thrill to that particular Sea Dragon magic by which they recognised the signature calling of one another's song across thousands of miles.

Just now, her lip curved in a fond smile and she murmured in fluid Dragoceanic, ≈*Go with him, o son of my wave. He'll be insufferable otherwise.*≈

Thundersong said, *First wave of the morn to you, Princess. Where's the blue Dragoness, Aria?*

Here, she said, rising from behind Dragon's right flank with a luxurious flexion of her butterfly-like wings. Oof. His jaw thumped down upon the white sand in appreciation. She fluted, *First wave of the morn to you, Thundersong the Elder, and Thundersong the younger.*

Dragon curved his muzzle to nuzzle her neck, possibly the least lethal part of a body full of spikes, sharp edges and serious warrior talent. The size differences amused him. Aria might be a little less than half his size and length, but he himself measured a mere quarter of Thundersong's eye-watering bulk. To his entire family's amusement, Azania had tried to pace out the titan's length while the family pod rested and told stories through the previous day. He had several times crooked his neck or curved his tail when she was not looking, leading to measurements ranging from 223 to 238 feet in length and a wingspan of some 261 feet – on the fourth measure.

One exasperated Princess!

The elder Thundersong had a sense of humour in keeping with the size of him.

Put him alongside Princess Azania, and it was clear she stood the height of his fangs, or thereabouts. Nibble-ish proportions. A miniscule morsel capable of monstrous mischief.

Just now, the aforementioned feisty nibble peered up into Thundersong the Elder's mouth. *Great-Grandsire, do you have something stuck in your gum?*

I do have a sore spot here, he admitted, touching his cheek. *Abscess, I think. Don't worry about …*

He gurgled with laughter as Azania folded her arms and tapped her foot. Even to Sea Dragons, her body language communicated perfectly.

Thundersong the considerably more minor, said, *Great-Grandsire, the female of the Human species is a most persistent creature when riled. I advise you admit her to your maw forthwith – and absolutely no swallowing!*

Wince. Guilty as charged; guilty of swallowing and regurgitating his best friend in all the world.

Never again.

Two minutes later, Her Royal Highness, self-appointed chief dentist to the Dragonkind, stood framed to either side and behind by a thicket of fangs fit to furnish the most epic ballad as she checked the innards of Thundersong's upper jaw. Mental picture. How his digits itched to apply brushes to canvas at moments like these! Her antics had already gathered a curious crowd of Sea Dragons.

Perhaps they were not used to toothpick-sized people poking about inside a titan's jaw?

Definitely something stuck in here. It's visibly swollen, she noted, pointing her talon dagger at the offending spot. *Haven't you had this seen to?*

No, because some *males refuse to admit when they need help,* Sirensong put in archly, glancing at her son as if to spread the accusation about – not without accuracy, he had to admit in the depths of his devious hearts. A mother's perfect instinct?

Thundersong grumbled, *I'm fine. It's no problem.*

I'll deal with it, the Princess declared.

Wait, the old-timer began to grumble.

At exactly the same moment, Azania said, *Just a little prick here and –*

PSSHHTT!!

With a yell, she tumbled backward on his tongue – drenched in greenish pus. Head to toe. Spitting and gagging, she threw herself between Thundersong's fangs and performed a high-speed evacuation of her stomach's contents.

Perhaps fifty or sixty Sea Dragons blinked in amazement.

Aah, Thundersong rumbled, palpating the spot with one massive digit. More pus oozed forth, decorating her previously bouffant curls with a decidedly noxious load. On the point of rising, Azania slipped and went down with a revolting squelching sound. He added, *That does feel better. You are a very fine dentist, Princess. I still feel something spiny in here, however. Could you –*

Could she? The Princess did what she did best. Clearing out her mouth with one final hawk and a spit onto the sand and then wiping the muck clear of her eyes, she returned straight to her work. Shortly, after checking with her audibly irked patient that she was not hurting him, she employed the talon dagger to extract a saw-edged piece of bone from the gum.

There we go! she brandished her trophy triumphantly.

Ah, a swordfish's bill, the Sea Dragons exclaimed in approbation and amazement.

Thundersong growled, *So that's what's been bothering me all this time.*

Quite, said the black-green, pus-splattered Princess.

Sirensong said, *Grandsire, you should gargle with seawater to clear out any infection.*

Gargle a Princess in my backwash? I think not! he boomed.

I've often been tempted, I must admit, Dragon announced at the same time.

Aria clouted him in the ribs. *I'll gargle you, if you're not careful. Despicable beast!*

Ouch? he wheezed mournfully. *I think you broke something. Poor, sweet little male.*

He roared, *EE-GNNARR-FFF OF THIS!!*

As the echoes of an enormous thunderclap boomed around the bay, he stretched his wings and flexed his shoulders. Thundertiddler, eh? At least he was a loud one.

Aria, Sirensong, the two Thundersongs and one intrepid Dragon dentist swam out to the edge of the reef, where the enormous Sea Dragon could find water deep enough to fully immerse himself, while the Princess availed herself of warm tidal pools left atop one section of the reef by the retreating tide. She did need to find a pool less frequented by spiny black sea urchins, however. Even a Dragon would think three times about stepping on a bed of such prickly customers.

After gargling seawater with the enthusiasm of a frisky hatchling and showing several of the hatchlings how far he could spit a stream of water, Thundersong the Elder returned to the group, saying, "So far, thirteen Songs and six Whisperers have approached me to ask if and when the Sea Dragons will fly with you on your quest against these Skartunese Dragon torturers."

Azania, rather more presentable than a few minutes earlier, smiled over the lapping waves toward the behemoth. "That's wonderful, Thundersong! Is it possible?"

"Possible for Sea Dragons to fly?" he growled.

"Aye," Aria nodded. "Or, to leave the great migration? I understood that was taboo?"

"Taboo? No. Not done? Mostly." Swimming closer with fresh respect for a budding dental wizard, the elder said thoughtfully, "After the theft of your egg, Sirensong, the Elders of the pod made an agreement not to allow contact with Humans or Dragons of the Air. You may not know, however, that the egg theft was not the only reason."

"It wasn't?" Thundersong and his dam chorused.

"No, it was not. I refer to the entanglement with the Terror Clan."

≈*I did not know this!*≈ Sirensong cried.

≈*I am sorry, I always assumed —*≈

≈*I blamed my song, grandsire! I blamed my being gullible and stupidly naïve … being the worst mother in all the oceans, in truth …*≈

She moaned in patent distress.

≈*Sirensong, my precious jewel,*≈ he said, drawing close to stroke her flank with a gentle paw. After humming a massively deep song over her, he continued, ≈*You have nothing to be ashamed of. This Dragon is so regretful he left you feeling solely to blame. That is not the truth. Our pod, and indeed, our entire nation, failed to protect a young Sea Dragoness from the Devastators' treachery — with respect, Thundersong. There was the matter of the Terror Clan's harvesting of our y'liss-al-horyam —*≈

He paused in his delivery, making Thundersong the

Younger pause in his translation for the Princess and Aria.

Switching to Draconian, he said, *I am sorry. This requires explanation. We Sea Dragons are foundational to one of the great physical and magical cycles that impacts all life around this world, by which I mean the life of the ocean, the air and the land alike. As we swim around the globe, our song cleanses and rejuvenates the waters, producing oxygen to breathe, food for our fellow denizens of the ocean to eat and renewing what we call y'liss-al-horyam, which is difficult to explain. It goes to the deepest, most mystical nature of a Sea Dragon … it is of course the reason we migrate, but… ah …*

Sirensong interjected, *Simply put, it is the reason that magic exists. We believe that without y'liss-al-horyam, our world would die. Dragons would fall from the sky. The oceans would turn dark and everlasting storms would ravage the lands and waters.*

Dragon nodded slowly, thinking of what he had sensed of the essence of Sea Dragon magic changing the nature of the waters. Aye, he began to taste the bigger picture – ah, however that linguistic slip-up worked. A Dragon tasted the fates. This was such a moment.

He ruffled his wings with a shudder and arranged them fussily upon his back. On that note, he mimed to Azania to clean out her left ear. A caterpillar-like trail of yellowish green pus had begun to ooze out of it.

Spare Azerim a rather ghastly sight.

Thanks, she said privately.

Stirring the waters with a restive talon, Thundersong the Elder said, *That's a good definition. There are many aspects to y'liss-al-horyam, one of which is the key interaction which we enjoy with Taramis, the white sun. She is the power behind our magic and the reason the Lumis Ocean is luminous. Anyways, put another way, our migration drives multitudes of great natural processes, such as the warming and cooling of the oceans that drive weather patterns all over the world. We believe that our work and our joy is a service to all creatures beneath the suns. As a result, however, we have perhaps been guilty of seeing ourselves as superior to other kinds of Dragons and other intelligent species.*

Aria said, *You're speaking of unforeseen consequences, o*

Thundersong?

Aye, I am, he said. *For example, shifting our migration path has led to fundamental changes in the waters around this Archipelago. There is less richness and abundance of life and, I would guess, more frequent and more violent sea storms. Is that correct, Ariamyrielle Seaspray?*

I believe so, she said respectfully, *but not all of my kind would agree with this view.*

Most certainly, an overabundance of Sea Serpents in the southern channel has affected the ships and trade of your Humans? he pressed.

The warrior Dragoness nodded. *Aye, most adversely. Trade with the mainland has come to a complete halt. My dam, who leads the Dragonesses of this Archipelago, says that the health of our Clan relies upon certain foodstuffs we always traded for in times past, which contain trace minerals essential to wellbeing and fertility.*

Sirensong said, *Birth rates?*

Down nearly thirty percent in the last decade.

Azania said, *That's terrible.*

Still falling, Aria said pensively.

Shiver his wings! Drawing close to caress his promised, Dragon inadvertently stepped off the steep edge of the reef and went under with a surprised '*glub!*' and a huge splash.

Elegance. Clearly a strong point.

Even better, a mighty paw fished him out like a hatchling steadied by his sire's grasp. He coughed unhappily. *Clearly, it is time for some youngsters to learn how to breathe underwater,* his great-grandsire said, not without a huge grin. *Sirensong, that's your task.*

She nodded eagerly. *Can't wait.*

Er … he could wait. Breathe underwater? Was that even possible without gills? Or not being an actual fish?

He spluttered, *One way I could escape –*

Unfortunately, at the very instant his thought popped off his tongue, his roving gaze happened to fall upon a certain cobalt Dragoness. Aria favoured him with a wordless glare that set him instantly ablaze with shame.

Sickly grin. Hastily, he put in, *Of course, I would not want to escape you, Aria!*

A pawful of razor-sharp talons threatened his sensitive nostrils.

Shall we discuss this in a cosy roost for two, my beautiful cobalt muse? he flirted brazenly, and had the satisfaction of being shoved back underwater by a speechless Dragoness who had just blurted fire across his muzzle.

Awesomeness.

Maybe he was a budding Thundersong, after all?

Still, even budding Thundersongs needed to take their courage in both paws and surface for air again. Usefully, his beloved did not swipe his head off his shoulders for that bold sally. She even appeared mildly impressed, if he read the colours of her emotions correctly.

Don't let that overblown ego pop, Azania suggested dryly in his mind. *Messy ending to the relationship.*

Oh, alright.

Raising his muzzle, he said, *Great-Grandsire, does this mean that the Sea Dragons will consider changing the migration path and even making a sweep through the southern channel this annum?*

I believe it is necessary to begin to re-balance the oceans, he agreed. *However, we must play the politics of the waves astutely.*

What does that mean? Sirensong inquired.

That means that we shall first swim off to consult with this Human King, Azerim of the Archipelago.

Four gasps greeted this news.

By my song, you're all as slow as sea slugs this morn, Thundersong grumbled, flicking out a talon to help Azania negotiate a tricky step over the reef as she returned to Dragon's paw to retrieve her clothing. *The main point being to remove* me *from discussions developing around these reefs. Once the wave of debate has reached a certain peak, we shall stage our return. We should also consult with your dam, Charielle Seaspray. You see, Thundersong, the return of your egg to our pod has taught this old Sea Dragon a new wave.*

It has? the smaller Thundersong asked. *Forgive me, but how?*

He said, *We have been neglectful of the wave of our interactions with our kin of the mountains and the Humankind of these shores. Always, the webs of interdependency surprise. That is why I will encourage our kin who are able to fly with you, even unto the waterless desert sands which are unimaginable to our kind.*

Thundersong and Azania exchanged incredulous glances.

The Princess whispered, *How can I ever thank you enough, Thundersong?*

Dragon echoed his Princess' thanks.

Never stop standing up for what is right, the old Dragon answered sagely. *In this way, we will swim a long ways toward restoring balance. Let me explain. Defeat the Skartunese and the Unicorn nation may stand a chance of not being wiped out, not to mention your T'nagrun people, Princess, and the Dragons and further Human kingdoms who would become enslaved ... so many ripples. Serve our kin of the mountains, and they may avenge us against the Terrors, who in the last five migrations have murdered seventeen of our young – we know not why. Where there is oppression, we must never fail to act. It is our sacred duty to swim – or fly – against.*

The small company exchanged grim nods.

Then, the mighty Sea Dragon said, *Swim with me. The tides wait for no Dragon.*

Azania said pertly, *But Dragons do wait for Princesses. Two minutes please, Thundersong?*

His brow ridges rose. *Why?*

Because I'd prefer to take on the forces of incalculable evil dressed in slightly more than my undies, alright?

Princesses. Can't take them anywhere, Dragon snorted, and had his lip smacked once more for good measure.

Ah, what a morning. Adventure beckoned!

CHAPTER 2

SCARING KINGS

THUNDERSONG SWAM WITH THUNDERSONG Junior. One cleft the waves as if he had been swimming for over a hundred years. The other – not so much, had he been pushed to make a confession.

Top of the class for effort, however.

≈*Copy me,*≈ his great-grandsire ordered brusquely. ≈*Make smoother strokes. Stop thrashing at the water and embrace the experience – oh, by my waters, it would be easier if we didn't need to pause to greet every Sea Dragon in the oceans!*≈

Sea Dragons were scarily sociable, he was learning. As in, they slept practically atop one another, spent all day chatting to one another and perfect strangers could be relied upon to give hearty greeting and inquire for one's life story – the extended version, naturally. In fives or tens, that might have been tolerable. By the thousandth time?

≈*I grow hoarse,*≈ he grumbled.

≈*Believe it or not, we are reaching the end of the pod,*≈ Thundersong chuckled. ≈*Now, you still have all the journeying ballads to learn. They will aid your swimming technique and stamina.*≈

Great. Keep the throat extra-raspy.

Mmm, maybe Aria would find a grating rumble desirable?

Raising his head, he sang a cheery greeting to a small

pod of hatchlings, who, at two weeks of age, were more than competent enough in the water to swim rings around him. By their seventh year of life, they would rival him in size. How depressing.

From her position upon Aria's back, Azania gave him a mental kick. *Warned you.*

Blergh! I can't even be a sackful of misery-guts in peace anymore?
No.

Wow. Talk about leaving a Dragon a modicum of wriggle room.

Drawing in a mouthful of water, he aimed and fired a decent spout at the Princess. Aria, flying just twenty feet above the waves, was wise to his tricks. She thrust out her chest to stymie the shot and bared her fangs lazily. Phew. Mouthful of daggers. A little higher up, Azania smirked royally.

Wretch!

At least she was no longer slathered in pus.

In keeping with the halcyon summery days of the Vaylarn Archipelago, the suns set the turquoise waters agleam. Clear skies stretched from horizon to horizon. The Thundersongs and Sirensong powered through the waves several hundred yards offshore of the islands, two singing the journeying ballads and one enjoying learning new songs. His great-grandsire was absolutely right about the rhythm and wording helping with the swimming – so much so, that Aria could no longer keep up and had to land upon Thundersong the Elder's mighty back to hitch a ride.

One unimpressed Dragoness.

The cobalt warrior was even less impressed but far more amused by his attempts to breathe water. This was another aspect of Sea Dragon magic which would take time to master, he concluded. Sea Dragons could breathe underwater to a degree, limited by depth pressure. In the shallows, they could remain submerged for hours, but his dam explained that the physical dynamics of gas exchange changed with depth, to the point where even Sea Dragon magic could no longer rid their bloodstream of toxins – which could lead to a toxic overload, if not managed correctly.

Sea Serpents swam effectively at much greater depths than the Dragonkind and laid their eggs on the sea floor. For this reason, a change to the migration path would take years to clear the Serpent menace from the shipping lanes, if at all. The Serpents would hide deep and their clusters of eggs would keep spawning year after year.

With the benefit of a warm current sweeping along the coastline, they made excellent time to the south, approaching Wave Dragonhome shortly before noon. He and Aria flew to the cliff tops in search of Charielle, meeting with another enthusiastic reception. One could reasonably conclude that there were no ill effects resulting from his interruption of her nuptials. However, they quickly learned that the leader of the Isles Dragonesses was not at her lair, having flown west to meet King Azerim at Zunityne, the Human capital city of the Archipelago. Perfect timing.

Aria grumbled that her mother would be playing at politics again.

Hmm. Having Charielle as a mother-by-oath might be far more palatable experienced from the other side of Solixambria, he was beginning to suspect. She was ambitious and no fool.

A number of curious warrior Dragonesses flew down to sea level with them to goggle in disbelief at the biggest Sea Dragon they had ever seen and to congratulate and bless Sirensong with a level of fervour that took him aback. He had not been aware that the tale of her loss had affected the Isles Dragons so deeply; nor had his dam been aware, judging by the soft apricot and umber tones of her emotions.

He could not imagine what it must mean to a mother to have her stolen egg return to her after twenty years.

How must Sirensong have felt? Guilt to crush the very soul. Despair deeper than the oceans.

When they swam on, he drew her to his side and nuzzled her neck tenderly. *I'm here now, mother. This is real.*

I … know! she sobbed. *Pinch my wings, son …*

He did as she asked, his joyful laughter throbbing in his chest as if seeking to dislodge an unbearable heaviness of grief.

As they swept down the southern edge of the isles, they hunted together. Thundersong and Sirensong taught them the wiles of Sea Serpents, how to flush them out of hiding and where and how to flame them or deliver a killing bite into the neck behind the skull.

For once, he was a better hunter than Aria, but he knew this was only because he was in his native element. He listened in closely as Aria questioned Thundersong and Sirensong. His cobalt muse wanted to learn every nuance and trick so that she and her Dragonesses could better protect Human shipping, which had also in the past served as transportation for draconic wares and crafts to Solixambria's mainland.

They hoped to revive that vital trade.

As evening closed in, for Azania's sake, they took a brief rest at the tip of the second island of the Archipelago. Sirensong coached her son through his first semi-successful water breathing experience. Basically, he did not choke outright. What a master!

He came up bubbling seawater and laughing.

"What's that all about?" Azania called from the beach. She had been practising sword techniques with Aria.

"The salt tickles my tongue! It feels amazing!" he boomed.

Sirensong shoved his shoulder. "You were terrible, son. Let's go again."

Blergh. Nice to have the truth rubbed in. While he practised wilful drowning – all of his senses kept screaming about the folly of attempting this Sea Dragon skill – Thundersong the Elder cracked open his jaw to have his wound rechecked by his personal fang hygienist and gum scrubber. Azania had him gargle again before reaching inside the wound to clean it as carefully as she could, squeezing forth several more handfuls of vibrant green pus. Mmm. Tasteful.

"I'm hungry," she announced, sniffing the air. "What's Aria doing?"

"Cooking you a portion of sea bass," said the senior Thundersong, with an appreciative inhalation that sucked the Princess' hair sideways.

Holding the two-foot fish up on the tip of her talon, Aria flame-grilled it skilfully.

"Smells amazing!"

Dragon dentistry being the approved way to whet one's appetite, it appeared. That said, he had a peckish fang or two himself, after all this swimming. He hunted for orange-striped grouper off the deep edge of the reef. Having excellent underwater sight was an incredible boon! Ten minutes later, his fourth attempted ambush netted him a five-foot specimen weighing perhaps three hundred and twenty pounds.

He popped his muzzle up out of water, calling, *Any other hungry Dragons in these waters?* No, he had his catch all to himself. Mmm. He licked his fangs in snackish anticipation.

Mother's methods are best, he complimented his dam.

Rascally ripple, she said, winking at him. *Go on, you stomach on paws. You've earned it.*

So this was why he had always suspected a form of camouflage magic. It was a Sea Dragon skill, albeit relatively rare – passed down through the Song line and several other pods, Sirensong told him. Once more, the magic was best activated by song. Sea Dragons spent much of their lives meditating upon and mastering the skill of song.

This latecomer was a mere twenty years behind his

peers. No pressure.

On the beach, Azania's dark eyes flashed in his direction – more a psychic awareness than sight, truth be told. Thinking aloud again? Such a bachelor Dragon habit! He really must work on tidying up his thought life.

With a congenial beach stop behind them, his next lesson involved snoozing on the wing, so to speak. One of the reasons Sea Dragons could circumvent the globe during their annual migration was an ability to sleep and rejuvenate themselves while on the move. Hatchlings learned this from their earliest days, nestled upon their dams' backs.

His job was to rest upon Thundersong's back and attune his inner song to the rhythm of his great-grandsire's semi-somnolent state. Sleeping, right?

Not quite.

Sirensong had wanted to lecture him on the correct cadence of maintaining an awareness of one's surroundings and direction of travel while still sleeping, but his great-grandsire insisted that the skill was best experienced rather than told. True to form, someone promptly struggled to fall asleep for several hours, before nodding off completely. Somewhat removed from the point of the exercise! However, when he half-awoke from a sleep cycle because Azania, asleep in Aria's paw, must have cried out at a bad dream, he was finally drowsy enough to let the song of his namesake's Dragon life soak up through his lethargic body – and that triggered the right state.

Just so.

Ripples of awareness expanded from his body. Suddenly, he knew exactly where the shelf of the reef started and that he swam a safe fifty Dragon-lengths from the shallows. He sensed movement all around them – his dam's presence alongside and, behind Thundersong's mighty wing, moray eels slipping into crevices among the corals and black-tipped reef sharks detecting the presence of Dragons and shifting away in a hurry. Resting in the same way upon Sirensong's back, Aria's life was brighter, a fiery pulse of draconic beauty. Fire incarnate! At last, he appreciated the comparison between yellow or red fires aligned to Ignis and whiter fires to Taramis.

Could the suns be a source of draconic life? Or merely an instructive symbol?

In this half-dozing state, Thundersong's slow, rumbling flow of instruction filled his mind with reams of fresh information. He learned how to read the tides and currents, how to navigate by the stars and how to set triggers and traps to warn and protect himself from potential predators.

Thus, they passed the night drifting upon the currents toward the Human city of Zunityne, covering many miles with no apparent effort whatsoever.

Fast asleep during schooling. Whatever next?

As a perfect dawn seared the lapping wavelets a brilliant, restless white, four Dragons and one Dragonish Princess woke up fully, terrifying the living daylights out of a few seals lurking in the estuary that served to protect the last few remaining oceangoing vessels of King Azerim's once-proud fleet. His shipyards were more than busy, however, in various stages of constructing twelve new vessels.

Thundersong the Elder purred, "Does your King scare easily, Princess?"

Azania smiled, whisking and shaking her unruly curls into a semblance of order. "Scare? No, Thundersong. However, I believe a creature of your magnitude should command great respect amongst the population."

"They'll flee like a frightened flock of fowl," Thundersong Junior translated.

"However, we don't want his parents to feel as if they

need to come down to the harbour in order to meet us," the Princess mused aloud.

"I predict widespread panic, mayhem and an evacuation of the city begun within minutes."

"Dragon!" she complained.

"Do I speak one word of a lie?"

"Not ... exactly. No."

Aria said, "In which case, I should fly ahead to announce you."

"Good idea," the larger Thundersong rumbled. The minute she had taken to the air with a deft flip of her wings, he grinned at his companions and added, "Whilst we sneak up to the Palace without terrifying these poor Humans. With me?"

Sirensong snorted, "Ever the troublemaker, grandsire?"

Azania rolled her eyes. "I know another one – he who sniggereth with great maturity beneath mine miniscule rump."

"I'll make you walk, Princess."

"Oh no, my noble carriage uttereth speech! What mystery is this?"

He almost fell on his nose, his ribs hurting with the strength of his guffaws.

Given the earliness of the hour, the city was only just coming awake. A few citizens stood upon their balconies, rubbing their eyes, as three Sea Dragons strolled up through the centre of town, one of whom hulked taller than a four-storey building. No warehouse could have housed his bulk. The entire width of the road barely sufficed to allow his paws room to pass between the buildings.

"Disappointingly calm," Dragon sniped.

"We Humans are not fowl to be chased about in a flapping flock," his Rider sniffed, "disproving the aspersions of certain creatures."

"Notwithstanding the undeniable entertainment value?"

"Do try to restrain yourself."

"I happen to know this Princess who rather enjoys making a grand entrance."

"Princess Yuali? Awful show-off, isn't she?"

With that, she had to explain to their companions the inexplicable affectation of Human culture in Amboraine, where fainting was a national pastime. This was punctuated by a royal wave for a trio of children who recognised Princess Azania seated atop his back, but their cries of joyous greeting turned into real cries a moment later as they saw Thundersong padding up behind, stepping politely over a cart that bumped into his foreleg before the carter quite understood what it was that he had bumped into.

Instantly, the poor fellow changed from brown Islander to paler even than any of the whitewashed populace of Hamirythe. Dragon sympathised. After all, had he not changed his scales from an unremarkable mud-brown colour to this much more fetching white?

A Dragon changing his scales – now that was how to wing straight past impossibility!

Much better self-talk there, my friend, Azania complimented him.

Gnarr.

If you say so. Step lively, now. Her Royal Highness demands a suitably impressive arrival.

I rather think you shall have it, he said dryly, eyeing up the commotion embroiling the Palace building at the top of the road.

He realised that the impressive azure building must have been planned to dominate the space at the top of town if one approached on foot. A wide road fringed with tropical trees, heavily in blossom, led straight up to the main gates – if one wasn't planning to burgle it from the air, just to pick a random example from nowhere in particular.

That said, infiltrating palaces as far afield as

Amboraine, Hamirythe, T'nagru and Zunityne was becoming a Dragon and Rider specialty.

Bringing a behemoth like Thundersong to overshadow these tiny Humans took the draconic awe to a whole new level. He measured up as a goodly fraction of the size of the entire Palace and could look straight over the top of it if he straightened his back. A few persons gathering upon the royal balcony should hardly attract his notice, but his great-grandsire seemed in a most genial mood, regarding the older and younger Kings and the Queen with genuine, lively curiosity.

Azerim did appear openly relieved to regard Azania riding upon his back. Good fellow. Unabashed admiration of his Princess was just what the Dragon ordered.

Tiny hands pointed, diminutive brown faces gawped at the Sea Dragons with amazement. The colours of King Varazim and Queen Vyioli's emotions reached his senses in popping bursts of pastel colours – awe, shock, respect. Even a touch of darker fear.

Thundersong paused before the ornate metal gate. *I cannot approach, great-grandson, or I shall destroy their pretty foliage and ornaments. Would it be possible to fetch the royals hence, that we might converse?*

Switching to the Human tongue, he greeted the gate guards cheerfully, assuring them that he meant no harm.

Forgive a *touch* of disbelief down there!

Plus, how was it possible that his kin spoke Human so well? Curious. A question for another occasion.

Minding his paws, Dragon stepped past, intending to conduct Princess Azania in a worthy manner right up to the front door. However, King Azerim was faster. He dashed out between the stiffly formal ranks of azure-clad guards, yelling Azania's name as he teetered and tottered about on his cane and heavily strapped foot in a most alarming manner.

Well! Top marks for the King, if her little heart's racing was anything to judge by.

Plus, the silly yelling, waving, blowing kisses and kicking his flanks as if he were an equine to make him go faster. Some mildly conceited creature might have considered slowing down, but then Aria zipped down from absolutely nowhere – he had no clue where she had been hiding – to land beside the eager young King and his paw tread quickened without further thought. Not that they had spent more than fifteen minutes apart, he supposed, but the picayune Princess had demanded a show. Therefore, a show it was.

Admit it, you love this too, she snorted.

Me? As if.

Catch me, please.

Dragon-swift reactions snaffled up the Princess as she leaped gaily off his shoulder, risking life and limb. Their telepathic connection turned impending disaster into a polished acrobatic manoeuvre. Catching her tiny waist lightly between his digits, he transferred her to the ground with an elegant swoop, before raising the diminutive Princess a foot into the air – wicked chortle – to present her lips to the openly startled Azerim.

Summoning up his manly courage, he did the necessary with gratifying zeal.

Dragon ignored the slobbering over and around his knuckles. Humans. Honestly, the whole kissing business turned a Dragon's stomachs, despite that he understood its importance in courtship rituals.

This Dragon became most learned on the subject of these small yet intelligent bipeds and their peculiar antics.

For his part, he risked the loss of a wingtip to caress Aria. She purred and arched her neck. This was a clear courtship signal to any watching Dragon – Humans would say, 'I'm with him.' In the Isles, this gesture was usually advanced by the dominant females, he understood, which could become entertaining once they re-entered his patriarchal Tamarine culture. Demure and Aria did not fit in the same sentence. Not without severe threat of bloodshed, anyhow.

Again, a problem for another day.

Azerim called, "Dragon, am I to understand you bring relatives in tow?"

"Aye. The smaller Dragoness is my dam, Sirensong, and –"

"Taramis be praised! What wonderful news!"

Ugh. Another kiss. He did appreciate Azerim bouncing on his good toes with excitement, however. Sometimes he seemed such a serious young man, but these boyish moments reminded him of the person beneath – similarly to his own experience, he reflected. This Dragon had developed so many crusty layers over the years, as a means of self-protection, it could be difficult to find a carefree young Dragon beneath. A King's untimely ascension to rule must pose similar challenges. Responsibility weighed heavily upon young shoulders.

Azania said, "Aye, she's – well, let's start here. Azerim, meet Thundersong, my Dragon. That's his proper name, the one given to his egg before it was stolen. To the left is his mother, Sirensong, and that slightly larger Dragon –"

"Obscuring half of my town," Azerim spluttered feelingly.

"– he's called Thundersong, too. They pass honoured names down the generations."

"Thundersong the Elder is my great-grandsire," Dragon put in.

"You are most welcome, noble Sea Dragons!" the King announced loudly, presenting bows all around. The Sea Dragons belled out an ear-splitting – and mercifully brief, judging by the Humans' reactions – musical salutation of greeting.

"You may call me Thundersong the Tiddler."

"Tiddler? Hardly!" said Azerim, boldly stealing an arm about Azania's waist meantime. "What does that make me?"

"Roguishly handsome," the Princess giggled.

"Riff-raff," Dragon corrected.

"Huh, I shall have to pass a law regarding disrespect of the Crown by certain Dragons," Azerim opined. "Good. Given our developing relationship with the Dragonkind, we built a new meeting area behind the Palace – however, we didn't quite have monsters of the deep in mind when we sized it up. No mind. I think we might be able to squeeze your great-grandsire into a handy corner – and look, here comes Charielle. We've made good progress on a number of issues since you left seeking Dragon – I mean, our Thundersong, Aria. Which brings me to an overdue apology, my friend. May I call you –"

"You may, friend."

He bowed from the waist. "Thundersong, I am sorry that my lack of forethought forced you into a difficult position. I regret the circumstances that preceded your departure and my part in them."

Dragon shuffled his paws. "I didn't do so well either that day, I regret to report. Are your parents well, Azerim? Your brothers?"

"As rascally as ever and my parents are getting stronger by the day, thank you."

"Your injuries?"

"Perhaps better if I didn't misbehave quite so badly," he admitted, kissing Azania's knuckles when she hissed unhappily at him.

They shook hand and paw gravely.

The King added, "So, would you like to bring your relatives around the back?"

"At once."

Pensively, he eyed how heavily King Azerim had to lean upon Azania's arm as they walked together inside the Palace building. Running on that foot had been foolish. Perhaps Aria's Dragonesses or the Sea Dragons could offer healing aid?

At the back of the Palace, artisans had built a pretty, shaded gazebo upon a raised platform perhaps six feet above ground level. Climbing roses rooted in wide pots were being trained to cover the frame. A gentle ramp at the back allowed the servants to scoot the Queen up to the dais in her wheelchair as the Dragons approached from a side gate that led into the beautiful ornamental gardens. He and Sirensong entered via the gate, wide enough even for his dam. Thundersong stepped cautiously over the top, raising his tail to avert danger of instant demolition. He tried very hard to keep to the path, but a few bushes did not survive the experience of ending up beneath his talons.

How the old-timer's lungs laboured in the air! Sheer size was likely why the older Sea Dragons could not fly – not without inordinate effort, he imagined, glancing up at the Elder with concern.

≈*I'll be fine if I can just lie down for a minute,*≈ Thundersong panted.

No over-the-top draconic pride from him?

≈*When you reach my age, you'll discover that even grumpiness is vastly overrated,*≈ the mighty Dragon put in, as if reading that thought effortlessly off the top of his brain. "May I settle here upon this patch of grass, o King?"

Leaning upon his cane, King Varazim said dryly, "Please do, o Thundersong. You honour our small kingdom. May we bring anything by way of comfort or refreshment?"

"A little salt water?" he suggested.

A cartload of barrels of seawater, Dragon thought to Azania, who leaned forward to whisper in King Azerim's ear.

Shortly, with minimal fuss, the representatives of three ancient and proud nations arranged themselves for a most unusual conference. Varazim joked about the decrepit state of the Human royalty, whilst Charielle showed age-respect deference to Thundersong by fussing over arrangements concerning his comfort. She greeted Sirensong cordially and promised she would always be welcome in Wave Dragonhome with the greatest honour – taking a moment to extol her prospective son-by-oath's derring-do.

The way she told it, boldly declaring his hearts for Aria during her nuptials was a courageous and honourable deed. A true warrior's path danced between the blades of death!

Warriors. Always so fatalistic.

Every smart Dragon ought to embrace wisdom. Unfortunately, he realised, he was rather too large to consider hiding behind his beloved in any forthcoming battles.

Maybe his place was beside her shoulder?

Nay, a talon's length behind. A thoughtful partner ought to give his beloved a chance to shine – first spoils to the Dragoness, razing everything in her path with extreme prejudice. His fires brightened. Aye, wisdom indeed. He'd chargrill anything she bothered to leave over.

Perfect plan.

From the platform, Azania winked at him. *Only the leftovers, Dragon? She's so fierce, you might starve.*

Farther back, and I'd most certainly be distracted out of any possible effectiveness in battle, said he, sending her a mental image of a daintily proportioned cobalt rump. *Mmm, leftovers are so ... tasty.*

Dragon, you're impossible! Standing behind Azerim's shoulder, she fanned her face, before checking his royal rump for blemishes. Finding none, but sensing Thundersong's amusement at her momentary lapse, she blushed the more heatedly.

Time for a political conference.

CHAPTER 3

HAVING A BALL

RESTLESS AND UNABLE TO sleep even though exhausted, Dragon burgled the Palace in the early hours. He and palaces were a thing. Castles, too. Sticky-pawed prowler that he was, complete with this new magical camouflage skill, he completed the feat with notable skill considering the sheer volume of paint he had just filched from their stores.

Time for a touch of recreational redecoration.

The ballroom was an impressive space if one considered Human scale, boasting a tall, arched roof and many beautiful columns and paintings hung on the walls beneath opposing balconies that ran the length of the hall. Above and around the entryway, however, the stone stood blackened by an unfortunate fire a year back.

King Azerim's priorities had not exactly included fixing up his ballroom.

Wonderful canvas. Seventy feet wide and rising from twelve feet tall at the edges to thirty-two at the hall's apex, the bare, grey-black expanse of stone simply begged to be transformed. His nostrils flared, scenting the old smoke. Very good. Picking up a few more filched supplies, the draconic prowler covered the floor with a paint-splattered roll of fabric which had evidently seen much use in years past and set about planning his masterpiece. Thankfully, a few lanterns in this great space had been left burning. He arranged them with pedantic exactitude to provide maximum illumination. Daytime was far better for art, but the preparation work did not require precision.

He visualised the images carefully in his mind. To his left paw, he would paint a verdant cityscape of Zunityne; there would be a range of gorgeous tropical islands over to the right and in the centre, a Sea Dragon migration streaming toward the viewer, above a tranquil underwater reef scene. No. Too much room, truth be told, for so simple a concept. He rasped at his scaly chin with a thoughtful talon. Blitz would go small. *Thundersong,* if he wanted half a sniff of a chance of living up to this massive name his Sea Dragon Clan had bequeathed him, should be far more ambitious.

Aye! He rumbled with pleasure as a new idea popped into the forefront of his mind. Left-paw, he'd blend in scenes from the kingdoms and locations they had already flown through. A condensed landscape of Solixambria. Right-paw begged for an artistic representation of beautiful tropical Zunityne and its surrounds – an Archipelago piece. Aye indeed and upward to the very suns!

With the enthusiasm of an artist who saw it all with absolute clarity, he set about splashing a first coat of paint onto the great wall.

Come the dawn, a passing servant was the first person to lay eyes upon his labours. The undercoat was already dry; he worked next with slate, sketching outlines with a sure paw. Here, the striking city and its hilly vineyards behind. Above the entryway's lintel, Thundersong the Elder's mighty wings flared, lending the architecture dramatic relief.

The manservant scurried off with a gasp.

Over the course of the following hours, he was only dimly aware of shuffling feet, whispered conversations and the movement of many times the number of feet he was sure this ballroom usually heard – unless a ball was in swing, of course. Imagine a ball taking place beneath the blazing gaze of his great-grandsire? He sketched many more Sea Dragons behind and around the mighty old-timer, sporting in waves that would become luminous … he needed to consider how he might achieve that effect. The Sea Dragons would be his family, of course. Did he dare to place Azania aboard one particular back?

"Ah, the artist at work?"

Azerim. He sounded … intrigued. Far from displeased. Behind him, a Dragon's acute hearing picked up the soft tapping of a dainty royal slipper. Someone, judging by the complex scent of her scattered emotions, was rather less certain about this endeavour. Tangs of horror, delight, embarrassment and shock all mingled together. Quite the mix.

"Inspiration struck," said he, splodging paint around his left ear canal as he forgot he was still holding a large brush in paw.

"So I see," said the young King.

"Forgive my presumption," he said, with a desperate lack of contrition. "Sorry. I –"

"Got carried away?" Azania murmured.

"Indeed."

"He does this, usually around midnight," she said. "Azerim –"

"A moment, my love." Standing back, he took in the sweep of the piece. Dragon was just now in the Kingdom of Hamirythe, outlining the distinctive curved turrets of the town. "I see our town and islands and a Sea Dragon migration … what's this part?"

Dragon grinned toothily. "This will be a condensed view of the mainland from Hamirythe down to the desert kingdom of T'nagru. That's tucked into the corner down over there. You can barely see it. You know, a kingdom so tiny, so insignificant, so very far away –"

"How's about I barely smack you?" the Princess hissed.

Feisty and furious this morning? he thought privately to her.

You can't just go – I mean, it's going to be incredible – but Dragon, you can't just walk into someone's ballroom and make it your own.

He understood.

"King Azerim, with your permission?"

Azerim grinned. "Forgiveness after the fact? Thundersong, you try my patience. This wall was an embarrassment. The only condition under which you are ever unlikely to earn my forgiveness for this awful transgression –" he paused for a dry chuckle "– is if you don't complete this masterwork to the highest standard."

"You … like it?" he stumbled.

"Like? What a terribly inadequate word. It's *amazing!*"

Azania muttered, "I can't believe you're letting him get away with this misbehaviour."

"I'm developing skills in delegation and other skills in turning a blind eye to goings-on beneath my nose," said the King. "Are you alright, Princess?"

"Slept badly," she apologised. "I'm not used to such a soft bed anymore."

"She's more used to sleeping with another male," Thundersong said and then bit his forked tongue as Azerim gasped and the Princess made a squeal of outrage. "By my wings, that's a Dragon-sized paw in the maw. I misspoke. I do understand that when Humans say sleeping, they don't actually mean *sleeping.*"

The Princess giggled, "Dragon, that's quite enough detail. You should also understand that we all know what we mean, we just don't say what we mean."

"Facing backwards in order to walk forwards?"

"Erm … I guess so?"

Turning to the King, he said, "So, Azerim, were you satisfied with the outcome of yesterday's conference?"

"Entirely. We all got to know each other and built a foundation for what I believe will be a most profitable collaboration. It's exciting to think about the shipping lanes opening once more and even more exciting to consider being part of an effort that literally circumscribes our world." Dropping a random kiss upon Azania's forehead, he added, "Of course, you understand that the Isles way typically is to quarrel about the details forever and a day. Expect many huffy, stuffy Lords and nobles to be stomping around this Palace over the next few weeks, bending my ear about the most ridiculous so-called issues. After a great deal of hot air has been expended, throats yelled raw and palms greased with money my treasury most emphatically does not possess –"

"I thought we'd solved that problem for you?" Azania said.

Her King raised an eyebrow. "You think? Then – with respect – you do not know our culture."

Turning back to his painting, Dragon chortled, "Princess, I believe this is a moment when you do call a talon a talon."

Azerim cleared his throat. "What are you two up to?"

"Kiss me."

The tall King eyed his intended as if she had just flown halfway across the known world to turn his life upside down – ahem. If that was the wave of his thoughts, then he was entirely correct and ought to get used to the idea. Yesterday. After all, he had first-paw experience to base his observations upon.

Kiss duly deposited upon upturned lips, he said, "Do fill me in, dearest. I smell perfidious plotting thick in the air."

"That's Dragon's natural scent."

"As if!" Thundersong snorted. "Eau-de-mischief is Azania's perfume. She applies it religiously every morning."

"Aye, and put the two of you together and you get a Dragon and Rider on the wall of my ballroom," Azerim realised aloud.

"What?" said the Princess.

He pointed upward. "Right there."
Dragon, you are *impossible.*
Mwaa-haa-haa!

Somewhat irritably, Azania said, "My Dragon and I merely suggest that you capitalise on Lord Gazaram's unfortunate demise by slapping your Lords and nobles into line. Firmly."

"I've always been fond of slow dismemberment," Dragon suggested, delineating several pretty corals for his undersea garden.

The Princess said, "I vote you see how many times you can wrap one of these fellows around your talon. I'm sure you can make them bend far enough."

"Disembowelment?"

"Defenestration."

Azerim exhaled slowly. "What's … that? It sounds evil."

"Tossing a person out of a window to their death," she smiled, sweeter than any honey.

"You've been spending too much time with bloodthirsty Dragons," Azerim said, trying for lightness of tone.

Smelling his emotions, Dragon was about to snarl at him when the Princess said, "So, what would you say if I told you I spent a month in the delightful confines of Vanrace's dungeons under threat of being forced to marry Prince Floric, beloved?"

The King said, "My fiendish heart would insist that the good Prince deserves a torture far more painful and infinitely more lingering than merely being hurled out of a window – even if the definition sounds evocative from a linguistic perspective. Indeed, I believe I could … grow most imaginative, the more I contemplate such a scenario."

She fluttered her eyelashes at him. "Really? How sweet you are."

"Call me Wicked King Azerim."

"Ooh, a kingly rogue!"

Predictably, more kissing commenced behind his back. Chuckling to himself, Dragon said, "I think I'll put you over here, Azerim, gazing wistfully over the glistening waves as you pine for your one and only beloved."

"Pining majestically," Azania said, sounding breathless.

"Be silent and kiss me, woman."

"Scoundrel."

Later that morning, a heated conference did indeed erupt somewhere not far from his painting station. Afterward, Azerim tapped down the corridor on his bad foot, grumbling a few words into his beard he might have been surprised to learn were not inaudible to a large Dragon lurking in his ballroom. Naughty, naughty, o King.

That reminded him, he ought to depart for his training in being nearly drowned. His dam and Thundersong the Elder awaited him offshore.

Poking his head out of the doorway, he called, "Azerim?"

Gnarr, said the royal.

Decent growl. Evidently, politics could turn good men into Dragons.

He said, "Why don't you come over here and have a little cry on my shoulder, Your Majesty?"

Gnarr! "Just working off some steam. Oh, I might as well tell you."

Kings had few confidantes. Thundersong could not have talon-tapped what it was about Azerim that he connected with quite so easily – perhaps, that he was the opposite of his brothers Brand and Brawl in so many ways? Taking a seat upon one of Thundersong's barrels of paint, the azure shade usually purposed for the exterior of the Palace, Azerim proceeded to unload a small archipelago full of frustrations. Burn his ear canals, he had no idea these nobles were such a clutch of self-absorbed, unhelpful, conniving sandworms! It was more than plain to them both that the kingdom's troubles had encouraged these men and women to take flagrant advantage.

How honourable of them.

Waving his hands, the royal finished up, "And you, Thundersong? What's weighing on your mind just now?"

"Actually, this will sound like the foolishness of hatchlings in comparison but, before you came, I was pondering how exactly to create the effect of the Lumis Ocean's shining in my artwork here – ha ha – I know!" They chuckled gruffly. "Matters of kingdom-shaking import, of course."

"Shell," said the King.

"That's vile," the Dragon snorted unhappily.

It took ever so long for the Human to make the connection. "Not eggshell! Seashell. *Ocean* shells, Dragon."

"Oh!" he chortled.

"We sometimes mix crushed shells into paint. Old, broken ones. It makes for a pearlescent sheen second to none. You can even make mosaics from shells."

"Excellent idea! I shall have to experiment. Thank you, Azerim."

"No problem. I only wish I could sort out my nobles as easily. Hmm. Crushing them into paint has a certain ring to it, doesn't it? Need any crimson?"

Obliquely, he replied, "Most creative. It is said that the way to a Dragon's hearts is through his hoard. Since there's no way under the suns you could accommodate their every wish and whim, my advice would be – don't."

"Don't?"

"Don't even try. You suggested that threatening them would only make matters worse. The way I see it, the issue is that they all think *you* are the one to fight with. So, here's a different idea. Set them up. Deflect. Make them bid against each other for limited space, slots, whatever works.

Any misbehaviour, they go straight to the bottom of the list."

"Attack them at the purse strings? Intriguing idea."

"I'm sure you'll think of something." He waved a paw absently, almost decapitating an unwary servant. "Oops. Sorry, little fellow. Make the bids public. Everyone wants valuable cargo space and you have but five ships. Who will protect the precious chattels; who will give their lives like the Sea Dragons are likely to when they try to wipe the Serpents out?"

"Pride and money?" Azerim chortled. "Oh Dragon, you are a sly one. You've given me hope!"

Blergh. Shiver his scales, what was it with Humans and the hugging?

Placing his paw upon the royal's shoulders, he said, "I suggest you talk it over with Princess Azania."

"Indeed I shall!"

"You see, my King, I have never met people who bargain like the desert-kind. To them it is not merely an art, it is mortal combat. You'd be wise to employ your intended in shaping the future of your kingdom. She's worth gold – literally."

"Which reminds me, we have a negotiation of our own to make – don't we, Thundersong?"

"I can assure you, that Princess doesn't come cheap."

"Cheap?" Azania huffed, eyeing them up as she strode into the ballroom. "Who exactly is cheap around here? Caught in the act! Are you two – do you dare to speak of my price?"

"Priceless Princess …" the King began to splutter.

She wore a pretty, full-length white dress in the Isles style, the upper part lacy and the skirts long, but light; many-layered like some of the desert outfits Dragon had noticed when they were last in T'nagru. On his advice, she had switched up her hairstyle, creating an artful swirling pattern of tight braids around the left side of her head and behind the ear, while the right side tumbled freely over her shoulder, and was adorned with tiny golden clips, each bearing a discreet cluster of garnets and diamonds.

Asymmetrical awesomeness, if he did say so himself.

A particular jeweller in the city being very keen to court new business.

Azerim's jaw developed a slightly dislocated look as he took in the change. "By the Isles, Azania, you look wonderful!"

"Keep digging yourself out of that hole," she grinned, not half as narked as she pretended, the scaly one judged. "Thundersong, you'd better thunder on down to the harbour area. Your great-grandsire is browbeating the populace down there, demanding to know when his prize pupil intends to show his tardy paws around the waves. Now, you scheming pair of desert ravens, what's going on around here? I demand to know."

With a wink at the Dragon, Azerim said, "O fabulous beauty, you are hardly in a position to make demands. You are but a captive Princess in a faraway foreign realm. Your captor and I were discussing putting you to work – to earn your keep, since I understand you have *extremely* expensive taste –"

She snorted, "As if!"

"– in Dragons, inasmuch as ambition to change our world," he finished smoothly, and raised his hands as if taking the rapturous applause of an adoring crowd.

Azania shot him a glare of fury mingled with admiration.

Ah. Four paws, each matched in splendour – or, something to that effect.

"I understand that you possess skills of value to the Crown, o Princess," said Azerim, rising to bow suavely over her hand. All the colours of her emotions sparked and shifted toward reds, oranges and yellows as he kissed her knuckles gravely. "May I take counsel with you?"

At that point, he suspected she might have been persuaded to sell Azerim the keys to her own kingdom, but a wise Dragon said nothing of the sort.

Instead, he murmured, "I was just leaving to go practise drowning. Wish me luck."

"Good luck as you duck," Azerim said.

"Soar, don't sink," Azania smiled.

"Teach those nobles and Lords some desert manners, Princess," he said.

He left them with the Princess' eyebrows doing their waggling dance. She had no idea what he had just suggested, did she? However, if he knew his wily Princess in the slightest, then said Lords and nobles were about to have their noses summarily tweaked out of joint.

Failing that? He flexed his talons meaningfully, holding them up to the early light to check their sharpness and breathed a hint of white fire about their gleaming tips. A whole pawful of persuaders begged to do a touch of tickling inside a few abdomens. He was quite certain that showing a few of the Lords their own intestines would focus their attention appropriately.

Winging down over the red-tiled rooftops of Zunityne, Thundersong brought the city to a standstill with a joyous rendition of a Sea Dragon journeying song. To his surprise, he several times heard cheers as he swooped down toward the harbour area. By his wings, this beast was in no way used to actual popularity!

One could grow accustomed.

Vanity. He dared to accuse the Princess of primping in front of a mirror? When he had just checked his reflection in every single window of the Palace as he passed by … *pah*. When had he become this beast?

When gratitude set his Dragon hearts ablaze as never before, considering his transformation. This was not only appropriate, but also the only honest reaction he knew to what he had experienced.

Sirensong! His five hearts bounced within his chest, matching the bounce of his wingbeat, as his dam rose from the ocean beyond the city to add her voice to his. Her power, resonance and musicality were extraordinary – Sea Dragons sang for most of their lives, he understood, and he had never heard voices to compare with a migration of ten thousand – but when Thundersong the Elder exercised his throat in a mighty song of dawn's greeting, he checked beneath in case the buildings started to collapse.

Silly Humans. The cheers only became more frenzied!

Extraordinary creatures.

Furling his wings, Dragon plunged into the turquoise waves a few tens of Dragon-lengths before his family, continuing the plunge until he touched down upon seaweed-dotted white sand, before turning, kicking off and powering for the surface. Breach! He hurtled into the air, thundering:

I – AM – DRAGON!!

Aggrieved seabirds took off in honking chorus for a mile about.

Maybe 'I am Thundersong' would be more appropriate in the future? He wondered if he would ever shed the habit of calling himself 'Dragon.'

Sirensong wing-slapped him fondly. ≈*Son of my wave! A thunderous Thundersong of greeting!*≈

≈*Very glad you* are *a Dragon,*≈ his great-grandsire put in drolly, supplying a wing-slap of his own. ≈*You use soundwaves as a weapon? This skill is new to me. Describe this power as we swim offshore, o name of my wave.*≈

≈*Oh, but I thought –*≈

≈*Today, we will teach you how to find Sea Serpent eggs – those deposited in the relative shallows,*≈ Thundersong explained. ≈*This is underwater breathing with purpose.*≈

≈*Very good, great-grandsire.*≈

How it warmed his devious Dragon soul to realise that Thundersong the Elder was just as pedantic about details as his namesake.

Chatting amiably, the trio swam a mile farther offshore, to where the bottom shelved off steeply. He described the unexpected combination of his powers and demonstrated how far he could expel fire – fifteen feet farther than his dam and with a considerably higher concentration of heat. Experimenting with his vocal powers, they bade him try different pitches and timbres of his natural voice, from ultra-low to painfully high, in order to tease out which effects worked best. He would have to train his voice like any other muscle or skill. Hmm. How come he had never considered this before?

Cloudless of sky and set alight by Taramis' pinpoint brilliance out-shining its much larger partner, Ignis, by orders of magnitude, the day was almost painfully bright. His weak eyes blinked and blinked again, but the moment they submerged, serenity and detail of sight returned to delight him afresh.

≈*Ready?*≈ Sirensong sang. ≈*Relax with the water breathing. We will not dive deep today, merely half a mile or thereabouts.*≈

≈*Half a mile?*≈ he spluttered, nearly losing his air right away.

Master of the waves, he was.

Reminding himself of Azania's pep talk on the perils of putting himself down, he shook his muzzle, girded up his scales and declared, ≈*I'm ready.*≈

Hope so.

Down, down, down they dived, moving from the crystal-clear waters near the surface into increasing gloom. Thundersong the Elder kept the usual flow of information coming. Dragon learned that due to the Lumis Ocean's innate properties, light penetrated to depths of almost a mile. Below that level, complete darkness reigned. Plants grew to a depth of about 1,200 feet but, even in the deepest ocean trenches, there were places where underwater vents supported strange, wonderful forms of life that apparently thrived without need of oxygen or light.

The deeps were a place dangerous even for Dragons. Sea Serpents, giant armoured squid with powerful electrical attacks and dozens of varieties of *lordûme,* a wild, aggressive draconic subtype with an extremely powerful paralytic toxin, made swimming deeper than a mile inadvisable. Even deeper, on the ocean floor proper, crustaceans dwelled, which were large enough to snack upon Sanbris Whales. They were also not friends of Sea Dragons, great or small. Sirensong told him that these were likely the source of fishermen's tales of monsters of the deep. Every so often, one took it upon itself to wander up to the heights of the world of air, destroying everything in its path in a fit of mad rage.

The pressure squeezed at his ears and body as they reached the ocean floor – here, an uninspiring, muddy grey slope strewn with furry-looking boulders. He had to force himself to stay relaxed. Just breathe water under high pressure. Nothing to it.

≈*Now, Sea Serpent eggs look like little silvery balls about the size of … well, your Princess' head,*≈ the giant instructed. ≈*We might have to search a ways along this shelf to find any. The best method we've found so far is echo-location, because even if they're buried in a layer of silt like you see here, they have a distinctive sound-reflection that the musical ear might detect. This method comes courtesy of our friends the dolphins.*≈

So saying, he voiced a high-speed stream of clicks and chirrups. The Sea Dragons wafted along, searching steadily through the gloom – a twilight colour, at this depth.

After twenty minutes, Sirensong said, ≈*I hear a cluster. This way. Thundersong, send your clicks out – good – and now listen for a more metallic 'pling' sound in the echoes.*≈

≈*Uh … how do I distinguish the echoes from the noise I'm making?*≈ he inquired.

≈*Practice and concentration.*≈

Ah. Put another way, this was like most life skills. One had to want it. Work at it. Focus and focus and *focus* until finally he imagined an echo, then clearly distinguished the echo and eventually, with his dam pointing her talon at the exact spot, heard the distinctive *pling*.

≈*Aha!*≈

His gleaming dam smiled. ≈*Good. Now, let's find the next cluster.*≈

So this was why Thundersong the Elder had been talking about a 'clean-up crew,' comprised of some of the oldest or injured Dragons, to stay around the Isles. Just in one small area, they identified five clusters of Sea Serpent eggs, numbering twenty to fifty eggs apiece.

≈*They really like leaving their droppings, don't they?*≈ Thundersong grumbled.

≈*Prolific,*≈ his great-grandsire agreed.

≈*What kills them? Dragon fire?*≈

Sirensong said, ≈*Not easily. Drying them out in direct sunlight is best. They crack and die after a day or two. Let's collect these eggs and take them to the surface. On the way, we'll teach you how to ascend from a depth without killing yourself. Ready?*≈

Marvellous. He really was a tiddler in this new world.

CHAPTER 4

DRAGON CHEF

THE FOLLOWING DAY, AROUND mid-morning, the Palace's Head Chef gaped at his visitor over the top of his kitchen worktop. His throat worked audibly. "There's a Dragon in my kitchen."

"We've been over this already," he rumbled politely. "I am a Dragon, aye; a Dragon who is concerned that you appear unwell, sir."

"Chef Mugizam, please just sit here," said the woman at his left elbow.

"There's a Dragon in my kitchen!" Wiping his sweat-streaked brow, the man stared across his kitchen with eyes turned glassy by fever. "Truly ... a Dragon ... in my –"

"Catch him!" he boomed.

"No!" the Head Chef insisted, swaying at the edge of his table as if ocean swells had unexpectedly attacked his legs. Most disconcerting. He slurred, "The nobles are dining today. I must ... make the ... sea bass special ..."

Clonk.

Sensible woman, that one lurking beside him. As the chef toppled, she sort of cuddled him down to the floor. Unfortunately, his forehead rebounded off the hardwood worktop, which could have been a great deal more damaging had she not acted quickly.

Singling out a scullery maid with a talon, Dragon said, "You. Get him medical help. Now."

"Me … sir?" she stammered.

"No, some other pasty-faced girl. GO!" Thumping up to the central worktop, he peered over it into the gap where the couple had fallen. "Loosen that ridiculous neck rope thing and bathe his face, woman – are you his wife?"

"Aye, sir."

"Good catch. I take it you are experienced in catching a husband?"

He winked at her.

For a busy kitchen, he could hear a mouse scuttling inside one of the cupboards.

"Joke?" he suggested, with an air that undoubtedly suggested they had better laugh at his humour or that would be the last thing they would do. Everyone chortled on cue.

All lovers of life.

Another man said, "What will we do? This is an unmitigated disaster. The sea bass is his speciality. No-one else knows the recipe."

The kitchen staff stood around wringing their hands, bemoaning the fates and splashing cool water on the sick man's face. Had he been hallucinating? Dragon snuffled carefully at his armpits. Nothing a good rest would not fix, he suspected.

Right. Straightening until his head bumped the roof, he rubbed his forepaws together. "So, who's ready to cook lunch for these pretty nobles?"

Blergh. Now they all stood about looking as gormless as worms.

Patience. Treat the yokels delicately.

He said, "I shall handle the sea bass. Now, you all have jobs, do you not? Simply get on with those while I occupy a quiet corner – oh, alright, while I take up half of your kitchen – and we'll soon rustle up a meal fit for royalty. Let's talk through the details. Breads, sides, starters, wines, sauces all taken care of? No? Come on, people, speak to me. I assure you, your tongues still work."

Among Dragons, he would have boomed and blustered his way through resolving all the issues the Head Chef had not yet addressed on his menu. However, having amassed all this experience of dealing with Humans since kidnapping Princess Azania, Thundersong did very well, by his own estimation. He only made three of the men cry. Nobody voided their bowels. Major accidents involving shaky hands, blazing ovens and freshly sharpened vegetable knives, did not occur. In fact, by the time lunch rolled around and he had envisioned a savoury culinary masterpiece created from the twelve sea bass offered to him, Dragon felt he had the situation perfectly in paw.

He had not even chewed anyone's head off for tripping over his tail, which had happened no less than a dozen times. Consummate self-restraint.

Marshalling his servitors – who must have been briefed by a servant thoughtful enough to ensure no further rounds of gasping, fainting and stammering explanation needed to take place – he set the meal in motion. The first course comprised great platters of succulent sea-themed nibbles, prepared, spiced and decorated to an artistic Dragon's rigorous standards, accompanied by a trio of choice wines and a selection of tropical fruit juices.

Curious as to the effect of his culinary efforts, Thundersong stepped outside to peek through the window of the first-floor dining hall. Azerim, with Azania seated at his right hand, held court, explaining how everyone would step up to support the kingdom as they reopened the shipping lanes.

Peering through his spectacles, he decided that the King might better have force-fed them platters of sea urchins, judging by the expressions around the table.

No, they would not be paid for their cooperation? What a tragedy in the making. Gracious me, they would be required to invest heavily before possibly seeing a return that would not be backed by the Crown's guarantee? Poor souls, how they suffered. Three vessels were reserved for cargo from the crafts-Dragons of Wave Dragonhome? Gasp, splutter, choke – somebody ought to hire this crew for a drama production. Surely, they complained, first priority should go to the Humankind?

Gnarr. Ungrateful troglodytes!

Directing his thoughts, he purred, *Azania, is it customary to compliment the chef?*

She jerked as if an invisible talon had tickled her ribs. *Aye, I believe so. Where are you, my friend?*

Nearby. Will you make that call when the sea bass special is announced?

As you order, Dragon.

I'm glad you're such a badly misbehaved Princess, he snorted, withdrawing to set the third course in motion.

Dragon? What are you up to?

Ignoring you, he chortled. The Princess demonstrated her growing mastery of the mental kick. *Feisty wretch,* he approved, even if it left him with a lingering headache at the back of his skull.

When the request arrived, the wicked scaly chef polished up his best grin and squeezed his way up the formal stairway to the first floor. Thankfully, this Palace had been constructed from solid blocks of stone. Nothing too serious collapsed beneath his tonnage – only one small section of stair railing demolished by an unfortunate twitch of his tail. Pausing out of line of sight from the dining hall, he checked with the servitors that the two metal trolleys holding the prepared, steaming sea bass were in place and that the shallow sauce bowls sat ready before each diner.

He nodded to the senior butler. "Would you announce me, please?"

The man grinned. He, of all the staff, acted well aware of the mischief under paw and had been fully supportive of all their efforts up to this point. He had also threatened to dice a few nobles up with the chef's favourite carving implements. Admirable notion, if done slowly with red-hot tongs, skewers and butchers' knives.

Throwing wide the doors, the butler sang out with evident relish, "Presenting our guest culinary artisan, Dragon Chef Thundersong, and his special one-time creation, tangy tropical sea bass flambé a la Dragon!"

Azania's face!

Never mind the frozen diners, hers was the shocked esteem he prized most.

Thundersong very carefully wriggled down through the doorway, with only the smallest scrape to the lintel, and straightened up to loom over the table. "I trust the meal is to your satisfaction, o King, Princess and guests?"

Snicker.

To his credit, Azerim was the quickest to recover. "Indeed, o Thundersong, seldom has a table been graced with such tasty and artfully presented fare. My hearty compliments upon your masterful efforts – is this not so, nobles of the Vaylarn Archipelago?"

They fell over themselves to offer their highest compliments.

The Princess barely contained her mirth. *Oh Dragon, I could wet myself laughing!*

Ugh. He had not needed to know that about Humans.

Adroitly, Thundersong bathed the fish platters in his white fire, before scooping up the flaming portions with his unsheathed talons and depositing them upon each plate, where they sizzled and bubbled in the rich, tangy sauce. Wide-eyed and unspeaking, the richly dressed nobles sat about the table and goggled at the Dragon Chef in action. Delicious, lightly charred fruity aromas filled the room as the servitors quickly added vegetables and savoury breads to the plates.

Applause! He bowed gravely.

At length, Dragon stepped back and addressed Azerim. "My King, I trust that these good noblemen and noblewomen have greeted your proposals with the same enthusiasm with which they appreciated my fare?"

"Ah …" he coughed delicately. "Discussions are … progressing."

The notables of the realm sat about the table squirming like a clutch of unruly hatchlings.

"Well!" he boomed heavily. "Here's what I expect. I and my kin are about to risk life and limb to reopen your shipping lanes, flinging the full might of our nation against the greatest army of Sea Serpents in the history of Solixambria. As we spill our life's blood, I expect our allies to demonstrate equal commitment, according to their capacity."

Step delicately now, Dragon. On the other paw …

Addressing the nobles, he said, "I will not demand your full backing for King Azerim, nor will I twist your arms into making oaths –" he cleared his throat with a loud rasp "– mostly because I would snap your frail appendages like twigs, which would be messy."

Dragon! Azania kicked him mentally.

"I'm sure that won't be necessary," Azerim said hastily.

"No, I am certain it will not," he said, gazing over the table like death unexpectedly possessed of four paws and attached to a foul attitude. "We Sea Dragons are grateful to have such fine allies as these Humans of the Isles – the very first Humans to ally themselves with the Dragonkind. Your vision and courage shall most certainly be marked in the annals of Solixambria's history. Please, do enjoy the sea bass before it goes cold."

He scraped out carefully.

Azania's mental voice reached him as he descended the stairs. *Azerim and I bow to you, Thundersong.*

Not a hint of irony in her tone; only admiration and deep gratitude.

Some Dragon might have been accused of strutting a touch as he returned downstairs. Ahem. Actually, he strutted so much, he cracked his muzzle a fine blow on the heavy ceiling beams. Very well, time to check on the dessert course before he left the kitchen staff to clean up. Job done; ambush executed with draconic style and subtlety.

He brightened. Maybe Azerim's men would already have brought sacks of broken shells for him to experiment with? An afternoon's painting beckoned before his double date in the evening; Aria and he planned to fly Azania and Azerim off for a break from royal duties. The King of the Archipelago needed to work on carving out time for himself, rather than acceding to all the demands placed upon him by his endless duties.

How did a Dragon end up missing his Princess so much?

His pride and preening evaporated, however, as he considered the future. That first renewed migration through the heart of Sea Serpent territory would be nothing short of brutal. Two days hence, Sirensong planned to bring a number of Sea Dragons to Zunityne to enjoy the types of treatment that Human-sized hands excelled at – wing stitching, parasite removal and care of longer-term injuries. They planned to train every Human healer, doctor and nurse in the Archipelago in the care of Dragons.

Furthermore, he was quietly convinced that the Skartunese army would bring new equipment, traps and weaponry when they arrived in T'nagru. Plus, the Terror Clan must have supplied them with more of their vile magic. This time, there would be no holding back.

Anhoyal Rangers, Isles Dragonesses and Sea Dragons who had little experience of flying through the air -. how did one forge an unstoppable force from such disparate elements as these?

By adding a woman in a wheelchair?

"Chanize!" he called happily.

"Dragon," she smiled. "I heard you were working here. Ah, it's now … Thundersong, correct?"

"Aye, that's right. Where have you been? Away?"

"Visiting my parents. Just arrived back today, actually."

About to pose the obvious question, he grinned toothily as none other than Sankir Farizam appeared, carrying her bags. The man smelled all citrusy – joyfulness oozed out of every pore; a literal truth where his unusual emotional senses were concerned, he reflected.

He said, "Has he been holding you as ordered, whilst I was away?"

"Never stops," said she, colouring prettily, at the same time as he chuckled, "How I suffer at the behest of your draconic paw, o Dragon."

Chanize said, "Last week, we exchanged vows before the village elders. Farizam is now my husband."

"Wonderful news. Congratulations!"

Stepping forward, he blessed them both in the draconic tongue. May she have many eggs? Most of it translated well, but not that piece. Oh. Did mammals have eggs? He knew they bore live young, but the process must be quite different to that of egg-laying Dragons, he assumed.

He said, "Having recently learned that Humans are not to be accused of sleeping together, I must ask, are you now … lair mates? How does one say this?"

Farizam said, "Oh no, we're definitely sleeping toge – uh, I see! Oops."

His wife smacked him fondly upon the behind. "*Not* sleeping is what this rascal means! Dragon, we've moved in together in my former apartment, here at the Palace. We hope to be assigned larger quarters in the future, but for now, cosy is best."

The man stooped to brush her cheek with his lips.

"I understand perfectly," he purred, enjoying their interplay. "Day after tomorrow, all the healers are being trained by the Sea Dragons and Isles Dragons. Will you join us, Chanize and Farizam?"

"Of course," they chorused.

"When we fly south – when that day comes – I want you both with us."

They bowed as one, holding hands.

Hmm. That reminded him. Azerim's armourers and leatherworkers needed to be warmed up post-haste if they were to figure out riding arrangements ... aye, which meant crossing a small continent's worth of cultural barriers with the Isles Dragonesses first. Never mind his Sea Dragon kin.

One paw-step in front of another.

With Taramis having shone for most of the day, an unusual semi-annual phenomenon, a blistering heat lingered into the early evening. Thundersong and Aria flew a short way north from Zunityne to a secluded beach recommended by the King, where he used to play as a boy.

The Princess chuckled as they swept into a landing upon the perfect white sands. "Why Azerim, the very beaches around these Isles sprout romantic meals for two."

"Even wine in a cooler," Aria fluted in amusement. "Amazing."

"Astonishing phenomenon," Dragon agreed.

"It's not every Archipelago where the very waters sing with magic, my friend," said the King, elbowing him slyly as he dismounted from his neck seat. He rubbed his behind tenderly. "Grief, I see why a saddle's important."

"Let me help you with that, my King."

Azerim's pure green eyes, startling in a face so tan, twinkled as he said drolly, "Why, Princess, your zeal takes my breath away." After another predictable episode of smooching, boldly essayed in the presence of two fire-breathing beasts, he said, "Alright, then. Doctor's orders; I am to try walking in the soft beach sand with this blasted foot – after which, I fear I'll be in sore need of sampling that wine."

THUNDER O DRAGON

"Go on, put your foot in it," Thundersong quipped dryly.

"And you can put a cork in it, Dragon," Azania echoed.

Miming swatting pesky Princesses into a beautiful sunset, he purred, "I thought the plan was for uncorking?"

"And copious glugging," the King agreed. "Gluggery, I am reliably informed, is completely unrelated to thuggery."

Azania snorted, "His jokes are as bad as yours, Thundersong." Evidently. He liked this King more and more! "So, tell us about your undersea trip, that turned up those eggs, and we'll tell you about your immoderately resounding success this lunchtime past. Deal?"

"Deal, Princess."

The young King limped up and down the beach, apologising every few minutes for leaning upon Azania. He scrunched his toes in the soft, hot sand as ordered, working the muscles and tendons. Tough work. The rebel Lord Gazaram had been making his best attempt to cleave Princess Azania in half when Azerim stopped the blow with his right boot. Unfortunately, that left his foot chopped most of the way through. Recovery would be challenging, but he was determined to fly south with the Dragon force to aid the desert kingdom and to seek King N'chala's consent for marriage.

Dragon sighed. Too honourable, if such a thing existed.

Marry the girl. Yesterday!

Aria nestled up against his flank, purring at the heat of the sands, and offered him a shrimp for his thoughts.

Ooh, warriors do biting humour? he murmured.

Razor wit, she chuckled.

Now now, beauty, no need to beat me over the head with belligerent pun-ishment.

You're a pawful of awful.

Mmm. The silliness must be infectious.

They chatted amiably, catching up on the news from Wave Dragonhome. Charielle had flown east to consult with the Sea Dragons regarding protecting their breeding grounds and helping them stave off the Sea Serpent menace. The Serpents had a nasty habit of trying to pick off Sea Dragon younglings; patrols from the air could offer early warning and better protection. Sea Dragon females of some of the family pods loved adorning their scales with imbedded jewels and jewellery – a fine trade opportunity, since the Sea Dragons could source metals and stones from the ocean depths which the Isles Dragons had no access to, while the male Isles artisans would have no trouble creating unique pieces for their new market.

Once Azerim finished hurting his foot, he sank into a chair with a groan, before making to rise to help Azania.

"No need," she scolded, with such fierceness that his eyebrows peaked and he sat back with a bump. "I'm a wild, independent Dragon-sitting sort of Princess."

"Dragon sitting-on?" Aria hooted.

Gnarr. "Makes me the butt of the joke, I suppose?"

Ah, the pleasure of hearing his friends guffaw. This Dragon glanced about him and reflected upon how fortunate a creature he was to be surrounded by such fine creatures and friends as these. He had always imagined he must face his fate alone, independent, strong – well, trying to be strong. One realised now that strength was not found in ways he had expected. The potential, the raw material, had always been there. Would he have been able to find the way on his own? Doubtful.

"Tell me," he said, "were my culinary exploits of service to the kingdom?"

"The nobles were completely fed up by your antics," Azania teased, handing the bottle of wine to Azerim for him to do the honours. "However, something in your touching the notes of history and honour spoke to them in ways that even His Majesty could not explain."

"No, I'm speechless," he put in.

Thundersong said, "Is that due to the Azania effect?"

Beaming mischievously at the King over her fluted crystal goblet of dry white wine, she chirped, "I must say, I am gazing at a very fine vintage of Archipelago royalty, full of characterful notes of zesty tropical manliness and a hint of flowery romance."

Azerim contrived to look as if he had been swatted by a thousand tonnes of the softest velvet.

Maybe she was the Devastator?

When apparently no words were in the offing – nor, perhaps, were they possible – she added, "Once the Lords and nobles decided to place themselves upon the correct side of history, the results were gratifying. I'll admit, when you sprang your surprise, I fully expected you to tramp in, Dragon, with your usual delicacy. Slightly misjudged, my friend. Sorry. It was like this." Deepening her voice, she imitated him, "Call me Dragon! It's the last thing you'll ever do!"

Over their laughter, he snorted, "I do not sound like that!"

"Catchy, though," the Dragoness purred beside him. "My warriors would fall over laughing if you said something like that during battle, but I rather fancy a chunky monster with excellent taste in catchphrases."

Oof. This would be the Aria effect, clearly.

Azerim said, "Maybe it was a secret mind-altering ingredient in your sea bass, Thundersong, but you created a landslide effect. By the end of lunch, they were falling over one another to declare and prove their loyalty to the Crown. I've more offers of finance, resources and workers scattered across my desk than I reasonably know what to do with."

Thundersong inclined his muzzle in a way he fervently hoped did not look ridiculously smug. "I am glad, my King. Suggestion? Delegate to your father."

"My father?"

"He's a wily old fellow and comes with the recommendation of succeeding in bringing up five rather excellent sons, plus plenty of governance experience. I'll bet he's thoroughly bored lying in bed all day. Fathers need to be put to work. There's no better medicine."

"Boredom is dispiriting," said he, scratching his fashionable bead with an air of calculation, before raising his goblet. "A toast!"

"I hope you're not trying to stand up again," Azania snapped disrespectfully.

"Very well, a seated toast. To friends new and old, and a future which is better because it has many Dragons in it. Everything –" he grinned at the T'nagrun Princess "– *everything* is better with Dragons. And wicked Dragon-Riding Princesses, too."

The senior King was indeed favourably exercised by the idea of capitalising upon his nobles' novel eagerness. He and his Queen – a devious creature in her own right – conspired with his advisors to initiate programmes that ranged from training teams of fishermen and women to support Sea Dragons in fetching and destroying Serpent eggs, to building a specialised medical facility for Dragons of the air and the ocean, and Humans too.

A Dragon scent sensed a hint of reprisal in the older King's doings. Revenge in the form of rebalancing, all for the good of the people? Perfect. He even involved the younger Princes in his schemes, relieving a great deal of the load from Azerim's shoulders.

That left Azerim and Azania free to fly down to the inaugural conference of healers, hosted by Imamate of the Whisperer pod, the acknowledged preeminent healer among the Sea Dragons.

Thundersong curved his neck to check on his riders, seated above his shoulders. "Kissing again?"

"Could not resist," Azerim opined.

"In-flight osculation is essential training for every rookie Dragon Rider," Azania said, wholly unrepentant. "I am pleased to report that I have a most attentive and able student."

"Attentive *and* able, eh?" Dragon rumbled, making both of his Riders blush.

"Since he isn't ready to leap off your shoulders trusting you'll catch him as yet," she said, "I thought to start with a few easy exercises. Now that he's warmed up …"

Was that smoke pouring out of the young King's earholes?

One matter up for discussion was how the Anhoyal Rangers would work together with either the Sea Dragons or the Isles Dragonesses, who boasted finely honed martial arts skills. Those skills did not include having Human support of any fashion, most especially not a Human seated upon them. Aria had already ruled out the neck. She said that their smaller bodyweight meant that the weight distribution, both in battle and in flight, would be thrown off by using that position. Plus, with their style of wing strikes, it simply wasn't safe for a Rider.

Atop the back? he asked.

More possible, but we simply aren't used to such a partnership. I fear a mounted bow would be impractical again, due to wing structures, but a more mobile archer or Ranger might indeed be a boon, if only I can convince my Dragonesses.

Perhaps they will only be convinced once they see the enemy we face?

Perhaps, but we must be ready. I will discuss different scenarios with my Dragonesses. I could see a kind of heavy artillery, borne by your Sea Dragon kin, and a lighter strike force of my Dragonesses, she mused. *However, based upon your descriptions of the ballistae and more importantly, that electrical discharge bolt, I think we shall have to think very carefully about how we arrange ourselves both for the strike and in support of those who fall. At all costs, we must prevent any further enslavement.*

Sharp, his Aria. Thundersong reflected upon his fears that the Skartunese would bring new, even more wicked weapons to their fresh assault on the Kingdom of T'nagru.

Fear, or premonition? How could one know? Perhaps Azania's little sister, Inzashu-N'shula, could have provided better intelligence, but they had not asked her.

A most unusual assemblage graced a broad white beach early that morning. Seventy-two Sea Dragons, twenty-five Isles Dragons and Dragonesses and over two hundred Human healers, doctors and medical staff were in attendance. Imamate the Whisperer, a hoary old Sea Dragoness who, at one hundred and thirty-five feet in length overshadowed everyone else, had each different team describe and demonstrate their main healing techniques. The Humans knew sophisticated herbal methods and remedies. Sea Dragons majored on the healing powers of song, vibration and restoration of systemic imbalances, while the Isles Dragons had developed numerous cunning devices to help with healing, bone-setting and surgery.

As the Humans swarmed over the Sea Dragons to learn about oceanic pests and parasites, Imamate approached King Azerim. "Where are your ill?"

"We – we didn't think to bring them," he admitted.

"You didn't trust us?"

"We didn't think it through," he said, meeting her burning gaze directly. "I considered our kind helping yours, but not – obviously – any reciprocal service, which is clearly an oversight on my part. Dragoness, I meant no insult and I am sorry if this appears one-sided."

Sirensong fluted, "Teething issues?"

Azerim said, "Aye. If I may, please have a Sea Dragon healer start with me. I am the King; I will set the example. Meantime, I'll ask Aria – nay, let me ask our Chief Medic here, which of our patients might easily be moved. I'll have people here before the hour's out, I promise."

Imamate the Whisperer leaned her massive muzzle close to scent his manner. Thundersong blinked. Could she have emotional magic, too?

She nodded. "Despite your youth, yours is a refreshing

and astute wave, o King. Let it be as you suggest. I myself shall attend to your wound; others among us are keen to learn what maladies and diseases afflict your kind. Of the … ah …"

Turning to Sirensong, she burbled rapidly.

Dragon blinked. What was *that?* Then, his Sea-Dragon brain kicked in and the translation entered his mind.

Sirensong said, "My wave-sister speaks a deep Sea Dragon mystery. Let me put it like this. When we learn to sing with new creatures, with new harmonies and songs, advantages accrue to all. What we learn from Humankind or the Dragons of the air will be of direct benefit to our kind – we believe in this holistic … ah, how do I express this in your tongue?"

≈*Serendipity-of-togetherness,*≈ Imamate whispered in Dragoceanic.

≈*Thundersong?*≈ his dam invited.

Allowing the song of this uniquely oceanic phrase to soak into his soul, he pondered the idea for several minutes, before saying, "Sea Dragons believe that destiny is not fixed, o King. I've learned that we believe that by working together in this way, we may shape a new song of beneficial destiny for all of our respective kinds. In this way, our harmony redeems the wrongness and evil in our world."

≈*Beautifully spoken, son,*≈ Sirensong breathed.

Aye, said Azania. *That's my Dragon.*

CHAPTER 5

MIGRATION

AFTER A WEEK SPENT in consultations with King Azerim, which included shenanigans initiated by Charielle that Aria successfully shut down after a raging argument, Thundersong the immensely impressive returned to the eastern end of the Archipelago to shape arrangements to his liking. His report arrived by Dragoceanic that very same evening. The wily old Dragon had measured and predicted the mettle of his kin with exactitude, confirming that the Sea Dragons had decided to circumnavigate the Vaylarn Archipelago before setting off on their annual migration. The burning question – as if Dragons had any other kind – was how much support they could expect from their kin of the Isles.

Thundersong the impressively paint-splashed, following his continued ballroom exploits, joined the discussion with his friends and dam at a spicy point that warm, partially overcast afternoon.

"That includes us," Azerim insisted heatedly. "Respectfully, ma'am –"

Sirensong smiled, "Thank you, o King. Charielle reported that her Dragonesses will be ready to fly in support. I understand you intend to provide ships?"

"Aye," he said, visibly subsiding. "We intend to provide

spotters all along the cliffs and mobilise every fishing vessel we have. We cannot support far into the ocean as yet, but we can help get injured Dragons to shore, bind wounds and provide mounted aerial support with archers and nets. We want to do our part – if you were able to provide some basic protection?"

"Our migration will be spread dangerously thin to cover the ocean at the depth and width required to make a real difference," the Dragoness argued. "I've been listening to the discussions up at the point. Charielle and my Thundersong have provided some excellent insights as to how we might organise to support one another, sweep up stragglers and so on. It means uncomfortable changes to our usual migration patterns. Therefore, a smaller number will thereafter undertake this year's full migration."

Planning on injuries? Thundersong cleared his throat uncomfortably.

His dam added, "Sixty Sea Dragons will fly south with you. At least three hundred shall remain around the Isles to provide shipping protection. We plan to sweep around the Isles, pause at the point for a day or two and then swim east as usual. The migration group will need to shift tail to complete the annual passage in time, but that is not beyond our capabilities."

He asked, ≈*Have you decided to migrate, o mother of my wave?*≈

She shook her muzzle slowly, her eyes shadowed but then brightening with white fires. ≈*Everdeep and I will not migrate. We will fly with you, if after the initial battle we are still able.*≈

≈*I had thought …*≈

≈*He is not so young anymore,* ≈ said she, reading the tenor of his thoughts perfectly. ≈*But he is a proud Dragon and he does not want to let me, or you, down. He has been training daily, flying three to four hours at a time. He also says – and I agree – that we must bury the talon between us and the Tamarine Mountains Dragons if the future is to be secured.*≈

He nodded slowly. A wise, challenging word.

Turning to the King and Princess Azania, he said, "My dam and I were just discussing arrangements. She and Everdeep plan to fly south with us after the first migration."

Azania inclined her head. "Respect."

Azerim bit his lip with a troubled air. Thundersong realised he would need more convincing.

Exactly a week later, the day came at last. Thundersong had rejoined his great family up at the point, experiencing for himself all the restlessness and anticipation as the Dragons prepared to depart a few days earlier than usual. For his part, he was so nervous he felt physically sick. No Azania, a short migration, during which the oceans were expected to run green with Serpent ichor and silver with the blood of Dragons, and then plans to fly south with an army.

Perhaps his biggest worry was a selfish one – would he be able to keep up with his kin?

As Ignis spread his orange fire over the waves, Thundersong the Elder raised his voice in an immense, haunting paean of the oceans.

Wave to wave and shore to shore,
The Song of Sea Dragons resounds evermore,
O'er spume and breaker, through storm and deep,
The eternal renewal of life we live to keep,
DEEPER! STRONGER! ECHOES AFAR!
OCEAN'S SONG WE WILL ROAR!!

The Sea Dragons began to walk from the land to the ocean, leaving the beaches where they had rested, laughed and laid eggs over the past weeks. They submerged in the warm, salty waves, shaking out their wings and calling eagerly to one another with snippets of song, encouragement and teasing.

Everdeep clapped him upon the shoulder. ≈*Come on, Thunderminnow! Shake one of those famous wings.*≈

≈*Thundertiddler,*≈ smiled a relative, Lovesong. ≈*Break*

the wave with me!≈

≈*Give us your roar, Thunderguppy!*≈ Lightsong said.

Taking a breath deep enough to cause his ribcage to creak, he bellowed, *I AM DRAGON!!*

Lightsong pretended to be knocked over. ≈*By my wings, now there's a wave! Is that what you used to impress that little Dragoness of yours?*≈

Grinning, he joined them in the lapping wavelets as, without any discernible signal, the Sea Dragons began to swim out in a curve, gathering off the point. As the waves splashed his eyes, his vision focussed and Dragon was able to see the same rippling motion repeated for miles and miles down the talons of the Vaylarn Archipelago. Odd idea! Throwing several paws full of seawater over his head, he realised that it was not only by being underwater that he could see better, but also when salt water sheeted over his eyes. Intriguing!

Everdeep rumbled curiously, ≈*What are you doing? The idea's to swim through the waves, my friend …*≈

≈*Testing my eyesight,*≈ he replied, explaining.

As he spoke, his great-grandsire Thundersong began to a sing a slow opening refrain. The Dragons picked up the melody, dipping their heads in the waves and shaking out their wings, before beginning to swim with slow, languid strokes that echoed the rhythm of his song. More voices began to join in, their beautiful timbre ringing both through the air and beneath the water. Despite the gentle start, his scales prickled in recognition of the glory of the moment as thousands of white heads dipped together, the movement undulating all the way to the horizon behind them.

Sirensong said, ≈*This first song is called the departing. It sets our course and allows the pods farther behind to catch up. We re-establish bonds of kinship and co-labouring – oh look, is that Aria and Azania?*≈

His neck twizzled. ≈*Oh!*≈

≈*Surprise.*≈

His lips curled back in a huge Dragon smile that probably sent every fish in the oceans ducking for cover. ≈*Suitably surprised, my precious dam!*≈ He waved a wing. *Thanks for coming, Azania!*

Azania waved right back, despite that she was over half a mile away, and he was one white head amongst thousands. Telepathy. Picked him out perfectly, the rascal.

Of course, she said smugly. *You are only the most awesome Dragon out there. Now, off you go and have fun with your family. We'll see you on the other side.*

Her mental state communicated concern that he should take care.

Tell Aria she shines.
Tell her yourself, mister 'I am Dragon.'

The hint of challenge in her voice was enough to bring him surging out of the water. His mightiest thunder yet belled out of his throat, *ARIA, I ADORE THEE!!*

The faraway cobalt spot jerked in surprise. Then, she did some kind of fancy somersault-into-spin manoeuvre that only a butterfly-winged warrior could have conceived of. This Dragon would have tied his own wings in a knot attempting acrobatics like that. Ha. Awesomeness.

On that note, he winged with his kin into the dawn, singing with a great deal more enthusiasm than skill.

His great-grandsire led the migration along the northern aspect of the Archipelago, a restless shoreline where not many Sea Serpents chose to dwell since they preferred the less stormy straits between the Archipelago and Solixambria's mainland. Still, there were a few abroad. The Sea Dragons hunted the light blue Serpents relentlessly, groups detaching to investigate every peninsula, bay and underwater cavern along the way.

In the late morning, the first group, who would stay behind, peeled off to begin sweeping the channel between the Dragon Island and the second major Island, which housed Zunityne. This was part of the plan. They did not expect to find many Sea Serpents here, as they preferred deeper water.

A few Dragon-lengths back in the pack of Sea Dragons, among his relatives, Thundersong found his rhythm as the mighty formation of Sea Dragons sang their way into the afternoon. He began to notice the ocean glowing around them. His personal glow increased as well. He could not have placed how the magic arose or how it worked, but it was more than clear by the trail they left behind that the passage of his kind fundamentally changed the waters of the Lumis Ocean as they passed through. The phenomenon became ever more vivid as the evening drew in.

By the early hours, the migration passed Mykita Lair where he had dive-bombed Aria's nuptials, snaffling her away from a loveless match to an admittedly exemplary male – he must not be too unkind, but that perfumed klutz was nowhere near the right Dragon for *his* Aria – and the Sea Dragons' course curved more to the south, beginning the run into the much deeper waters of the great Lumis Ocean. Until now they had kept to the coastal shallows, but the ocean to the west was so vast, deep and powerful that even a neophyte Sea Dragon sensed the difference straightaway. The swells became longer and more formidable. Fresh, evocative tangs teased his nostrils and tickled his throat. He heard the melancholy song of a family of Sanbris Whales carrying from faraway in the deep and startled as a pod of dolphins came to play alongside the Dragons for a while.

Next, Thundersong the Elder's song surged through the deep, assembling the Sea Dragons by family pod rather than in a single great flying wedge. This truly was an unusual manoeuver and it showed in a good deal of restive complaint and fidgeting which he did not take offence to. The Sea Dragons pivoted around the farthest southern peninsula of the Archipelago, beginning to spread far and wide as they cut across the ocean, the farthest-ranging heading all the way down to Hamirythe, over four hundred miles away, to take up their positions for the vital first sweep between the two opposing shorelines.

What no Dragon liked was the waiting. Ordinarily, they would be on the move now for most of the year. Slowly, over the course of hours, reports echoed back from further and further away. Some pods had already clashed with Sea Serpents. Big ones. Thundersong adjusted the lay of the pods to compensate.

Finally, by late the following afternoon, a loose curve of Sea Dragons stretched all the way from the Archipelago to the coastal region of the Kingdom of Hamirythe.

Thundersong the Elder submerged and sang out his instructions.

The Sea Dragons floated in massive array, waiting for the suns to dip into the ocean.

The Song pod had lined up nearly one hundred miles offshore of the Archipelago. Previously, no Dragon of the Air would have approached this stretch of open ocean without the greatest caution – apart from a couple of mad ones, namely Aria and himself. He remembered how he and Azania had agonised over making this crossing, exhausting themselves in the examination of tidal almanacs and gathering the best possible advice. All of that seemed laughable now, the foolishness of hatchlings. Still, he realised that a different danger lay ahead, one he and the Princess had not appreciated until they ran into a large Sea Serpent guarding the only landing patch in several hundred square miles of ocean. These brutes were big, tough and aggressive. They would not give up their territory without a fight.

At the stroke of sunset, the Sea Dragons began the eastward surge, their massed song cutting through the darkening ocean. Almost at once, he saw yellow eyes wink open in the deeps as Serpents reacted to the threat.

THUNDER O DRAGON

The first attacks developed within minutes. A knot of over a dozen medium-sized Serpents threw themselves at Thundersong the Elder. These light blue creatures slipped with ease through the waters, their large underslung jaws cracking open to snap at wings, tails, limbs and necks. The Sea Dragons responded by counterattacking in tight echelons. The smaller Thundersong flexed his wings to parallel his dam's attack as she sheared a Sea Serpent off his great-grandsire's left flank. He swirled in more tightly, searing a Serpent with a burst of his white flame before catching it in his talons and tearing it loose. Despite the writhing, entangling coils, his reflexive bite found the base of the neck. Fatal.

Surging back again, his fire cut the water a second time, boiling it instantly as it sought out the enemy. Two Serpents broke off their attack on his great-grandsire. The immense white jaws punished the Serpents for a second's inattention. Bitten in half, they fell slowly toward the ocean floor. Melodic calls resounded back and forth as the Dragons came under attack in many locations.

Others of the Song pod curved in behind them, diving deeper to try to reach and burn out the egg sacs of the killed Sea Serpents. They must have an eye on the future.

Surging up behind his dam, he cut a small Serpent off her tail. ≈*One more – watch your left wing!*≈

Yanking her wingtip out of harm's way, she gouged the Serpent across its eyes with her talons. Thundersong caught it as it whipped free and delivered the killing bite.

≈*Here comes a big one,*≈ she called.

This behemoth measured over twice his length. The immense jaws snapped left and right as it charged into their formation; the Dragons scattered before it, never quite lingering to receive the dangerous bite. The coils snaked about violently, throwing them off their attacks. Sirensong narrowly avoided the entangling coils before Everdeep raced through, gouging massive trenches in its back in search of the spine. He found himself climbing its back, digging in his claws as he slowed it down, joined now by his dam and several others as the massively powerful serpent tried to throw them off.

≈*Incoming!*≈ Thundersong the Elder buffeted them with his mighty wings as he swooshed through. He clashed fangs with the Serpent four or five times before the wily Dragon cuffed its head aside and sank his enormous fangs into its face. ≈*Everdeep!*≈

The great white Dragon struck smoothly, gripping the Serpent's neck with his left paw while quarrying away with the open talons of the right. He gouged repeatedly at the flesh, digging like a mad miner. Green ichor clouded the water as the Serpent fought back, but with many Dragons slowing it down, it was only a matter of a minute before Everdeep's talons severed the spinal cord. He checked farther down its body for the egg sac, cut that open, and burned out hundreds of silvery eggs.

≈*If you can disable their jaws and avoid the coils,*≈ Thundersong the Elder said, ≈*the rest is relatively straightforward. Good work, family. Reform ranks. Let's swim!*≈

Several of the Song pod had serious bites on their bodies already. Their great-grandsire ordered one injured female, Spraysong, to join the group farther back. He did not want to risk lives unnecessarily.

The next cloud of smaller Sea Serpents waited for them just half a mile ahead.

Again and again, they clashed with the Serpents. The sea water grew murky green, cut by the billowing white fires of the Sea Dragons as they fought an attritional battle. Every hour brought fresh attacks. Thundersong the Elder was immense in the forefront, rallying them with mighty cries and swimming far and wide to the aid of other pods. His song kept the migration on track as they slowly swept up the coastline toward Zunityne in the north and past Hamirythe in the south. As the channel narrowed, the fighting grew more intense, the attacks more frequent and brutal, fronted by the largest Sea Serpents he had yet seen.

Suddenly, furious roars rolled over the water from above. Dragonesses skimmed over the surface, their blades slicing and dicing the Sea Serpents before they could react. Precision cuts disabled many. The butterfly wings fluttered so fast their edges were a blur as they retained a tight formation, sweeping the waters in search of potential victims.

Thundersong!

Ariamyrielle Seaspray!

The Cobalt Dragoness broke formation and skimmed toward him, her wingtips kicking up spray off the stippled water surface. Her blades stabbed sharply as a Sea Serpent tried to ambush her, a fatal error.

She said, *We've taken in over a hundred wounded already. When you advance, it disturbs the Sea Serpents for several miles ahead of your position. They tend to surface to check what's going on. That's been their downfall. It's been quite the slaughter closer to the Isles. Tougher going out here.*

Guess that would be his great-grandsire through and through. He had selected his position in expectation of the worst. Did that make him a pessimist or merely wise?

She said, *How's that sonic weapon of yours? Have you tried it underwater yet? They say sound conducts far better below the surface.*

He stared at her. *Uh ...*

Scoring top marks for sounding intelligent, judging by her expression.

No regrets, Dragon. Go mix it up! You want to know who you are? What you can do? Waving her swords furiously, she shouted, *I'll gladly bite you in the butt, Dragon, but your destiny won't. So get out there, seize the fates by the scruff of the stupid neck and make a difference, DO YOU HEAR ME?*

Interesting warrior philosophy!

Drawing himself up, he barked, *Loud and clear, ma'am!*

Aria raced off after her battle group of Isles Dragonesses, not without a sassy wriggle of the tail that he knew was meant for one Dragon in particular. Best set about impressing her, especially since she was right – and in the future, try better application of the alleged brain matter, Dragon!

Dipping his head beneath the surface, he called, ≈*I'm going to try a few sonic effects. Protect your ear canals, all Sea Dragons!*≈

One hour later, having lost count of the number of unsuccessful attempts, he finally hit his pitch. A detonation of sound raced out of his maw, causing Sea Dragons up and down their line to cry out in pain. A swathe of Serpents ahead of them jerked and slumped in the water, unconscious or badly hurt.

Mwaa-haa-HARRGGH!!

He and the Songs mowed through the dazed enemy ranks, leaving carnage in their wake. This was more like it! He swaggered through the dark seawater for a mile or so, enjoying relative peace for a few minutes.

≈*Thundersong, I hope you have a few more of those left in you,*≈ his dam called urgently.

≈*I do indeed!*≈

≈*Good, because our echo soundings tell us that every Sea Serpent within a hundred mile radius now thinks you're the preeminent danger in the ocean.*≈

≈*So they're fleeing before my undoubted majesty?*≈

His great-grandsire gave him a withering, fiery stare that stopped up his boasting as if his vocal cords had been cut. ≈*Not quite, youngling. They're converging on you in their tens of thousands. Your dam's right. You'd better get out there and start booming your little lungs out or we're all dead Dragons.*≈

He said something rude and sulky. More sulky than rude, to be fair.

Then, he pulled on his brave scales and surged off to war, starting with a forlorn, ≈*My apologies, every Dragon. I obviously did not think this through. Let's try to make the most of it, shall we? Close your ears!*≈

By the time he had produced over two dozen thunderclaps, mowing down plenty of Sea Serpents but simply enraging an even greater number, he knew that this technique was doomed to failure. It concentrated them beautifully. Serpents wriggled toward him from all quarters, their bodies creating phosphorescent trails in the dark ocean as they made to greet him with snapping jaws and cunning coils.

His family and other pods nearby grew tired of rampant slaughter. His throat burned like fire and the numbers of azure Serpents were endless. Already, he had failed to produce his sonic thunderclap twice, the second time almost causing him to be swamped by four of the granddaddies of these creatures. They had neither been shy nor slow about teaching him the error of his ways. He now sported new holes in the scales in his left hind leg, tail, right flank and lower neck. He was still sensitive about his fresh white scale-job. The serpent venom burned something vile, too.

What would Azania do? Something sparkling and ridiculously clever, of that he had no doubt.

Princess, I need an idea, he admitted.

No answer.

The Sea Dragons swam beneath the waves toward the next, monstrous knot of Sea Serpents. A wall, in truth. He realised that the sea floor shelved upward here. They must be close to the route he and Azania had taken. The flaming yellow eyes winked like stars beneath the surface. So many.

Like … myriad stars …

A thought slowly percolated through his large brain and introduced itself to his mental processes like a bolt of lightning. ≈*Aye. AYE!!*≈

Why exactly was he trying to do this alone?

He was a Thundersong! A Song! His entire Sea Dragon family knew how to sing far better than he ever could. All they needed was a tap in the right direction of the magic required to compress the sound and unleash it as a sonic weapon. They were more than built for this. They were born to it, besides which, most of them had lungs twice his size.

He spun about in the water.

≈*Family! Songs! Hear my lead! This is what I want you to do …*≈

≈*Thundersong, behind you!*≈

≈*No, listen to me. Feel this magic! I'll picture the concept, show you how it feels in your chest and throat –*≈

≈*Thundersong!*≈ his dam wailed, throwing herself toward him.

BRRROOOAAMM!! Everdeep's powerful explosion pummelled a huge Sea Serpent mid-ambush. The backward-sloping fangs scraped right off his back as the stunned creature failed to execute his killing bite.

How had he not noticed the danger? Nor reacted?

Moron!

Sirensong swept on past, her own explosion thudding out of her throat in an oddly deep timbre. The sea waters shook at her power, and the Sea Serpents collapsed or writhed under the onslaught. Suddenly, there were explosions up and down the line, spreading across the miles of water as more and more of the white Dragonkind discovered this new ability – merely a riff upon their outstanding musicality, in truth. Here was a life lesson he had hardly imagined. One needed to look for the truth within each creature, each person, not just within oneself. This was what Azania had done so beautifully for him. She had changed his destiny. He could do the same for others!

The Sea Dragons hammered over the underwater ridge as one beast, savaging the enemy every wingbeat of the way as the great flyers of the oceans rejoiced in this new skill. At last, they could take on the biggest Sea Serpents on something like equal terms, rather than having to gang up on them five or ten to one in order to subdue the immense creatures.

In the distance, Thundersong heard Aria's Dragonwing pass by again, their swords clattering off flesh and bone. He heard a scream as a Serpent ambush took one down, biting the Dragoness to death before she was ten feet beneath the surface.

A faint cry came on the wind, *Thundersong, incredible! Aria!*

No, the territory was not easily taken. Bruised, bloodied and oftentimes dazed, as much by their own sonic booming as by the aftereffects of battle, the Sea Dragons gathered again by the talons of the Archipelago and all along the southern shoreline and counted the cost of the night's work. Over eight hundred Sea Dragons would never migrate again. Great numbers carried smaller and larger injuries. Thundersong the Elder ordered the worst of these to be separated out. They would be carefully swum down to the new medical facility near Zunityne. The Humans of the Isles were out in force all along the shoreline, helping, carrying, binding and stitching. Some cried when they saw the worst injuries.

Costly as the victory was for the Dragons, the Sea Serpents had been utterly decimated. So many dead littered the waves, the Lumis Ocean lapped green rather than pearly white upon the shores and might do for days yet.

Dragon dragged himself from place to place, helping where he could with the wounded.

One secret fear lived in his hearts. Where was Aria? He had not seen her for hours. No-one had any news of her. At length, he took to the air and flew down the coast toward Wave Dragonhome, searching as best he could with his miserable eyesight. Four hours passed. He helped three Sea Dragons find their way onto the beaches, hurling himself airborne each time with fresh determination.

Then, he saw a patch of cobalt a couple of miles out to sea, gleaming in the last rays of Ignis' fiery light. To say his hearts turned over in his chest was an understatement. All five combined to give him such a wallop that he clean forgot how to fly for a minute.

ARIA!!

A white head rose a little out of the water beside her, reacting to his cry.

A Sea Dragon helped her? Why was he swimming so badly, and Aria worse? Was she unconscious? Clapping his wings together in a serious of tremendous beats, all exhaustion forgotten, Thundersong sped out to sea.

As he neared the pair, he realised that the Sea Dragon's right wing draggled at his side, clearly broken. A vicious battle had left him bloodied, bruised and exhausted, yet he nonetheless carried Aria upon his shoulders, holding her nostrils above the waterline.

As he neared the pair, the injured Sea Dragon called in a weary voice, ≈*I am Bluewave. Your Dragoness is injured but alive, Thundersong. It is my fault. She came to help, seeing me injured, and risked her life to save mine. She took a heavy, heavy hit upon her neck as we tried to escape.*≈

So perfectly Aria. Never shy on the courage.

≈*Thank you for bringing her in, Bluewave,*≈ he said warmly. ≈*Ah, let's bring you –*≈

≈*If you can be my right wing, brother, I believe I can make it along the current to Zunityne. I fear Aria will need help. She has not woken as she should.*≈

Furling his wings, Thundersong dived for the water beside his Sea Dragon brother. As he smashed deep, raising a mighty wave, he reflected upon what a privilege it was to have ten thousand brothers and sisters. What a family!

For this, he would be any Dragon's right wing.

CHAPTER 6

SECOND MIGRATION

THE HUMANS FOUND THEM long before Thundersong, Bluewave and Aria made it to Zunityne. It transpired that Charielle's males had set up a communication system along the cliffs that worked with messages passed by mirror, lit by Dragon fire and magic. Naturally, nobody had told him that he and Aria had been the object of concern and much correspondence for the hours that they swam gently along the currents.

Aria had woken twice, disoriented and in severe pain. He and Bluewave winged through the water to the accompaniment of a song they sang together, with Thundersong's left wing draped over his brother's shoulders and the splintered bone of the right resting upon his. They swam steadily but effectively as a team, each working the outside wing.

Thundersong! Thundersong, are you alright?

Princess! Doing well, he called, raising his head to look about for her. Here she came, clinging to the shoulders of none other than Imamate the Whisperer as the mighty pearl-white Dragoness cleft her way toward them.

Four other Humans upon her back? Ah, healers. Of course.

He called, *No Dragon left behind.*

We were just talking about that – Sirensong's idea, actually, came her reply, tinged blue with relief upon his senses. *Azerim just messaged the bigger Thundersong to suggest we should ask the Sea and Isles Dragons to run a few patrols and search –*

Thundersong jerked in the water as his great-grandsire's mighty song boomed all around him, practically making the waters froth, as he demanded to know if there were any Sea Dragons or Isles Dragons left out in the waters. Almost immediately, a reply came from fifteen or twenty miles farther offshore. He could not quite tell the direction, but Imamate clearly could. She surged toward them, calling that she would drop off Azania and the healers, if they were alright to swim to shore by themselves?

Bluewave said at once, ≈*We are fine. That Dragoness needs help more than we do.*≈

Brave. Thundersong chuckled as Azania made her impetuous leap over to his back, unlike the healers, who were far charier.

She knelt, stroking his scales. "You scared me, you beast."

"Scary beast is all part of the plan," he lied heartily. "I am sorry to have caused you concern."

With urgency evident in her every movement, Imamate examined Bluewave and Aria. "This is a bad break. We need you onshore, Bluewave," she pronounced. "Aria may have a fracture of the neck vertebrae." Dragon swore morosely. "Aye. Don't let them shift her neck without first setting a brace, alright? Healers, clear on that?"

"Aye, ma'am," said the oldest lady of the group. "We did not bring splints out here."

"Could we not use her sword sheaths and swords as a temporary measure?" he blurted out.

"Good idea," Imamate fluted. "I must swim on now."

THUNDER O DRAGON

≈*I am coming with all speed! What's your name, Dragoness?*≈
≈*Tealripple. I'm hurt …*≈
≈*Keep calling directions,*≈ the healer Dragoness ordered, swimming away at top speed.

It was an hour before dawn by the time the double-Dragon team managed to reach the beaches of Zunityne. The beach heaved with people and Dragons. In fact, it was a miracle nobody got stepped on in the chaos, but that appeared to be somewhat down to King Azerim and his brothers, each of whom was seated upon a male Isles Dragon. They dashed about from place to place, directing, organising and distributing supplies. Azerim came over to check on Aria, who stirred just in time to complain about having her neck stuck straight out and to have everyone yell at her to lie still.

"Thundersong? Is this your doing? Murder is too good for you!"

"I know, I totally agree."

Her prismatic eyes blinked in surprise. "Am I dying?"

"No! Don't you dare. No and ten thousand times no, do you hear me?"

"What …" she wheezed

"You may have fractured your neck vertebrae," he advised. "Do you have a pain in the neck?"

"Aye, I'm looking at him." Before he could growl a response, she added, "There's sharp pain here, just below the skull. Maybe a splinter of bone?"

"Maybe you're right, Thundersong," he smirked, copying her accent rather poorly. "Maybe I should do what I'm told for a change and not set about murdering anyone for the rest of the week, at the very least."

Aria showed him a few fangs. "Why, you do care."

"Just another of my many failings."

"Did you fly far to find me?"

"Bluewave did most of the work, but it was a job to get you both to shore safely."

She smiled at him with her eye fires. "Thank you."

Dragon helped two Sea Dragons lift Aria off Bluewave's back. They laid her on the sand. A large packing crate went beneath her neck and muzzle, helping her to keep the spine perfectly straight after a couple of adjustments. She gritted her fangs and hissed in pain. Leaving the medics to check her over, he moved to help Bluewave. One of the unfortunate features of Dragon bones – he was not sure if Tamarine Mountains Dragons were similar in this regard – was that they tended to splinter rather than crack. Bluewave had four shards poking out of his hide. Thundersong helped press the bones back into place and to hold them still while the healers packed the wounds with herbs and sang their magic, before starting the much longer binding and splinting process.

By then, a Human doctor had opened Aria's neck with a scalpel and, with Chanize's able help, very gingerly extracted a five-inch bone splinter with a pair of pliers. He peered inside the hole with some kind of goggle or scope. "That'll do. I suspect a similar injury on the next vertebra, Dragoness. Ready for another cut?"

She began to nod, before saying, "Aye."

A younger Sea Dragoness healer, Firewhisperer, came over to brief them. "Dragon spinal injuries of a superficial nature often heal well. We are more robust than Humans, we are learning, especially since we have a quintet of nerve bundles where Humans have just the one. Chanize will flush out the wound and stitch it up. Total stillness for five days is required. I mean that, Dragoness." Aria came in for the many-fangs treatment. "Total! After that, we will begin to test your movement slowly. All being well, you should be moving more confidently and may start exercise within a couple of weeks, but none of your crazy whiplash battle manoeuvers for a month. Understood?"

When Aria nodded contritely, Thundersong realised just how worried she was.

Once Firewhisperer had left to attend to other patients,

Aria said quietly, *Go help the others, Thundersong. I'll be alright here.*

He said, *I'll be keeping a fiery eye on you, my beauty.* "Thanks, Chanize. Are you alright up there on that crate?"

She nodded. "Wheelchair brake clips are on."

The doctor raised his scalpel. "Alright, nurse. Ready to clamp open?"

Not the least terrifying moment in a Dragon's life. He wandered off to find a T'nagrun Princess to annoy. Otherwise, he might just need to think about that scalpel digging into his beloved's neck.

Azania found him first. "Dragon. *Dragon!* Get your sorry scales over here!"

"What is it?"

"There's been a call heard from way to the southwest, a Sea Dragon youngster. We're not the closest, but we are the fastest. Thundersong wants us out there. Five hours ago."

"What happened?" he asked, flicking the Princess carefully onto his neck.

"Apparently, she was swallowed whole and only just managed to dig her way out of the Sea Serpent's gut, is the word," she explained. "Go!"

Gnarr-blasted … brave! he thundered, turning a swear word into an exclamation of amazement.

Rather than blast white sand all over the open wounds on the beach, Thundersong opted to run out into the water before springing aloft with a mighty leap. Strong beats took them up into a clear morn, but in true Islands style, he noticed a squall building to the north in frowning ranks of clouds.

"She can't swim back?" he asked meantime.

"No information, but the current seems to have taken her quite far out to sea already," Azania said. "She's only three years old, Dragon."

He growled quietly beneath his breath, steadying himself on course before flexing his weary shoulders.

THUNDER O DRAGON

"Alright, girlie, let's blow past this Isle. Ready?"

Tiny hands and legs tucked in close behind his skull. "Do what you do best."

After four hours on the wing, they outpaced a pod of Sea Dragons racing in the same direction along the coastline of the last Isle, the tail end of the Archipelago. From a height of over three miles, he could not see them, but Azania had filched a spyglass from the King's stores and she told him that she thought they numbered about a dozen. She also noted that there were many azure serpentine bodies washed up along the shores in this area, to the carnivorous delight of the already large saltwater crocs that inhabited this swampy bay.

"I think we need to head over the tip and a little more west," she said, helping him adjust his heading. "If you could start a long swoop with a thought to getting us lower …"

He noted, "We really need to find her ahead of the storm."

"Right."

"We might need to be swimming to call to her."

"Maybe try a sonic blast from a height?" she suggested. "I can't see anything in the water yet, but the last word of her position put her about thirty-five miles off the point."

Dragon paused to twizzle his shoulders and shake out his wings before setting himself into the most streamlined flying position he knew. He accelerated into a shallow dive, crossing the end of the Isle. Only the open ocean stood before them now. Thousands of miles of luminous seawater, in which a young Sea Dragoness would be just a white speck in immensity. Sensing Azania linking close to him to ease his pain and strengthen him as she had done before, he thanked her quietly. This was another secret of their Dragon Rider relationship they had yet to share with Aria and Azerim, but there had not been opportunity yet. He hoped Aria's injury did not delay their departure.

She's already suggested travelling by ship, the Princess told him in her mind.

Truly?

She does not want to be the cause of delay, she said. *By then, the only thing she will be required to do is rest. Being the stubborn sort of female —*

I happen to specialise in stubborn females, he purred archly.

— she says a hot, sunny deck is more comfort than any warrior deserves. Azania kicked his neck for emphasis. She balanced the spyglass atop his head, scanning the water. *Nothing yet. Keep flying.*

Tough stuff, that Dragoness. Plus, the racy cobalt scales. Mmm …

Dragon. Projecting.

Sorry.

I'm going to start picturing scales on Azerim in a minute, she growled.

What, like this?

Dragon! I did not need to see that.

They searched farther. Azania used the celestial navigator to gain an accurate location, which confirmed they were on the spot. No Sea Dragoness.

They agreed to take Her Royal Highness for a little swim. Thundersong promised he would not dip deep and he did land gently in the ocean to avoid knocking her about too much. She told him she appreciated his tender care for the state of her royal snout.

He called, ≈*Dragoness! Dragoness! Where are you?*≈

≈*Here …*≈

Without taking off again, he drove through the water in that direction with an over-wing or butterfly stroke Sirensong had taught him. Undulating his body strongly, he flipped his wings up over to the fore, almost touching the tips ahead of his muzzle before driving them backward down toward his hind paws. Given a Dragon's innate strength, this stroke led to a low flying motion across the waves – indeed, as he picked up speed, he discovered he could take off on a low, skimming trajectory. Neat trick.

≈*Danger! Don't come,*≈ the youngling called weakly.

≈*What is it?*≈

≈*Creature …*≈

That's helpful, he growled beneath his breath. *Azania, spy forward!*

No need, she returned rapidly. *I see an island rising out there – some crustacean thing – there she is!*

Her voice hit a pitch of excitement and fear. Darn right. Beyond the speck of white highlighted by Azania's mind, a lobster-like crustacean had taken an interest in their target as well. He sensed its mind orienting upon them. The deep-water monster, at least the size of a small island, surged through the turquoise water, its mandibles waving hungrily as it raised a bow-wave in pursuit of its intended lunch. Why could she not flee?

Thundersong jinked to change the angle of attack, aiming to sweep more crosswise as he snaffled up the small Dragoness. He saw that the mite appeared to be entangled in a cocoon of grey, organic threads. Unable to swim. Almost unable to breathe!

Suddenly, a massive orange pincer surged up beneath the youngster, struggling to gain a pinch grip on her twenty-foot length as she wriggled madly. Another pincer rose toward her neck.

"Not good!" Azania shouted. "Dragon –"

Close your ears! he shouted, trying to throw his magic around the youngling and Azania at the same time. *BEGONE!!*

His thunderclap cracked across the water, smashing the enormous crustacean's pincers apart and blowing the wrapped-up Dragoness back into the water. A Juggernaut-approved tail-snap manoeuvre won him clean passage past the falling digit. The Princess clung to his neck like a limpet. Reaching out with his paws, Thundersong snatched the young Sea Dragoness out of the water and swerved as the creature erupted in a paroxysm of rage, nearly blinding both him and Azania with a psychic bludgeoning. No need for dignity here. He fled as fast as his wings could carry him, trying to protect all of their minds from a withering series of blows.

Ouch. Talk about a monster headache!

Five or six miles away, he slowed and landed in the water, rolling the young Dragoness into his front paws.

≈*What's your name?*≈ he asked gently.

≈*Livingwaters,*≈ she fluted.

Let's just cut this off you, shall we? Azania said, whipping out her talon dagger.

Don't eat me! Livingwaters blurted out, snapping toward the Princess.

Hey! she snatched her hands back. *I'm — sorry? I meant that I'll cut you free of this rubbish. I've no interest in your hide apart from keeping it intact.*

I ... can't see.

Oh! he and Azania chorused.

The youngster explained that she thought the strange, rubbery sheeting was something from the Sea Serpent's gut that it used to subdue its meals. She showed them how she had managed to force one talon out and used that to try to saw her way free. However, the toxic gut acids had affected her eyes, causing them to swell completely shut. Perhaps that was for the better, Azania put in quietly, helping his paws to release her head and neck. They worked their way carefully down the torso, which had been wrapped up in multiple layers of the tough material. No way to escape this mess on one's own.

Shortly, the Princess had sawed her wings free. Dragon helped her peel the strange substance down off her sleek back, freeing up her hind legs. After that, it was like wriggling out of Human clothing. Easily done.

"You should alert the Sea Dragons," she reminded

him.

"Good idea."

Submerging his head, he called out in his new tongue, sharing the good news far and wide. Yet this incident puzzled him. Was this some new capability on the part of the Sea Serpents? No-one had mentioned a parcelling effect like this before, nor had they seen Sea Dragons use it during the migration assault. He resolved to discuss the matter with his dam, Aria and Azania later, in private.

After a few minutes, congratulations started coming back from the closer Sea Dragons. It was only once they were underway, with the exhausted youngster resting upon his back in the approved Sea Dragon fashion, that his great-grandsire's thanks arrived in a tingling ripple of sound. How strange it was to have these delayed conversations, he reflected. Say a few words, wait twenty minutes or half an hour for a reply, then say something more. Azania would never cope.

Just now, the tiny Princess sat upon his back, holding the youngling's paw and telling her stories about the desert.

Quality. Just plain quality.

Having returned to Zunityne with an escort of additional Sea Dragons, the Dragon Rider team dropped Livingwaters off with the healers to have her eyes treated, before checking in with Aria.

"I'm a stiff-necked Dragoness," she complained.

"Nice headgear," he complimented her. "I see the wings also took a beating?"

"Fourteen broken struts. That Serpent was not out to make friends."

"I trust you left him the worse off?"

She chuckled softly. "I've never been a creature's chew

toy before. I suppose this is where I say, 'I'll be back, stronger than before,' but they've given me something against the pain that's putting me to sleep. Will you stay beside me tonight, Dragon?"

"Of course."

"I won't be much company …"

The Isles warrior's eyelids fell shut with a slight clicking sound.

"Wow, I didn't think it was possible to fall asleep mid-sentence, especially not for Aria," Azania said. "Right, I think I'll go find some dinner."

"Spelled, 'kiss Azerim?' " he suggested slyly.

"No, he's *King* Azerim," she giggled.

"The King of Kissing and Lord of Lip-Locking, not to mention the Reigning Royal Rump Tweaker?"

Azania threw him an exasperated but decidedly fake glare. "I've been known to make dessert out of Dragons that suggest such things. On that note, want to hear my latest joke?" He nodded. "What did the Dragon have for breakfast?"

"I don't know. What did the Dragon have for breakfast?"

"Flamefast."

"Oh … *groan*," he chortled.

"You thought I was going to say beast-feast, didn't you?"

"Double groan! Say, Princess, what kind of tales do Dragons like best?"

"Cobalt blue ones?"

"Ah, sneaky as you are, it should be clear that all Dragons fancy an epic tale."

She wandered off chuckling about that one. He did not tell her, but Thundersong kept an eye and then a thought upon her until she found King Azerim. Even the most self-respecting Dragon worried about his Princess when she was out of his sight. This business of having another male in her life certainly took a dint of adjusting to. Since the night had begun to clear now, after a brief but violent tropical squall, he counted stars until he reached the number 5,219, but that did not induce the sleep he craved. He mentally checked over his progress on the artwork in the ballroom. No matter how much his paws itched to return to it right now, he had given his word to Aria Seaspray.

Absolutely no succumbing to any bouts of artistic inspiration just now.

Poor Dragoness. Her neck had been clamped into a wooden brace that reached from her shoulders to her skull and, though it should not have, it reminded him painfully of the head cages worn by their Dragon kin under Skartunese control. Dragon thralls. He needed to find the right time to start briefing the Dragons who would be flying south – and with that, he pictured his brothers' faces at the sight of him and Aria leading over one hundred Dragons, plus one deadly pint-sized Princess, into Tamarine airspace.

This time, he fell asleep smiling.

Three days later saw him flying up to the talons again, together with Sirensong, Everdeep, Azania and Charielle, to see off the migration proper. They chatted on the way up and then spoke at length with Thundersong the Elder and the other aged Sea Dragons. Already aware of the strange netting which had captured Livingwaters, they also speculated that this development might somehow be related to the Terror Clan Dragons.

Charielle promised to start scouting the large bay in Northern Solixambria between Mornine and Terror Lair, while the Sea Dragons made a firm decision to skirt the Terror Clan's waters much more widely than usual before they headed out East on their usual migration route.

THUNDER O DRAGON

Considering all the injuries, the Sea Dragons would leave over one thousand of their kin behind this year, under the command of Imamate the Whisperer. This unprecedented number, plus all the fatalities, had become the cause for much grieving over the last few days.

Gazing about at his relatives, many sporting bite marks and scale abrasions from the battles they had fought with the Sea Serpents, Thundersong felt an almost unbearable urge to throw everything aside and dive into the water with them. This was his place. He should be singing the journeying songs with his kin, thrilling to the lightening of the waters as they cleft them with each mighty wing stroke, resting on the wing beneath a starry sky and hearing his song echo in the eternal deep. Despite that he knew his destiny lay in another land far, far away from this place, he shivered with longing.

Azania touched his neck. "It goes deep, doesn't it?"

"Aye."

Even though he had only experienced this synchronised swimming once with his kin, the loss felt unbearable.

"Perhaps another year," he said quietly. "Do you understand, Princess?"

"I do."

Taking his leave of Thundersong the Elder, he said, ≈*Great-grandsire, why did you …*≈

So much grief and loss. So many left behind. He could not bring himself to say the words, appalled so deep in his Dragon hearts, the pain robbed him even of the power of speech.

≈*Thundersong, it is simply that we had to. There are times in this life upon the wave when it takes all our courage simply to be true — true to ourselves, true to our heritage and true to who we are. If ocean did not rise, we would be the lesser creatures for it. One day, every Sea Dragon here will learn what we have demonstrated to one another and to our allies. We rise because we must. What other choice is there?*≈

What great wisdom! He could only incline his muzzle in acknowledgement.

With that, the great Dragon touched him upon the shoulder. ≈*Remember to be true, o my Thundersong. I know you will.*≈

He watched as they walked into the ocean once more, as the many, many variances on the beautiful white spread across the lapping waves, and the Sea Dragons began to sing their first song. As before, they flexed their shoulders and began to call encouragement to one another, but this half-Ocean half-Mountains Dragon, who waited behind upon the shore, heard the sound of a different song, one he had not appreciated so clearly before.

This was a poem of epic love.

CHAPTER 7

CULTURAL SURPRISE

UPON HIS RETURN TO Zunityne two days later, Sankir Farizam co-opted a certain Dragon into assisting in ironing out a few loading issues up at the wharf, where King Azerim's fleet of eight oceangoing vessels made ready to depart. He thumped large-pawed over a few priorities and sniffed about a few cargoes, determined that one Lord had rather stretched the bounds of his remit and thus made everyone, bar the offending Lord, a great deal happier.

Problem solved with dictatorial delicacy. *Gnarr.*

Another problem of the cobalt sort presented itself in addition. He nipped down to the beach to put his life on the line by helping to convince Aria that she needed to have her infected neck wound cleaned out and spend an extra day in the neck brace.

Alive by the mere skin of his fangs, he retired to put finishing touches to his artwork. Dragon thanked every ancestor he knew that paint brushes did not speak back, stomp their tiny dark feet, threaten murder in the name of love or indulge in devious political shenanigans behind his back. Paint could be relied upon to act like paint and brushes brushed. Just the sort of predictability he preferred.

At least Azerim's family – no, there it went. Shouting match up in the royal apartments?

He gritted his fangs together so impressively, a couple of lads mopping the ballroom floor absconded in a flustered rush.

Shortly, the King and his much-improved foot came stomping down to the ballroom to inspect the Dragon's artwork by the light of the lamps, blazing now, as a gorgeous but early tropical evening set in. That would be, to let some steam dissipate. Azerim parked his rump on an overturned, dry paint bucket to contemplate the deepest mysteries of his boot toes.

After a while, he threw up his hands. "Parents!"

"Parents indeed," Dragon agreed. After adding a few judicious finishing touches to the desert down in the corner, he added, "They're going to miss you."

"I know. I might even come back half-married."

"Half? How does that work?"

"By virtue of our crazy laws which state that I must first be wed according to the laws and customs of her culture, then mine, before it is all recognised and official."

"Oh." Dragon absently painted his nose desert-black while thinking this through. "I mean, why don't you just mate the girl already?"

"*Mate* the girl?" Azerim choked out, turning a rather darker shade of his usual tan.

"Aye. Why not? You love her, she loves you, you can't peel your eyes off her in tight trousers, she drools when you walk past. What's the issue?"

"Dragon, we do not just 'mate the girl!' Whatever –"

"I should think not," Azania said breezily, entering the ballroom.

Her betrothed almost exploded with embarrassment. "Princess Azania, I – uh – well … this isn't what you think –"

"What a fascinating conversation," she said, stopping beside King Azerim, who did not fail to notice her hips approaching his nose. He hurriedly corrected his errant gaze. "Were you boys swapping cultural notes? Do fill me in."

"So we were," Dragon boomed. "In Tamarine culture, one is free to sample the buffet, so to speak. Azerim was just expressing his immense frustration at having to wait – " the King made a half-strangled squeak which he grandly ignored "– to seize your person with desirous paws and – ah, is that an inappropriate turn of phrase?"

The two Humans spluttered various things. Not a sensible syllable between them.

"It isn't that strange a custom," he added, sensing an opportunity for further education of his tiny friends. "The Isles Dragons follow a tradition of matchmaking before solo sampling. I believe matches can change in rare circumstances. Tamarine Dragons will occasionally seek out only one partner and make their vows early but that is unusual in our culture. I suppose Isles Dragons and you Humans are more culturally similar in this regard."

Azerim said, "Aren't you concerned that another male might make … moves upon Aria?"

"That would be an awful mistake and very messy to clean up," he chortled, wondering at the King's question. He had not tapped Aria's thoughts on this matter. "No mind. We are promised and I have made my intentions absolutely clear. I am being respectful of her culture, see?"

Was he? Or was he being a honking great coward?

As he considered the imperative there had been to have her nuptial status resolved before she set out on her first exploration flight and the attempted ambush of a wedding he and Azania had broken up, Thundersong wondered if the drive to resolve her status might not be stronger than he had imagined. Hmm. He eyed Azania and Azerim, who exchanged a thoughtful courtship glance of their own. No. A plotting glance. His emotional sense never lied. They must be thinking about their own future together. He understood this yearning. After all, did he not long to be with Aria? How could he navigate these complex currents and do right by her?

"Sire!" Sankir Farizam jogged in. "I'm so sorry to disturb, but there's a matter down at the beach that requires your attention."

Azerim cleared his throat in annoyance. "Sankir, we were just enjoying a congenial conversation. Can you not attend to this matter and spare me for once?"

He said, "I fear this is beyond my station. Charielle and many of her Dragonesses have arrived in force and they appear riled. Something about the loading protocols, treatment of the wounded … it's not pretty, sire."

"Dragons. Never short of a fiery temper, eh?" He elbowed Thundersong in the thigh. "What do you say, my friend?"

"Aye, that's a truth," he grumbled. Charielle and her devious ways! He could only imagine what trouble she might have stirred up this time. "May I offer a swift wing down to the beach, o King?"

"Appreciated."

"Only if it's *two* wings and not one," the Princess inserted deftly.

Sharp as his talons, that one. He had no desire to fly in wonky spirals either. Who knew what it did to one's digestion?

With Azerim, Azania and Farizam safely aboard, he flipped up into the air above the Palace building and sped eastward into a sky of glorious oranges, pinks, carnelians and golds. Forgot his glasses, to his annoyance. He could drink in this scenery all day long.

"Azania, did you pack in my spectacles?"

"I'm sorry, I forgot," she said. "Let me just climb up here and clean your nose. You do look a little silly for diplomacy. Were you painting yourself or the wall?"

"Artistic frenzy," he murmured.

Makeup? she suggested privately.

Roast Princess for breakfast?

"Sounds hazardous to the health," she chortled, scrambling up onto the bridge of his nose, cloth in hand. "It's almost finished, isn't it?"

"The urge to tinker and perfect is never-ending," he admitted, gazing about at the Isle. "Hmm. Is the ocean a little lighter than usual out there?"

"The bodies and blood must be clearing," the Sankir said.

"Still, there's a perfectly ghastly mess around our reefs," Azerim noted. "I'm secretly hoping we set sail before the stench of rotting meat really hits. Very kingly of me to abscond beforehand, but I suspect it will be indescribably foul. Now, shall we play at guessing which Lord has managed to insult the Dragons this time? Any bets?"

Chatting amiably, they completed the short flight down to the medical beach. Heaving with Dragons, he noticed. Plenty of Humans about, too, swarming the beach like an infestation of dark-haired sand crabs – *mwaa-haa-harrr*. Nice image.

He waited impatiently for Aria to come into focus so that he could see her past Azania's tiny rump, which from his perspective took up half the sky in his right eye. Azerim should try this view. That would get his blood pumping. Oh, Charielle and Aria were engaged in earnest conversation down there. Her Dragonesses lined the low grassy dunes above the beach, doing their best to look ominous and imposing while the portly males scurried about, fetching and carrying, tidying and mending and caring for the wounded. The disparity in their roles still struck him as incredibly one-sided. Tamarine Dragons were far more equal. To her credit, Aria had always treated him as her peer, even when he had been cast out and dishonoured.

His five hearts warmed pleasurably at the thought,

while his chest swelled to dimensions that approached painful fullness. To have captured such a Dragoness' regard was a triumph and an honour he must never take for granted. They had taken the neck cast off. Chanize cleaned her wounds with care, leaning out of her wheelchair to reach across her neck. Aria still held her strapped wings awkwardly but the struts, at least, should be healed in a day or two.

She and enforced inactivity were not best acquainted.

He saw Everdeep and Sirensong emerge from the breakers a few wing-lengths down the beach, seawater sheeting off their flanks. Ah, a romantic evening swim for two? The huge male treated his dam with tender respect. It was clear from their draconic body language how much they adored one another. This pleased him mightily.

One thing he did not observe was all this fuss the Sankir had alluded to.

"Sirensong and Everdeep look as if they've been indulging in a little sampling," Azania noted dryly.

"Princess!" the King gasped.

"Well, I do believe she may be correct," Thundersong agreed heartily. "There's a mischievous ochre gleam in his eye and see how she leans subtly against his flank? Those are clear wooing signals, my friends. The Sankir knows this for a fact."

"Ahem!" he cleared his throat, smiling at Chanize as they landed neatly nearby. "I believe I do."

The girl smiled in puzzlement.

He said to Azerim, "The foot's improved?"

"Greatly, thanks to Imamate's stretching routines and your Sea Dragon song magic," he replied. "It still feels weird and stiff but I can actually balance and put pressure on it now. We're considering crafting an insert for my boot to compensate for the twist in the – oh? What's going on here?"

Thundersong scanned the throng in growing bemusement. Now what?

THUNDER O DRAGON

The Isles Dragonesses had begun to hum, a low, droning sound which was not at all unpleasant. They shuffled together as a massed group, curved at the ends so that all eyes gazed ... well, toward him? Or Azerim? The Humans on the beach glanced up and began to gather around, as did the Sea Dragons and Dragonesses, standing around and between their patients. Few were a simple white, he noticed idly – tints of rose, blue and green were common - and the pearly white of his Clan stood out, even a hint of lustrous grey in Imamate's case.

Song issued as if in reply from the waters beyond the reef. Dragon tweaked at least a dozen of his neck vertebrae in a fast-rippling sequence as he whirled in shock. "Oh? But I thought – by my wings!"

Quite without warning, the entire ocean out beyond the reef appeared to shiver and lighten and then thousands of Sea Dragons breached toward the deepening evening sky, an immense congregation that thundered a song greeting to the gathering upon the shore. Thundersong's jaw thumped down upon the sand. The Isles Dragons, female and male alike, roared back in concert as the oceanic Dragons crashed into the surf, churning the entire ocean into frothing white mayhem in an instant. At once, the Isles males all launched heavily into the air and began one of their elegant dances. Ooh! They wore all their finery, he had not noticed before. The Humans – several thousand, indeed – cheered like mad. How they loved a parade and a show. It really was a cute cultural affectation.

"Thundersong?" Azania's voice broke into his distracted thoughts.

"Aye, Princess?"

"Aria would like to speak with you."

"Aria? Of course." He had taken all of two paces down the soft white beach sand when an incredible prickle seized his every scale. He stumbled to a halt. "Azania, what are the Sea Dragons doing here? Aren't they ... uh?"

Smiling at him in her most mysterious, feminine way,

she said, "Thundersong the Elder decided that the oceans needed cleansing. Your kin made another circuit of the Isles over the last couple of days, putting their magic to work. They have just now returned and paused here."

"The migration doesn't pause, Princess."

"Doesn't it?"

He stared suspiciously at her. "What are you up to? I scent-sense your mischief, little Princess."

"Dragon," she laughed merrily, tweaking his questing nose with her fingers, "why do *you* think everyone's here this evening? What special event do you think might gather all these people and Dragons in one place?"

"I don't rightly know."

However, his voice cracked on the last syllable as he took in Ariamyrielle Seaspray's expression. She beckoned him with a dip of her eye fires and coy twirl of her wing surfaces. *Whadda-whomp!* His hearts burst into thundering joy. His body knew; only his mind scrambled to catch up.

Aria?

Thundersong. Will you join me?

Aria — Ariamyrielle Seaspray, what are we — are we? Say we are!

The crimson notes of concern in her eye fires evaporated, swallowed by whites, yellows and blues of joy. *Surprise?*

Oh, I am — reaching her side, he touched her delicately beneath her eye with the tip of his right fore-talon — *suitably surprised. I do believe I've just been royally ambushed. Is this what I think it is?*

She shrugged gracefully, taking care for her neck. *I wanted something small and simple. We still have simple, but small — that flew beyond the stars a long while ago, thanks to my dam. It was right that your family should be here and we Isles Dragons would not miss such an event even though they aim to circumnavigate the world in time ... and so they changed the migration pattern once more for us and ... Dragon, my Dragon, my Thundersong, are you willing to make public the promises we've already made privately to each other?*

Willing? he spluttered, his gaze moving to Charielle, who stood close enough to listen in.

Rascally plotter! She nodded in a way that assured him he had just been outplayed and he had better make the right moves, or else unspecified, uncountable tortures would swiftly be inflicted upon his unworthy being. Sirensong, too. No pressure; only ten thousand creatures or thereabouts looking on. An entire migration had halted for this moment. He breathed out slowly through his nose.

Good thing his mind was already made up then, wasn't it?

Willing? Terrible word, he continued, struggling to induce a couple of rational thoughts to collide somewhere deep inside his cranium. *Why, my fires – this Dragon burns for you alone, Ariamyrielle Seaspray. It has been so since that first day you demolished Juggernaut the Grinder's entire training course in front of my disbelieving eyes.*

As Charielle raised a jubilant bugle to the fiery skies, he added, *I can't actually feel my paws, mind, and I feel as if I'm drifting through a strange and wonderful dream.*

This is real, my beloved, she whispered ardently. *As real as it gets. You don't mind a surprise?*

I could be persuaded to forgive you, he teased.

I can be very persuasive, the Cobalt Dragoness said, flicking his scales with a pert wingtip. *Shall I show you just how much?*

As long as it doesn't involve hurting your neck.

Ah ... true.

Shall I show you how happy I am?

You're already glowing like a star, Thundersong. That tells me everything.

Oh. So he was. In other odd tangential thoughts, betrayal could turn out to be positive.

When she smiled in radiant invitation, however, he threw back his muzzle and launched four bolts of white fire into the sky, where they exploded with shattering detonations that scattered smaller fire trails in wide spherical bursts of light. Fireworks! Pitching his voice upward as well, he thundered, *I – AM – DRAGON!!*

What a Dragon you are. She quivered deliciously against his scales, a frisson of excitement that did things to him he would never admit in any company, polite or none. *How you ignite my every fire, Thundersong!*

The feeling is mutual. He nuzzled her flank tenderly.

After the songs and dances of celebration from the Isles Dragons and songs of conjugal blessing from the Sea Dragons, Charielle, Sirensong and Thundersong the Elder came to them to lead the couple in speaking and receiving the respective oaths and blessings particular to their kinds. He barely knew what he said, even though every word was poignant and laden with promise and meaning. All he could think was that he had once been a Brown Devastator Dragon, Blitz, who was called the Fritz, on account of his propensity for making a ridiculous Dragons' breakfast of everything worthwhile he had ever attempted, and now look where destiny had whisked him. He enjoyed the company of the finest of friends, a family that beggared belief and he stood upon the cusp of a marriage to the most striking Dragoness beneath creation's stars that promised to unite not just two, but even three, Dragon nations and to bring Humanity into the fold.

Ah, only the most minor ambitions.

One must strive not to strain a talon in the doing.

Gazing deep into Aria's shining eyes, he wished this extravagant happiness for Azania and Azerim as well, all the days of their lives. They deserved no less.

After taking their formal oaths, his Sea Dragon kin led them through the songs of promise, love and fidelity and, at last, a rollicking ballad of the oceans that more than hinted at what they ought to consider doing amongst the waves next. Aria giggled merrily as he translated a few of the choicer phrases for her. To be frank, he was a little shocked that even the Sea Dragon younglings knew this song. Really, the Elders should know better.

Then, he and Aria received the congratulations of all her kin, the Humans, including the senior King, Queen and Azerim's four brothers, who must have sneaked off long before – oh, that extremely fake argument, he realised now? When he tossed this amused accusation toward King Varazim and Queen Vyioli, they chuckled in turn and told him that aye, he had been taken for a royal ride. After all, these Isles had a tradition of mischief which had admittedly been absent for a few years but now promised to return in full force. Varazim reminded him pointedly that large Dragons were not exactly guiltless of misbehaving around his Archipelago, right?

He liked this King more and more. He could not wait to negotiate Azania's ransom price with him and Azerim. The trick would be to wrestle honour out of what could otherwise be a tricky conversation.

When at last all the congratulations were done and his kin had departed with thunderous odes of joy – hopefully migrating in the right direction for a change, which he only checked a dozen or so times – he and Aria lay on the warm beach sands together and cuddled for a very long time just being together, watching the play of his white glow through the glorious, butterfly-like patterns of her wings, listening to the contented purring of her fires, talking of their hatchling days, their hopes for the future and her fears about this injury.

"When a warrior is all one is, one fears to become less," she said softly. "I know that isn't right, but our hearts don't always obey reason, do they, Thundersong?"

He said, "Since when were you only ever a warrior?"

She chuckled knowingly. "Ah. Do I sense a deep thought coming?"

"Do you mind?"

"Never."

"Thank you. So, a warrior is who your culture and upbringing say you should be," he said, letting out a breath he had been holding. "Inside, however, you are Ariamyrielle Seaspray. You are a restless explorer. A wanderer. One who refused to accept the status quo. You knew that if you did not do the impossible, crossing the ocean and the length of Solixambria, the King and Queen would die – and so you gave of your own blood for the Humans and changed their fate … and mine. There's more to you than a pair of blades and a ferocious scowl, Aria, and if you can't see that, well, this Dragon shall simply have to remind you from time to time. Forcefully."

Ah, he dared!

"A pair of blades and a ferocious scowl? You flatterer," she smiled, her eyes softly agleam. "More to you than a paintbrush and who your family painted you to be, isn't there?"

"Touché."

"I love your great heart, my Dragon. I've longed to be yours … forever, it seems. I feared at first my scent sense of your nature could only be infatuation, for it came upon me like a summer squall, but everything since has gone to prove you are so much more than anything I imagined."

"I adore you, Aria. Will you be ready to sail on the morrow?"

"As long as it's with you, I'd sail around the world. What's a little jaunt to Solixambria compared to that?"

"How is it you are already precious to me?" he murmured.

"Hold me, Thundersong."

He slipped a wing over her back and touched muzzles with her, listening to the quicker, lighter rhythm of a far smaller Dragoness. Scenting the charred fragrance of her breath and the deeper emotions of her hearts, he thought upon her description of a summer squall. Hard to believe how profoundly he cherished Aria, even after such a short time together. Could love truly be like this?

At last sleep snuck up on them, a soft-pawed thief in the night.

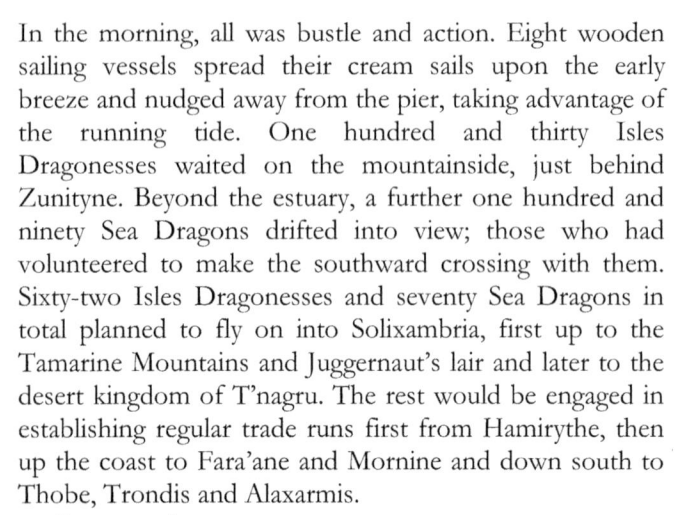

In the morning, all was bustle and action. Eight wooden sailing vessels spread their cream sails upon the early breeze and nudged away from the pier, taking advantage of the running tide. One hundred and thirty Isles Dragonesses waited on the mountainside, just behind Zunityne. Beyond the estuary, a further one hundred and ninety Sea Dragons drifted into view; those who had volunteered to make the southward crossing with them. Sixty-two Isles Dragonesses and seventy Sea Dragons in total planned to fly on into Solixambria, first up to the Tamarine Mountains and Juggernaut's lair and later to the desert kingdom of T'nagru. The rest would be engaged in establishing regular trade runs first from Hamirythe, then up the coast to Fara'ane and Mornine and down south to Thobe, Trondis and Alaxarmis.

So many plans.

With the benefit of steady trade winds, the crossing ought to take around three days for the ships, enough time for him and Aria to start what she called the shakedown of their forces. The three hundred Anhoyal Rangers of King Azerim's command would be practising Dragonback every day. Sea Dragons flew longer stretches in the air and the Isles Dragonesses would land to take rest both upon the sailing vessels and upon the backs of their assigned Sea Dragon partners. Once they took to dry ground, she planned to expand their training regimen.

The oceangoing vessels were not many for this first voyage, but King Azerim had no doubt that the merchants would be very keen to add their own vessels to future trips – for a fee, naturally. Aria had cracked open a gleaming jaw full of fangs at this point to murmur, 'After all, he who enjoys the favour of Dragons, enjoys the spoils.' True. To this end, Azerim planned to deal in the first instance with

Lord Ivarn and Lady Ishana, Yardi's parents. Hamirythe could have first pickings. After that, the wheels of trade ought to grease themselves with gratifying speed, for to his best understanding, many Humans appreciated the scent and sight of gold just as much as avaricious Dragons.

After clearing the port, the sailing vessels spread their sails and headed out to the healing beach, where Dragon was forced out of an artistic reverie, involving cream sails snapping in the breeze, to face his first issue of the day – namely, his mate.

"I am not being carted down a beach and loaded like a crate onto a ship," Aria snapped. "I will walk!"

"The neck brace goes on, then," Chanize said.

"Says who?"

"Imamate said –don't you be growling at me," the young woman smiled grimly. Not without courage, Thundersong approved. "You're my responsibility during the voyage, Dragoness. I take my responsibilities very seriously indeed."

"Did my mother threaten you?"

"She said a few words, aye. So, you are not climbing aboard. You will be lifted – and aye, you will listen to and obey all my orders while you are healing. No exceptions."

"Fine!" Aria snarled.

"Fine," Chanize snapped back. "Farizam, would you help me fit this blasted brace, please?"

That was the right tone to take with Aria. Thundersong and Everdeep carefully paced her as she walked down the beach. A clenching of the fangs betrayed her weakness. Out in the surf, the larger male submerged to position her upon his shoulders while Thundersong transported Chanize and Sankir Farizam out to the vessel which would carry his Cobalt Dragoness, Azerim's square-rigged, four-masted barque, the current flagship of his fleet. He had plans in the works for bigger vessels.

"Land there on the foredeck," Farizam pointed.

"Why not ask me to land in a spider's nest?" Dragon

complained.

"Hear the singing? Those are some jovial mariners," said Chanize, apologising as her long blonde hair fluttered in her husband's face.

Dragon said, "You're not supposed to eat a woman's hair, man."

Farizam chuckled gruffly, "Oh, you know about women's hair, Dragon?"

"More than you may think. The Princess Azania taught me something of the culture and care of hair – and its pitfalls. I understand that in your culture, this light golden colour is regarded as a woman's treasure hoard, correct?"

"Correct."

Trimming his wings, he swooped toward the vessel, planning how to land without destroying something essential. "Tell her how you prize it."

"Dragon, you're so pushy," he snorted. "Chanize, your hair is indeed a treasure, one of the many outward features I love –" he must have noticed the deep green melancholy tones of her emotions, because he added "– and that includes your legs. Aye, I know it is more than complicated, but I want you to know, Chanize, that I've loved you from the very first. We all have our scars; it's just that some of us wear them on the outside."

She made a sound like a soft sob.

Thundersong sighed. He had by no means intended to prompt this conversation, yet its implications reverberated in his own hearts. How many years had he seen himself only as a worthless, unwanted, deformed worm and no Dragon at all?

Still, the snuggling going on upon his neck gave him hope. Indeed, the crook of his neck was becoming quite the bastion of Human romance nowadays. Intriguing. Slowing further, he aimed his muzzle at a gap in the tangle of ropes, stowed his wings and lifted his tail as he swept over the railing.

A cabin boy darted in front of him, avoiding Azania's

reflexive grab. She screamed, *Dragon!*

He was fully committed to the landing. In trying to avoid the lad, he slammed down hard and clumsily, gouging a splinter from the deck as he twisted his left forepaw at the last second to avert flattening the boy – that wretched fool! *Gnarr!* Farizam leaped down toward the lad with a cry of fear but realised that the small brown face peering between the Dragon's talons was turning neither purple nor crimson. Thundersong's paw flashed up to steady Chanize as she began to topple sideways. He popped her into the wheelchair Azerim held ready for her and then shifted paws to let the lad up.

"Sorry, mighty Dragon!" piped the lad, apparently undaunted and indestructible.

He growled, "Lad, never run beneath a landing Dragon. I've no desire to scrape your inch-thick remains off the decks."

"Aye-aye, sir!" he saluted cheekily.

Thundersong mimed a nip toward his backside. The lad got the idea with a leap and a wail and thus, righteous order was restored in all Solixambria, so to speak.

"That was deftly done, Dragon," Azania said brightly. "Welcome aboard the *Royal Wavecutter*."

"You are looking suspiciously nautical, Princess," he approved.

"Nautical or naughty?" Azerim put in.

She wore white knee-length shorts, a short-sleeved shirt and a smart white bandanna that tried, but largely failed, to tame her vivacious curls. Barefoot, she could easily have been mistaken for that cabin boy, unless one looked more closely. The desert people might have thrown a fit over the bare calves but here, the Princess fit in perfectly.

"I don't see you scaling the rigging, my King," she retorted, dimpling of cheek.

"Teach you how to set sails?"

"I thought you'd never ask. Catch me if you can."

"I grew up around sailing ships – but not if you cheat.

Thundersong!"

"What did I do?"

Azerim waggled a finger at him as he chased the Princess up into the rigging with an eager chuckle since she had a twelve-foot head start, thanks to his helping paw. Turning about, he watched Everdeep and Sirensong paralleling the vessel's course, bringing Aria alongside. Curling his tail about a mast for support, he leaned well over the bulwark, bracing his hind legs so that he did not crush the wood. Leaning over in a way that made the vessel groan and heel over until the wooden cross-spars threatened to dip into the water, he gathered Aria into his paws and lifted her onto the decks with a minimum of jostling.

Ooh, I fancy these muscles, she purred.

Mmm, he agreed, not posing in the slightest.

He backed up carefully and set her down where the Captain indicated. Sailors needed to get around her; in addition, the foredeck would be used for landings and takeoffs by the Isles Dragonesses.

"Welcome aboard, Aria!" the Captain called, snapping into a smart salute.

"Thank you. I look forward to our voyage," she said. "Please let me know if I'm ever in the way."

Rolling forward, Chanize said, "How's the nerve pain?"

"Bad," the warrior said quietly.

Why had she said nothing so far? What was it with warriors and this need to pretend they felt no pain?

The healer said, "I'll mix up some herbs and shall I ask Sirensong to sing over you?"

"Thank you, Chanize."

With the most precious cargo safely brought aboard, the sailors struck up another of their shanties as the helmsman spun the wheel. The sails luffed for a moment as they turned, before swelling with the breeze. He saw Azania and Azerim high up in the rigging, helping to set additional sail. All the ships' crews were doing the same, unfurling additional canvas. The vessel's timbers creaked as it made headway. They rejoined the other ships on a fairly straightforward downwind run that should sweep them all the way to Hamirythe without pause.

Everdeep's sonorous song called the Sea Dragons into a protective echelon, sweeping ahead and to the sides of the ships. Everyone assumed that a few Sea Serpents would have avoided the first mighty sweeps, hiding in the deeps as they loved to do, and they were right. The first attack came within an hour of setting out. The Isles Dragonesses flying above sang out warning. Everdeep showcased his new sonic skills by smashing the Serpent with a blast that Thundersong felt through his paws and four of the pod tidied up behind him with snappish zest.

The sailors cheered but many looked as green as the ichor spreading in the water at the carnage.

After seeing to Aria's comfort, she told him her mate could go fly with his family.

"Your mate?" he purred in delight.

"Aye, she's your first mate," said Azerim, popping up beside them.

"I am not any kind of *first* mate," Aria corrected waspishly. "I am his only mate."

"My only mate, my date and about that, there's no debate," Thundersong put in, deciding that if he was to win points, he ought to do so in poetic style.

The Dragoness winked slyly at him. "Go play in the waves, mate, and don't come back late." Turning to Azerim, she said, "Right, shall we set up the rest schedule for the Dragonesses? There's limited deck space. Also, do you want your Rangers to try flying with them, as yet?"

Thundersong slipped smoothly over the railing and let the seawaters close over his head. His mate. Phew. Maybe cooling off for a minute was a good idea.

Much to contemplate.

CHAPTER 8

HAMIRYTHE

BENEFICIAL WINDS AND HALCYON weather took the unusual fleet skimming over the channel to Hamirythe in record time. Barely two and a half days into the historic crossing saw the boy in the crow's nest crying out the traditional, 'Land ho!' Soon, the glorious white cliffs hove into view, seeming to raise Hamir Town out of the blue-in-blue depths from their perspective on this blustery but clear early afternoon. Azerim sighed as his eyes grew a touch dewy about the edges. A tiny sailor girl held his hand and asked if he should like to drop by the Ociane family's place for dinner.

Dragon supposed that the sight of eight tall ships cutting through the extraordinary light teal of the Lumis Ocean, cream sails billowing in the breeze, would have been enough to stir hearts up there in the town. Throw in the mighty draconic escort and they enjoyed simply the most explosive reception he could have imagined. Thousands upon thousands of people lined the wharves, the cliffs and even the rooftops to goggle at the sight. They cheered lustily and waved blue and white scarves above their heads. Aye, they knew what this meant.

"Thundersong?" Azerim inquired.

He raised his muzzle toward the ship's railing to inquire

archly, "Is the Princess' penchant for the grand entrance rubbing off on you?"

"Unfortunately," he said.

The Princess smacked him impolitely.

"I am merely taking lessons," he said at once. "On that note, to avoid outright scandal, my dearest, would you care to go change?"

She stomped off in a huff.

"Phew, females," he said, wiping his forehead.

Aria promptly threatened his kneecaps with her talons. To his evident consternation, she immediately turned the gesture into a lingering stretch and commented that she would start light exercise when she had a chance.

"Starting with the King's kneecaps?" he asked.

Wilful and innovative interpretation being the order of the day.

Azerim stepped over her paw with exaggerated dignity. "Let's go make arrangements to *our* satisfaction, Thundersong."

"I suggest we wait for the Princess."

"Oh. Very wise."

"Otherwise, she tends to turn into a Dragoness and bites your head off."

"I'd wish to avoid any such awkwardness."

Princess Azania never had been one to linger over wardrobe issues. Today's ensemble returned her to the martial warrior Princess of the desert – tough leathers, weaponry to spare and a fierce smile for King Azerim as she leaped from Thundersong's paw onto his neck. Scandal? Merely a different sort for this Dragon-riding, knight-bashing, kingdom-toppling black Princess.

Now, why did Humans say 'black-hearted' when black was obviously the best colour?

Skin colour made no person a rogue! What bigoted foolishness lived even in common sayings in one's language!

His Rider stole the front seat with an emphatic wriggle

of her rump. Azerim did not appear to mind. Indeed, a discerning Dragon may have noted that his neck had, once more, instantly turned into a boudoir of palpitating Human romance. How bizarre. Dragons *caused* romance? He must claw to the bottom of this curious behaviour in the species, for it did not strike this Dragon as logical.

The ways of one's hearts being wholly logical, naturally.

With a pleased chortle, he climbed the forecastle with care for the byzantine tangle of ropes that made these wooden sailing vessels work. There, Thundersong spread his wings and swooped off the gunwale with more of a lurch than intended, given as he misread the vessel's motion on the waves. Three mighty snaps of his wings avoided a humiliating splash-landing and sent him skimming over the ocean surface like a seabird. He pretended nonchalance by dipping in his talons and wingtips, raising white sprays until rainbows danced in his wake, before he tilted his wing surfaces and took them shooting skyward in a spectacular climb at top speed. Azerim wheezed unintelligibly.

Someone to impress, Dragon? Azania's mental voice asked warmly.

Is she looking?

I believe the phrase you are looking for is 'slack-jawed approbation.'

Murr-hurr-hurrggh! he chortled gleefully, levelling out as he accelerated toward the white cliffs. Salty spray hung in the air where the waves crashed upon the rocks but he spied plenty of sandy white bays the Sea Dragons would enjoy making their own. The Isles Dragonesses would likely prefer the cliff tops, but he and Aria had remarked upon a minor rash of gleaming-eyed sizing up between several of the burly male Sea Dragons and the sleek female warriors. Just wait until they started training and flying together. Dragon predicted trouble. Aria agreed.

Stop them? Might better try to stop waves from breaking upon the shore.

As they neared the town, he said, "O King, shall I announce you?"

"Shut your ears," Azania said immediately.

"As you wish," said he.

PRESENTING … he let the thunder roll away into the distance *KING AZERIM OF THE ARCHIPELAGO … AND … THE PRINCESS AZANIA OF T'NAGRU!!*

The pitch of his sonic blast rolled over the city like an invisible wave, fluttering flags, ruffling hair and silencing the crowds. Thousands of faces gazed upward, dumbfounded. Hushed.

"Oops," he muttered.

Then, they went wild. A minor echo of thunder roared up from the frenzied throng as they danced in the streets, hugged one another, screamed at the top of their lungs and generally behaved like complete idiots. Thundersong gaped in amazement. He would never understand Humans as long as he lived. This species was quite, quite mad.

Azerim patted his neck. "Nice work."

"Scared the pants off them," the Princess said.

"I like the sounds of that, my darling."

"Azerim, behave."

"Absolutely not," he snorted, kissing the back of her neck. Thundersong felt her shiver against his scales.

"Alright," he growled. "Humans are crazy. What is it about Dragons that makes you lot go all smoochy-romanticy the minute you climb onto my back, eh? A special tingle in my scales? Loss of brain function at altitude?"

"O, thou wingéd paragon of all passion," Azania declaimed.

Gnarr, he disagreed.

Azerim said, "She has a point. Perhaps it is something about the visceral thill of even the nearness of a mighty beast of fiery magic, perhaps an element of imagination, mysticism and enchantment that makes us Humans respond to Dragons in the way that we do. Basically, you get all the poets in a knot and nab the best parts in all the legends which is thoroughly annoying. Dragons are breathtaking. Even draconic tyranny, cruelty and lust for treasure is somehow washed in rosy hues by silver-tongued minstrels, turning your kind into admirable villains. Alright. We're hopeless."

"Royal seal on that?" Thundersong chortled.

"That'll be the day you accept the nickname Thunderteeny."

"Did you just swear at me?"

"Foul-mouthed royal," Azerim chuckled. "Go on, give them another one. Make them quiver and quake. Healthy respect for their new allies, being closely followed by more advantageous negotiations, do you follow?"

"Perfectly. Ears?" *I AM THUNDERSONG!!*

Another crack of thunder set them off again. Truly, a Dragon could grow accustomed to such a rapturous reception.

With that, he landed beside an important-looking building in the blue-roofed town, where important-looking people had gathered upon the steps to make important pronouncements. Naturally, they were all suitably cowed by His Majestic Scaliness and amazed and delighted to welcome King Azerim to Hamirythe and all the – subtext, highly profitable – trade he would bring. Lord Ivarn bowed impeccably over Princess Azania's hand while the fourteen Lords behind him threatened to expire at the scandal of a woman, and a Princess at that, wearing actual trousers.

Quite beyond belief.

"My dear Princess, how delighted I am to see you safely returned to our Kingdom," Ivarn said meantime. "May I invite you to my mansion to freshen up? King Azerim! It has been far too long. I am mightily pleased to welcome you back onto our shores. What a day! Truly splendid!"

Azerim clasped forearms with him. "Azania and I are

honoured by your lavish welcome, Lord Ivarn. We are betrothed –"

"Congratulations, lad! Simply terrific news! We shall crack open a little something by way of celebration this evening, shall we? Good journey?"

"Smooth sailing, thanks to our allies," said the King with an elegant sweep of his hand to indicate the escort – every inch the diplomat, Thundersong approved.

Clearly, the nervous Lords were not accustomed to seeing over a hundred Dragons rushing toward their town in gleaming array. "We have some immediate requests, my Lord, after which we should catch up properly. Those include landing rights for the ships, warehouse and wharf space, arrangements for a place for the Isles Dragonesses to rest and beach space for our Sea Dragons."

"All doable, my King!" Ivarn boomed cheerfully. "May I make a proposal, an order of business, so to speak? First a few light refreshments, then a working lunch over which our Lords and your Archipelago representatives shall discuss and agree upon high-level trade arrangements. Details can follow. I'm sure my Lords will be champing at the bit to set their own vessels in motion and attend to the needs of the Vaylarn Archipelago which are many, I trust?"

"I have a fat list."

"And we have fat purses!" he chuckled, clapping Azerim on the shoulder. "Your ships are riding low in the water, are they not?"

"I know I can trust you to lighten them, my Lord."

"Indeed, much enlightenment shall surely be forthcoming," said he, managing to find Azania's hand once more with the miraculous ease of a man born to diplomacy. Thundersong approved of his pun with a generous purr. "Congratulations upon your engagement, o Princess of T'nagru. He's one lucky son o' the Isles, may I say?"

"Ooh, I think I snaffled up a fine deal myself," she

said, casting Azerim a teasing sidelong glance.

Had his knees just lost the ability to hinge properly?

However that worked, he looked as if he were still at sea, riding the swell.

"Could not agree more. You make a handsome couple. Now, may I introduce you to my colleagues? How much space would your Dragons require? Meat and fresh water? Charbuz! Run and inform the Harbourmaster that King Azerim's vessels require anchorage and request that he find and secure all the space needed for the goods." He shook his head in sorrow. "Our warehouses are in a woeful state. Nothing but rats and dusty echoes."

Sniffing at Azerim's emotions, Dragon sensed that, despite his pleasant smiles all about, he was not at all overwhelmed by this effusive welcome. Furthermore, he kept the Princess close to his side. The plan was for Azania to lead the charm offensive while guiding the negotiations with the skill of the desert-born. These Lords would not know what had hit them.

Azerim said, "Thundersong, we'll take a carriage up to Lord Ivarn's place in a moment. Would you want to see to Aria and the Sea Dragons?"

"Thundersong?" Lord Ivarn exclaimed. "You've discovered your name, o Dragon – and how well it suits!"

"I am honoured, my Lord," he purred, essaying a Human-style bow. It seemed to go down a treat with the Lords. "Aye, I found my dam amongst the Sea Dragons. I shall introduce you later."

"Perfectly smashing!" Ivarn enthused.

Ha. Which part of this conversation involved smashing things? One needed to beware when asking a Dragon to start smashing – oh, of course! Mistake. He must mean that this was an acceptable arrangement, correct?

He bestowed a broad, flashing Dragon smile upon them.

Good to remind the Lords of their mortality.

"Thundersong, will you join us up at the mansion

later?" Azania said, quietly reassuring the Lords that this was a draconic smile and not a prelude to snack time.

"I shall."

With that, he winged back down to meet the incoming ships.

Since the royals were up in town shaking hands and charming their eager clients, it fell to the Dragons to make practical arrangements. He, Everdeep, Sirensong, Aria and Shellmyrielle, assigned to command the Isles Dragonesses who would stay to start patrolling alongside future shipping runs, held a quick five-way conference. They agreed on patrol schedules up and down the coast and around Hamir Town's harbour and he suggested that the Dragonesses spread out around Lord Ivarn's mansion until such time as a more permanent roost location or caves could be found. They would simply appropriate the desirable beaches until someone complained.

First spoils to the Dragons.

He wondered idly if there were any caves or old Dragon roosts in these great white cliffs. Such a view of the radiant Lumis Ocean would be unparalleled, the quality of the light ... suns-sets over the ocean ... amazing! He filed the idea for future reference.

"Strict orders not to sup on anyone who comes to gawk at you," Thundersong teased.

Everdeep chuckled, "We'll return visits to their homes. Peep into their windows while they're sleeping and suchlike. What do you say?"

"A flawless, no-fail strategy to gain the trust of the locals," Aria grinned.

The mariners started up a show of their own as they began to reef in the sails in preparation for making port. They sang vigorous shanties as they raced around the rigging, coiled ropes and bellowed contradictory and sometimes ludicrous orders, apparently some sort of game or tradition. He could not make head or tail of the nautical terminology. Some of the mariners who had volunteered for this first journey had relatives here on the mainland, he had learned; several had been separated from their families for years by the Sea Serpent menace.

He volunteered to swim up to the harbour to locate the Harbourmaster. He found the harried fellow kicking behinds in various directions, a pursuit of which any Dragon wholeheartedly approved when it came to considering how best to treat Humans. Dragon politely introduced himself and asked if there might be any separated families he would consider allowing onto the wharf?

The Harbourmaster dusted his hands firmly. "That's a fine idea, Dragon. I'm sorry I can't spare a man myself but if you walk up that line of warehouses there, you'll find the main gate. I'm happy to let people in on the basis of family connections. If anyone gives you trouble …"

He looked the Dragon up and down. Fifty fangs smiled at him.

"Trouble being extremely unlikely, I suspect," he corrected hastily. "Hmm, do you think I might usefully employ a Dragon or two? I'm sure the productivity rate around here would treble."

"I'd be happy to bellow at a few people for you."

"I'd appreciate that. Shall we go talk to my warehouse workers? The bunch you see lazing about over there. They're keen on overtime pay and the day's scarcely touching noon."

"I'll gladly help them to reconsider their priorities," Dragon promised, rubbing his forepaws together with a loud rasping sound.

The Harbourmaster said, "Anytime you need a favour in return, Dragon, just ask."

"Thank you."

Having left an astonishingly zealous warehouse crew to their imitation of a severely disturbed ant nest, he strolled up to the gate in a fine mood. Ah, nothing like a good thunder, bellow and bluster to clear the airways of cobwebs. It had admittedly helped that Everdeep turned up right behind him at the instant one poor man began to grumble. First a monster Dragon, then a monster nearly double his size. Bad day for those who enjoyed complaining.

Everdeep took this in very good humour.

Having identified three women and one man who had been separated from their families, he ushered them, together with an infeasible number of children, up to the ships to see if he could not reunite their families. This went smoothly. He deafened everyone and made several of their children cry by roaring out the names after which, he plucked the mariners off their ships and brought them to shore ahead of the mooring process. A small storm of Human hugging, leaking, wailing and laughter ensued. Quite the fuss. Dragon glanced up as another woman cried out from the rigging of Azerim's flagship. Ah, she was the mother of that reckless cabin boy whom he had nearly flattened.

"Dragon! Oh, Dragon – there he is! My husband!"

Springing into the air, he plucked the pair out of the rigging and gave them their first Dragonride. Aye, he was that mushy – at least in one of his five hearts, he told himself. The other four were untouchably draconic and overstuffed with mighty draconic pride. This one heart was an exception.

It did introduce a prickle to his throat to see the husband sprinting madly down the wharf with just one thought on his mind. Oh, and granny and grandpa in tow, it appeared. High-speed hobbling with canes, which struck him as an alarming pursuit.

Ah, sweet, he purred to himself as the family sort of collapsed in a heap. A cane popped out and rolled away. A thoughtful paw stopped it before it tipped over the edge into the water.

He grew mighty in romance and family reunions – what could this Dragon not accomplish?

THUNDER O DRAGON

His answer arrived very shortly. He could not convince Aria to take any form of transportation at all up the cliffs to the Lord's mansion.

I will walk. Slowly. Even if it kills me, she informed him, in her 'I'm dauntless and ever so dangerous' tone of voice. *I need this, Thunderstrong.*

Thunderstrong? He flicked her wingtips with his talon. *Why, you brazen flirt.*

Aria began with an exasperated glower before a self-conscious grin asserted itself. *Slip of the forked tongue, beloved, but I cannot say that it doesn't suit you like the scales suit the Dragon. I … apologise if I am over-serious at times. One of the things I best value about you is that you help me to laugh.*

He nuzzled her with care. *Come on, o song of my hearts. Let's see you walk.*

Aria walked down the gangplank; he did not dare. No piece of wood would thank him for being stepped upon. They paced steadily up from the docks, stopping in a few places to inquire for directions to Lord Ivarn's place. This business of moving about on paws was so undraconic and roundabout. He itched to take to the wing and fly straight to his target, especially since Aria had slowed considerably, despite that they now walked along a road which ran across the green tops of the cliffs toward the familiar mansion with its pristine blue turrets and white walls.

Water break, he announced, leading the way aside to a small brook.

Lowering her muzzle to drink, she said, *This is much harder than I thought. I'm blowing like a whale.*

Exceedingly small and good-looking for a whale, he corrected slyly. *Aria, I'll carry you up to Juggernaut's lair if needed. That'll build my strength as well. You'll be flying before you know it.*

How can I lead … like this?

No one respects you less because of an injury you sustained saving another Dragon, he said. *Now, do you have another mile left in you? Two hundred servants shall wait on you paw and fang, offering delicately spiced nibbles upon silver platters while cooling your fevered brow with large, feathered fans.*

Aria nudged him fondly. *Cosy spot under the suns for two? Taramis is about to emerge.*

Perfect.

They completed the walk side by side, the hulking white Dragon and his far smaller mate. Was she even one-third of his tonnage? Azerim and Azania had a considerable size difference for Humans, over eighteen inches in height, he understood. The disparity between him and Aria was on another scale altogether, her twenty-nine feet in length being only a touch more than half of his fifty-three feet. She was slender and sinewy, all sleek lines and hypnotic wing structures that afforded her bewildering disguise when she attacked. He was still not convinced she had only the one set of wings. For his part, Thundersong felt he had bulked out even since he had met her, as if the shedding of his brown coat of scales had released additional physical potential. Plenty of swimming helped too, of course.

When Aria stumbled over her own paws, he caught and steadied her without so much as blinking.

He said, *Maybe a gentle flight off the cliffs tomorrow?*

Good idea. This neck is improving. The nerve pain is better today and I have more flexibility.

Excellent. I should practice with you on my back as well.

Why?

Was she asking seriously? Or having a gentle rib at his earnest care? He said, *We don't know if or when that scenario might come in useful, even as a surprise factor. Any of our Sea Dragons could carry an Isles warrior upon their back. Why carry an Isles Dragoness? I've no idea.*

Aria said, *We'll rehearse the scenario. We want top-class teamwork and some of my Dragonesses are resistant to the idea.* She nudged him playfully. *Don't look so startled. You are brains above brawn.*

Ha. He strutted ostentatiously for a few steps before subsiding with a chuckle.

THUNDER O DRAGON

At last they found their way up to the house where a liveried servant showed them around to the patio where Thundersong and Azania had previously met the Lord and his guests. Aye, and that racist relative had called her a black toad – a low growl filled his throat as flame spurted up his throat. Controlling a flow out of his nostrils to relieve the unbearable pressure, he related the distasteful incident to his mate. Aria clenched up so badly that she ripped up several flagstones with her talons and then put a paw to her neck.

Bad? he asked at once.

Tweaked something. I need to rest.

He set her to rest, Hamirythe style. The servants brought bolsters to brace her neck, fresh water and several whole grilled fish. Aria accepted all the fussing with a wry smile at her incapacity. With Taramis now ascendant, they offered to set up an awning for shade but Aria said she preferred the heat. Two minutes after downing her fish, she was asleep.

Over the course of the following hour, the Lords gathered inside. Smart thinking from the Lady Ishana had a buffet table set up along one side of her formal reception area, attended by ten servants, and informal, comfortable seating for the Lords just inside the shade line indoors. Eventually Azerim and Azania strolled in, hand in hand.

Dragon caught his breath. *By my wings, you look fabulous, Princess!*

Thank you, Dragon.

She smiled shyly at him before sashaying forward with Azerim to greet the guests. The couple wore matching white outfits in white Isles cotton with azure block patterns at the collar, waist and trouser trim for Azerim, while Azania wore a floor-length white cotton dress that set off her dark beauty to exquisite perfection. The ensemble was light and ethereal as if she had stepped out of a fairytale. White sea pearls adorned her wrists, neck and elegantly braided hair. She must also be wearing platform heels, he assumed, because she stood at least seven inches taller than usual, if not eight, her petite head just reaching Azerim's jawline. Azure makeup with silver highlights made artworks of her eyes.

He turned upon a Dragon sense and caught Aria's eye open the tiniest crack, through which she watched him. He purred, *Warrior power nap?*

She grinned lazily. *I assumed you'd want to take a nice afternoon snooze through the politics, Thundersong?*

How well you know me.

I'll wake you if something interesting happens, she purred. *I put the chances at nil. Sleep well.*

CHAPTER 9

WARRIOR POWER

THUNDERSONG'S NAP LASTED UNTIL he started snoring in keeping with the size of him. That was enough to drown out a minor thunderstorm, let alone a meeting.

His dam thumped him in the ribs. "Hush!"

"Fas-snore-ating topic," he murmured. "Aren't you done blathering on yet? It's the dulcet drone of your voices that's kept me sound asleep so far."

"Dragon!" various voices admonished him.

Princess Azania said, "Thundersong, we were planning to wind up – apologies for disturbing your snooze, o most vexing quadruped – but became stuck on the thorny topic of –"

"Oh, split the costs down the middle and be done with it!" he snorted. "Honestly. Is that even a question?"

Oddly, one of those moments developed where everyone looked at everyone else and somehow worked out at the same instant that they really were arguing over nothing. Lord Ivarn started the round of guffaws, followed closely by all the Lords and Azerim. Even the Sea Dragons and Aria joined in. Azania eyeballed him coldly, her foot tapping beneath the conference table.

Lord Ivarn said, "On that brilliant note, I believe that we should conclude a profitable afternoon with a toast to the particular and peculiar genius who is Thundersong!"

"Hear, hear!" shouted the Lords.

Everdeep chortled massively to the far side of Aria. "To Thundersong!"

Azania's glower deepened.

"Come now, dearest," Azerim said, making to hold her arm. She snatched it away. "It's a perfect solution."

"So it is," she said and, as if she had flipped instantly from brown scales to white, her radiant smile returned. Rising, she joined the toast, but said privately, *In the desert, a person would have their throat slit for such disrespect, Thundersong. Be grateful it worked so well here.*

He swallowed hard.

By the ambient light, he realised that the shadows grew long. The meeting must have lasted for hours.

Aria whispered to him, *I'm sorry. I put the idea in your mind first.*

No matter, beloved. Rising to his paws, he said, "I honour those who labour so diligently for the good of their people. I meant no disrespect but only to leave the policymaking and affairs of state –" he gazed directly at his Dragon Rider "– to those far more able than I."

Her black eyes flashed.

He realised that he needed to expunge the fires from his hearts before he did something foolish. Disrespect? Was that not the very last insinuation he meant toward Azania or Azerim … he saw how his behaviour could be characterised by those who did not understand his motives but repudiated that in the depths of his hearts. This was not his skill! He blundered through subtlety and niceties like a runaway boulder. Why could creatures never see and value him for who he was?

Far more upset than he had pretended to Aria, wasn't he? Paws turning, before the rest of him realised his intent, he walked up off the patio toward the cliff edge several hundred feet away. This was no great distance for a large Dragon. Freedom beckoned. With a sound far closer to a whine than a roar of draconic hubris, he charged toward the edge.

Out there? Nothing but freedom.

Dragon. Dragon, wait!

Azania!

His paws clenched at her mental wail. Plowing a furrow through the soft, bright green grass toward the edge, he realised belatedly that he could not halt his momentum in time. Whipping a glance over his shoulder, he saw her running after, but the long dress and impractical shoes made that a hazardous affair.

He toppled over the edge.

Snuff his mortal fires. No Blitz the Fritz! Not today!

Snapping out his wings, he caressed the air and turned his ungainly tumble into a swoop that approached actual elegance. A strong breeze rising up the cliff helped him gain altitude at a tremendous pace. From his Rider's perspective, it must have been as if he vanished, only to rocket up into the lowering rays of the suns, backlit by glorious white light, and then his tonnage kept on rising improbably into a wide somersault that brought him back over the double-pentagon, castle-like building, before he completed the loop by swooping back toward her with a blast of air. A deft aerial jink avoided the edge of the roof. Several servants ducked and scattered like startled fowl.

Azania froze like a mouse unexpectedly faced by a cobra. Panic flashed through her expression. Then, her body language changed from fear to realisation. Bending her knees, she sprang lightly into his lowered right forepaw as he caught her up at high speed. A deft flexion of the wrist – courtesy of Juggernaut once more – won him a light catch, a jolt that was far from knocking the breath out of her.

Shooting low over the grass, he burst off the cliff edge even faster than before.

Carefully, he placed her upon his neck. The wide cotton skirt made her seating straightforward, once she tucked up the material and wriggled a few times.

She rubbed his neck. "Are we alright, Dragon?"

"Excuse me for one moment," he said. Tilting his head to the side, he expelled a massive rush of billowing white fire. On and on it raged, until his inner rage subsided and with it, more rational thought returned.

"Better?"

"Ironed out a few kinks in the innards," he admitted.

Leaning along his neck, she said, "That was a deathly dull meeting, even I'll admit. Like dancing with a circle of stones."

"I meant no disrespect. That's the last thing – Azania – it's the way I *never* want you to feel!"

"I know. I … should have realised, been less touchy." Laughing shakily, she held his neck with her arms and rested her forehead against his scales, a tiny, slightly cooler touch. "I don't ever want to drive you away again. Sorry. I panicked. Look. I'll try to explain. Azerim and I had just disagreed quite sharply and I felt ill-advised and small because he did not respect my position and then you popped up and solved everything in a moment's bleary-eyed confusion and everyone agreed you're a genius and jealousy – heck, it bites deep sometimes, doesn't it?"

"More than," he admitted gruffly.

Spreading his wings, he glided out to sea.

After a long time, she murmured, "What a beautiful evening."

"Not a time for disagreements," he suggested.

"I don't believe we're disagreeing anymore, my Dragon. I apologise. Neither the best foot nor the best paw forward today from us, was it?"

"No. Tell you what, in the future, I will attend and not snore through any meetings at which you require my presence. I will respect you – but you need to realise that disagreement does not imply disrespect."

She chuckled softly. "That's hard."

"Aye, I imagine it must be, having grown up in a

culture where no-one hears you because you're a woman, and a titchy one at that, and having been lectured for years on how your only worth was to keep your mouth shut, marry for wealth and be a good little brood mare."

"Ouch."

"*Blergh!* See? That's my best diplomatic tongue."

"It's accurate, even if expressed like the cuff of a large paw." Her tiny arms squeezed as hard as they could. "Dragon, you and I need to be more confident in who we are. Heavens' sakes, we're the first Dragon Rider team in history! We're not supposed to have petty squabbles and –"

"Be Human? Or Dragon?"

"Aye!"

He chuckled massively, squirming in the air to work the tension out of his neck, through his shoulders and down his tail.

Imitating Yarimda's aged tones, she said, "My girl, it's not about whether or not you have disagreements. Those, you will have. It's about how you solve them and move forward."

"Ooh, watch out. You and I might become infected by this wisdom bug."

"Dreadful fate."

"Thank you for running after me, Azania. It means a great deal to this Dragon."

"Told you, I was not letting you go anywhere this time. You are mine, my Dragon, period. I think I might have been planning to leap off that cliff after you. Is that weird?"

"No. It's … cute."

"Cute? Thundersong, I am not cute!"

"Oh, you're a mighty cute Dragon Rider. This King of a faraway Archipelago I know told me so. Now tell me, o cute package of singular awesomeness, how many times did you skewer our friendly Lords with your rapier desert negotiation skills?"

"Dragon!" she snickered happily. "Three times, if you must know. I'm small, but I bite hard. Even Azerim was impressed."

"If he wasn't, I'd bite him personally."

"Permission granted. Anytime."

"Wow, why that tone?"

She sighed. "He can be a bit bullish, Dragon. Maybe he's not used to having a partner who speaks her mind? I guess he's used to being the King and here comes this know-nothing desert girl saying things he clearly wants to say for himself – I don't know. Is this the 'little me' speaking again?"

"Perhaps. You're almost into a quality of Thundersong self-talk, there."

"Ahem. Sorry."

He purred, "Maybe a desert Princess needs to learn to use all her wiles and cunning."

"What do you mean, Bl … uh, Thundersong? There are still times I want to call you Blitz."

"Fair enough. I was Blitz for twenty years." Exhaling gustily, he began to turn, sweeping across the face of a glorious, Taramis-dominant sunset. He said, "Look at how the suns create the effect of a flower with a white heart and many fiery orange petals spreading across the sky, laced with pure white stamens."

"I love how you see the world," she breathed.

"Fuzzily," he chortled. "I meant, Azerim worships the ground you float above in those crazy shoes."

"Aren't they something? Nine-inch platforms. The designer wanted to create exactly that floating, otherworldly look."

"Fashion requires risking breaking one's ankles? Count me out."

"I still only reach five foot five in these," she groaned. "Azerim's so tall."

"*Mwaa-haa-haargh,* but look at how tall you are on the back of a Dragon! You can use me for a lift when you want to kiss him. Anytime."

"Thanks, I feel suitably elevated in heart."

"So, it is very simple. All you need to do is to seduce him with one flutter of those dark, dusky eyes and purr, 'Oh, Azerim, I'd be so honoured if you could ask for my input during meetings.' "

"You wretched beast, I don't behave like that!"

Putting on his best Azerim impression, he added, " 'O Azania, my gorgeous muse, my one and only, what's your opinion?' Or, 'My precious as yet un-ransomed Black Rose of the Desert, how do you feel these costs ought to be handled?' "

She smacked his neck. "Those Lords would fall over laughing."

"Stronger together, Princess. This truth defines us."

Gnarr.

"Perfect," he said. "Now, *shh.*"

Silencing even the breeze wuthering over his wings, the Dragon treated his Rider to the evening's beauty, a silence of vast aerial spaces beneath the spectacular fiery vault of the sky. They soared upon the softest of breezes, gazing over Hamirythe with its new colourful population of Dragonesses resting upon the cliff tops and beaches that appeared from this height to have grown a population of lumpen white boulders overnight. Tilting his axis, he brought them sweeping around for a light landing upon the grass in front of the mansion, catching Azerim and Ivarn in the act of uncorking a skein of his finest vintage with unmistakable gusto.

Aria had appeared asleep, but once more, she watched him with a feline expression, one eye open a crack. He glided forward to acknowledge her regard with a wingtip touch. A soft, wordless purr constituted her response.

Lady Ishana bustled over with motherly intent, calling, "Oh look, it's my favourite Dragon-Riding Princess. The Lords have left. Come, Princess Azania, let your hair down a little with us."

"Is that something like letting your scales down?" Dragon asked suspiciously, offering Azania a courteous paw as she dismounted with care for her dress.

"Ooh, naked Dragons? I shudder," the Princess giggled.

"It means to relax with friends," Ishana smiled. "Considering the service you rendered first my family and now our nation, I should most certainly like to consider you friends."

"That we are," Azania smiled, standing on her tiptoes to kiss the Lady's cheek. "You've been so kind to us. Dragon, remembering how I snuck out last time to sleep in the crook of your neck, Lady Ishana kindly offered me chambers which open to the outside, so that we may be close to one another."

"Most thoughtful and appreciated, Lady Ishana," Dragon rumbled, inclining his head.

"Oh, it's nothing," she said. "A goblet of wine, Princess?"

"A small one, please," she said. "Otherwise, I stand no chance in these heels. Actually, Azerim, would it be terribly undiplomatic of me to declare aching feet and go barefoot?"

"When on the Islands, do as Islanders do," Lord Ivarn said. "Servant –"

Despite a servant appearing at the Lord's elbow with almost prescient timing, Azerim raised his hand to stop him. "This is my duty," he said, steering Azania to a comfortable chair before kneeling at her feet. "Ah, now why does this pose strike me as familiar?" He stroked his fashionable beard, deep in supposed thought. "Must be that I knelt before the most beautiful woman in Solixambria just the other day, pleading for her to promise to be mine …"

"And her smelly feet didn't even chase you off?" Dragon inquired, with a massive guffaw.

Azania howled, "Dragon, I'm so going to paste you

from here to T'nagru!"

"Nay, not even the feet," said Azerim, handling the ankle ties with aplomb. "Fresh as a … well, a zesty ocean tang, one might say."

She pretended to thump him beneath the chin with her other foot.

"Although, dear one, you really do not want to experience the insides of the royal boots. That's on a whole different level."

"We've a local secret," Lord Ivarn said. "Back in the day, I discovered the same issue. Spending all day long in a hot climate wearing formal leather boots can lead to some truly memorable odours and, shortly thereafter, nasty infections of the fungal sort."

The Dragons all gasped in concert.

"Dragons don't have any such issues?" Azerim asked.

"Scale fungus can result from prolonged immersion," Everdeep noted succinctly.

The Humans all winced.

Thundersong said dryly, "Only the best of friends could be this well acquainted with the delights of one another's bodily fungi … Ivarn, you were saying?"

"*Barzuga* herb." Winking broadly at Azania, he said, "I shall give you a supply before you leave. It neutralises odours and keeps the feet from sweating too much –"

"And is thus a failsafe recipe for marital bliss," his wife put in.

How they roared with laughter!

Half an hour before dawn, a large white paw cunningly slipped the Princess into the bed she had not used during the night and even tucked her in with a deft touch. Fast asleep. By his wings, this Dragon knew how to handle a Princess, he congratulated himself.

THUNDER O DRAGON

Then, he joined Aria Seaspray at the cliff edge. They tipped forward onto the breeze. He queried her health anxiously.

Flying is better than walking, she said.

The cuts are healing well.

Good. Still, let's take this one paw at a time. With a ripple of her wings, she rose above him and then executed a deft landing on his back. *How's this? Not too heavy?*

You, heavy? he snorted. *I could carry you all day.*

You may need to. Aria took off again, supremely graceful in flight. *Warrior training today? The Lords wish to meet separately. Depending on how that goes, they'd like to carry on with Azerim this evening or tomorrow. That means we've time to start smacking our Dragon army into shape — warrior power exercises, teamwork training and even practising that snatch you showed us with Azania. All of that would be very good to start with.*

Isn't Chanize coming to check on you?

Aye, I forgot about that.

She nudged him with a naughty curl of flame in her eye. *So?*

So? he echoed.

There's two of us all alone in the wide, wide sky.

Dragon stared at her, tingling in every bone of his body. She surely didn't mean ... Aria wriggled closer and mimed a bite toward his neck. Her wings rippled in a way that turned his male brain into a pile of steaming hormones.

Up here? he blurted out.

Where else? she inquired, caressing his flank with her wing edge.

Uh ... well, Tamarine Mountains Dragons disappear into a cosy lair for two, he spluttered. *However, Sea Dragons do this underwater — and I wouldn't want to drown you, so I ... suppose we should —*

Enough talking, Thundersong.

Aria —

Catch me if you can! she called, flexing her wings to

accelerate into a vertical climb.

Cheat!

They flew up toward the suns together, a pair of Dragons who adored one another profoundly, and no doubt made both Ignis and Taramis blink in shock at the naughty things they did right beneath their brilliant eyes.

Sirensong nudged him as they winged down to roust up the Sea Dragons, who were late for their day's training. One did not want an unimpressed Aria. Oh no.

≈*Good flight this morning, son?*≈

≈*Energising,*≈ he rumbled.

≈*You flew high.*≈

≈*Parts of me still feel as if they haven't come down yet.*≈

≈*Oh?*≈ said his dam, before clearly making the right connection. ≈*Oh! Thundersong. Was she alright?*≈

He opted to give her a huge, slow wink. ≈*Let's just say, the oceans are deep and the sky is high, but ocean always rises.*≈

≈*Thundersong!*≈ His dam's fires blushed audibly. ≈*You're just like Everdeep. So inappropriate. Let me say, gladness swells my wave to see the two of you together and, the more I observe you, the more certain I am that you could not have chosen better. She … she sees you.*≈

He pondered this as they dropped through the air.

≈*You are good for her, too. She might have dominated another male, in their Isles way, but I do not believe that type of relationship would have brought out the best in her. She respects your innermost fires.*≈

≈*Thank you, mother. I value your wisdom.*≈

≈*So formal?*≈

He chuckled self-consciously. ≈*What I meant was, I value your perspective more than my poor words made clear. My sire's family knew me twenty years, yet in many ways, did not know me at all.*≈

Sirensong voiced a soft, keening wail.

He comforted his dam with a wingtip caress and many fond and fiery words.

Then, roaring in tandem, they thundered at the tardy Sea Dragons to wake up and shift a wing. Up top of the cliffs, they consigned their kin to Aria's tender mercies. She worked them – and her warriors – until they were ready to drop. The three hundred Anhoyal Rangers joined in midmorning, practising Dragonback. They tried the teamwork exercises and ended up with one broken leg, a freak accident to one of the young Dragonesses when she collided with another mid-air.

Please don't leave me behind, Aria, she almost begged, her eyes awash with dark colours of pain. *It's just an ankle. I can fly!*

Aria considered her plea. *Thundersong, this is doable, right?*

Let's have Sirensong and Chanize examine the break, but I don't see any major issues with her continuing up to Juggernaut's lair, he said. *Let's have the Sea Dragons work on the back carrying. We may need that.*

The back carry? asked one of the other Dragonesses, Faryrielle.

Aria said, *It's a teamwork exercise, as well as a manoeuvre that may grant the element of surprise.*

I am not being carried by some other Dragon!

Dragon nudged the Dragoness slyly. *Is Farsinger not burly enough for your taste?*

I resent your implication! she barked.

He said mildly, *Ah, I see. Maybe we should change up the pairings, Aria?*

His own siblings – the two males, Lightsong and Eversong, and his three sisters, Echosong, Farsong and Ripplesong – all stared at him as if he'd grown curly horns and started running about bleating like a sheep. Did one not favourably arrange romantic relationships among Sea Dragons?

Never mind – a question for another time, for just

now, he had a different problem, by the name of Faryrielle. She threatened his nose with a pawful of talons, demanding, *Are you calling me incapable?*

How did one deal with this level of female belligerence?

His mate pushed between them. *This one's mine. Go flirt with some other male; just leave him in a fit state to fly, alright? Day after tomorrow, he still needs two wings attached to his body.*

The other Dragoness chuckled curtly, *Is that all?*

Filling her lungs, Aria roared, *Right, Dragonesses, let's test these Sea Dragons' warrior power! Every Sea Dragon will take a warrior on his or her back. Everdeep, was that a snigger? That's two for you! You will take off, fly around the town and back again. Top speed! Drop one Dragoness and you're fodder!* As her Dragonesses began to chuckle, she added, *And after that, we'll swap around! See which of my fine warriors can actually lift a Sea Dragon off the ground!*

As the flight of deeply displeased Dragons lifted off – both sets being displeased for different reasons – he turned to find Aria glaring at him. She tapped a talon pointedly.

Oops. He inquired, *Me?*

With a sinuous wriggle of her hindquarters, she suggested, *If you can't beat them, no more skyward trips for you … you big, bad, broad-shouldered beast.*

Quite unexpectedly, my motivation levels appear to have smacked into the suns, he confessed. *Shall we show them how it's done?*

I know you can, Thundersong.

CHAPTER 10

TO THE MOUNTAINS

TWO DAYS LATER, THUNDERSONG checked in with Chanize and Farizam before takeoff. The husband-and-wife team would fly with Sirensong as her Riders, a task for which his dam had volunteered. He examined the fit of the modified saddle on her neck.

"Straps all good, Chanize?" he rumbled, plucking the thick leather straps buckled below her knee stumps. "You can reach these?"

"All good," she smiled.

"How's your saddle companion?"

"Gorgeous," said Farizam.

"I didn't ask you, riffraff," he growled with mock aggression. "How's the lateral fit?"

"Solid on the waist," she replied, demonstrating. "It's a good design. I'll sing out if I sense any trouble, Thundersong, but I suspect Sirensong could smash through waves and I wouldn't be going anywhere."

"Good. How's Flinryielle?"

"The ankle patient? Farizam helped me to figure out a perfect splint," Chanize said. "The bones are well set. As long as she doesn't try landing on that paw for a couple of weeks, all will be well."

"Good."

Thundersong eyed the Rangers balefully and then gave the incoming weather front his even more special fire-shot eye. The eye of ire, Dragons called it. The brisk wind promised to push them along from behind, but it was also moist. The Isles Dragonesses predicted rain before the day was out.

He bellowed, "Everyone, check your saddles one more time! Mount up! Let's get this outing underway before evening, shall we?"

From over on Everdeep's neck position, Azerim chuckled, "You'll have them misty-eyed with memories of their basic training, Thundersong. Keep going."

"Should I? As you wish, o King." Raising his voice to a thunderous pitch, he roared, "You pustulent runts of dune rats' litters, shift your skanky behinds before I thrash you over the very suns!"

The Anhoyal Rangers rushed about with redoubled zeal as Azerim bent over, trying to disguise his laughter as a coughing fit. Apparently, a certain Dragon had been reading too many scrolls. Thundersong growled at him that he and Azania had been ready for over an hour and would have been halfway to the ruined Kingdom of Taribonli by now.

Taribonli was indeed their first target, tomorrow evening's stop at their predicted speed. Neither the Isles Dragonesses nor the Sea Dragons possessed anything like his swiftness and stamina – through the air, he reminded himself firmly. In seawater it would be another matter. The Sea Dragons had power aplenty. Rising with them, he sent Everdeep into the point position of their formation and began his instruction of the Sea Dragons and his observations of the Isles Dragonesses' technique.

Curious. He could not fathom the anatomy of their shoulder structures which appeared to support double, independently mobile forward wing bones, while secondary muscles controlled two sets of strut-like bones farther back. Mini shoulders. Plus, further muscles on the wing surfaces, where other Dragons had none, gave them the ability to create that butterfly-like rippling motion. All that combined to give them a ridiculous level of control and flight characteristics that defied scientific explanation.

Descending from Hamirythe's clifftops toward the inner end of Hasnorne Estuary, the Dragons flew over the coastal marshes, great patches of silvery water broken by dark khaki sedge grasses. Hordes of idiotic water birds posed a real menace. A number clattered into the flying Dragons and eventually, one caused a minor wing injury. Thundersong ordered a climb and took Aria upon his back. After putting down for a rest on a low grassy hill toward noon, they flew steadily until evening, passing the last of the marshes and crossing a low line of stony hills. Less miles than he wanted.

The following morning, getting underway was even more chaotic. Tired people, tired Dragons, everything sodden with the overnight rain. He wished them a fine morning at a merry volume and set course for Taribonli.

≈*There's a river just past the city,*≈ he called to the Sea Dragons.

≈*Flying is overrated,*≈ Everdeep grumbled.

A chorus of Sea Dragon grumbling followed. His brothers and sisters were among the most vocal. Family. Could not fly them anywhere. With rising irritation, Thundersong snarled, ≈*If you can't handle this, how are you planning to handle the desert?*≈

≈*It can't be all that bad?*≈ said Sweetsong, one of his extended family.

His half-sister, Echosong, said, ≈*It sounds like some kind of hell reserved for the unholiest of creatures.*≈

≈*That's my Rider's home you're talking about!*≈

Azania patted his neck. "Thundersong, on a rampage this morning?"

THUNDER O DRAGON

Gnarr.

"The enemy's far over the mountains, my friend."

GNARR!!

"I could not agree more," she said, with an infeasible degree of cheer. "I'm cold and wet and we're flying up into the freezing mountains. Can't wait."

Right she was. Thundersong shook off his curmudgeonly mood and focussed on the mission. As the cloud cover lifted during the morning, their companions peered ahead at the white-tipped peaks spreading across the horizon. The Sea Dragons said that they were just like the mighty underwater mountain ranges and the ice, like the permanently frozen ocean of the far North. The Isles Dragonesses flicked their wing edges uneasily, while the Rangers chattered excitedly. The Archipelago dwellers had never seen snow before – only Azerim, and that over five years before.

One of the female Rangers yelled, '*Yeee-haaah!*' as her Dragon dipped unexpectedly through a thermal pocket and then surged, breaking the silence and making many laugh.

Her Sea Dragon mount, Truewave, snorted, "I am not some animal to be '*yeee-haaah-ed*' at through the air, lady."

"No. Animals don't talk back either," she responded, "and you're only … well, at least bazillion times more awesome than any animal, Truewave. Give or take."

"Mmm, I like you, girl."

"Hey, get your big paws off my girlfriend," complained the Ranger behind her.

The seventy-foot Sea Dragon chortled, "Then you'd best get your paws on her fast, my friend, because this one's a treasure of the waves."

Ah, that gave a Dragon an idea. Clapping his paws together sharply, Thundersong roared, "Sea Dragons, let's have a journeying song! Dragons and Humans, pick your partners! Rangers, you may dance upon your Dragon's back! Sea Dragons and Isles Dragons, pair up! Let's shake those wings and show off our moves."

Azerim made his move first and fast. Snapping his buckles open, he clambered up onto Everdeep's back and then, as the huge Sea Dragon swept over, he jumped onto the pair of shoulders behind Azania with aplomb. A few Rangers applauded ironically.

He bowed with a show of elegance. "Milady, may I have the honour of this dance?"

"I should be –"

Everybody startled in fear as a Ranger pitched overboard with a wild yell, but with over a dozen warrior Dragonesses in hot pursuit, a landing on the ground half a mile below never threatened. Everdeep set the Dragons singing with one of the bouncy, frothing songs about sporting in the waves and … well, other naughtiness, one might argue. Thankfully, that part could safely remain lost in translation. Several beats in, seventy Sea Dragons struck up in multipart harmony, filling the vault of the skies with an incredible concerto of voices. Passing above a small village, Thundersong saw through his spectacles sixty or so tiny white faces rushing outdoors to gawk at the sight of one hundred and thirty-three Dragons winging directly southeast into the foothills of the Tamarine Mountains with people dancing on their backs.

Oops, there went another Ranger.

Aria began to swoop, but she pulled up in a spasm of apparent back pain. Dragon immediately dipped beneath her with a warning to his dancing Riders. To their credit, they flexed their knees and stayed onboard as he caught up with the Cobalt Dragoness and eased her into a landing upon his back.

She groaned softly, *Oh, that was brutal. Chanize did warn me.*

Warn you of what? he asked anxiously.

Nerve healing in Dragons can trigger these unexpected cramps. I've numbness and tingling all the way down my right side, but it's starting to ease already.

Do you need Chanize now?
She has an oil extract which should reduce the pain.

Turning, Thundersong called, "Sirensong, toss Chanize over here, would you?"

"I – Dragon!" she howled. "I'm not anyone's throwing game!"

"But you are," he said. "Never fear, you're still strapped into your saddle. Shall we practice an aerial transfer? Aria needs you."

"Remind me why I gave up needlework again?"

"Because you prefer to *needle* Dragons in your spare time?"

Ooh, smooth answer. Even his dam had a chuckle for that one.

Shortly, they organised a low toss of about thirty feet. Chanize screamed her way into his paw but then emerged with a chuckle, "Oh, was that all? What fun! Boost me up to Aria please, Thundersong."

Still seated upon Sirensong's neck, Farizam extended his arms. "I want my wife back!"

"Easily arranged," she grinned, making a come-hither gesture.

A few seconds later, the leader of the Rangers hurtled through the air, yelling something about galumphing Dragons and their overweening ways.

Thundersong caught him deftly. "Do come join the party, Farizam."

"I'm definitely awake now," he growled.

Steady flying won them a sight of the tumbledown towers of the old city by late afternoon. Taribonli had famously been sacked by Zobar the Warlord after its foolish King Azarkal had despatched his entire army into the Tamarine Mountains, meaning to take revenge upon the Smiter Clan for kidnapping his daughter Amonette. Azarkal's name was now a byword for foolishness.

History could be cruel, especially to fools.

Winging over the ruined city, largely covered now in

briars and thick undergrowth but with the main roads and buildings still visible, Thundersong led the Dragons to a landing on the banks of the Taribonli River just beyond. A frisson of excitement gripped the Sea Dragons as they eyed a frothing series of waterfalls and deep riverine pools. Minerals from the glacial runoff turned the waters a striking teal colour. Decent trout frequented this river too, as he recalled.

"We'll make camp here," Everdeep called.

Weary cheers greeted his announcement. How were the Rangers tired? They had been sitting all day. Was it just the travel? He could not wait for his fetching, insect-splattered dusty travel-greyish colour to return to white again. How did Sea Dragons ever keep their colour? He had always been fastidious about personal cleanliness but to be frank, brown hid the dirt rather better than white with the golden-brown flares.

Besides, he had a mate to impress these days. Best get scrubbing and polishing, Dragon!

Soon, the river turned into a ripple of colours as the Dragons and Dragonesses vied with one another to decimate the local trout population, some of which came ashore for the Rangers to share as well. Sankir Farizam said that this was the life and that his soldiers would get lazy not having to hunt for themselves. Ariamyrielle promptly proposed that his Rangers, on the days following, could take hunting shifts with her Dragonesses to work on their aerial shooting skills.

Thundersong and Aria showed some of the curious Dragons how they put their Humans to bed for the night, tucked up in a cosy nook between their bodies, with wings overhead sheltering them from the cold. Natural draconic body heat did the rest.

"Better than any tent," he averred.

"Over the top it goes," said Azania, pulling on his wing to hide her and the King from sight.

"Oh, and what's going on under there?" Farizam

inquired.

"Sleeping," Azerim replied, all innocence.

"Only his lips are still moving," Thundersong put in slyly.

"I'm snoring."

"None of us believe you," Farizam said.

"Exactly," said the King, sounding muffled as Azania applied herself to distracting him.

Thundersong added, "It's easily done with either one or two Dragons – one, with Humans held in the crook of the neck with a covering wing or with a pair of Dragons lying in this configuration. Dragons often sleep like this either for a couple's intimacy or simply to increase body warmth in the lair. Cold stone in a deep mountain winter can be miserable otherwise."

Privately, Azania said to him, *I know, but everything's better with a Princess in paw, isn't it?*

Except the considerable financial outlay, he teased.

Rascal. Feeding you would stretch any Kingdom's budget, never mind a Dragon army.

That reminds me, we ought to talk about supply lines to T'nagru.

True.

The following morning, Thundersong bellowed his now familiar wake-up routine over a campsite of Dragons dozing on the sands and in the river and Humans either sleeping in the low, compact Ranger tents or tucked up next to the amenable Dragons. What had come so naturally to him and Azania seemed a much slower, more awkward process for many – except for Farizam and Chanize, he noticed, who emerged from a suspiciously comfy-looking married person snuggle between Everdeep and Sirensong.

Oho. His infallible nose for mischief tingled furiously.

Up the river they flew.

"Wake up, you miserable, slouching crew of slackers!" Thundersong cried early on the fourth morning of their journey. A chorus of groans rose from everyone. At the top of his lungs, he bawled, "It's a beautiful morning for climbing into the mountains! Let's see you shake those legs and paws, ladies, gentlemen and beasts of all descriptions!"

Someone yelled, "You're the beast around here!"

"Aye, I'm the beast of the beast of the beast!" he thundered back. "Hunting detail, where's my breakfast?"

"You're turning into a morning tyrant," King Azerim complained, emerging from his bedroll looking laughably mussed of hair and half asleep.

"Azania's influence, of course!" Dragon boomed.

"Me? Dragon's just discovered his inner Princess, everyone!"

"My – my *what?*" he spluttered.

"Your inner Princess! What a progressive Dragon you are."

"You pint-sized pest! You whispering mosquito in Human clothing! Just wait until I catch you!"

Azania sprinted away at high speed and dived behind Everdeep's legs. "Can't catch me! How does it feel, Princess four-paws? Are you primping your hair over there? Polishing your gorgeous white scales again? How's the makeup coming on?"

GNAAA-GRROOARRGH!!

Chortling, snorting and thundering threats fit to split the mountains apart, he chased the rascally Princess all around the camp. Inner Princess indeed! He had never been so perfectly and hilariously insulted in his life. Half of his attempts to catch her failed because he was laughing so hard, he kept tripping over his own paws. Eventually he managed to catch her and he made a show of bending over her hand to Dragon-kiss it, which involved smooching her arm right up to her elbow, his lips were that large.

"Ew, save it for Aria," she complained.

"Preferably not," said the Cobalt Dragoness, with a shudder of not entirely simulated horror. "Thundersong, are you done playing at Princesses over there?"

THUNDER O DRAGON

"Toy Princess, toy King," he needled.

Azerim called out, "On that note, Human-Dragon relations hit an all-time low."

After a light breakfast consumed for the Humans' sake, the flight of Dragons began the hard, steep climb into the mountains proper. Dragon had not realised how much the increased altitude would affect particularly the Sea Dragons, who laboured hard in the thinner air. Thankfully, they were tremendously fit as a result of their migratory lifestyle or they might just have collapsed somewhere along the river's course they followed. Taking a break every two hours, the army soared up to the shores of Yazinti Lake, a gorgeous montane lake lying behind the first range of peaks in the broad Tamarine Range. There was no snow on the ground in this season, but the precipitous drop in temperature had the Anhoyal Rangers scrambling for the fur-lined cloaks and warm trousers they had scoffed at back in Hamir Town.

Thundersong did not bother with an 'I told you so.' Instead, he told them that they had a couple of even steeper but shorter climbs ahead, crossing the great vaulting passes into the central Tamarine Range, but they should soon grow accustomed to the altitude. Meantime, they would rest and train here beside the lake and negotiate the first pass on the morrow.

"You did well today, Aria," he said, helping her to slide off his back onto a comfortable spot on the dark sand by the lakeside.

"Aye, much better. I'm knackered now, though," she said. "Thanks again for the rides."

"Anything to show off my brawn."

She nudged him tiredly. "Aye, because you're that shallow. I believe you, of course. If there's a fish or two going spare, I'm really hungry, but in all sincerity, I couldn't lift a talon –"

"Aye, because you're the kind of Dragoness who never lifts a talon," he said archly. "Rest. I'll find you a snack."

"This is not easy for me," she whispered.

"How may I encourage you?" He cracked a fang-filled smile. "I can be very ... encouraging."

Her eye fires brightened at once. "Ooh, you're a *bad* Dragon."

"So bad, I'm good," he purred, and had the satisfaction of hearing her subdued fires growl into fresh life inside her chest.

That evening, Thundersong gathered his tropical and oceanic troops and delivered a lecture on the care of paws, tails and wings or fingers, toes and noses in the extreme conditions of the high mountains. Frostbite really did bite, no question about it. This led into a briefing on male-dominated Tamarine Mountains Dragon culture. Ariamyrielle laid down the law on not completely filleting, dismembering or murdering any males who made inappropriate advances upon the physically smaller Isles females. Just break a few digits. They'd soon get the right idea.

A couple of the Sea Dragonesses chuckled among themselves at the idea of any thirty-five-foot males – barely half their size – strutting their stuff around such massive females.

"Just watch where you sit," Thundersong put in. "No accidental flattening of my relatives, you see?"

They guffawed heartily.

"Although, if you meet my half-brothers Brand and Brawl, please do feel free to rearrange their tiny egos with extreme prejudice."

"Dragon," Azania admonished.

"Oh, alright. Correction rather than outright crushing, please. That might be hard to explain to my sire."

True to the way of the world, Thundersong noticed a few pairings beginning to solidify amongst the different Dragons – both friendships and romantic pairings. Faryrielle and Farsinger acted laughably skittish around one another, constantly sparring and teasing. Flinryielle, with her broken ankle, had no less than five Sea Dragon males hulking about her and her sister, Asurimyrielle – hmm, including his half-brother Lightsong. For a quiet fellow, he could certainly turn a female's head.

Tomorrow, they would fly through various Clan territories – first the Smashers, then the Wreckers and Obliterators before they reached Juggernaut's lair in deep Grinder territory. Azania loved the Clan names. He had to admit that they held considerable amusement value. As subtle as a straight right punch to the jaw. Sheer numbers should see them make this flight untroubled, he suspected, but any diplomacy required would likely fall upon his shoulders.

On that note, he walked over to Everdeep to speak with him about how to handle the Devastators' likely reaction to Sirensong's presence.

Everdeep shook his great head slowly. ≈*I am not naturally an aggressive Dragon, Thundersong, but if your Clan mistreats or maligns my Sirensong, I will say this: deep waters move powerfully.*≈

≈*I understand and I would stand by your side,*≈ he said.

≈*She is your dam.*≈

≈*Aye. Any dishonour ...*≈ He clenched his paws and admitted, ≈*I have no idea how I might react, but I suspect it would not be pretty. Much depends upon how the Devastators approached Blaze's admission that he sired my egg off Sirensong. Before, they closed ranks and pretended it never happened.*≈

Everdeep clapped him upon the shoulder. ≈*Shall we hold one another's waves accountable, brother?*≈

≈*I'd appreciate that, brother. Thank you.*≈

What a strange thing. Twenty years with two brothers and he had never realised what brotherhood actually meant. Thundersong shook his head slowly. He would have wanted to say that Sirensong made a mistake with his sire, Blaze the Devastator, but then ... he would not exist. Even that betrayal must have a purpose.

He clenched his right forepaw into a fist. Aye. His task

was to turn that error of judgement into a treasure hoard. A Dragon might stand tall, but he would stand far taller still upon the shoulders of others – or, as the Sea Dragons said, a rising wave lifted all Dragons.

Better still, he must be the wave.

CHAPTER 11

BREAKDOWN

RISING IN HER SADDLE, Princess Azania waved in the huge Dragonwing. "Just as we practised, Thundersong?"

"You and your memorable entrances."

"We agreed to shake the power hierarchy here in the mountains. You're not about to shake a tree by smiling at it, Dragon."

"Nor does one kidnap a Princess by smiling at her."

"Oh, and here I thought you were smiling at me all those months ago. Was that just constipation, you poor thing?"

"Azania!"

"Shh, don't wreck the surprise."

No danger of that. They hid just shy of the rim of Juggernaut's massive sinkhole, watching the stirring sight of all the Sea and Isles Dragons, together with all their Ranger Riders, rushing toward them in a mighty battle formation beneath the partially overcast sky. A mountain squall threatened, he judged, but the volatile summer weather made it hard to judge for certain. Chalice the Grinder, the Yellow Dragoness who had spied them from miles off in her familiar role as sentry, grinned at Thundersong from nearby.

How's Juggernaut? he asked bluntly.

She blinked in her coy way. *Wonderful, Thundersong. I understand you and Aria wing together?*

We've made our vows, he smiled. *What about you?*

I think he might be waiting upon your return, she said, even more bashfully than before. *Juggernaut has no immediate blood relatives to speak for him before the Clan Elders.*

What about my status?

I believe it should not matter. More importantly, whatever happened between you, he feels a sense of connection. Will you speak with him?

Aye – excuse me. Close your ear canals, Chalice.

Rising into the air, but staying well out of the way of the lowest wedge of Sea Dragons who, like him, were not the most manoeuvrable of creatures when speeding through the air, Thundersong drew breath and ignited his inner fires with a thought. As the mighty Dragonwing pummelled the air overhead, he paused in anticipation of a clear space before launching his fireworks over a quarter mile into the late afternoon sky.

Phew. Pyrotechnics! This developing skill might come in useful in the desert.

BLA-DA-DA-BOOM!! His volley shattered whatever peace there might have been inside Juggernaut's lair which, for his students, was always a debatable point. His training methods were famously robust.

Even before the echoes had finished rolling back from the mountains, the Sea Dragons unleashed a volley of their new, shattering sonic weapons. Reaching out a swift wingtip, he righted Chalice in the air with a low apology – how her eyes bulged with wonder!

He chuckled softly. *Noisy bunch, aren't they? Ears again, please.*

With that, he winged over the upper edge of the cliff, thundering, *JUGGERNAUT! STRENGTH TO YOUR WINGS!*

Below, on the sands of his training ground, Juggernaut

had assumed a martial pose, primed for action. Many other Dragons of other Clans stood frozen in the act of fighting, wrestling, trying on armour or practising solo with weapons. The famous dark orange Dragon relaxed visibly as Thundersong made his appearance, Azania waving madly off his neck and yelling a welcome, even though she could not possibly be heard from that height.

"Dragon, look over there – isn't that Yardi and Garan?"

"Plus, all their brood. That is a *lot* of Human children."

"What's this tone for?"

"I'm feeling snackish, Princess."

"I won't even dignify that with a comment."

"Why's your jaw moving then?"

Swinging off her saddle straps, she contrived to kick him near the base of his jaw. "I'll show you a moving jaw, Dragon."

Trick riding? His pet Princess grew bold.

Chuckling like a pair of parakeets planning to overthrow a kingdom, they led the way down to the sands. The Isles Dragonesses and Sea Dragons spiralled in behind them. In swift succession, they landed in the open space and peeled away at a jog, clearing more space for those coming in behind. Shortly, the massive Everdeep shifted a great deal of air as he winged in to make the heaviest landing of all. His chest heaved with the effort.

Drawing himself up, the hundred-and-ten-foot Sea Dragon bowed toward Juggernaut the Grinder, who at forty-two feet in length, suddenly looked like a hatchling in comparison. "Juggernaut the Grinder," he rumbled. "We are honoured to meet you. I am Everdeep of the Sea Dragons of the Lumis Ocean. This is Sirensong, my mate."

Juggernaut raised his wings in the Tamarine fashion. "Everdeep, Sirensong, be welcome in my lair."

"May I present King Azerim of the Vaylarn Archipelago and his betrothed, the Princess Azania of T'nagru, whom you know?"

Again, the warrior bowed. "Princess Azania, my Dragon hearts warm with mighty pleasure to see you safely returned from your epic quest across the ocean. I am honoured to meet you, King Azerim. I trust your parents have recovered?"

"Aye, they have, thank you for asking," said he. "They are still often abed but gathering strength every day. Juggernaut, thank you for what you and these Dragons are doing for my Princess Azania – indeed, for T'nagru and by extension, for the all the noble Dragons and Humans of Solixambria."

Juggernaut nodded. "Wingtip to wingtip, we soar."

Everdeep said, "We bring with us three hundred Anhoyal Rangers of the Archipelago, sixty-two Isles Dragonesses under the command of Ariamyrielle Seaspray –"

"Aria," Juggernaut acknowledged her with a formal arch of his neck.

"– and seventy Sea Dragons, under the command of Thundersong." Gesturing with his paw, he said, "My mate Sirensong is honoured to be Thundersong's dam. You knew him by another name before. The congregation of Sea Dragon Elders saw fit to honour him with a name of mighty renown among our kindred, a name that, as you heard, though not bestowed upon this Dragon for twenty years, fits him with prophetic perfection."

"Thundersong!" the warrior's eyes gleamed. "A mighty name indeed."

"Strength to your wings, Juggernaut," he repeated.

Princess Azania dismounted to join King Azerim. They bowed to the four cardinal compass points as Azerim said, "We are honoured to make acquaintance of the mighty Dragon Clans of the Tamarine Mountains. Our mission here is peace toward the Dragons and death to our mutual enemies!"

The Dragons raised a great roar of approbation at his statement.

Azania said, "Hearing of the great threat toward the Dragons and to my nation, the Dragons and Humans of the Archipelago joined forces with the Sea Dragons in order to bring this army to the mainland. We shall join your campaign as you fly south against the dread Skartunese. Together, we shall prevail. Death to our enemies!"

Thundersong led an even louder roar.

Still, his five hearts sank a touch, for, among the Devastator Dragons, he saw his brothers, Brand and Brawl. Two sourer faces could hardly have been imagined. He nodded briefly to them. Only Brand nodded back; Brawl tilted his muzzle aside as if disgusted, while the others ignored him with stony expressions. That boded ill. No doubt, a message would be winging its way south before evening. The question uppermost in his mind was how much the dynamics would have changed in his Clan. Did Indigofire or those who supported her now have the upper paw? Where was his sire? The Devastators held much sway around these mountains, but no Clan was as large as this force he and Aria led, not to speak of the thousands of Sea Dragons they had left to roam the oceans of the world.

Walking over with a formal, stiff-legged posture, Juggernaut greeted Aria respectfully and thanked her for bringing many more to join the cause. They could camp in an area around the springs, he said, as no cavern lair of his could possibly hold creatures of the size of Sea Dragons. Great as his sinkhole was, this number of Dragons would strain its capacity to the limit.

Dragon gave the warrior a friendly shoulder-bump. "It has become busy indeed around here."

He said, "Thanks to your recommendations, we suddenly have fifty or so Blacksmiths about the place. I've lost count. They are excellent – don't tell Yardi I said that."

"I will, Mister Juggernaut, sir," piped a tiny voice.

"Tixyti," he chuckled, tapping a dark-haired Human girl lightly upon the head. "Seven years old. What she doesn't know around this lair isn't worth knowing."

Tixyti grinned up at Thundersong, all twinkling blue eyes, disorganised light brown hair and a mischievous smile. "My mommy Yardi said you was coming, Mister Dragon, but she forgot to say how huge-mongous you been. And ma'am, you are so awfully pretty, you are," she said to Azania, "and why did you bring giant butterflies? Or are they Dragons?"

"We are Isles Dragons," Aria smiled down at the earnest little face.

"Gosh, you're a gazillion times more beautiful than any butterfly, lady," she chattered on. Aria's eyes twinkled at the artless compliment. "My mommy – she's new to being a mommy, you see, but she's ever so nice – told me not to be scared of Dragons so I'm not really afraid because you look so pretty-ful and girly but your friend here is so very colossal I just have to be a teensy bit worried in the corner of my heart, do you know what I mean?"

Aria's eye fires brightened farther still at being called pretty and girly. Thundersong thought he might save these compliments for later teasing. On second thoughts, he might not survive the experience.

The Cobalt Dragoness said, "Well, I think you're pretty too. This is my Thundersong. He's called Thundersong because he can be very loud. I'm Aria, like a song. The biggest Dragon over there, he's called Everdeep and he's a Sea Dragon."

"Oh. Oh wow!" she squealed. "He's a real giant!"

"He's kind to all little things," Thundersong put in. "Garan. Yardi! Glad to see you made it to the mountains."

Garan caught Tixyti up in his arms and gave her a quick tickle. "Making friends already, are we? Did you know that Azania is a real Princess? She loves Princesses."

"No, you is not, lady. I mean, you *could* be a Princess because nobody's beautifuller in all the wide world that I ever done seen," she explained earnestly, "but *real* Princesses wear floaty dresses and do their hair up with ribbons. Also, they are not little girls like me, they are proper grownups."

Azania giggled merrily at her sally.

At this moment, Azerim arrived. Bowing elegantly to Tixyti, he said, "Well, I am King Azerim and I say that you are a secret Princess."

"Ooh, a real King!" Tixyti's eyes flew wide. "This is the most amazingest day ever! I'm totally blowed to smithereens, I am."

Garan sent her on her way with a fond swat upon the behind. "Go on, do your chores. It's nearly dinnertime."

Azania gave Yardi a hug and introduced Azerim. Aria left for a few minutes to send the Isles and Sea Dragons in the right direction and to speak briefly with the Rangers. Chanize dismounted by means of dropping into Farizam's arms. Since the arena sand was no place for a wheelchair, Everdeep and Farizam walked over to the side nearest the cave lairs, where the ground was iron-hard sand or boulders and clean-swept.

Garan already eyed her chair with interest and went over to introduce himself. "Ma'am, I'm Garan Blacksmith. I might have a few ideas for getting you around this place a bit easier. Thicker wheels to start with. Shall we talk when you've had a chance to settle in?"

"Thank you," she said. "I'm Chanize and this is my husband Farizam, the Sankir – ah, that is the leader or captain – of the King's Rangers."

"Honoured to meet you both," he said.

With Juggernaut roaring his much larger group of students back into action, Thundersong wandered down to the hot springs to see if Aria needed help. Not so much. Their group had lost no time claiming a swathe of sandy hollows and spaces between the pools. A couple of Sea Dragons already tested the waters, although there was a fair deal of chuckling over the size of the pools. Not exactly oceans. Not for Dragons of their dimensions. Eversong, his half-brother by Sirensong and Everdeep, made a show of cleaning his wing-pits from all the grime of travel and bemoaning how he'd ever keep himself clean in this dry climate. Several other males ribbed him loudly for his alleged air-Dragon pong.

Seven lakes lay not far away in the mountains, however. Mental note. Make sure to wean his kin off their dependence on water before they headed into the desert, or not? Thundersong scratched a scale itch thoughtfully and then sneezed an unwary bug out of his left nostril with a curl of fire. Discuss that with Everdeep later – he yawned hugely – the water, not the crisped bug. For a mite, that thing had produced a memorable stench.

Time for a power nap?

"Oh, Thundersong," Aria purred, approaching him through the trees. Mmm! His fires frisked about as if he had children playing inside his belly. He should not admit this thought anywhere near the two-legged sort. Awkward. "Juggernaut would like to talk about Dragon armour and weapons options. Coming?"

"I had a few other ideas," he admitted.

The Dragoness rubbed coyly along his flank as she twirled beside him and led the way. Oops. Isles behaviour, he guessed. She threw over her shoulder, "Did you, now? I could not have told by that desirous gleam in your eye. Later, my hearts' fires. That's a promise."

Why did people and Dragons say 'later?' Worst word in the world.

He nipped her tail fondly. "Am I following your tail or are you following mine?"

"That would be telling."

With Azania's help, Juggernaut spread out a map for them

that evening and showed Everdeep and Aria the agreed hunting grounds to the East of his lair and the route to the Seven Beaded Jewels. Thundersong realised that for the Sea Dragons that would be much more of an overnight outing, at their speed. Maybe a good training flight. The warrior Dragon warned them strictly against disturbing the arboreal Serpent Dragons in the valley of rainbow springs. Eyes only. Wild albino ice yaks roamed the area and were good eating for several Dragons apiece, but the Grinders were jealous of that food supply and had already been rumbling about ensuring that they would not be wiped out by this venture.

No mind. He had established supply lines with several of the Northern kingdoms, thanks to Princess Yuali of Amboraine. Large herds of cattle and deer had been driven up through the mountains – almost straight into the Dragons' bellies, the Orange Dragon chuckled heartily. Armies were already on the march around the western fringes of the Tamarine Mountains and had been underway for several months. Having established contact with their friend Tarangis Lionbaiter in Chakkix Camp, supplies should be stockpiled there by the time they arrived.

Juggernaut said, "One disappointing aspect, however. Vanrace has been a thorn in our sides. Of the more southerly Human Kingdoms, Garome, Ayren, Trondis and Alaxarmis have all responded positively to the threat. Lymarn and Vanrace, not so much."

Azania rubbed her hands and said jauntily, "We should pay Prince Floric a visit."

"No, that's not a good idea," Azerim said. "I don't want you going anywhere near that cockroach, darling. Enough of him for one lifetime."

"Thundersong and I could pry his treasury open – trust me."

"We are not into regicide!"

King and Princess faced off across the map, spread on

the ground just outside Juggernaut's personal cave lair. Two lanterns, held high by Everdeep and less high by Aria, lit the four-foot square parchment and the angry faces beneath.

Yardi said, "Peace, Azerim. She wasn't suggesting any killing. Just … encouraging him."

"Well, I forbid any such *encouragement*," the King said acidly. "We should look for a diplomatic solution. Once our armies start marching through their kingdom, King Tyloric and Prince Floric will be forced to see reason."

"Azerim," the Princess' voice shook audibly, "you don't know them as I do. They will not –"

"Enough, Azania. I don't want to argue with you over freaking Floric, of all people!"

Thundersong, speak to him?

His eyes shifted to the Princess. Her emotional colours flickered all over the place, too quickly for him to evaluate, but he had a general sense of humiliation mingled with fury.

He replied, with rising anger, *I can only imagine how awful that time in the dungeons of Vanrace was for you, my precious Rider. I thought captivity most painful to free creatures of the air. Never would I have wanted to learn differently, but now I have. I can speak to him, but I may not speak well.*

We are too deeply invested in one another –

To see reason. Aye.

Aloud, he said, "King Azerim, Vanrace will need to be dealt with and it may not be as cleanly as you wish. All our supply lines cross their claimed territory in one way or another. Dragons may simply fly over, but all ground troops must pass by near their capital due to the terrain."

Azerim gave him a sharp look, one that did not wholly appreciate his support for Princess Azania. "True."

"What would you do, Thundersong?" Everdeep rumbled.

With a macabre chuckle, he said, "I can't help but picture tossing father and son into their own dungeon.

Mouldy bread crusts and stale water for a few months ought to adjust their attitudes."

Most laughed at his enthusiastic suggestion; Yardi even suggested Azania might volunteer as their jailor. King Azerim, however, appeared to be in little mood for banter, remarking that an instable Vanrace would be no service to anyone, given their proximity to T'nagru. After agreeing to return to the issue at a more opportune moment, the meeting proceeded to discuss other matters, starting with securing food and water for the Dragons, to training schedules and a potential date for flying south.

Thanks, Thundersong, Azania spoke softly in his mind.

Are you alright? he probed gently.

No, but I appreciate you asking. I will speak to him later. Give me courage, Dragon.

Duly passed over – a Dragon's portion, although I've never known you to possess less. Do you know that?

She gave him a mental hug. *You're the best.*

Very late that evening, long after the meeting had wound up and most creatures were asleep, Thundersong awoke suddenly. Had he heard a faint shout? Could someone be attacking his Princess? Rising in an instant, he flung himself into the air – remembering at the last instant to mask his presence as best he could, with his chameleon ability. Winging over to the cliff edge where Azerim had been given a chamber beside, but not connected to, Azania's, his wingbeat stuttered as he saw a tiny dark form momentarily silhouetted against lamplight in a doorway.

Assassin! His hearts thundered in his chest; white fire swirled behind his fangs. No, only Azerim's silhouette, looming behind her. As Thundersong veered off, gnashing his fangs in annoyance at his reaction, his draconic hearing caught voices raised in bitter argument:

"Azania, be reasonable –"

"I am being reasonable! What's plain is that you don't care a rotten fig for my feelings, or for T'nagru, for that matter!"

"Oh, please. All you want is revenge and you'll manipulate that Dragon into getting it for you. Azania always has to have her way, doesn't she? Does he even realise what you are doing to him?"

"How's that true, Mister 'talks over his betrothed in every meeting?' I have a mind, Azerim, and I don't need you to make it up for me."

"I've always treated you as equal."

"Have you? Why do you have to put me down in front of others all the time? Does that make you a big man? Maybe you'd prefer one of those pretty Archipelago girls who don't talk back or dare to raise a peep in the great Archipelago King's presence, for that matter? Well, comet flashing over your skies, my King, that's not the woman you asked to be yours."

"No, that woman has a viper's tongue, I'm learning! Go – go run off to your Dragon like you're always doing. I've heard enough. Goodnight, Princess."

She bowed sardonically. "Goodnight, Your Majesty."

Even a Dragon flinched at her tone.

Azania stalked away across the training ground. Thundersong tracked her progress across the dark sand with his weak eyes, uncertain of when to intervene or perhaps he might fly back to his spot near Everdeep and his dam and pretend to be asleep? The Princess was clearly coming to be with him.

That was when he saw a familiar burnt umber shadow moving between the trees along the edge of the sandy training area. Brand!

He was not the only creature tracking her.

Talons glinted in the moonlight. Scenting his brother's strangely dark and rank emotions, Thundersong clipped his wings to pass silently, unseen and unheard, above a Princess consumed in her own fury. As the Princess trudged furiously into the shadows of the treeline, taking the path down toward the hot springs, Brand slithered forward with predatory intent, drawing back his paw to strike. Furling his wings, Thundersong hit him like lightning from a clear sky. One massive punch atop the cranium. Done.

Azania began to scream but stifled the sound with her hand. He saw that she had bravely drawn her talon blade, although the chances she would have survived his brother's ambush for more than a few seconds were slim indeed.

She relaxed as she recognised him, and shuddered. *Thundersong! Oh ...*

It was Brand. No idea what he thought he was doing, but – he's not a Dragon in his right mind.

What? You're defending him?

No. Come, let's leave this fool to sleep off his headache. Are you alright, my Rider?

Not really. How much did you overhear?

After asking Aria, who had also woken to the sound of his attack and Azania's scream, to set several guards for the night in case of further mischief, Thundersong curled up around his mate and his Princess and listened to what she needed to say. He could not erase Azerim's accusation from his mind, however. Did he truly allow Azania to trample over him, manipulating him into doing exactly as she wished? He would like to think not.

His unsleeping gaze asked the stars very many questions that night.

CHAPTER 12

TERROR EFFECT

VERY EARLY IN THE morning, Brand appeared through the mist to offer the most un-Brand-like apology Thundersong had ever heard. He claimed he did not know or truly remember why he had tried to slay Princess Azania the previous night. Hard to believe – almost as hard to be convinced about an actual apology emerging from his brother's mouth.

I swear it upon my own fires as a Dragon! he insisted.

I understand. Could this be some influence or doing of the Terror Clan? Thundersong asked him.

Some Tamarine Dragons did fly out to investigate, his brother said, feeling his tender skull. *They have not yet returned from their mission. Our sire was one of them.*

Ill news.

Indeed. We fly to the Devastator territories today to convey tidings of your arrival to Indigofire, he admitted. *She now rules the Devastators by what was understood to have been a close vote amongst the Elders.*

Great. Eyeing his brother's departing rump, Thundersong realised that he had several more concerns to share with Azania and Aria.

That was enlightening, Aria whispered to him.

Aye. Are you thinking what I am?

I believe so.

They batted the issues back and forth for several minutes. The only rational explanations were uncomfortable ones. Brand had turned to evil, he lied through his fangs or he had acted under an influence they did not understand. Nothing to like here. Aria felt that the only answer was increased vigilance until they could learn more about the Terror Clan's methods.

Restless now, Thundersong slipped to speak with his dam and Everdeep, awake just a Dragon's stride away beside a small hot spring. Sankir Farizam popped his dark head up to join the consultation. Reminding her son of his own story, Sirensong suggested that he contact his Great-Aunt Ignita.

"Ooh, excellent idea," he murmured.

"With that many flashing fangs involved?" she smiled back.

Chanize stirred, moaning, "Uh … oh no! Fari … where are you? I lost you? No!"

"Here, darling." he said. Kneeling at once by her side, he stroked her brow. "Nightmare?"

The younger woman woke groggily, rubbing her right temple. "Bad. Ooh, my head. I feel as if I've been hit by a hammer. Sorry. Was I – I dreamed I couldn't find you, Farizam. Something was chasing –" Spying three Dragons all watching her in concern, she blushed self-consciously and whispered, "And … I feel silly now."

Thundersong said, "No need. If she's sensitive –"

"Aye," Everdeep rumbled. "This is far from my realm of expertise, but we Sea Dragons have a power of song which may winkle out or defeat such malign influences or destroy them –" Chanize's breath hitched audibly "– aye, little one. Allow me to fill you in."

As the camp came awake, Thundersong strolled up to the forge, as he had agreed, to check over their Dragon bow-mounts and to speak to Yardi's developing 'chemistry corner' as she called it, where a few of the young adults who had come through Garan's programme were experimenting with variations on basic oil or smoke bombs. Acid, wasps and toxic smoke had already seen good success. A cheery, 'good morning, Mister Dragon!' trilled from Tixyti as she came scooting out in a state of infeasible excitement, ignoring a call to finish her breakfast.

Before either he or Tixyti quite realised it, he caught her in his paw as she tumbled headlong toward his ankle.

Thundersong peered in through the doorway. "Yardi, did you happen to lose a small packet of mischief?"

"I'm not mischief, I aren't."

"Ooh. A runaway mischief, I believe," he chuckled, reaching in one long limb to deposit her on an open seat amidst the chaos that passed for breakfast in this family. "Eat up."

Tixyti scowled rather fiercely at him. "I'm so not hungry no more."

"Then is this bread roll for me? Or what about this leg? Can I have your knee for a morning snack, little girl?"

She squealed as he prodded her side experimentally. Oh. Ticklish was a fascinating reaction. Dragons did not respond the same way at all, as best he understood.

"No, but you can share my bread?" she offered.

"Why, thank you." Such a charming mite! He popped the proffered crumb into his mouth. "Now, which of your brothers or sisters do you recommend I eat for breakfast?"

Wide eyes! Garan, seated at table with his crew, had to quickly assure a few of the younger, shyer ones that no, the big mean Dragon was not about to eat them; he was just being funny. In the background, Yardi mimed crying. Oh, did he really have to act like a Princess?

Gnarr, served up extra spicy.

Well, some other inferior brand of Princess, unlike his superb specimen. One must congratulate oneself on kidnapping nothing but the best. Mighty Dragon and all that.

Now, to the task at claw.

Covering his face with one forepaw, he produced a very fake sob. "Oh, boohoo, sob sob, I so wanted a nice roast child for breakfast." Ahem. That would be as far from an Azania line as he had ever heard. Never mind. Since many of the children tittered, he added, "Oh please, just a little one? Sobby-sob-sob?" Plucking one of the boys up between his talons, he said, "This one smells of bravery. Is he brave?"

Everyone yelled, 'Yes!' and 'Put him down, you big brute!' while the boy acted … very uncertain.

He sniffed around the wriggling legs. "Mmm, far too many tangy heroic qualities over here. I shall have to find something far sweeter."

Pretending to cast about the room, he settled upon Garan. "What about you, my little sweetmeat?"

The Blacksmith acted horrified as his children burst into peals of laughter.

"Come here, sweetie," he crooked a talon.

"Why Yardi, how you've changed," he called back. That broad, bearded face could not have grinned any wider without cracking in half. "My, what big eyes you have."

Oh, that old tale!

"The better that I might see you, my sweet," he purred assertively.

"My, what a big nose you have," Garan continued.

"The better that I might smell you, my sweet!"

"And my, what big teeth you have!"

"The better that I might eat you, my sweet! *GRROOOAARGGH!*"

What merry pandemonium! Breakfast being so much improved by having children hiding under the tables, shrieking in – well, delight or terror? Perhaps both? How odd. Did Humans enjoy being scared out of their wits?

This might also have been a leading reason why, when Azania and Aria joined him about an hour later, a certain Dragon had transformed into a local piece of children's playground equipment. They scrambled over his back, played house between his forepaws and slid down his carefully tilted wing with shouts of excitement. 'More! Again!' Tixyti actually tried to climb onto his tongue to peer down his throat in an attempt to find out where Dragon fire came from. Thundersong gently discouraged the child from climbing too far into the cavern. He did not want his swallow reflex to kick in.

Far too embarrassed about a certain memory regarding swallowing his Princess …

"Working hard on the weapons design, I see?" Azania greeted him.

"Working, aye. Did you know that Human children are as energetic as Dragon hatchlings?"

Garan the Smith emerged from his forge, rubbing his hands on his thick black apron. "Greetings, gracious Princess. Thank you for lending us this almighty distraction. Children! Time for work and chores!"

"Aww! Come on!" they yelled.

"Say thank you to the nice Dragon."

"Nice is a four-rune word," Thundersong informed him balefully. "I prefer awesome, splendid, remarkable, amazing, talented or magnificent –"

"Or indeed, a scroll inked in gold leaf describing all of the above?" Azania suggested. "Ooh, ouch! Something just whacked me on the nose."

"Erm … what's that?" he rumbled.

"Your ego."

Harrghh-harr-HARRGGH!! he chortled. "Good one. Run along now, little children."

One of the brown-haired boys waved a metal pair of forge tongs in his direction. "I am not little! On guard, you wicked beast!"

"Ah, it's the tasty heroic one!" Dragon exclaimed. "You'd better be heroic, waving that toothpick beneath a mighty Dragon's nose, boy."

"I'm a Dragon slayer, I am!"

Garan said hastily, "Torban, that's not the best choice of game around these parts. Sorry, Dragon."

"Oh, I guess not," the boy grinned.

"You can be a Dragon Rider," Azania suggested.

Torban gasped as if he had just been offered a slice of heaven. Or, was that caused by the Princess' smile? "Could I? Oh, please please *please!*"

The Princess stamped her tiny foot. "Thundersong. Remove this young pretender from my presence at once and bring him back a newly minted Dragon Rider, would you?"

He blinked.

Take him for a flight, you nitwit.
Oh. It's still early. Brain now fully engaged.
Makes a change.

Sweeping grandly past her fire-snorting companion, who was not half as aggrieved as he pretended, Azania greeted Garan, glancing sidelong toward Azerim's quarters meantime. No sign of the King yet. Thundersong hoped he emerged in a better mood than last night's stinker.

Turning to Garan, the boy asked, "What did she – oh no – no *waaaaaay!*"

"Which way?" asked Thundersong, already two hundred feet in the air and beating his wings hard.

"I don't want to die!"

"Don't be rude," he growled. "Besides, this is what it feels like to be truly alive." Lifting the lad in his forepaw, he placed him with due care upon his neck. "Grip with your legs and arms. A Dragon Rider trusts his Dragon to do the flying while he, safely seated upon his neck or back, surveys the mountains with a suitably majestic air. Come. Where is your bravery now, lad?"

"I think I left it down there," he quavered, pointing.

Aye. They departed the training ground at pace. Even the Sea Dragons grew smaller.

"No problem. I believe I have a portion of fresh courage right here in my paw." Tapping the lad's back, he said, "There you go. That's a Dragon's portion, Torban. Use it wisely."

After this, he took the lad on his first flight – not a long one. Just long enough that by the time they returned, he hopped off the Dragon's neck yelling, "Whoa, that was incredible! Did you see what I just did? Somersaults! Garan, Princess – *wow!*"

Azania grinned at him. "Dragon Rider Torban. Returned from scouting the area? Report, please."

"Princess Azania!" he wheezed. "I – wow – I …"

"To work now, lad," Garan said.

The lad rushed into the forge feeling five miles tall, by the looks of him.

Thanks, Thundersong, she thought to him.

No problem. Only about forty other children who'll be begging for rides before we know it.

Hmm. Well, we do need to get them down to Chakkix Camp somehow. Plus, all their equipment.

That'll take some arranging.

Aye, she agreed. Turning to the Smith, she said, "How were you planning to move your entire operation to Chakkix Camp, Garan?"

"I don't rightly know," he said. "Sooner is better, however, before we get too settled in here. We already have a fearful load of weapons and armour to transport. We travelled to Juggernaut's lair by cart through the mountains, but I'm told the trails beyond are much more difficult."

"Non-existent, the Grinder Dragons say," Yardi put in, coming over to slip her hand into the Smith's elbow. "Plus, the passes are far too high. Were you thinking about Dragon transportation, Azania?"

"If they were willing?"

Aria scratched her neck scabs thoughtfully. Dragon told her off immediately.

Baring a set of needle-sharp fangs at him fit to put the largest shark to shame, the Cobalt Dragoness said, "We're a bit lightweight for such work, I fear. My Dragonesses could each carry a smaller load, but we'd be looking to the Sea Dragons to do the bulk of the lifting, maybe using cargo nets?"

"Perhaps equipment could be lashed onto pallets and lifted by rope?" Thundersong put in.

"It's tonnes," Garan said bluntly. "We Smiths don't do light."

"Why don't we test how much weight the various Dragons can lift and fly along with? Then we can make calculations," Azania suggested.

Thundersong chuckled, "There go the good old days of soaring over the mountains with only a titchy Princess in tow. I guess I had it easy."

"Easy is a four-rune word, Dragon."

"Oh, you're sharp today, Princess. Verbal talons."

She mimed scratching out his eyes.

Unfortunately, King Azerim emerged from his hibernation to catch the tail end of their exchange. A muscle in his jaw twitched before he smoothed it out into a suave smile, greeting everyone as if nothing had happened. No apology? He doubted that would sit well with Azania.

A Ranger brought over breakfast for the King. Ah, the joys of having staff. His Highness barely had to chew for himself, did he? Aria sat Azerim down and briefed him on recent events and discussion. With three-quarters of an ear canal attuned to that conversation as he and Azania examined a Dragon bow-mount and made a couple of suggestions for the mobile joint upon which it sat – the mechanism was too loose, meaning there was real danger during battle manoeuvers that it could swivel and smack its operator in the teeth – Thundersong picked up on the King's reaction to Brand's attack on the Princess. Cold fury. Guilt. Sadness.

Still, when he rejoined them, it was with a maddeningly urbane exterior. Thundersong was on the point of biting him just to raise a reaction when he caught Azania's mental headshake. Projecting his feelings again? To his surprise, her response encompassed an easing of the tension palpable in the set of her shoulders and a rising of ochre-rose colours of her emotions. Contentment?

Now, a wink?

Unfathomable jolly Humans!

By way of explanation, she sent him an image of a dark Princess tossing a King into a dungeon cell. 'I prescribe a strict diet of filthy rats and miserable isolation until you worship my feet,' declaimed the apparition.

He had to mask his laughter with a fake coughing fit.

Working out how to resolve the cargo issue was where the teasing and posturing started. Tamarine Dragons were beasts renowned for being full of their own airs. This task was no exception. The Isles and Sea Dragons helping him came in for a barrage of mocking laughter and unpleasant commentary, ranging from being compared to goods carts to being called aerial donkeys. Mid-afternoon, three Crusher Dragons rushed up from the hot springs in a rather hotter and more bothered state than a bath would have justified, as the state of their fourth companion shortly made clear. All four had taken a thrashing; the fourth Dragon was semiconscious and bleeding from a large cut in his flank. Green intestines trailed out of the four-foot wound.

"What happened here?" Juggernaut demanded.

"The Isles Dragonesses attacked us," the first hissed.

"A dozen!" said the second.

"At least two dozen," said the third, whose left eye had already swollen shut.

How to tell a credible story in three easy sentences, right?

Faythrielle came strolling up from the hot springs, too. The coppery female had several broken wing struts, but otherwise appeared unharmed.

Juggernaut made an unmistakable huffing sound.

"What happened?"

She said, "Those four tried to corner me, is what happened. One – that Green – seized my haunches. When I protested, the four tried to become physical."

"How did that work out for you?" the warrior growled bluntly at the three still standing.

"That's a lie," the first stated.

The Tamarine Dragons growled at the Isles Dragonesses, who did not back down one inch. Aria stood amongst her kind, appearing as fierce and narked as any.

Faythrielle roared, "I will not be called a liar! I'm calling you out. Single combat to the death!"

Juggernaut said, "My lair, my rules. I remind all Dragons here that you stand on Grinder territory. If we fight among ourselves, only the enemy wins. Now, healers –"

"Here," said Chanize.

"Ready," Sirensong put in.

"See to the wounded. Aria of the Isles and Strongfist the Crusher, consult with me. Now."

Aye, that could only have been seen coming from a hundred miles off. Only Aria's orders had prevented outright murder.

Leaving the squabbling of hatchlings to Juggernaut to resolve, Thundersong returned to the task of working out how they would carry nets and pallets of the heaviest items and perhaps, sacks slung over Dragons' backs.

The bickering did not stop there. Clearly, it was far beneath the dignity of any Tamarine Dragon to lift a paw to carry anything. The Sea Dragons did not let their scornful opinion of their smaller mountain kin go unheard. Only the Grinders refused to fit the mould – willing to do anything, they said. Famously contrary they were, yet Thundersong found himself wishing it was his own Devastator Clan who could have been less hidebound and more accommodating.

THUNDER O DRAGON

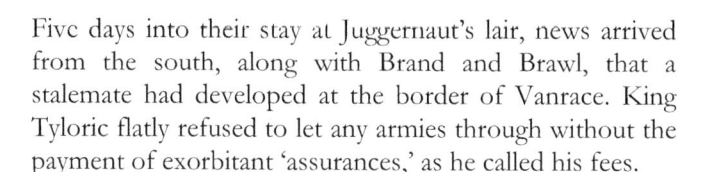

Five days into their stay at Juggernaut's lair, news arrived from the south, along with Brand and Brawl, that a stalemate had developed at the border of Vanrace. King Tyloric flatly refused to let any armies through without the payment of exorbitant 'assurances,' as he called his fees.

Azania did not speak a word regarding the subject when it came up, but something must have flared again between her and Azerim, because that evening did not pass without further heated words. When the Princess arrived back at Sea Dragon camp without being accosted by any rogue Dragons, she flung herself upon his neck and wept bitter tears. Thundersong comforted his Dragon Rider as best he knew how. Hugs of the paw that did not crush a person. Gentle words breathed without calming flame upon her hide. He even tried to stroke her hair without slicing it off with his talons.

While he was trying to put his distraught Rider back together again, Aria arrived in a flustered rush. She said, *I'm sorry, Thundersong, but firstly, the Grinder Dragon Elders had arrived and wanted to speak with you regarding Juggernaut. Secondly, your sire has returned from Terror Isle. He is wounded, appears dazed and will require urgent treatment. Thirdly, Indigofire is reported to be flying up from Devastator territory.*

Oh, is that all? he snarled.

The Cobalt Dragoness stiffened in indignation. *Who'd want to be the messenger?*

Blergh! Sorry! My fires are all in a knot. He touched Aria with an apologetic wingtip. She remained fierce of stance but had a slow wink of her left eye for him. Alright. She could take the heat, was what his mate wished him to understand.

That's physically impossible, Azania put in, with a miserable giggle.

Thundersong perked up. *Watch this, every Dragon. My*

THUNDER O DRAGON

Princess is about to show you her Dragon power.

Eh? the dusky Human asked.

He said, *Watch ... wait for it ... any second now ...*

Giving her swollen eyes one last swipe, the Princess smiled around at all the Dragons watching her – Thundersong, Aria pressing against his flank to show her solidarity, Everdeep and Sirensong close to his shoulder, half a dozen others of the Song Clan and many Isles Dragonesses besides. Her little arms twined across her chest. Her foot tapped the sand lightly as she appeared to scent their mettle.

Raising her definite chin, the Princess said, *Well, Dragons, what are we waiting for? Battle calls! Who's with me?*

There it is! Thundersong guffawed.

Azania scowled, *What?*

Aria said, *Azania, how do you do that?*

Do what? What are you all – you Dragons – laughing at?

How you summon up an ocean of inner strength and charge off to do battle in the very next breath, the Dragoness said.

Every female has this power, she smiled. *You just have to summon up your inner –*

Princess? Thundersong guessed.

His mate elbowed him with a very sharp foreleg elbow. *Don't you dare!*

Azania's face developed a smile of wicked perfection, almost like an Aria preparing to slice an opponent into ribbons. *Whatever works for you, Thunder-sweetie.*

With a massed roar of laughter, the Dragons walked up from the hot springs to the training grounds led by one tiny, feisty Princess of T'nagru. Meeting Aria's eye for a second, Thundersong shared an amazed, amused headshake with her. That girl had gumption to spare.

THUNDER O DRAGON

His sire looked ghastly.

Thundersong almost fell over his paws as they approached. All jollity froze in the Dragons' veins as they beheld Blaze the Devastator and seventeen other Dragons of the thirty-one who had flown out to investigate the Terror Clan's activities. Not one was in a fit state to even speak about what they had seen or where they had been. They shivered uncontrollably, staring at nothingness, their eye fires as dark as he had ever seen in a Dragon. Many were wounded, bites and cuts from fierce Dragon battle in the main. He could only imagine that they had seen or been subjected to unspeakable horrors.

Whatever he had expected of seeing his sire once more, this was not it. These Dragons had survived by the skin of their fangs. What had become of the others?

Other Tamarine Dragons, regardless of Clan, had gathered around the returnees. They acted equally shocked. What had happened? How had they even returned, several asked? They touched the limp wings and stared into the empty eyes of their kin. They drew aside to make space for Sirensong to approach and make her examination. She began to shake her head in profound dismay; her mate steadied her with a kind word and a firm paw upon her shoulder.

≈*Beloved, we will find a way.*≈

Sirensong whispered, ≈*This is perverse and wrong.*≈

≈*Aye.*≈ Everdeep said soberly, ≈*My kin, we can thank every star in the heavens above that our migration resolved to avoid Terror Lair by a very wide margin this year.*≈

≈*Aye, Everdeep.*≈ Thundersong could not keep from flicking his wings in agitation as he inquired, ≈*Mother, what is the matter with them? Why won't they speak or even respond?*≈

≈*This is some deep disturbance of draconic magic,*≈ she said. ≈*I've never seen or treated anything like it. We will try something. It is little-known oceanic magic, a kind of way of sharing the effect of* y'liss-al-horyam *with other Dragonkind. It … may help. I can't think of any other approach.*≈

Chanize said, "I could try a restorative herbal brew and several stimulant tinctures the Isles healers taught me. What do you think, Sirensong?"

"Let's do that," the Dragoness agreed. "I wish we had Ignita the Devastator here, however. From what my son has told me, her knowledge of these more esoteric areas of Dragon lore and treatment is unparalleled. Perhaps between us we can restore these Dragons to a measure of health enough that they may seek Ignita's further help?"

"We can only try," said Chanize. "Farizam, can you help me heat up my cauldron? Time to bubble and brew."

He gave her a strange look. "Don't say that around the more superstitious Human kingdoms."

"Why not?"

"They'll think you're brewing up witchcraft."

"Farizam, that's ridiculous," his wife protested, yet her face became pensive. "Do Dragons think this way?"

"A few," Juggernaut admitted, "but mostly of our own kind. There's a deep, visceral fear of – by my dam's egg! A fear of what you see right here. Dragons dread few things but losing one's mind, one's magic, even one's very Dragon soul to the powers of dark magic … that is why the Terrors are called the Terrors."

Thundersong saw many Dragons' muzzles nodding all about them. Aria commented that her kind detested the Terror Clan, but not in the same way. Still, he saw how troubled her warriors were by these Dragons' appearance and behaviour, how one's Dragon hearts could not help but be touched by superstitious fear. Aye. A foul miasma lay upon them, especially his sire … moving forward, he touched his father's flank and drew him close.

Sire, speak to me. What is wrong?

Blaze, once so mighty and vital, stared ahead of him as if he were a wood carving of a Dragon.

Blaze. Blaze the Devastator … why will you not speak? Panic clamped his chest like pincers. *What happened out there?*

Aria moved close with a gentling wingtip touch.

Strength, my Thundersong.
Green mists. Always … the mists …

Every person and Dragon present jumped at Blaze's sepulchral hiss. Though Thundersong spoke longer with him, his sire made neither motion nor gave any sign of further reaction to anything happening around him. Meantime, Chanize soon had a cauldron steaming on a tripod over a small log fire, which Azerim tended, while she moved between the stricken Dragons with Everdeep's help, administering one tincture to the eyes and two separate restorative oils upon the tongue.

"The eyes?" Azerim asked quietly.

"Excellent absorption into the bloodstream and firestream circulatory systems," Sirensong said quietly. "Chanize has learned her craft well."

The young woman glanced over. "I only know enough to know how much more there is to learn."

"You are gifted," the Dragoness stated.

Chanize ducked her head.

Next, Sirensong gathered the Sea Dragons and bade them stand in close array. Speaking Dragonish for the benefit of the pensive Tamarine Dragons, she explained that, just as the migration gave rise to the glow that showed their oceanic magic was at work, this magic should rise best when Sea Dragons stood and sang in close array. Thundersong had wondered why he no longer glowed white. This explained the phenomenon – yet, he also knew his glow had arisen from the deep anticipatory joy at his mother's approach despite the thousands of miles separating them. His dam described the magical process of cleansing the oceans and her hope that it might do the same for these afflicted Dragons.

Then, Sirensong led the singing over their mountains kin.

Thundersong stood shoulder to shoulder with Sirensong and Everdeep, feeling overshadowed but, nonetheless, part of the larger family which shuffled closer and closer around them, wings resting upon one another's shoulders, muzzles touching the back of the Dragon in front. Behind him, his sisters Ripplesong and Farsong, healers like his dam, rested their muzzles upon his lower back. He faced Blaze directly; to his right paw, Azania stood with Aria, both watching intently as the Sea Dragon choir found its rhythm and voice. A mighty sound swelled within the ambit of Juggernaut's lair, echoing off the tall cliffs with extraordinary resonance. Thundersong was not the only Dragon who developed a case of the shivers at the gorgeous vocals. Even Azerim rubbed his arms and grinned a silly, boyish grin.

Thinking upon his Princess and how she had changed him, Thundersong found he was the first of the Sea Dragons to break into light. That was the best way he could describe it. A fantastical ripple of sensation warmed from his hearts outward, causing his body to burst into such a blaze of radiance, a number of his kin's songs hitched noticeably before they picked up with renewed zest.

The light was catching.

Four or five beats later, Sirensong warmed against his flank. Everdeep made a basso rumble of pleasure as his body waxed like a star gathering its brilliance in a deepening night sky. Their kin looked on in patent amazement. He especially enjoyed Aria's bright-eyed wonder. The radiance shimmered through the throng until they all blazed with one light.

Even Azania? Thundersong wondered if that was a reflection of radiance, the way the light played upon her flawless dark skin or whether a magical process – like her sudden development of a command of Dragonish – was underway in her body. Fascinating. Could it be that something deeper had begun to take shape in this novel relationship between Dragon and Rider?

WHAT IS THIS?

With a massed roar, Tamarine Dragons dropped from

the sky. They landed fast and heavily beside Blaze and the others, snapping their jaws in anger.

As the song faltered and ended, Thundersong realised it was Indigofire who had cried out.

Eyes ablaze with fury and beautiful scales shimmering in the light cast by the Sea Dragons, Indigofire cried out, *Who are these foreign Dragons and what have you done to my Blaze? Blaze, o Blaze!* When he made no response, her neck snaked about as she sought someone to blame – Thundersong sensed her emotions clearly. *You Sea Dragons! Is this your revenge? How dare you! MY MATE!*

Thundersong said clearly, *The Terror Clan Dragons have struck my sire and these others, Indigofire. We were trying to heal them.*

Heal? Heal? she screamed, utterly beside herself. *You are the outcast, are you not? So, who are these with you? Sirensong! Do you stand among these white slugs? You traitor, you mate-stealer, you treacherous siren of the deeps, I'd know the stench of your enchantments from a thousand miles off! Raise a wing if you dare!*

I am Sirensong indeed, his dam said calmly.

Indigofire seemed to swell to an impossible pinnacle of rage. Then, talons bared and fangs gnashing, she launched herself at the throng of Sea Dragons.

CHAPTER 13

GREAT GRINDER

EVERDEEP MOVED, BUT NOT quickly enough. It was Thundersong who lunged between them, his shoulder lowered into a braced position Aria had taught him during combat training. Indigofire rebounded off his chest and mounded shoulder muscles as if she had run into a granite boulder.

He roared, *TOUCH MY DAM AND DIE!!*

His sonic blast rolled off the nearby cliffs in a secondary detonation, returning to pound his stomach before rolling off into the distance like a thunderstorm having its final word.

Thundersong gazed at the Devastator, Windchaser and Obliterator Clan Dragons he had shovelled together in a heap. A terrible urge for revenge gripped his hearts. Very slowly, aware of the touch of Azania's alarm and an unspoken plea on her part, he breathed through the white-hot wrath and allowed it to pass through him without harm to any others.

Very softly, he hissed. *I am Thundersong. This is my true name.*

Indigofire rolled over slowly, pulling herself off Dauntless Obliterator's tail and up into a distinctly wobbly stance. She wheezed, *Thunder ... song?*

He said, *I am Thundersong, o Indigofire the Devastator, and these are my true family, just as Blaze is my true sire. I swear upon my mortal fires as a Dragon, we have not come to the Tamarine Mountains seeking revenge nor do we seek to pick a fight with any here. Now, pick yourselves up and behave like the Dragons of honour you are!*

"What's happening?" he heard Azerim ask the Princess.

"He's giving them an honourable path."

Rising, the Tamarine Dragons drew together in a confused, indignant mass. He knew he must speak first to retain control of the situation.

Our grief and fury are reserved for those who would attack our kin in such a craven manner! Thundersong snarled, stalking toward Indigofire in a way that made her draw back in fear, lips peeling back from her fangs. *This – all this is the work of the Terror Clan and I see already how they have succeeded in dividing Dragon from Dragon and egg from egg. Do not for one second think any of us are immune, as Brand will confirm.*

His half-brother had the ill grace to act shocked at being singled out, but after an awkward pause, he said, *He speaks truth. Their power twists a Dragon's mind.*

Indigofire appeared to deflate.

Before any Dragon spoke further, Blaze's head jerked strangely. *Where … where … I hear – son? Where are you?*

Blaze was blind? Unbelievable! Or … no? From his body language, Thundersong realised he must be seeing other things, perhaps a reality known only to him. If he recognised auditory cues, then his mind must in some way be accessible – just now, he complained shakily about a thunderclap in his ear. Had the sound shaken him free, somehow? Had the singing before been effective?

Either way, he barely felt his paws as he shifted forward. *Sire, I am here. Indigofire, Brand and Brawl are all present in support of you. Can you tell us what happened out there?*

Blaze rambled on about the mist, how it seeped and crept and confused, how it had crawled down his ear canals and burned his brain, as best they could make out from the fragmented words. Two of his fellows became disoriented and aggressive; other Tamarine Dragons held them down as they bellowed, struggled and spit gobbets of green-tinged fire, meantime asking of Thundersong what should be done.

Addressing Indigofire, he said, "The Sea Dragons have a cleansing magic which already appears to have made some steps toward restoration. If we could speak with Ignita, that would be a great help. Could the Devastator Dragons arrange that? I assume she is too infirm to fly here?"

"Too infirm," said another Dragon voice.

"Talonfire!" Azania cried gladly. "How's Sapphira?"

Many of the Tamarine Dragons murmured amongst themselves, amazed that she knew the details of a particular Dragon family in the mountains.

Clearly aware that he spoke in front of several hundred interested Dragons and people, Talonfire – once one of the Smiter Clan, whom the King of Taribonli's forces had all but obliterated – said, "My sweet hatchling is well and flying again, thank you, Princess Azania. Truly, Bl – ah, Thundersong – saved her life that day. Now, Indigofire, perhaps we should allow our kin to try singing over Blaze and these others. Dragon healing magic is powerful, is it not?"

Somehow, in the intervening moments, Indigofire had regained her composure. Haughtily, she said, "As long as it has nothing to do with dark magic."

Talonfire said, "From what we heard, I trust their intentions."

Ergo, Indigofire most clearly did not and his Clan looked to her for their lead.

Thundersong rejoined the singing with his oceanic family, but his hearts remained unsettled, even distressed. It took a long while for his glow to return. Sirensong directed Tamarine Dragons to stand with their troubled kin by Clan. They sang for over an hour, by which time many of the returnees had fallen asleep on the training ground sands. This, in itself, was remarkable. As the assembly broke up, he heard several Dragons commenting favourably on what had transpired. Indigofire, however, had a parting glare for Sirensong. No, this particular battle was most certainly not over from her side.

In his five hearts, he knew that this incident might only be the start of their issues with Indigofire. How it must gall her that her old rival was the one treating her mate!

Juggernaut brought seven elderly Grinder Dragons over to meet him.

So, this is the loud youngster? one teased, pretending to check his left ear canal. *Couldn't quite hear you earlier, Thundersong. Still can't – HAR-HAR-HARRRGH!! I am Hammerfist the Grinder, Elder of the Clan. These are my Clan-kin, called Annihilate, Destructa, Overkill, Meteorite, Gale and Fireblaze.*

Ah, Grinder Clan names. Poetry and song, right?

Turning to Juggernaut, Destructa the Grinder said, *Off with you now, youngling. Go destroy a few things.*

He clacked his fangs and strode off.

Thundersong said, *Strength to your paws, mighty Grinder Elders.*

We're always strong! Annihilate barked. He was a male Green Dragon built like Juggernaut, solid as a gold ingot in the beam. He clapped Thundersong upon the shoulder. Wince. *You're a titchy one, aren't you? Are you planning to grow as big as your relative there?*

That tiddler? he chortled heartily. *Aye, he's a beast on paws, by my fires. That's Everdeep, my dam's mate.*

So, can we speak? Hammerfist put in.

Gale grinned, *It's time and past time to make an honest Dragon out of that stubborn old hunk that calls himself Juggernaut! You keen to help us, Thundersong? See, he has no living direct relatives. That means another must speak for him – preferably a Dragon whom we all are growing to admire as showing truly great Grinder qualities – and propose him formally to the Council for the oaths. Are you willing?*

I am, indeed, he rumbled. Ha. So he had Grinder qualities? Quite the compliment.

Good! the Grinders all chorused. *Let's go grind some yak bones!*

As it turned out, Grinders were called Grinders because they settled all important matters over a shared meal of yak meat – several lowing animals having been dispatched with brutal efficiency – while gnawing the bones between their back fangs. Grinders could grind with the best of them. Thundersong summarily failed to crack open his portion of bones for the marrow, earning a great deal of teasing and jollity. Along the way, they explained the simple ceremony to him. His part was essentially to praise Juggernaut beyond the heavens, convincing Chalice's supposedly sceptical relatives of his value to the Clan. Tough one.

Took a real beast!

He swaggered off. Time to find a Princess to impress.

Hmm. Was that an apologetic smooch, a make-up smooch or a who cared, just smooch me smooch? Gurgling with amusement at his own joke, he snuck up behind the oblivious couple. What did Humans enjoy about sucking one another's faces like leeches? *Blergh.* Finally, Azerim and Azania appeared to be seeing eye to eye, mostly because that waif of a Princess had co-opted a handy boulder into raising her to a suitable height.

He flicked out a devious talon and prodded Azerim's behind with its freshly sharpened point. "Mmm, can I grab some of this, too?"

"Help!" he yelped.

"Dragon!" Azania complained. "That's my royal behind. Paws off."

"So I see. You were definitely exploring the territory, but does that mean it is now annexed to the Kingdom of T'nagru?"

"My very next move," she confirmed.

"Excuse me, this is still Isles property," Azerim said, patting his trousers.

"Not for long, if this desert Princess has her way – and that, my dear sandy-toed Isles love, is absolutely inevitable."

"Doomed?" he asked.

In a deeper voice, she intoned, "Doomed, she boomed, that monster from the desert one entombed in Vanrace –"

The King cut in, "So, Thundersong, all arranged on the Juggernaut front?"

Not in a mood for joking, was he?

Perhaps the kiss had been a wish for better relations between them? Thundersong contemplated swatting the King into compliance, a surefire way of resolving all these relationship shenanigans.

Ignoring Azania's mental prod, he said, "Quite, Azerim. Tomorrow, an hour after dawn, we are all to pretend to be incredibly surprised by goings-on. I'll make a speech and he'll get the Dragoness. That simple."

Haggard, sleep bereft and feeling decidedly like hitting something beyond the moon, Thundersong rose at dawn and staggered into the nearest hot spring the following dawn. Huge splash.

"Ah, much better."

"Keep it down to a dull roar, would you?" Everdeep grumbled.

"Thanks for half emptying the spring," Azania said, appearing from behind a boulder where she had been doing that peculiar Human ritual of hiding her hide. They had wholly inexplicable rules related to when one showed hide and how much of which particular part. Oddly complex social mores.

A cheeky desire filled his Dragon hearts to toss Azerim

and Azania into the same space, minus all this silly clothing, just to see what would happen. Call it a cultural experiment. According to Everdeep, Farizam and Chanize were quite naughty about clothing when they were hidden in their between-Dragon space. Close the eyes and ears, every Dragon!

Hsst. Thundersong. Want to fly? Aria whispered.

Ooh, speaking of which … *I'll leave the water for you, Azania. See you in an hour.*

You two are going flying? she inquired.

He shrugged. *Just a bit of alone time as mates. Maybe she has something important to discuss?*

Alright – but don't be late for Juggernaut's event.

His Cobalt beauty did ask him about all the bellowing and keening during the night, which came from the eighteen returnees suffering from awful nightmares. His sire had been particularly tormented. After that, however, once they disappeared behind a handy mountain peak and were hidden from the sentries, there was rather less talking and rather more airborne frisking. Unfortunately, due to a mutual excess of enthusiasm, Aria tweaked her neck midway, which had the salubrious effect of returning them to the sinkhole in the nick of time.

Ahem.

He claimed unavoidable distraction.

Obviously, that was entirely the attractive warrior's fault and nothing to do with his woeful dearth of actual willpower.

Thundersong made a light-hearted, yet honest, speech in Juggernaut's honour, extolling his prowess as a teacher who could turn the most stumble-footed Dragon into a real warrior. With Chalice's family being suitably – and very unsurprisingly – impressed by his legendary qualities, they proceeded to put on an energetic Grinder nuptial dance which involved using bones for drumsticks and yak ribcages for xylophones.

Azania commented to him, "That's memorable for

reasons I'm not sure I want to talk about."

"Juggernaut's rather sprightly of paw, isn't he?"

"So he is. Doesn't Chalice look adorably happy, too?"

"Quite. I'm glad we were able to play a part in this, Princess. Aren't you?"

"More than," she agreed.

"Your turn soon."

"Aye," she said aloud, but in her mind, she clarified, *I'm not so sure, Thundersong. I wish I knew what the problem with Azerim has been. It just doesn't feel the same anymore. I can't figure him out; it seems I've done something wrong and I've no idea what it is. He isn't telling.*

Touching his chest, Thundersong considered the collywobbles in his hearts introduced by that pensive statement. He clenched his right forepaw. *Princess, if I can help in any way …*

Thank you, Thundersong. This looming war has us both on edge. Where's Inzashu? he asked.

Yardi told me she travelled with Princess Yuali's forces. Our estimate is that she might be in Ayren soon, if not heading into Garome – but that is as far as they'll get until we swell King Tyloric's coffers.

Gnarr-blasted-death! he cursed furiously.

My feelings exactly. Azerim and Juggernaut are trying to find a way to break the stalemate.

This will need our paw, Princess.

Aye. I just don't know … how to, without infuriating Azerim beyond reason. He's such a stick-in-the-mud regarding how things ought to be done. War isn't pretty, Thundersong! Our enemy won't stop to inquire if we've applied all the seals to the scrolls in the right order.

Aye. I need to ruminate upon this. They both chuckled as his stomach voiced its own version of rumination.

Icky tummy, my Dragon?

Just wishing a certain flatulent Prince were digesting inside –

Dragon! You aren't a cannibal.

Loftily, he replied, *A cannibal eats one's own species. Eating a Human — now, why haven't I tried it with you?* He pretended to lick his chops. *Mmm, fresh desert rose. Yum!*

She elbowed him in the thigh. *Joker.*

Still, I do have to point out that eating Floric would be a service to all Humankind.

I'm not supposed to agree with you, but … aye. I wish there was some neat way to set him aside that doesn't involve your digestive juices. That would be a trick.

Musing over this thorny issue as the celebrations proceeded, they fell to silently discussing the loading procedures, how large a force ought to fly south to Chakkix Camp and how many Dragons to leave there just in case the location became a target for the Terror Clan. Perhaps they ought to fly farther, to T'nagru, to check the situation on the war front with Skartun? Or head West to connect with the armies marching south around the Tamarine Mountains, perhaps to bring her sister Inzashu-N'shula back to see if she could not help these stricken Dragons? So many competing variables! However, he discovered that Azania had a mind like a perfectly organised scroll rack. It purred along smoothly, evaluating different factors, checking with his thoughts on a particular issue — indeed, all accomplished at the speed of mental communication.

Shortly, they had knocked out a solid plan.

He said softly, *We're good together.*

I'm … so grateful, Thundersong. I only wish Azerim — she bit the thought into silence.

So challenging to think upon how a creature could stand right next to another and yet feel completely isolated. For his part, he resolved to be more open with Aria. Now, how could he best support his Princess to find a way past or around this stumbling block? Could Azerim be putting himself under inordinate pressure to resolve everything, command everything, carry every burden — as he had for his family and nation ever since he assumed his kingship? As an expert on Human psychology — *harr-harr-harrgh* —

could he make such a diagnosis?

If Humans were anything like Dragons, the twists and turns of the psyche might prove inexplicable and utterly perplexing.

Once the ceremony was over, the Grinder Elders bundled Juggernaut and Chalice into his lair for what they, with flashing grins, called a private celebration. Several of his Clan roared helpful advice to speed him on his way.

The warrior popped his head out and roared right back, "Get back to your training! I despise lollygagging and dillydallying while the suns are already high!"

Chalice hauled him back inside by his tail and kicked an inner door shut with a loud bang, raising thunderous gales of laughter. All part of the fun.

A long morning's bruising training led into a longer afternoon working with Garan, Yardi and Everdeep on the preparations for loading. With a mere three hundred of the King's Anhoyal Rangers at their disposal, the staging area very soon came to resemble an anthill populated by busy brown Islanders. Farizam rolled up his sleeves and joined his teams doing the hard labour, while Chanize and Sirensong attended to Blaze and his Dragons. He observed no substantial improvement yet, apart from a greater sense of calm.

By late afternoon, they had amassed a huge pile of supplies, armour, weapons and equipment ready for transport. Azerim and Azania made the tallies.

"Two trips," they agreed.

"One for Everdeep and one for the rest of us," Thundersong said.

"Lightweight," Everdeep teased him.

Juggernaut and Chalice finally made their appearance from his private lair, one swaggering and the other acting comically self-conscious.

Pausing to survey the scene, the warrior bellowed, "My beautiful mate and I –"

The Grinder Clan exploded in raucous cheers,

drowning him out.

"My matchless mate and I –"

More cheers, thundering and congratulations!

"My soulmate and I –" after allowing the pandemonium and laughter to subside, he said, "– thank you for attending our nuptials. I am the happiest Dragon alive! Now ... what are all you looking at? GET BACK TO WORK!"

Chalice nipped his shoulder for that.

He mimed a couple of snaps right back at her, whereupon a touch of naughty necking developed. Grinders loved to show off in public, to the vocal embarrassment of many of the other Mountains Clans.

After working late into the night to pack up the entire forge operation, the Dragons woke early again to start the loading. Thundersong took his leave of Aria, Everdeep of Sirensong, Farizam of Chanize and Azania of Azerim. The King and Aria would oversee Juggernaut's lair until they returned for the second trip. Sirensong needed to attend to her patients. Meantime, several healers planned to consult with Ignita, while other Tamarine Dragons flew farther afield to check on the progress of the Human allies and armies.

Privately, Aria had promised to both him and Everdeep to look after Sirensong. Powerful as she was, his dam was not primarily a warrior. Aria was also the only reason Everdeep was prepared to leave her in what he had, in a moment of deep frustration, called enemy territory. Not all the Clans. With many Grinders led by Juggernaut flying south, bound for T'nagru, those they privately agreed were staunch allies would be many less in number.

Quickly back.

Half an hour later, a huge flight of Dragons lifted off – fully three-quarters of the Sea Dragons, thirty Isles Dragonesses and twenty-five Grinders, including Chalice and Juggernaut. Azania rode Thundersong, together with Tixyti in the foremost position her sister had often taken.

The mite had not stopped twittering like a little bird yet. So excited!

The first climb was the hardest, two vertical miles up to the lip of Juggernaut's sinkhole. More than sufficiently warmed up, the Sea Dragons, especially, groaned in relief to spread their wings and coast out over a high snowy plain beneath pristine turquoise skies. Dragging his own six-tonne net through the sky, Thundersong dropped back to check in with his kin. The flight included one hundred Rangers, seventy-five to remain at Chakkix Camp, while twenty-five would continue down to T'nagru to make preparations for the larger army's arrival.

After resting on the wing for a few minutes, his sisters Ripplesong and Farsong struck up a journeying song. Trailing their heavy nets or carrying bulging sacks tied to their backs, the Sea Dragons led the way with the more lightly loaded Isles Dragonesses fluttering alongside and above.

Thundersong clapped his paws loudly. "Rangers! Let's learn this tune in Dragoceanic! Dragonesses, join in." ≈*Repeat the first verse, my kin.*≈

≈*Plenty of miles to go, o frothy wave,*≈ Everdeep chortled massively. The huge bruiser carried no less than eleven tonnes on a solid cargo pallet, some of the heaviest individual pieces of forge equipment.

Yardi and Garan's children had the best time. Spread out over the Dragons, each with an adult or two in attendance, they gaped at the scenery, spread their arms to flutter their hands as pretend Dragon wings and prattled and laughed constantly in high-pitched voices as the flight of Dragons swept over the plain toward the first pass, several miles distant. Eventually, Thundersong called in a rest stop.

"Is this the lecture on altitude sickness?" Azania chirped brightly.

He gave her a stinker of a glare. "Listen up, everyone, the Princess has a few things to say."

"Never stops," Sankir Farizam grinned.

Arching an eyebrow, Azania grinned, "Farizam, go supervise the children while Yardi and Garan have a break."

"Oh no, how can anything be worse than my Rangers?" he groaned.

After that, the Princess of an extremely flat, sandy, waterless desert land gave a creditable lecture on the dangers of freezing cold and altitude sickness in the high mountains. There. Who said a woman could not be taught?

She kicked him upon returning.

"Projecting my thoughts, Princess?"

"No, it was your expression this time, you rude reptile."

"Next, you'll be claiming you kidnapped me."

"Why, but I did. Having with incomparable cunning set up a scenario in which this motley brown Dragon believed he was kidnapping a helpless victim to the King's heinous plan," she elaborated, "the wicked Princess took over the Dragon's lair, stole all his artworks and flogged them to the highest bidder for a fine profit. The Dragon, having shed his scales in shock at the Princess' impudence —"

"There's a fine line between history and fiction, Princess."

"Too much?"

He grinned, "Just a toe over the line. Beautiful toe, however."

"Why, you flatterer." She batted her eyelashes at him and gave him a simper that was as far from the real Azania as Ignis was above the mountains.

After that, they laboured up and over the pass. Numbers of the Sea Dragons and Isles Dragonesses began to exhibit altitude sickness on the way, but Thundersong taught them how to protect themselves from the worst effects of oxygen deprivation. The drain on his own resources arrived with surprising swiftness, but Azania joined with him to share her strength. Together, they struggled up and over the saddle, passing so low that his net dragged through the snow a couple of times.

≈*Alright there, Thundersong?*≈ Everdeep panted.

≈*Aye. That was rough.*≈

≈*Forgot the drain of magical work?*≈ He nodded. The Sea Dragon said, ≈*Want to see if you can teach some of us that shielding trick? Might come in useful against any green mist.*≈

He stiffened. ≈*Oh. Good idea!*≈

Azania said, "What's the matter, Thundersong?"

Spreading his wings with the others, he glided for a space, catching his breath. The thin air at this altitude did not help. "The Malnoose Pass still lies ahead. It's even higher, Everdeep. No less than twenty-five thousand feet. We'll rest and train before tackling that beast. Azania, we were just talking about gas shielding against that green mist my sire kept talking about."

"You're a brain!" She patted his neck warmly. "Nice one."

"Everdeep's idea, actually."

"I –"

"Take that back and I'll swat you," he warned.

Azania giggled merrily, causing Everdeep to gaze strangely at them. "You two – how do I ask this?"

Thundersong said, "I could imagine that gas shield could come in handy around Prince Floric, don't you think, Azania?" *Shall I tell him?*

"Indeed," she chuckled. *I guess. I … I see it as something special between us. We should share.*

≈*Are you talking in your minds, like those mated for the longest time are said to do?*≈ the Sea Dragon asked, switching languages out of courtesy, he realised. ≈*Sirensong and I have only just begun. It's regarded as unusual at our young age, a sign of singular intimacy. Does Azerim know?*≈

He's guessed already, Thundersong told his Princess.

She smiled over at Everdeep and nodded soberly in acknowledgement. His eye fires swirled with surprise. As the Princess bent to chat to Tixyti who, like her, was deeply wrapped up in blankets against the cold, Thundersong gazed at the other Dragon. He knew what he was thinking. How was this even possible with a Human?

For that, he had no answer.

CHAPTER 14

TAKING THE CAMP

THE FLIGHT OVERNIGHTED BESIDE the fifth of seven lakes, one of the Seven Beaded Jewels of the Tamarine Mountains. Stocked with tasty giant carp which had no business living in deep lakes in the middle of fairly much nowhere, the lakes at last provided the Sea Dragons with a familiar environment. After unloading their sacks or setting down the cargo pallets and nets, the oceanic Dragons dived into the icy waters with bugles of joy. The Tamarine Dragons gazed at this activity in open startlement. Water from hot springs, aye. Freezing-your-talons-off temperatures? Not generally the first choice of bathtub for one's rump.

"Spending weeks or months in desert conditions will be interesting," Azania observed.

"I do hope some of your cisterns are a good size."

"They're ... maybe up to a hundred feet across? Fairly deep, as I recall. Getting into them might be a challenge. Either that or we can teach your kin to swim in sand?"

"Excellent idea. Pure friction."

"I'm itching for a sand bath myself."

He chortled, "Sounds awfully dry."

"Dry wit, do you mean?"

"You're killing me, Princess. Stop before I *desert* you."

THUNDER O DRAGON

"Burying you with a flurry of stinging humour?"

"Ouch, I remember that incident all too well. My bad jokes have clearly rubbed off on you."

"So, Thundersong, how you dune?"

They agreed this was at the low end of potential humour and left it there.

The way that Garan handled his massive brood never failed to impress. Everyone down to the youngsters had a task, apart from the two infants. Their job was to be coddled by a rotation of minders, supervised by a young woman married to one of his graduates, a nurse by trade. On that note, beyond the Rangers' fires, he observed Eversong, a sixty-five-foot young adult Sea Dragon, chatting up Jainrielle, a pretty light green Isles Dragoness. Ah, sharing his fresh catch with her? This was a clear courtship signal across all kinds of Dragons he knew.

As the evening deepened, Azania told the children a bedtime story in her dramatic desert style, a tale of a T'nagrun Prince who fell in love with a magical creature of the far south, called a Fey Wisp, and followed her to the waterfalls at the end of the world.

Weary from their day's travelling, everyone dropped off early, save for a sentry rotation organised by Everdeep. Good awareness, Thundersong decided, his eyes lidding. He tucked Azania into her customary place in the crook of his neck and drew a wing over her, making sure its curvature trapped the hot outbreath of his nostrils in order to provide additional warmth.

A few minutes later, Yardi came over. "Tixyti's too shy to speak directly to you, but she's asking if she could sleep with the 'bestest by a bazillion miles Princess in all the realms tonight.'"

"Plenty of room. Bring her over," Azania smiled.

"Seems you've made a conquest," he said.

"Three conquests?"

Three children indeed. Yardi shrugged with a long-suffering air.

Ten minutes later, Thundersong said drily, "The 'bestest by a bazillion miles Princess in all the realms' wins the popularity contest. We're up to fourteen girls."

"What can I say?"

"You could tell Azerim you want fourteen kids of your own."

"I'm worried he might just agree!"

"Hmm. Aye. Save it for next time you want to scare him – how do you Humans say it – right out of his trousers?"

"No need to be crude, Dragon. Good night."

Opening his left eye a crack at her verbal smile, he checked his newly extended brood. Fifteen girls tucked beneath his wing. Maybe he was the winner around here, broody feelings and all. Few male Dragons would ever admit to such feelings, but to his surprise, he was content. Maybe he and Aria would start a new tradition with the male being allowed to brood over the eggs while the female guarded the lair – that said, what did Isles males do? Was he ready to discuss the delicate matter of eggs with her as yet?

A question for another day.

From the lakes, it was a tough battle to fly over Malnoose Pass, beating and gasping with the exertion to outfly a squall bustling in from the northeast. They picked up an excellent head of speed on the long rocky descent beyond, riding a zesty tailwind. Thundersong worked the group hard but not unfairly, demonstrating and coaching all the Dragons in streamlining and wing stroke techniques which maximised both energy conservation and power.

Juggernaut growled at all the Tamarine Dragons to follow his lead. When a couple of rumbles of dissent rose, he roared, "I'll still beat the stuffing out of him in ground combat, but he knows his stuff in the air. You have to see his combat sprint."

Eventually, a combination of tiredness and dangerously high winds forced them to land at the northerly head of the same valley where he and Azania had once met a group of women from Vanrace. Recalling that incident, he shared the memory with his Princess.

She said, *My Dragon, Azerim wanted me to promise we'd do nothing to King Tyloric on this trip. I –*

You promised on my behalf? His mental voice boomed in indignation.

I did.

Azania!

I'm sorry; I'm just now realising what a royal mess I made of that. I ... gave in too easily. I only wanted things to be better between us.

Gritting his fangs, Thundersong said, *Are you blaming him?*

She hung her head. *No. I walked wide-eyed into that one. I said you and I would not touch a hair upon his head. Nor Floric's –*

Everything below the hairline being fair game?

Dragon – she chuckled miserably *– I'll try not to presume next time. Forgive me?*

Alright; what's done is done. Let's get your girl posse under cover before the rainstorm hits, alright?

Thank you for understanding, Thundersong.

He would likely have done the same. Sighing, he raised his wing and tried not to picture a scaly twenty-tonne mother hen gathering her chicks into safety. Ridiculous image. With a low, drumming roar, the rain came sweeping in and with it, at least two dozen children in a shrieking charge to take cover before they were soaked.

"Your turn," Azania told him.

Curling up so that his body worked as a windbreak and the rainwater would run down his angled wing rather than pour over the children's already wet heads, Thundersong warmed up his rapt audience with a number of Dragon tales that his kin loved to tell hatchlings.

When the squall eventually eased up, Garan and Yardi came over. "Ah, so this is where the party is," Yardi commented drolly.

"Thundersong's the best!" said one of the boys.

"No, Azania's the best!" chorused the girls.

Before anyone could get more than a few verbal digs in, Yardi held out a small sack that appeared to hold cloths. She said, "You may thank Thundersong for his hospitality by showing him how you buff scales. If you can buff a weapon, scales are no different – just follow the way they lie."

Ah. As his horde of little helpers set to work, Thundersong stretched out luxuriously. This was the life. What a wonderful all-over sensation! White scales picked up every smudge of dirt. An artistic Dragon did like to look his best. Not that she whom he wished best to be impressed was anywhere near their place of rest, but why not imagine a future with a bevy of Human servants to polish his scales every day?

Ahem, said a voice in his mind.

Image instantly erased, he purred right back.

Aren't you the sweetest Dragon?

No!

Everdeep strolled up. "What does a Dragon need to do to earn this treatment?"

"You way too big, mister!" Tixyti called.

"Am I now?" he rumbled, touching her shoulder with a talon longer than she stood tall. "Want to ride with me this afternoon?"

"No, Thundersong's the bestest. I'm sorry, mister Dragon. Don't be sad. He just is."

The Sea Dragon looked nonplussed as the mite rejected him outright. Thundersong bared a few fangs in an apologetic grin. Everdeep just chuckled and shook his head.

On and on they flew, dragging their loads southeast through the mountains to skirt the highest peaks, passing just one range west of the headwaters of the Skaggar River, which Dragon remembered very well. The following day, they zigzagged along a descending valley, that would eventually merge into the much lower badlands that abutted this eastern corner of the Tamarine Mountains. From here, it was a straight run down to Chakkix Camp over the tan wasteland, dotted a deep green where the stands of tall, prickly multi-branched cacti grew in profusion.

The Sea Dragons tasted the dryness in the air uneasily. Thundersong understood. They flew over a land that would soon, beyond Chakkix Camp, turn into a demesne as far from their experience as anything imaginable – the subtle, beguiling, lethal desert where water was so precious, it was anathema even to spit in the sand.

Stark as it was, the desert was also beautiful.

With a sigh, Thundersong handed his spectacles to Azania. "Clean and polish, please?"

"What's the sigh for?" she asked.

"The fact that we plan to fly only as far as Chakkix Camp."

The Princess said, "My kingdom can wait. Even with all their vaunted magic, the Skartunese will not have been able to make the crossing in the heat of summer. For my part, I would like to enter T'nagru with Azerim at my side."

"Do you think Nahritu-N'shula will be back?"

"Do the desert winds blow?"

"Do the oceans rise?" Everdeep said softly, flying just behind and to Thundersong's right in his slipstreaming position. "Juggernaut will shortly be in T'nagru, Princess. He can be trusted to give a sound report."

"Aye, Everdeep," he agreed. They would use message hawks between Chakkix Camp and T'nagru, but the passes up to Juggernaut's lair were considered too high for their kind.

"We need my sister," Azania thought aloud.

"Hmm," he said blandly, as a few fires flickered to life in his brain.

Idea generation in Dragons did not resemble a

headache as much as a head fire. The sensation first raced through his substantial cranium like a lacework of white-hot fires before the whole mass heated up inside his skull. Times and dates whizzed about, rearranging themselves. The Dragons intended to take three days at Chakkix Camp to set up operations under Taragis Lionbaiter's beady eye. The Grinders would fly south as soon as they were not needed. A fast Dragon could sneak off and rejoin the return flight before anyone was the wiser … right?

Aye. That evening, as they rested in a dry, sandy riverbed, he put his ideas to Azania. They should hunt down her little sister and cast a beady Dragonish and Rider-ish eye over developments in Vanrace, before returning via Ignita's lair, despite it lying within the southerly edge of Devastator territory.

"Do we or don't we break a promise?" Azania asked.

"It's for my sire's sake."

"I realise that; I just don't see how we can do this with integrity. There's the Vanrace issue and does your Great-Aunt Ignita ever step paw out of her swamp?"

"Not easily," he said.

"Let me think about this, Dragon."

The following morning, the flight set out for Chakkix Camp, about six hours in the air at their speed. The Sea Dragons were wing-weary after travelling many miles dragging heavy loads. Temperatures soared during the course of the morning, a foretaste of the desert proper. Ignis blazed unrelentingly in a white-blue sky. They rested at a small spring mid-morning, taking turns to slake their thirst before taking off once more for a low line of hills toward the horizon where the camp was located.

Half an hour out, Thundersong squinted through his spectacles. "Azania, isn't that rather a lot of smoke?"

She peered ahead. "Juggernaut! Everdeep! What's happening ahead?"

Several of the Isles Dragonesses shot skyward in near-vertical climbs to check the terrain. They came down nearly as fast, calling, "Green Dragons attacking an area out there. Maybe ten, fifteen miles distant."

"Terror Clan!" Azania hissed.

Everdeep said, "Juggernaut, it's your wave."

"Command us," Thundersong agreed.

"Down and land!" he bellowed. The entire flight of Dragons appeared to lurch as one as they descended rapidly. Several children began to sniffle or cry. "Offload the cargo. Yardi, Garan, you're in charge here. I need five Dragon volunteers to stay and cover our team – land there, beside that dry streambed. Looks doable. Break out the Dragon bows! This is war, Dragons and Rangers! Be ready for action!"

As they lost height, Juggernaut quickly divided the force into three, designating Thundersong, Everdeep and himself as the leaders. Everdeep would lead a frontal attack, Thundersong should circle more to the east and Juggernaut planned a surprise attack using the hills to the west as cover. No quarter would be given, but if they could capture a couple of the Terror Clan alive, that would be a bonus. The Dragons should protect the Humans of the camp as best they could. Under no circumstances were any Terror Clan to be allowed to escape to warn their fellows.

"Any last ideas?" he barked as the unloading proceeded at full pace.

Azania called, "Don't breathe in any green mist!"

Many of the Dragons snarled, baring their fangs in recognition of what she meant.

Good thinking, he approved.

They might not like it, but it had to be said, Azania replied grimly, affixing a Dragon bow to his upper spine spikes. *Feels just like old times, right?*

Aye. Now, we know the Terrors are working talon in sheath with Skartun.

The Princess' eyes widened as she breathed, *Aye.*

Juggernaut bellowed, "Rangers! Did you forget your earplugs?"

THUNDER O DRAGON

Farizam ran among his men and women, distributing the wax plugs they had decided upon. They were ill-prepared, but the entire operation took a mere fifteen minutes before the Dragons were ready to take off once more. Twenty-five Sea Dragons, including Thundersong, carried Dragon bows upon their shoulders. Everdeep sported a Juggernaut invention, an oversized monster bow worked by three engineers, a treble-loader that shot bolts almost as long as a Knight's lance.

One hit would punch a Dragon clean out of the sky.

By this time, dense black smoke billowed up from numerous individual fires in the camp. The Dragons swept in low and fast, trying to use the broken terrain for some cover. With a hoarse cry that carried plaintively over the badlands, Everdeep bade his eager Dragonwing slow a touch to give the pincer movement time to take shape.

Peering one last time through his spectacles, Thundersong handed them to Azania to be stowed safely. "Maybe a couple dozen Terrors?"

"Aye."

She scrambled up onto his shoulders, swapping places with two Rangers armed with bows. The camp appeared to be giving a reasonable account of itself against the Dragons. No surprise that there might be some aerial defences hidden amongst the tan and brown tents or upon the ridgeline above the Chakkix Camp, for the nature of the place attracted the types of Humans who tended towards paranoia in their security arrangements.

"Mist check?" he growled.

"Nothing so far."

"Stay sharp – all my Riders." Raising his voice, Thundersong called, "Isles Dragonesses go in higher, as we trained. Isolate and take down the Greens. If any try to flee, sing out."

"There's Everdeep's signal," Azania called.

"Battle speed!"

Preoccupied with flaming tents and fighting the ground

forces, the Terror Clan Dragons did not spy the incoming Dragonwings for long, vital seconds. It must have been the last thing they could have expected – a substantially larger force of Dragons appearing from nowhere to roll over them in a wave of fury.

Six-foot Dragon bow quarrels spat briefly over the gap toward the openly startled Terror Clan before the Sea Dragons thundered their mighty challenges. Several Terror Greens dropped immediately, stunned or fatally pierced by the six-foot quarrels. Azania cried out in triumph as she slid a quarrel smoothly into a Green Dragon's throat. He was dead even before three Isles Dragonesses introduced him to their blades from above.

Thundersong weaved past a green paw that appeared from nowhere amidst the smoke, trying to scrape the Dragon bow off his back. Whirling, he pounded the departing Dragon with a tail strike that shuddered her to a standstill. Riding the centrifugal force generated by his motion, he rotated up over her back to grip her head and neck between his paws. As she roared in fury, he drew back his right hind knee and smashed her in the mid-skull region with all his strength. *Blam!* This knee strike was a move Juggernaut said he had developed from watching Human fighters.

The Dragoness dropped like a stone.

Everdeep stormed by, savaging a Terror Green with his huge jaws while his Riders released a trio of lances. They spitted an incoming Dragon like an unfortunate kebab. He spun and dropped at once.

As the Greens broke and tried to flee, Juggernaut and his team came rolling over the ridgeline in an avalanche of furious flashing jaws and gushing fires. Quarrels pounded home before the forces even collided. Two Sea Dragons caught a Green by the tail and neck and pounded him into smithereens between them. Eversong's Ranger team struck with their third shot, sending a Green spinning into the path of Juggernaut. That ended badly for the enemy

Dragon.

"Gas!" Chalice shouted, swerving past her mate to grip the offending Green before he fell into the camp.

"Watch downwind!" Juggernaut bellowed, pointing.

Two Sea Dragons caught the dying Terror Clan Dragon. He expelled a plume of strange, oily green gas from his jaw as they attempted to drag him out of harm's way. Thundersong saw how they held their breath and tried to shield themselves. Had it touched them? Or not?

Shooting up to him, Jainrielle slapped his right wingtip sharply. *Dragon! Look high – one escapes!*

I –

Azania pointed. *Straight up, Thundersong, I see a speck – two specks!*

LET'S GO!!

The Isles Dragoness tried to keep pace. He left her staring in amazement at his departing tail. Full sprint! Thundersong gritted his fangs at the exertion of maximum acceleration. His Riders groaned at the forces upon their bodies, but that eased as he found his flying rhythm. The pair of Green Terror Dragons tried to outfly him for a few minutes, but they were no match for his speed. Thundering in defiance, they swerved apart before returning at high speed for a direct attack.

No more dishonourable fleeing? He taunted, *Little Dragons want to play?*

Highest pitch sonic attack! Azania ordered. *Left is mine. Right!*

"Rangers, close your ears!" she shouted. "Target left!"

Seconds separated them. Drawing breath, he shaped the sonic scream they had worked on. *WHEEE-BOOM!!* His cry rang out, but the Greens did not appear to respond or be incapacitated in any way. A quarrel and two arrows pinned the Dragon to the left, but the right barrelled straight on through. At the last instant, Thundersong raised his wing and swerved, taking a heavy but glancing blow to his right flank. Shallow cut. He was on the point of drawing breath when he spied a haze of green moving against the prevailing wind, back toward them. He backwinged powerfully out of its path, dispersing the gas while discovering his flank had just gone numb.

Poisoned talons? Merely the shock of a wound?

Azania reloaded at high speed. *That gas – did you see?*

Aye. Hit them! I'm going low …

Daring to breathe at last in clear air, he readied another attack. As a Green jaw opened for a bite at his outstretched left wing, he changed his mind in a fraction of an instant and shot a firework down his agape throat into his gullet. A dull explosion ensued. *Whomp!* A rather stupid expression entered the other Dragon's eyes as his wings folded without strength. Thundersong threw a long, straight right punch that did the rest. The Dragon plunged out of the sky.

Instinctual trust made him act instantly upon the Princess' mental command. He dodged a sharp attack aimed at disabling his right wing. Watching out for the green gas, he stalked the other Dragon through the sky. The enemy jinked to avoid Azania's bolt, only to have two arrows sprout instantly in his neck. One must have hit something important, because he jerked and started to fly in an ungainly circle.

"Dragon bow again?" he inquired, leery of closing the distance.

"Gas!" one of the Rangers cried.

The strange gas crept out between the Dragon's fangs, behaving as if it were somehow under mental control rather than dispersing a physical element ought to. It wavered before accelerating determinedly toward the Dragon and his Riders.

"Ready," the Princess said.

"Ears," he commanded. "Three, two, one, *GRROOARRGHH!!*"

Azania's bolt smashed home just above the Dragon's left eye. The enemy had dipped his head into the shot. His own shaped, focussed sonic blast struck the other male spinning, ripping the amorphous blob of gas apart. It still managed to attempt to draw back together again and make one more feeble attempt to reach them, before dissipating.

Paralleling the other Dragon's falling body for a few moments, he checked and double-checked for gas before reaching out and slitting his throat.

"Quick, the other one's about to land in the camp," the Princess called.

Upending himself immediately, Thundersong called, "Hold onto your hair, little Humans!"

The Rangers groaned as he dived.

CHAPTER 15

FLYING SPRINT

CHAKKIX CAMP WAS A mess. A dog's breakfast, according to Sankir Farizam, referencing the delightful canine habit of sick dogs eating grass in order to throw up – then, more likely than not, consuming their own vomit. Thundersong had always seen dogs as affable, if rather stupid, creatures which were rightly terrified of Dragons.

Dog's breakfast? Mammals and their bodily functions were nothing short of gross.

Thoughtfully, he dropped his final victim in the scrubby brush a hundred or so Dragon paces from the dusty outskirts. Fond memories? Indeed, the local smells were just as appetising as he recalled, only a little more charred around the edges. He was not sure if the locals liked the idea of more Dragons descending upon them, but Tarangis had apparently advanced the eloquent, 'Our butts are not being burned anymore, so this has to be a better outcome' argument in support of his new visitors.

Thundersong glowered at him as the man bent over Princess Azania's hand. "Your Highness, what a pleasure it is to see you again."

He struggled manfully, but his eyes gave up an unequal battle to check her outfit over at least once. Honestly. They needed to find this man a wife. Fast.

THUNDER O DRAGON

Azania politely pretended not to notice. "Tarangis Lionbaiter, I hope business is good?"

"Far better, Princess, thanks to your timely rescue from this treacherous ambush. Dragon! I see you have not lost one iota of your smoking glower. You look well. Larger than last time we met, I'll warrant."

"Tarangis," he bowed his muzzle cordially.

"Needless to say, rumours of impending war appear to be well-founded," the man said ruefully, thanking him as Dragon extended a paw to steady his sliding wheelchair. "I received messages. You were bringing cargo and smiths?"

"We dropped all that a few miles out, before rushing to your aid," Azania said. "Are the forges still available?"

"Very much so. Everything was ready until an hour ago," he apologised.

The Princess said, "Here are Garan and Yardi and their crew. Let me introduce you."

"Yardi!" he exclaimed. "And … husband? Holy heavens, this camp is no place for children! This cannot be right."

Giving him his best evil Dragon leer, Thundersong purred, "It had better become so, Tarangis, and fast. This is a package deal. We've moved this entire family of smiths right across the Tamarine Mountains merely to support the war effort. The quality of their work is unsurpassed. Plus, they will be working with three Grinder Clan Dragon blacksmiths."

"You certainly like to shake a place, Dragon," Tarangis smiled, but his eyes conveyed doubts.

"I'm just the heavy backup for Azania."

"Right …"

With thirteen new patients following the battle, Thundersong realised that their priorities had shifted once more. Five Dragons and eight Rangers had succumbed to the curse of the green mist – they acted sick and lethargic but were nowhere near as mentally confused as the Tamarine Dragons had been. Less exposure? Would their condition worsen or remain stable?

He and Azania helped organise a couple of flights of Sea Dragons to pick up and return the remaining cargo, which they placed where directed outside Yardi's old premises. Meantime, the Isles Dragonesses cleared up and helped to put out fires, terrifying everyone with their belligerent glares and huge swords. Garan and Yardi's teams swarmed into the five adjacent forges Tarangis had secured for them, examining the offerings and making plans.

Soon, Juggernaut cornered him. *Listen, I know you're itching to get out there.*

Out where? Thundersong asked innocently and earned a bruised shoulder for his trouble.

Leave this mess to us, youngling. I can see it in your eyes. You take your Princess and skedaddle. I don't know where you're going, but if you're a betting Dragon, I'll take your gold right now with a pinpoint guess. These Dragons and Rangers need help urgently, right?

Aye. Thank you, Juggernaut.

You can thank me by fixing this lot up. Now, get out of here before I boot you out.

He gave Juggernaut a mighty clap upon the shoulder. *Get back to work, Great Grinder! Azania?*

I heard.

She spoke briefly with Sankir Farizam. Soon, he heard her say clearly, 'I promised. That still stands, Sankir.' The man shook his head slowly but clasped her shoulder. No, he could not stop her. He might not like what they were about to attempt, but he had eight men and women down with the Terror infection.

Walking over with Azania, the Ranger said, "Fly strong and true, you two. Azerim will kill me, but he'll simply have to understand."

"He will," the Princess promised.

"I know you'll take good care of one another," he said. "See you soon, Princess?"

"Sooner than you think," she smiled mysteriously.

His bearded face assumed several confused expressions before realisation evidently clanged home. "Princess, you can't –"

She mimed shutting her lips.

"Take a few supplies, at least," he said promptly. "Stock up with quarrels for your Dragon bow, ma'am?"

"Please," she said.

"Bow and arrows?"

"Check."

"Feisty and furious attitude?"

"Double-check, right, Thundersong?"

"That's just my Princess," he grinned. "Sankir, will you speak to Juggernaut about setting up patrol schedules? We're all allergic to surprises."

"Noted," he said, with a smart salute.

Talk about a flying stop. No more than ten minutes later, having briefed Everdeep meantime, Thundersong took off with his nose pointed to the West. Time to shake the dust off his wings.

All that afternoon, they flew toward the lowering suns. Taramis blazed right into their eyes. Azania asked if he was flying with his eyes closed.

"Mostly," he admitted.

"Warn you about any mountains jumping randomly into our flight path?"

"Sure."

"Say, Thundersong, what does a Dragon prefer for lunch?"

"Eh? No idea."

"A fry-up."

He chortled along for a few miles, each chortle bouncing them through the air.

An hour after nightfall, they swooped into a neat

landing in the canyon cavern where he had performed his crazy backflip manoeuvre for Aria. Dragon and Rider bathed beneath the waterfall, sloughing off the dust, grime and smoky smell of long travel.

"I'll admit, Princess, even I feel like a good scrub every time I leave that camp." *Blergh!* "Nasty place."

"Too right." She shook water through her curls. "I gave Tarangis quite the lecture about looking after the children. Missing Aria yet?"

"Some. It feels better than I imagined to be just the two of us again. I've missed … the quiet."

"Me? Quiet?"

He gave that an obligatory snort. "Chattering chaffinch, you are."

"Dragon demagogue."

"Ooh, how perniciously you wound me. Missing Azerim, especially in your nude state beneath a waterfall?"

"Do you think he just doesn't like a strong, independent woman?"

Hmm. Nice avoidance of the question there, Princess. He said, "Oddly, I'm not sure he knows what to make of your independent streak. I wonder …"

"You? Wandering about like a lost goat? Nope. Not the Thundersong I know."

"Aye, don't wander too far, you might get lost." Scratching his chin with a talon, he mused aloud, "Random Thundersong-ish theory of the day? Maybe he wants to protect you, but he doesn't know how. Isles women, after all –"

"*Protect* me?" Throwing up her hands, Azania protested, "So, all this restricting my movement and choices, binding me to ridiculous promises and talking over me in meetings is an expression of protective love? I don't feel claustrophobic at all. Oh, come on, Thundersong, sell me another barrel of tripe. Please. I'm begging for it."

"*Blergh!* It was just an idea."

"Oh no, not the sulking! Please! No fifty-foot Dragon

should sulk like that."

"I do have a very large lip to drag about when I do."

"True." She gurgled with laughter, and then gurgled for a different reason as he scooped up a double pawful from the shallow pool to properly inundate her. "So, are you still game to fly overnight?"

"My wings do feel oddly light after dragging tonnes of fine steel all over the mountains. I'm more than ready."

"Excellent, right along with the male Dragon chest-thump to underscore your masculinity – sorry, your almighty draculinity."

Gnarr-scrambled-Princess-on-toast.

"I'll wake you around midnight, Thundersong. Get some sleep. And – thanks."

"Thanks for what?"

"The theory. It might just explain a few things. Oldest brother of five, always protecting the younger ones. Early kingship over a troubled kingdom. A deep fear of losing those he loves, exacerbated by recent events – it could all make sense, actually."

"By my wings, a Human actually making sense? Historic day!"

She smacked his neck open-handed. "You'd better zip that lip and start snoring, Dragon, or I'll lock you in a dungeon with Prince Floric for the rest of your life!"

Since no nightmare could possibly be worse than that, he slept like a hatchling.

Rising at the appointed hour, Thundersong flipped a wing out into the canyon that separated Vanrace from its claimed territorial possession of the land all the way east beyond Chakkix Camp. Nobody took that seriously, but since nobody actually wanted the badlands either – no problem.

Riding a brief thermal up into a clear night sky salted to the point of breathtaking brilliance by thick bands of stars, he prepared mentally for their next trick, a long, straight flight out over Vanrace that should take them all the way to the border of the Kingdom of Garome in one monumental bound. How did they plan to find the border? Azania suggested spying on any army movements from above. A border snarl ought to be visible from a great height. There might be opposing ranks of soldiers, perhaps a tent camp. Trust Humans to stand around waiting for a problem to solve itself rather than clobbering one another until someone pushed the resulting carcasses out of the way.

Draconic methods were so much tidier.

Well, messier in terms of the body count, but tidier in terms of results.

Setting a flying rhythm according to new patterns he had learned from Thundersong the Thumpingly Thick-Thighed, he sought to replicate what he and Azania suspected he might several times have achieved purely by accident, sleeping on the wing yet remaining aware of his surroundings. This was a Sea Dragon migratory skill. Periodically, he noticed the stars changing position, wheeling through the clear heavens as he winged along with smooth, steady strokes. He imagined slow pendulums swinging either side of his body. His awareness expanded to encompass Azania tucked into her slipstreaming position upon his neck. A tightly buckled leather harness held her in place in case she fell deeply asleep, which appeared to be the case now. Other straps held the Dragon bow flush against his left flank.

As dawn rose behind his tail, Princess Azania stirred and woke. Thundersong greeted her with gladness. They passed directly over King Tyloric's castle, a mile and a half overhead. Perhaps King Tyloric dreamed of a draconic shadow crossing his grave? Mmm. He mentally picked out flowers for his final resting place. Nice ones. After all, the best flowers grew on dung heaps.

With a cackle of pure pleasure, Azania hugged his neck. "You're both ridiculous and the most wonderful friend a girl could wish for."

He bounced through the air for a good few miles on the strength of that comment.

This Sea Dragon skill was incredible. Feeling fresh and stuffed to the ear canals with vim despite travelling for more than half the night, Thundersong imagined he could practically fly across the world – although, to be fair, one would need to stop for food and water. As a frisky tailwind picked up, he accelerated his wingbeat as well, hitting his full sprinting speed. Azania whooped and encouraged him as they zoomed along beneath a morning sky full of delicate wisps of cirrus cloud slowly turning from pink to white.

By late morning, grey smoke rising from multiple cooking fires alerted them to the probable position of the opposed forces on Vanrace's western border. Resting his wings, he swooped in a long decline, peering ahead through his spectacles. Two armies camped on the one road that connected the two kingdoms, facing one another across a short distance. Nobody had even bothered to form up in ranks to annoy one another with the traditional trading of insults the ballads were so fond of. The Vanracian camp had green tents, the Garome one, a smattering of different colours.

"Morons," he muttered.

"Exactly. Still, we know precisely where to land so as not to break my promise to Azerim."

"One scale beyond the middle, aye?"

A few moments and a spot of wriggling later, she said, "Oh, go on then."

"Go on what?"

"Earplugs duly inserted."

"Ooh, goody!" He rubbed his paws together with glee. "First, my dear Princess, you have to approve my introduction. What do you think of this? 'I am Dragon! My rage shakes the portals of fate!' "

"Ahem. Very … literary."

"Shame we aren't keeping those notes on our deeds

anymore."

"Says who we aren't?" She patted her left saddlebag fondly. "Can't wait to write that one down. 'Thunder, o Dragon!' 'Aye,' he roared, 'for my rage shakes the portals of fate!'"

He inquired knowingly, "Not too conceited?"

"Oh, no. A Dragon, conceited? Who could imagine such a character trait?"

Upon that note, he shook the sleepy, not very standoffish standoff with his customary bellow of welcome. Uprooting a swathe of green tents with the violence of his blast – totally accidental, of course – Thundersong swept to a landing between the two armies, taking care that not even the tip of his tail transgressed over the boundary line someone had helpfully marked with a random post which stood innocently at the roadside wondering what under the heavens all the fuss was about.

"Who's in charge around here?" Thundersong demanded.

"I am," said a soldier on the Vanracian side.

Dragon glanced over his shoulder. Several hundred men gathered behind a green-robed fellow in a dazed formation of sorts. Awful shame about the rude awakening. Oops.

Turning to face the Garome side, he asked more loudly, "I said, who's in charge?"

"I am," said a grizzled knight, raising his right hand. "Commander Arroc of Garome at your service, mighty … oh! Do the very heavens rest upon our earth?"

Stepping off his paw with an insouciant air, Azania, in a millisecond, wreaked far more damage than a recently arrived large white Dragon had just achieved on the other side of the border.

She smiled sweetly. "Commander …"

Apparently, the poor fellow had just expired and winged among the very stars, judging by his expression. The hundred or so knights behind him were no better.

Simpletons, he sniffed. Wearing tin plate helmets in this heat had obviously baked their brains beyond redemption and these were men firmly steeped in the tradition of outright worship of dark, beautiful Princesses.

Be nice, Dragon. I am merely establishing utter dominance of the situation. Understand?

By my sire's egg, what a little Dragoness you are!

Aren't I just? Introduce me, please.

Thundersong said, "Commander Arroc of Garome, may I present her Royal Highness of T'nagru, Azania, the Black Rose of the Desert?"

She smiled, "Noble knights of Garome –"

As one, the men crashed to one knee, cracked their right hands upon their solid metal breastplates and roared, "All honour to the Princess of T'nagru!"

"I say!" she said brightly, beaming about her with radiant delight not exactly reflected in the darker tones of her emotions he scented. "It's not every day that a Princess earns such a welcome to a kingdom around Solixambria. I do believe Garome shall be my new favourite. Thank you, noble knights. I am honoured and, indeed, overwhelmed by the warmth of your welcome."

Expecting me to write this slop down? he complained.

Do be quiet, Thundersong. We are simply oiling the wheels of diplomacy. Attend.

With the drool of a hundred men or what?

She giggled mentally.

Touching her hair, although it needed no attention despite them having flown all night and most of the morning, the devious rascal gave them one last, coy glance before turning toward the border, where the stiffly formal leader of the Vanrace force awaited her. This one tried to resist her charming smile. He worked hard, clenching his fists and biting his cheek, Thundersong judged, struggling not to melt into a puddle of goo.

Messy, but inevitable.

"Captain Surabic," the Princess cooed. "How lovely to

see you again."

Surabic appeared to be clenching his buttocks in order to secure something – he shuddered to think what – against an unfortunate accident.

"I believe we last met in the dungeons beneath Vanrace's castle?"

"Your Highness, ma'am!" he barked.

"How is your wife, Surabic?"

"Much improved, ma'am, thank you!"

"I'm glad."

"Ma'am!"

Aye. His brain had just become stuck on 'ma'am,' just like one hundred knights behind her – Garome's finest – had become fixated upon the royal rear view. He stepped up behind her, both to smile at the unfortunate Captain and to break the spell cast by her legs. He understood. Too much staring at Aria's wings or hindquarters tended to unhinge his brain, too.

Azania said, "I've come to resolve an unfortunate misunderstanding. Captain Surabic, why will you not allow these armies to pass through on their way down to aid my kingdom against the Skartunese invasion?"

"King Tyloric demands assurances," he rapped. "Too much – I mean, much gold. Without payment, passage cannot be allowed."

She locked gazes with him.

Thundersong smelled his terror stench from twenty feet away. Vanrace was definitely the kingdom of rich, ripe, redolent smells. Truly an olfactory bouquet. He smiled at the enemy force in an attempt to further thicken the air with their horrid stench.

"How unfortunate," the Princess noted drily.

"Extremely," he said. "It is not a popular policy, but I have my orders."

"What will become of all that gold, I wonder?" she added.

The men behind the Captain muttered darkly in

realisation of the truth, but they did not back up an inch. Tyloric was famed for throwing lavish parties in his own honour and claiming to own the largest wine cellar in Solixambria.

May I, Princess? he asked politely.

By all means. I'm trying not to gag over here.

In a deep, amiable voice, he said, "Last time I was in Vanrace, Captain Surabic, I was taking my rest upon the tallest tower of your castle when I became aware of Princess Azania's plight in the room just below. The King and your Prince Floric advanced the most uncivilised proposal to the Princess. I myself am a peaceful creature, but their abominable behaviour roused me to wrath – a wrath that even now, sets my Dragon hearts ablaze."

Allowing his voice to rise in volume and heat, he continued, "You will know me as the Dragon who destroyed that tower and kidnapped the Princess. Long have I pleaded with her to take my vengeance upon the Kingdom of Vanrace, for as you know, Dragons' memories are unfailing and their ire at dishonourable, despicable deeds – aye, as you just heard, and felt, my thunder shakes the portals of fate itself! I have brought with me no less than seventy ruthless kin, not one of whom is my lesser in size, and if you stand in my way, nothing in all creation will be able to save your little kingdom from total annihilation!"

"Dragon, peace," Azania put in mildly.

"PEACE? I WANT WAR!"

The Captain staggered backward several steps at the blast.

"Dragon, please. We agreed to desist for the sake of the innocent people of Vanrace."

"Desist? What is this craven pleading, this accursed word that burns in my ears? Why do these foolish Humans not simply remove this King and install another?" Surabic frowned. Apparently, the idea of treason took a touch of processing in the woefully underutilised space behind his thick skull. "I mean, Princess, I have sniffed around Vanrace –"

Isn't that like cauterising your own nostrils? she slipped in.

Thundersong grinned hugely. Thankfully, Surabic and his men appeared to interpret that as a terrible threat. One man had a dark stain spreading down his trousers. Most pleasing to a Dragon's ego.

"Please, noble Dragon," several soldiers began to beg, "spare our noble kingdom."

"You could please me," he said loftily, "by tossing that vile King and his foul son into their own dungeons and hurling the key into the deepest sewer you can find! Princess Azania, you are far too kind to these peasants."

"Peasants?" she protested. "These noble men of Vanrace suffer great injustice under the reign of a tyrant."

How did she lie so glibly?

Dragon narrowed his eyes at her. This Princess would bear watching.

Addressing Captain Surabic, Azania said, "Good Captain, I apologise. Dragons see the world in such simplistic terms."

Thundersong clenched his paw before it wandered off on its own accord to swat a cheeky royal over the nearest tent camp. *Gnarr* –

"I'll admit," she added, ignoring his rumbling ire, "it will be extremely challenging to restrain these vengeful Dragons, for they are rightfully incensed about the fate of their many kin who are being held captive by the Skartunese. I myself would not want to be the creature standing in their way. However, in my role as T'nagru's Roving Ambassador to the Dragons, I do hold some small sway. We travel now up to Garome to consult with our armies and allies."

Not a subtle hint, but then, these Vanracians were about as subtle as their body odour.

Stepping right to the edge of the border, she put on her most brilliant, fragile smile yet for the soldiers of Vanrace.

"I care for your people, truly I do. We are neighbours. It is indeed regrettable that King Tyloric acted so dishonourably toward me, locking me in his deepest dungeon for a month –" she squeezed out a large tear, which trickled slowly down her cheek, leaving a glinting trail that appeared to exert a mesmeric grip upon her audience "– where it was so dark and lonely and terrifying … and then he threatened with many harsh, contemptible words to force me to marry Prince Floric!"

To a man, the Vanracian contingent flinched.

Dragon decided that this was their one redeeming behaviour so far.

She wept softly, "It was the most terrible time in my life. I'm sorry. I'm quite … overcome. Thundersong, take me away, would you?"

The Princess leaned heavily upon his paw, sobbing as they walked back through the lines into the Garome encampment. That girl! Judged her performance to perfection. As they passed amongst the tents, they both stopped in surprise.

"Brand the Devastator!" Azania gasped, wiping her eyes.

"Indeed," purred the Umber Dragon. "A most enjoyable performance, Princess. Although, if any Human creature called me simplistic, I would decorate my lair with their bones."

Thundersong clenched his jaw. "What do you want, brother?"

Ten minutes later, the fully recovered Princess sat with Commander Arroc beneath an open tent, sipping a cool goblet of fruit juice. She commented politely on how beautiful the Gemwoods looked in this season and inquired about the disposition of the other armies or bodies of Knights. He listed armies from ten kingdoms of the seventeen, including Hamirythe. Some were still on the march and would not arrive for another month, but a substantial body now camped outside of Garome itself, including Princess Yuali and her sister, Princess Inzashu-N'shula, waiting for the border to open.

Azania sketched the battle over at Chakkix Camp for them.

"More injuries like our sire?" Brand growled.

"Aye, brother," Thundersong said. "It appears that the Terror Clan have discovered some new, dark magic which confuses and sickens the minds of both Humans and Dragons. The gas they expel almost appears animate, sticking together and moving against a light breeze, for example. Not all the Dragons can do this magic, but at least four or five, of the two dozen we encountered, were capable."

Azania said, "Brand, you could really help us."

"As if –"

"Thundersong, a moment. We really need my sister Inzashu to consult with your Great-Aunt Ignita, Brand, in order to help your sire and all these Dragons and people," the Princess explained. "She might be young, but Inzashu enjoys an unparalleled power of magical healing. However, as you know, Thundersong is forbidden to enter Devastator territory. If we flew to Garome, would it be possible for you to fly up to her lair and bring her down to the edge of the mountains?"

He bit his forked tongue until he tasted blood. Ask his brother for help? How this galled his pride!

Brand nodded slowly. "I agree, Princess. For the sake of our sire."

"We appreciate your help." Mentally, she prodded, *Thundersong?*

He grated, "Thank you, Brand."

The other snarled slowly, "For what it's worth, brother, what my dam did with your egg was a wicked and shameful misdeed. I will neither pretend to like nor to understand you and your undraconic ways; however, we are blood kin and bound into this war whether we like it or not. Truce?"

Thundersong had to rescue his jaw from an impending collision with the ground. "I – ahem – of course, Brand! Truce."

His half-brother nodded. "I see how you and the Princess labour unceasingly for the Dragonkind, brother, and indeed, for all the peoples of Solixambria. No paw can undo the past, but we can shape the future. If there is nothing more, I shall fly on to speak with Ignita and then up to Juggernaut's lair to deliver my report."

They spoke for a few minutes longer, but with little else substantive to discuss, it was mostly pleasantries.

Thundersong buzzed quietly with surprise at his brother's gesture. Was Brand growing up? Might he be positioning himself advantageously as a future Devastator Clan leader? As his brother winged off to the North, he pondered long upon the matter before his thoughts eventually wound their way to what Blaze the Devastator had done.

Maybe his sire's casting him out and latterly revealing the shameful truth of his past actions were the best things he could ever have done for his son.

Now he could become the Dragon he was meant to be.

CHAPTER 16

ODDLY PLEASING

OFF THEY TOOTLED TO Garome, a local expression to which Commander Arroc had introduced them. Thundersong was mightily unimpressed. Noble fire-breathers of the air did not tootle anywhere. Especially not since they were able to accomplish in one afternoon a journey that armies on foot or horseback would take three days to cover. Sixty-five miles to Garome?

Barely a tootle. Closer to a footle.

Soaring over the magnificent emerald Gemwoods, Dragon and Rider shattered the local peace by practising his sonic attacks as Everdeep had been coaching him. The high-pitched attack had not appeared to affect the Terror Dragons, but it might work on armies. He practised his full singing range from soprano notes the envy of the most musical Princess – which did not include Azania, despite that all proper Princesses in the ballads out-sung songbirds, at the bare minimum – to subsonic rumblings which they hoped might do nasty things to the sand under an army's boots. Having terrified the local bird population into stunned silence or desperate explosions of feathers as they raced off to the horizon, he and his half-deaf Rider winged in to the forest fortress of Garome, a pretty town of five linked fortified hills with thick forest lying between.

"What was that?" Azania yelled.

"Take out your earplugs!" he boomed.

"Alright, alright, keep your scales on, Mister Rip-Snort-Blast. I hear you."

"So, how do we find your sister in this warren?"

"I do happen to own the loudest Dragon on this continent."

"Own? Wash out your mouth!"

"I can't hear you," she chuckled, poking her ears. "These things really work a treat. They'd even stop me from hearing your snoring at night."

"Do earplugs come in a larger, Princess-proof size?"

"You could use my foot."

"That'd definitely be putting your foot in, well, a place you never want to put it."

They coasted down into Garome through golden evening skies that burnished the tops of the Gemwoods a magnificent, fiery emerald colour. White pigeons nested in the treetops, while light green treeswifts flitted about in great numbers, darting in and out of the foliage.

Time to inflict minor heart attacks on the local birdlife and the slightly larger Human life too. Sucking deep of the cooling evening air, Thundersong bellowed, *I – AM – DRAAGOONN!!*

Thunder from a clear sky. Little white faces popped out here and there and rushed into the streets to see what was happening.

INZASHU!! he thundered for good measure.

"That looks like the castle," Azania said, pointing to the hilltop to their right side.

"I like castles."

"Paws off, Dragon. These are nice people. Allies."

"Please tell me that these are the kind of allies who need an occasional clout about the earhole to keep them honest?"

"Sadly, not even that much."

"You're no fun."

Privately, he reached out with his mind. In a few seconds, a mental blast of excitable greeting made his wingbeat stutter. Well, hello there, scarily powerful little Princess with a wicked enchantress for a mother. He could not wait for her to meet Sirensong. What they could not accomplish together …

"She's at the castle," he confirmed.

"How do I look, Dragon?"

"Like the usual amount of trouble, Princess."

"Perfect. Bring us in – oh, what do you know, it looks like they have a training field inside the castle grounds there, behind the keep. See? Plenty of space for even the burliest Dragon's wings."

"Mmm, have I told you how much I like you, pretty girl?"

Flicking his wings, he adjusted to take them in right over the top of the keep. The sentries upon the rooftop turned as pale as white linen as he whispered past just a couple of feet above their heads. Smooth as silk, he tilted his wing surfaces to cup the air and executed the lightest landing he had ever managed. Barely disturbed a grass blade.

However, an entire cohort of soldiers, who had been practising archery at the end of the field, promptly fainted in graceful concert.

"Aha, that'll be the Amboraine contingent," Azania noted.

"How do they ever fight a real battle?"

"I have no earthly idea."

"Azania! *Azania!*"

"Off you tootle then, Princess," said he.

"Blasted buckles. How does anyone ever – there we go. Inza! I'm coming, Inza!"

Leaping down to the ground, she sprinted over to her sister, who wore her customary flowing cream-coloured desert-style robes. There was hugging and squealing and happy crying – as opposed to sad crying, overwhelmed crying or plain terrified crying. Humans had so many excuses to leak. He greeted the younger Princess warmly. So many fond memories of flying, camping and battling together. Inzashu promptly wet his scales with her salty dripping. No mind. The ocean was salty and he had swum in that. How was biological saltiness any different?

Next, Princess Yuali of Amboraine turned up to collect her hug, most certainly not from the Dragon. Ah, and here came a larger delegation of people dressed in fancy clothing that, amongst Humans, proclaimed their high station.

Recognising the redheaded young man in the lead, Dragon said heartily, "Ah, Prince Faratic of Garome! Last time I saw you, you were – *oof! Gnarr!*"

Mental cudgel to the alleged brain, Azania said pertly.

You rotten little trickster.

The Prince stopped in his tracks. "Have we met, mighty … large Dragon?"

A clear memory of Faratic's pale buttocks fleeing downstream at top speed flashed through his mind. Aye, they had met, in a manner of speaking. Very briefly, it had to be said, since the Prince was a great runner. Truly gifted when encouraged by a Dragon's smile.

Azania giggled merrily meantime, saying, "Indeed, Prince Faratic, it has been a while. This is Thundersong, my Dragon. He has changed colour from brown to white since last you met him up in the mountains."

He inclined his muzzle. "And this is Azania, *my* Princess."

Young Faratic clearly put two and three together and made a sum total he did not enjoy.

Aye. Fancied himself a Dragon slayer, did he? Giving the Prince a glower that assured him how any ideas of such a nature might be greeted, Thundersong rumbled, "As a modern Dragon, I have been known to venture upon occasion into the realms of forgiveness, my Prince. Azania has impressed upon me how staunch an ally you have already proven to be. We are grateful. We bring encouraging news of a Dragon army flying south and perhaps less encouraging news on the border front."

Exhaling loudly, the Prince said, "May I offer refreshment, o mighty Dragon Lord?"

Mmm, the title of 'mighty Dragon Lord' had a certain ring to it. Maybe one day, when he reached a quarter of his great-grandsire's size!

He said, "I do have a corner in my stomach which is crying out for a portion of the succulent venison for which your kingdom is famed, but please, see to my Princess' needs first. May we brief your key personnel?"

"Fresh water and a light snack will suffice for me," Azania said.

"We were just meeting over a small meal," Faratic said. "Will you … uh, join us?"

His tone clearly suggested the question, 'Is this safe?' Dragon would have liked to assure him that it most certainly was not. Too much politics or diplomatic chicanery and he would start nibbling on a few ankles and work his way up. However, Princess Azania slipped her hand into the crook of the young man's elbow and bade him lead on.

In other exciting news, Human males were able to float in his Princess' company.

Since he could not possibly fit though the archways that linked the central keep to the battlements, he stepped up onto the stonework with liquid menace that clearly terrified the soldiers on patrol. To his surprise, several hundred people had gathered outside the keep's gates. They gasped and pointed at him. Hmm. Flex the muscles? Make a speech? *Blergh.* Feeling the venison's call rather more loudly than the desire to posture upon a stone wall of dubious stability, he walked around to what Faratic – the word 'frantic' kept popping into his mind whenever he regarded the imprudent young man –had called the reception area, an outdoor gazebo-like structure in a private courtyard, where a dozen or so important people in their fancy robes and uniforms forgot all about their meal as they gaped at the visitor.

"Good evening, little Humans," he said politely.

Two fainted onto their plates. Amboraine, of course. Remembering not to show too many fangs, as they might get the wrong idea and perish rather than faint harmlessly, he introduced himself and Princess Azania as she appeared through another archway. King Aramic, a redhead like his son, welcomed the Dragon to Garome in a pleasingly unsteady voice and invited him to join them. He clutched the table as if he feared his furniture might be the first thing to disappear down a certain capacious throat, swiftly washed down with a portion of the royal personage.

Servants bustled about adding places and making arrangements. Inzashu popped over to ask if they had made it over to the Archipelago and how Aria was.

"As beautiful as ever," he said. "We are mates now. It's quite a story."

"I'd love to hear it."

"Perhaps tomorrow, as we'd like you to fly with us?"

"Just when I was growing accustomed to having my feet on the ground," she joked. "How can I help, Dragon? Is it an urgent matter?"

"More than," he said and filled her in on what they knew about the Terror Clan's disquieting new weapon. She was most intrigued and excited by the prospect of being able to work with Sea Dragon healers. "So, we'd fly you to Ignita, then down to Chakkix Camp and up to Juggernaut's lair —"

"I just left and took the long way around the mountains," she chuckled. "More snow and cold?"

"I'm afraid so. This could be critical, Inzashu."

"I ... understand."

"No pressure," said he, suiting actions to words as he squeezed her gently in his right forepaw.

"Didn't feel a thing," she lied cheerfully, with an

appreciative chuckle for his empathy. "So, all's well with Aria? What about … King Azerim, wasn't it?"

"Aye to Aria but it's a little more complicated with Azerim," he admitted softly. "They're betrothed but they've been having a rough patch and we're sort of on the run, trying to change the fates without flouting promises Azania made to him. Be gentle with your sister, please."

Inzashu smiled, "Thanks for the warning."

Shortly, a servant appeared at his elbow to inquire in trembling voice exactly how many deer the mighty Dragon Lord would like and in what form? The mighty Dragon Lord declared that he was not fussy but perhaps out of concern for his dinner companions, the meal ought to be brought dead and not bleeding all over their freshly swept flagstones. Having been appraised that these deer stood the height of a man's thigh, he inquired if a mere three might be possible? Anything for the mighty Dragon Lord, the servant promised.

Loudly and long did he purr in approval.

"Thundersong?" Azania inquired from the table.

Slinking forward like a predacious Dragon stalking a meal, he settled with his jaw upon their gazebo, bringing his eye line well above the tabletop. "I was merely expressing my appreciation for King Aramic's most excellent hospitality."

"Ah, the servants may have mistaken your response for anger," she noted.

"You." He crooked a foreclaw toward a young male servant, who trembled as if he were about to set a new record for the mile dash. Hmm. Was sprinting a Garome talent? Very odd for a people who lived in deep forest, for he was convinced such a sport would lead to multiple unfortunate accidents involving unsuspecting trees. Thundersong said, "Please inform the other servitors that I am delighted with your generosity and extend my compliments to the kitchen staff on the artful presentation and delightful scent of the victuals upon the table. Truly, this is a table fit for a King."

The young fellow scampered off, touching his neck as if to reassure himself that it was indeed still attached to his shoulders.

Now, to stay awake and alert. No snoozing through this meal.

Azania's thought broke in, *Once bitten, twice shy, Dragon? It's alright. I'm also learning.*

We Dragons say, once bitten, bite back twice as hard.

The Princess promptly choked on whatever nibble she had been chewing. Inzashu swatted her firmly upon the back. A swig or two of water and muttered apologies later, everyone was fine. A massive platter of venison portions arrived for the mighty four-pawed one.

"Ah, my private buffet," he joked, raising nervous laughs from around the table.

He tucked in, trying to be polite about picking up pieces between his talons when he could have just tilted the platter and slid the lot down his throat in a second. Commendably tasty. Succulent young animals had been selected for the Dragon's dinner. Mmm! The meat practically melted on his fangs.

The talk turned to the armies still on the march. The latest news from T'nagru, now a week old, was that the Skartunese armies were not yet on the move but scouts had reported that they lay massed in the underground cities just beyond the hottest zone. One speculation was that they might be digging permanent tunnels beneath the desert.

Just then, a servant dashed in. He bent to whisper in the King's ear.

"What? Say that again, lad?" Aramic demanded.

All eyes turned to him.

Passing him a message scroll, the servant whispered again.

In a moment, the King said, "Attention, everyone. We've just received a fast message hawk from the

THUNDER O DRAGON

Vanracian border. In summary, the forces under Captain Surabic have packed up their tents and marched back toward the capital."

"Surely not, father," Prince Faratic said. "Tyloric made it abundantly clear he would never open that border, not even if encouraged with all the gold in our treasury."

King Aramic inclined his grizzled head. "This message also says that they left a note nailed to the border post. It says, 'Welcome to Vanrace.'"

Thundersong led a chorus of disbelieving guffaws.

"Further, Commander Arroc reports that their actions may have had something to do with the visit of a certain Dragon Rider and Dragon this afternoon. What did you say to them, Princess Azania? Did you two raze their camp or threaten to eat their – pardon my expression – children?"

"Nothing of the sort," she protested.

Thundersong put in, "We merely suggested – delicately – that if Tyloric is truly such an awful king, they might want to consider their options. We were very polite, weren't we, Azania?" She nodded eagerly. "We stepped neither foot nor paw upon Vanracian soil nor threatened regicide nor suggested anything uncouth whatsoever. Word of a Dragon and his Dragon Rider."

They continued to stare.

Azania shrugged. "I shared my experience of staying in their dungeon."

"Apparently, you two are masters of persuasion," Aramic said dryly. "The border lies open. Our scouts and spies are already en route to the capital."

"Astonishing," Thundersong rumbled.

Azania echoed, "Amazing." For him alone, she added, *Nice fake rage and bluster back there, partner.*

Nice fake tears, partner.

Quite the sob story, eh? Her rich laughter tickled his mind. *I rather suspect King Tyloric is even less popular than we thought.*

Wonders will never cease.

Peculiar but pleasing result, all told.

The meal proceeded to take on a rather more jovial note than before as servants lit pretty metalwork lanterns about the gazebo. King Aramic proposed a toast to Azania and Thundersong which they all took up with excessive enthusiasm, he felt, before he excused himself for a few minutes to set the military minds in motion for an early start the next day. By then, he should receive word from Vanrace, he said, as his spies there had not reported in for two weeks. Tyloric must have been busy in his own right, keeping things very quiet.

Time for a change of residents inside his dungeons?

The Dragon said, "There's that noise again. What's happening outside the gate, King Aramic?"

"I'm not rightly sure," said he. "Faratic –"

"At once, father."

Curious how so many in this kingdom were light of skin and blonde or reddish of hair, Dragon noticed, but the servants did show a smattering of dark tan faces. Lymarn and Ayren were said to be browner of skin, but even darker Human peoples lived beyond the Obsidian Desert in the far south. How had it come about that Azania's people were so prized for their beauty, he wondered? Of course, Dragons also made beauty distinctions by scale colour. Was this wrong? Or a natural process followed by intelligent creatures? What made a society collectively decide upon certain hallmarks of beauty, such as physical size, face shape, wing structures or indeed, skin and scale colour or sleekness? Why had an aesthetically pleasing woman like Chanize been overlooked simply because she lacked legs beneath the knee?

Nor were Dragons guiltless in this regard. A wounded or wing-disabled Dragon would certainly be looked down upon.

"Dragon's deep in thought," Azania's voice broke into his reverie.

"Sorry," he rumbled. "I was ruminating upon the

character of what amongst our respective species passes for attractiveness and why and how we make those judgements."

"You're a philosopher?" Prince Faratic asked.

"Amongst his many gifts," Azania said. "The Tamarine mountainscape you have hanging in your hallway, my Prince, is one of Thundersong's works."

"You're the artist?" The Prince flushed richly. "I ... I meant no disrespect. The agent assured me it was a genuine work created by a Dragon artist – done in a style so unique, I purchased it at once for my parents' fortieth wedding anniversary."

"A superb choice," Queen Shariza said, speaking almost for the first time that evening.

She was a lady of some sixty years, Dragon judged, reserved in manner, yet with clear blue eyes that took in every nuance. She sat very straight-backed to Azania's left, receiving word from a servant who had hurried off to check on the disturbance.

"Thank you, o Queen," he said.

The Queen said, "The people beg for sight of the famous Dragon who sacked Vanrace and flies with a Princess. Might you be willing? They've been cheering for ever such a long time in the hope of seeing you close up."

"One teensy tower hardly counts for a sacking," he protested, illustrating with his talons.

"Plus, a cow barn," Azania pointed out.

"I did steal a cow, I suppose. That must count for something."

"It sat right on your nose – takes bovine stupidity to a whole new level."

"True. Moo-sical temptation has always been my downfall."

"I didn't know Dragons had a milk tooth."

The Princess giggled as they both realised the amazement with which everyone else at the table regarded their conversation. She suggested a smidgen of entertainment for the locals, if Thundersong was willing, and maybe Prince Faratic would like to help them meet everyone? The Prince looked most displeased by this idea and even less pleased by the time a Dragonish paw deposited him atop his twenty-five foot battlement. At least he was not sprinting away over the horizon on this occasion, minus any stitch of clothing.

He hopped up onto the battlement alongside the Princess of T'nagru, instantly silencing the crowd. The Prince took the opportunity to greet everyone and to introduce their guests in ringing tones that carried right to the back of a crowd of perhaps two or three thousand largely light-haired Humans. A loud cheer rolling back caught him by surprise, clenching his talons and ripping a large block of stone out of parapet.

Dragon set it aside carefully. "Oops. Sorry about that, Faratic."

"It needed repair," the Prince said quickly. Seemed this fellow wanted to stay on a Dragon's best side on this occasion. Good boy. Fast learner.

Azania greeted the people with a cheery wave, setting off wild applause.

Dragon flashed a grin. Silence.

"Must you?" the Princess teased, reaching up to pat his neck as if to reassure everyone down there that they were not about to be eaten. Not happening. She called out, "Now, my Dragon will breathe fire for you!"

"Am I some performing animal?"

"Dragon, you are always one big performance. Now, will you please humour me by producing a plume of fire to amaze the nice people?"

GRROOOAARRRGGHH!!

A skyward spout of white flame lit the houses for hundreds of feet around. At the sight of mortal danger, the silly Humans broke into crazed adulation. Wild cheers and shrieks of approval! His chest swelled with pleasure. Thundersong quickly sheathed his talons before he demolished any more of the ancient stonework. How very peculiar. If he aimed closer, would he earn a greater cheer?

"See? Oddly pleasing reaction, isn't it?" Azania murmured to him.

"Hmm?"

"You're glowing."

"Oh, this is embarrassing."

Gesturing for silence did not achieve much at all but another fang-filled grin stilled the crowd. Pretending that he was reading from a story scroll, he told them about the annual migration of Sea Dragons that passed through the Lumis Ocean and how his kind breathed white fire rather than the orange of the Tamarine Mountains Dragons. The admission that he was not large at all for a Sea Dragon gave rise to many gasps of disbelief. Then, after issuing a caution not to be afraid, he produced a series of his exploding fireworks for them. By concentrating very hard, he could shoot a ball of fire, about two feet across, over a thousand feet into the air where – for reasons unknown to him – it promptly exploded. Altitude? Internal explosion? He had tried to teach this skill to the other Sea Dragons without success.

Judging by their reaction, he had just been promoted in rank to the most awesome creature on four paws.

Suited him just fine.

CHAPTER 17

IGNITA'S ROAR

OVERNIGHT, A SOAKING RAIN arrived. By shifting and curving his body, Thundersong created himself a puddle in the courtyard where he had slept and drank deeply. Aye. He must remind his kin that their fire could run out if they did not keep properly hydrated. Having lived over ninety-nine percent of their lives immersed in water, the Sea Dragons might not imagine this scenario.

Azania popped out of the castle to let him know that Inzashu-N'shula had a team of royal servants scouring the town for certain herbs she was low on. By the time this job was accomplished, the Princess roused him from a very pleasant dream about cosying up to Aria, and the rain had stopped.

She reported that another hawk message had come in. Azania gave a very un-princess-like caper and a fist pump. "The reign of King Tyloric has ended!"

YEEEERRRSSSS!! he thundered.

Three windows up in the castle's turrets shattered at the reverberation. Glass tinkled down.

"Dragon, any chance we could think before we bellow?"

Gnarr-t a chance.

"I understand perfectly. Anyways, it is the best news

since Ignis and Taramis decided to smile upon Solixambria."

He displayed at least fifty fangs in a grin so huge, the stretch caused his jaw joint to pop loudly. "Who's the replacement, may I ask?"

"Lord Harikic, who happens to be married to Queen Shariza's younger sister, Immiriza."

"What is it with Humans and rhyming names?"

"What is it with Dragons and silly Clan names, like Crusher, Grinder or Obliterator?"

"That's what they do."

"So practical," she teased, inflicting a hug upon him. "Is it bad of me to feel vindicated? Before you ask, this man is a very different prospect. He –"

"Knows what a bathtub is?"

Consumed by a fit of helpless giggles, she gasped, "Dragon, I love you!"

"Oh dear. Does Azerim know he's lost your affections?"

"Not like that, you ridiculous reptile."

Placing his right fist over his heart, he moaned in a high-pitched, knightly voice, "Oh, say it not, Azania, my verimost muse, for I have loved thee most fulsomely since the very first day I clapped paw upon thy peerless person! Woe, thou breakest at least one of mine five hearts. How shall this scorned creature ever become whole again?"

This was too much for the Princess. She guffawed so hard that tears sprang into her eyes. She folded up in his paw, apparently unable to stand. He eyed the girl wriggling in his paw in a perfectly undignified state of hysterics. Ah, so this would be 'rolling with laughter' in Human parlance. The problem was that it was catching. What was it about yawns and laughter that was more infectious than the worst disease imaginable? Very soon, his roars of mirth shook the castle. Another two windows gave up the unequal battle and dropped their leaded glass into the courtyard with a loud crash.

Inzashu, the Prince and at least twenty servants rushed out to see what the commotion was all about.

"Celebrating Tyloric's downfall," Azania managed to explain between hiccoughs.

Thundersong said, "This would be the same Tyloric who clapped Princess Azania in irons in his dungeon for a month, hoping she'd break and agree to marry Prince Floric."

"Floric the Flatulent? Gods, no!" several servants blurted out.

One man ducked aside and deposited his breakfast in a nearby flowerbed. "Sorry …"

"I understand perfectly," Azania said.

On that memorable note, the younger sister declared that she was packed and ready. The girls disappeared into the castle to take their leave of Princess Yuali and the royal family. Thundersong apologised to the servants for his random acts of unintentional destruction. Forgiveness must be proportional to the size of the beast causing the trouble, for they were incredibly eager to assure him that it was no trouble at all.

After that, they loaded up, which for two titchy Princesses was not saying a great deal. Thundersong welcomed Inzashu back aboard as they winged into a sky clearing from the east.

She patted his neck. "Storytime?"

"I thought you were too old for bedtime stories?" Azania teased. "How have you been, sister?"

Inzashu said, "I have been in every kingdom from here to Amboraine and I can tell you, Dragon flight is far, far superior to riding horseback. Yuali and I have become good friends. King N'chala will be delighted at her arrival, I am sure. Seriously, my tale won't even take a minute. We rode a long way, the end. What about you two? Tell me everything, especially the romantic bits."

"How is Yuali's father, King Harilan?" Azania put in.

"The latest news has him recovering well – it has been

hard, but he's walking with a stick and beating people with it upon occasion."

"Excellent," said the older Princess. "Dragon, talk."

"Everything since we parted. Remember, I love detail, just like you," Inzashu chirped.

"Oh, is that so?" he growled, amused.

Thundersong flew steadily that morning and into the early afternoon, telling Inzashu the tale of their crazy ocean crossing, treachery, interrupted nuptials and homecomings. Azania chipped in regularly, putting across her perspective or adding details. They headed a few hairs north of perfect northeast, at least if one considered hair less curly than that of the Princesses.

It was a good eighty miles up to the mountains against a light breeze, but at Thundersong speed, they crossed into the foothills within five hours of flying and spent a further hour searching for the river fork where eventually, Inzashu spotted a pair of Dragons, umber and green. Sort of green. Great-Aunt Ignita's natural disguise was breathtaking. Had they not known where exactly to look for her and had they not spotted Brand first, there would have been no chance of identifying her as anything but a patch of bushy grass from a height.

Thundersong swept into a neat landing on the grassy patch between two burbling streams.

"Huh. About time you turned up, lazybones nephew," Ignita yawned widely, showing off a still impressive set of dentures. "At least you've brought my favourite Princess in the world, which is a point toward your redemption. Make me some tea, will you, dear? You always did it best. Oh, but who's this, by my wings? Multiplication of mischief?"

"I'm Inzashu-N'shula, Azania's younger sister – her half-sister," the girl said shyly.

"Nothing half about your beauty, child, nor about the magic I scent upon you," Ignita creaked. "Do you make tea as well as your sister?"

"Definitely Azania's job," Thundersong teased.

"Cheeky hatchling. Off with you! Go fetch sticks for a fire. Run along, now, great-nephew. I've important catching up to do with my *two* favourite Princesses in all of Solixambria."

"You only know two," he pointed out.

She thundered, "Shut your fangs! Are you still here?"

He might have changed his scales, but Great-Aunt Ignita had not changed in the slightest. He had never known her to be any different. By the time he and Brand returned with several paws full of dry sticks for a fire, she had Inzashu and Azania scrambling to write down her wisdom, recipes and ideas. Ignita had, of course, insisted that Brand bring down her favourite teapot. While his brother helped to brew the tea, she questioned Thundersong expertly about his impressions and observations of the green mist. He reminded Azania of its use as what the Skartunese soldiers had called coldstones, the verdelite crystals which had allowed them to keep cool enough to survive a desert crossing in adverse weather conditions.

"It all seems to be related," Ignita grated. "Where's my tea?"

"Almost ready," Azania promised.

"Write down this list, child. Quickly. Brand, I'll need you to fly up to my lair to fetch a few things. Be quick, youngling. One does not keep royalty waiting."

Even Brand did not dare to gnash his fangs.

The minute Azania had a bucket-sized barrel of Dragon tea ready and Brand had winged off, Ignita blew on her tea, gulped the lot, demanded more and said, "Children, listen closely. All of what you have told me fits into a disturbing pattern but points to a danger I cannot yet fathom. These Green Dragons must be imbuing green verdelite with magical properties. Some have even begun to exhale green mist. I'm thinking a few things. One, the Terrors stumbled upon and have been experimenting with a power they do not understand."

"Scrolls always talk about some ancient evil dug from the bowels of the earth," Thundersong quipped lightly.

"There's a reason for that, youngling!" Ignita snapped.

His eyes flicked to Azania. It was unlike his Great-Aunt to act so disturbed.

She nodded. "Extra honey with your tea, Ignita?"

"You're such a darling." The old Dragoness, covered in swamp muck and plants, patted her upon the head. "Aren't you planning to grow anymore?"

Inzashu cracked up.

"I'm afraid I'm past the growing age," she admitted.

"The biggest trouble comes in the smallest packages," the Dragoness snorted. "That's exactly why my great-nephew likes you, and this petite Aria Seaspray, for that matter. Interesting how the Terrors have been able to concentrate draconic magical power into small packages – these stones. I'd give half the treasure hoards in the mountains to understand how they achieved that. You see, it's a fundamental law that magic doesn't like being forced into containment structures or systems."

"Organic or inorganic?" Inzashu asked alertly. "By what mechanism?"

"Oh, good girl." The Dragoness petted the younger sister upon the head. "Glad to see that your tiny cranium guards a respectable brain."

Inzashu gave her sister a nonplussed glance. Azania made a 'simmer down' gesture.

"Inorganic has always been said to be impossible," the Dragoness mused aloud, clearly losing track of her patting. Thundersong quickly nabbed the girl out of harm's way as Ignita illustrated her point by thumping the ground with her fist. "Impossible! Verdelite should not hold magic."

"Unless by organic means?" the girl put in.

"Hush! Can't you hear that I'm thinking, child?"

"That's your stomach growling, Great-Aunt Ignita," Thundersong noted accurately.

"Oh, what a pretty white colour you are," she cooed,

making him blurt out a horrified snarl. "So, it has always been held that draconic bodies have certain processes that control the flow of magic – similarly to how the Human bloodstream functions, in fact, or how the conscious mind is said to be grounded in physical brain matter. Bleed a Dragon out – well, we don't lose magic from blood loss or gain it by drinking another Dragon's blood."

"Ew," Azania spluttered.

Thundersong gulped back a surge of fire and bile at the thought.

"Sorry, dearie, but that's been tried and disproven by the Terrors. Where's my tea?" As the Princess made a show of checking the large, steaming aluminium teapot on its tripod, she added, "However, it is clear that the magic stream has properties which sustain, clarify, concentrate and control draconic magic and it definitely interacts with our psychic processes. Thought controls magic."

Thundersong said, "Does that mean that the Sea Dragon singing was pointless, just sound without effect?"

"No," said Ignita. "Imagine something like a fungal infection of the blood or perhaps a contamination. From your description, the singing process clearly helped – the Dragons returned somewhat to their right minds but remained sick. Let's say that the spores or infection or whatever it is resists Sea Dragon magic. You'll need to work at three levels simultaneously, girlie –" she smiled at Inzashu "– mental, magical and physical. One, clarify the mind, which will begin to restore a Dragon through their natural defensive and self-curative abilities. Two, cleanse the magic or bloodstream or both. Three, winkle out the infection or neutralise the contaminant, wherever it likes to reside in a Dragon's body. This interplay of factors creates considerable complexity."

"Could it be a brain infection?" Azania asked.

Ignita sniffed toward the teapot. "That Blaze the Devastator. Even as a hatchling, he had a yen for flying straight into the worst trouble he could find."

"Maybe verdelite is somehow a carrier of the infection?" Thundersong put in, wishing to move on from the subject of his sire. "Lichens prefer certain rocks. Maybe this is something that grows on verdelite, maybe on its dust?"

"Or could it be another life form or entity, something unfamiliar to us?" Inzashu mused.

Ignita said, "All good ideas. Keep thinking and keep sharp, children. I'll run you through all the herbal lore I know as well as eight types of ores which could be ground up and ingested to help with cleansing processes. Dark magic is very strong on refining toxins, including by psychic magic. You have a good number of patients – not that I approve – so, divide them into groups for testing the different methods and combinations. The Sea Dragons will have additional lore you may draw upon."

"Tea's ready, Ignita," Azania said.

"Not now, dearie. Can't you see that I'm very busy?"

By nightfall, both Princesses had very sore wrists and they had covered every scrap of parchment they possessed with dense notes. Brand brought a great number of bottles, gourds and hessian storage bags from Ignita's lair. She fussily arranged and explained everything. Azania turned her travel cloak into a bulging sack to hold the bounty.

Since the old Dragoness did not want to overnight anywhere but her own lair in the swamp, they took fond leave of her and a more formal leave of Brand. His brother promised to see her safely back.

Ignita clouted him over the ear canal. "I'm the one looking after you, young Dragon. Safely back to the lair indeed. I am not enfeebled yet!"

"Great-Aunt –"

"Don't forget my teapot. Hurry up. Night waits for no

Dragon."

Thundersong winked at his brother behind her back.

"Don't you cheek me, newly lily-white great-nephew with the artistic golden brown scale décor," Ignita snorted without even turning. "I'll have your gorgeous hide for a lair rug if you aren't careful! Take care of my girls, alright?"

"Always," he rumbled.

Gorgeous lair rug, Azania snickered in his mind.

Shut it or I'll stuff you and mount you on my wall, Princess. That's a promise.

I used to be a trophy Princess, she pointed out.

Of course, Azania, I kidnapped you purely for your decorative properties or didn't you know?

With that whopper of a lie, they flew a couple of hours south, down to the theoretical border of Vanrace, before pausing for a break. Even Princesses needed to water bushes from time to time, Azania claimed. The girls leaned against his flank and chatted for a while, sharing a light meal of nuts, fruit and bread, washed down with water from a nearby stream.

Then, he repeated his flying through the night trick.

Somewhere toward midnight, Azania sat straight upright and said, "We should post Prince Floric a herbal remedy for his stomach, sister."

Inzashu murmured against her sister's shoulder, "I'll brew one … right away …"

The older sister said, "Nice joke, right?"

"Hilarious."

Sleep conversations? Thundersong was not convinced that either of his Dragon Riders had actually woken up. Fascinating on the one wing and weird on the other. Had they not been breathing slowly and evenly in the rhythm of Human sleep, he might have been able to question them about all their secrets. After checking briefly, by the stars, that they were still headed in the right direction, he allowed himself to drift into that somnolent sleep-flying state and only woke as they passed over the canyon that separated

Vanrace from the badlands.

The girls stirred as he landed neatly beside their favourite waterfall. The sound echoed loudly in the open grotto high up in a grey-green vertical cliff, which was perhaps what woke them.

They both stretched and yawned.

"Despite the padding, my behind has gone all numb," Inzashu groaned.

"What padding?" he asked, prodding the region inappropriately.

"Get off!" she squealed.

Snatching her up in his paw before she could escape, he flipped her about and pretended, with exaggerated movements and much chortling, to massage the blood flow back into her behind and legs. Poor Inzashu. She did not always know how to react to humour. Thundersong could not imagine an upbringing like hers, where she had always been one factor in the ambitious plans of a powerful enchantresses whom she had learned to fear and never to love.

Family humour was not always easy – as he should be well-placed to know. Stay on the right side of waggish, Dragon! Humour could still treat its object well, without belittlement or hurt.

Popping her back onto her feet, he laughed openly at her scandalised expression. "Azania has Azerim for this service, don't you see? You need help."

"He doesn't! Surely not?"

"Would you care to explain, Princess?" he said shrewdly.

"Inza, kissing involves use of the lips, hands and –"

"La la LAAA!" Inzashu yelled, covering her ears.

Dragon said, "So, what did you two think about sending Prince Floric a little dungeon-warming gift?" They stared at him in startlement. "Do you remember discussing it last night?"

Apparently not.

They had plenty more creative ideas, however. Nothing that a lifetime's supply of soap would not help to fix, for starters.

After an hour's pause to restore feeling to the royal derrieres and relax his shoulder muscles, they took to the skies once more and set course for Chakkix Camp – not for the first and certainly not for the last time.

Well before their arrival, they spied several lookouts shooting the breeze and lurking along the ridgeline and concluded, by a swift count, that the Sea Dragons had not yet departed for the North. Juggernaut's crew had flown out that morning, they learned, as an agog Tixyti yelled up at them before Thundersong even completed his landing. He helped Inzashu and Azania alight from his neck, more a courtesy than a need, to be frank.

Tixyti almost swooned at the sight of Inzashu-N'shula. "She's a real Princess!" she squealed.

"And I'm not?" Azania asked, mildly exasperated.

"No, you're a wicked amazing Dragon Rider, you are," the youngster explained. "That's *totally* different."

"I see."

"And you got no Princess dresses. Even so, you're littler than her. Like me, see?"

Logical according to a child's mind, a Dragon supposed, casting about for the patients. Everdeep greeted him from a cavern entrance a couple of hundred feet further along the ridge at a volume that could be heard across the camp. He called together a briefing for Inzashu, who was openly overawed to meet the huge Sea Dragon contingent.

Leaning close to the young Princess, he whispered, "This is when you wipe that, 'but what can I do, I'm only little,' look off your face and get to work. The truth is that this is new to everyone. No-one knows much."

"Dragon …"

"I know I'm being annoying, but I'm also right."

"Alright. I'll try."

THUNDER O DRAGON

After introducing Inzashu to the gathered Dragons – a susurration of approval ran through their ranks as they recognised her resemblance to Azania – the girl asked each Dragon to recount what they had observed, felt about or speculated upon regarding the green mist. This generated fruitful discussion. After that, she walked up to the largest of the ridgeline caverns Tarangis had procured for them, where the patients had been placed.

Sweetsong, his female kin, was the most experienced Sea Dragon healer here at Chakkix Camp. She spoke at length with Inzashu before the two walked inside to start interviewing the patients by lamplight. Most had responded positively to treatment but remained physically sick and weak; sign that some malign influence worked upon their bodies.

Azania said, "Inza, the fact that it affects both Humans and Dragons must be significant, right?"

"Right," she agreed.

Sweetsong said, "Meaning it might not merely be a magical malady? A most eloquent wave, Princess. Also, since our sick include three Sea Dragons, one Tamarine Dragon and one of the Isles, we also know it isn't specific to one type of Dragon. My measurements indicate that this affliction might indeed be consuming their magic – feeding off it, perhaps – hence the signs of illness. Could it be that all Humans have latent magic?"

"Not too loud," Azania cautioned quickly. "Some Humans and indeed, some Dragons, would take great offence at such a suggestion."

"Curious," said the Dragoness. "No mind."

Thundersong found Azania updating Sankir Farizam and Everdeep on recent events. They were both keen to start the return journey the following day. He and Azania agreed. The season's turning could not be reliably predicted. When it came – usually within the following month – the change was often rapid, the Princess had told them, the average daytime temperatures dropping from over 140 on the Fangheat scale to around 110 to 115. That still meant a brutal trudge through a waterless desert in broiling heat but at least it would not kill a person within hours. They could not imagine enough coldstones existed in the world for the entire Skartunese army to use that method of travel.

Surprises tended to be unhealthy. As everyone kept telling him, one could never be too prepared. They planned and evaluated as obsessively as a clutch of kleptomaniacs.

On that note, he wandered off to become a children's playground for a while.

One must keep up one's air of draconic gravitas.

A scream and a bellow of fury from the healers' cavern snapped him up onto his paws before his brain had a second to catch up. Azania sprinted over toward the entrance. And … he caught three flying children with a dint of fancy paw-work and another two landed upon his outspread wings. How had he flicked them into the air? No mind; they thought it was all part of a game - a good scare.

"Back in a moment, children," he said, hastily setting them down.

Watch the paws!

High-stepping his way out of trouble and minding his tail for good measure, he charged over to the cavern, arriving in time to hear Azania yelling at her sister that infecting herself in the name of science was totally not the idea.

"Inzashu!" he cried, rushing inside.

"Keep your distance," the girl said bravely. By his sire's egg, she looked swamp green! Kneeling quickly over a bucket, she threw up violently. "This bug is nasty."

"Oh, Inza!" Azania wrung her hands.

Sparklefroth, the Sea Dragoness nearest her, said, ≈*I'm sorry, Thundersong. I could not stop it.*≈

"The Dragoness was asleep," Inzashu said at the same time.

Sweetsong said, "I also tried to stop it, Azania, but the youngling was standing right next to her mouth. It moved over too quickly."

"It felt like swatting a sponge with my mind and slipped through before I could find a way to grapple with it," Inzashu explained apologetically. "Inside, it's … different. Somehow, it's soaked in and become part of me, which is highly frustrating. I'm working at it, believe me."

Thundersong said, "Sweetsong, Inzashu, I'm thinking that this is either an animate entity or an inanimate infection that spreads towards strong sources of magic. What do you think?"

The Dragoness replied, "That's meant to be impossible …"

"But we need to consider all possible vectors," Inzashu finished for her.

"Absolutely," Sweetsong sighed heavily.

"What a mess. Alright." Azania rubbed her temples unhappily. "Consider this a learning point, with the added bonus that Inzashu now gets to experience this thing firsthand."

"I will crack this before it cracks me."

Stout words from the young Princess, but as the others nodded, Thundersong realised he knew better.

He said balefully, "Or, like Brand, before you end up attacking someone without even knowing what you're doing." Everyone shouted and growled at him. He snapped, "Just saying! We still haven't figured out how that *directed* attack came about. That's why I'm still wondering if this stuff isn't somehow sentient."

"Oh, Dragon!" Azania groaned.

He said privately to her, *As in, could it have been developed by her mother, perhaps to capture the daughter again?*

Aghast, his Rider could only gasp and gape at him. Even her command of mental Dragonish deserted her momentarily.

Aye. What a talent he had for thinking of the worst possible outcomes.

Privately, the Princess hissed at him, *We're taking her with us. Whatever happens, Thundersong, that woman is never, ever again getting her paws on my sister!*

When a person is evil, they become an animal with paws? he flashed back.

I … misspoke – but what does that matter right now? My sister's infected! We need to get her to Sirensong, don't we?

Swallowing back his fury, he said, *We do, but first, we need to do everything we can here, then figure out how to move her with minimal danger to ourselves or others –*

Fly back on our own. Just the three of us, with her in a cargo net?

Aye. Might have to, at that. He swore angrily beneath his breath. *We've barely seen battle, as yet, and this Terror Clan power is whipping the scales off our bodies.*

Thundersong, we faced down a Jabiz. If this does not pass on its own, we will make it pass!

How he loved that flare in her eyes, the dark of the pupils shot – at least in his imagination – by fire every bit as powerful as that of a Dragoness. If only she could learn to see herself as he saw her!

She chuckled, *Alright, if you're going to project your thoughts, why not wallop me with a sledgehammer while you're about it?*

Blergh! Sorry.

Sorry for what? Dragons never apologise, right?

Azania raised her hand. He paw-slapped it. "Alright, everyone. Let's work this out. Inzashu, I'll get you as many Rangers as you need. You and Sweetsong treat the patients but leave all the running to the Rangers. How many scribes do you need? Get that head out of the muck and start commanding, girl."

Inzashu threw up into the bucket one more time, groaning.

She said, "Right, I'm ready. Give me a dozen. I need parchment and scribes. Tell them to keep at least fifteen feet from us patients at all times, hear me?" The girl stood up and staggered against Sparklefroth's flank. "Ooh ... not good."

Sparklefroth said, "I'll help. My wave is feeling far more –"

The Dragoness bit her tongue in realisation.

"You're feeling as if you're no longer infected?" Sweetsong clarified for her. "I can test that. Sing with me."

A few minutes later, she confirmed that Sparklefroth appeared to be clear of infection and that Inzashu must therefore be the lucky recipient of a wholly unintentional gift.

Thundersong had once considered himself a Dragon of enormous patience. Having slept poorly, he woke early to see the returning Dragonwing off. After that, he mooched around, generally getting in everyone's way, until Azania kicked him over to the forges to help out with weapons crafting and testing. With his new fires, he could heat a forge to temperatures that impressed even the crustiest Grinder Dragon blacksmith. They promptly decided he had better speak with the local Sea Dragons, ten in number, who formed part of Chakkix Camp's new anti-Terror Clan protection unit.

Recruiting living forge bellows? Bring it on!

Aye, they needed the heavies.

The white fright, Azania laughingly called them, and then booted him in her favourite spot on his ankle when he called her the black slack. Wholly untrue, but she was not the kind of character to let any creature get away with that sort of nonsense.

Especially not since he got to be the local Dragon sky wagon.

"Does that make Azerim the brown clown?" he

inquired mischievously.

She kicked his ankle again. "No, it makes someone who says that racist. Even as a joke."

"Why, is there more than one Human race?" he asked, narked. "Ridiculous idea if you think about it. Of course, all creatures group together and discriminate based on perceived traits within their race … but if you cut a few Humans or Dragons open to compare, I can guarantee you aren't about to find any substantive differences related to skin tone or hide colour. All Dragons bleed the same." She began to speak but he raised a paw to forestall her. "Listen, I'm not trying to whitewash the issue – pun intended – I … I just find the idea of being against your own race backward and idiotic. Says far more about the accuser than the accused, is what I mean."

She said, "Dragon, you are sweet and language is stupid. The end."

"Eh? This is far from the end."

"You nit-picking, insufferable old reptile. You need to follow what I mean, not what I say."

"Human females being so simple to understand," he goaded.

Azania swung a third time at his ankle, but this time he dodged smartly, making her fall on her backside. He burst into a round of thunderous guffaws.

That was how a four-foot-eight black Princess came to be chasing a fifty-three-foot white Dragon around Chakkix Camp, yelling blue murder. Clearly, a very colourful issue.

CHAPTER 18

IN A FLAP

WHY, BY HIS WINGS, was murder *blue?* What did the colour blue have to do with murder? Thundersong pondered this crucial philosophical question as he winged up from the wasteland two days later, once more bound for Juggernaut's lair. He had two Princesses in tow, one figuratively and one rather more literally – to wit, Azania perched upon his neck while Inzashu dangled below his left forepaw from a thirty-foot rope, her dark face peeking out of her carrying sling with a pensive air.

He must remember to land her gently and not stomp upon her head when he arrived.

"Charming image, Dragon," Azania murmured.

"I major on the charm," he lied glibly. "Imagine all those brains squishing and oozing between my talons?"

"I see why Aria loves you."

"So, Princess, why does a person scream *blue* murder? Why not crimson for Human blood or something … logical at least?" When she shook her head at his unnecessarily testy tone, he added, "Well, murder doesn't necessarily have to do with turning blue while drowning, does it? Humans turn interesting colours when they're deprived of air, such as when a Dragon stands upon their chest or –"

"Dragon, change the subject. Now."

"Do black people turn blue in such circumstances?"

Azania kicked his neck. "If a certain Dragon maintains this line of questioning, a certain black person will indeed kick him black and blue. Time for a joke. What's white and brown and red all over?"

He scratched his chin, pondering this conundrum. "I don't rightly know."

"A suntanned Thundersong!"

"Most witty," he chortled. "I wonder what the colour of amusement is?"

"We Humans love colourful allusions," the Princess noted. "We say a person's green with envy, white with fear or rage or seeing crimson; we call a person a yellow-bellied coward or say we're feeling blue – and aye, many kingdoms apparently use the saying that black is beautiful."

"So, about blue murder – does rage or aggression imply oxygen deprivation in the brain?"

"Says the local fire-head?"

Murr-hurrr-hurrrgh! he gurgled appreciatively. "Aye, our thoughts can be all *fired* up."

"Gives new meaning to the phrase, 'you're fired,' " the Princess chuckled. "Alright down there, Inza?"

She chortled, "To join in the awful jokes – and you two are terrible, by the way – I should say something like, 'I'm at a bit of a loose end.' "

"Slinging jokes upward?" her sister chimed in.

"Ooh, that's impressively bad," Thundersong purred appreciatively. "So, anytime you need a comfort break, Inzashu, you can just do an airdrop."

"Ew! Dragon!" squealed the younger Princess.

"Shall I demonstrate?"

For that, she gifted him a mental swat that made him wobble in the air. Illness had clearly made her bristlier than usual.

An overheated badlands day rolled into a stultifying late afternoon, the sort where oppressive heat and thunderheads building in the sky made two Princesses wish for the weather to break. No such joy. After a sticky, sweltering night spent camping within sight of the mountains on the horizon, the three travellers unanimously decided to put a few miles behind them at a height guaranteed to be cooler than the previous day.

The dangerously infectious younger Princess kicked her feet a couple of miles over nothingness, watching the immense range of white-capped Tamarine Mountains unfurling slowly ahead. She looked a shade less green than the previous day, Dragon decided. Full-on swamp scum reduced to a milder case of swamp algae? Close enough.

He and Azania spent hours working with her on ideas to combat the Terror Clan contamination without making significant progress.

After a brief ground break in the early evening, he picked up and flew due north once more, settling into his snoozing-on-the-wing rhythm. Having picked a height at which he could not possibly fly straight into a mountain peak, he settled in for a doze of suitably splendid draconic majesty, which was a quality he fully intended to achieve, perhaps not by next week, but certainly by his eighth decade of life. One must have octogenarian goals. Essential.

What woke him was not a dream of Jabiz Urdoo attempting to flash-fry his innards with an electrical torture device but a change in the weather.

Quite suddenly, the air temperature dropped a dozen degrees and a surge of turbulence made him judder sharply. Moist, tangy air crowded into his nostrils. Surprised? How was a half-ocean Dragon supposed to be surprised when Sirensong's mantra was that water was just like air, only thicker? Snorting and shaking his muzzle as the previously reliable airstream suddenly sucked away beneath his wings, he winced as his passengers woke up with identical howls.

Terrifying the Princesses was absolutely not the idea

but this turbulent weather was having none of his alleged mastery of the air, let alone his sense of righteous draconic majesty. *Whap! Wham!* He flailed his wings as, out of the blue, a gale pummelled them downward and sideways.

Azania shouted, "Alright, Dragon?"

Inzashu clutched her stomach. Without needing to look, he could feel her turning greener than Aunt Ignita's best tea back there.

He fought through air that cuffed him like monstrous fists, he bulled through the change and turmoil, smoothing out the flight for his Riders as best he could, expecting that at any second normalcy must return. It did not. Instead, with a howl like a demented animal, the wind picked him up and hurtled him into an otherwise pristine sky.

His neck creaked as he surveyed his surrounds, never more shocked. Nary a thunderhead in sight. Sweetly rosy colours pinked the eastern horizon, harbinger of an otherwise tranquil dawn.

Whap-whurr-snap! The impossible weather attacked his outspread wings. Gritting his fangs, Thundersong raged, *Gnarr-stupid-wind!*

Azania screamed, "Thundersong! You have to –"

"Hold tight; we'll get through this!" he boomed.

"Ooh, I think I just tasted my own intestines," Inzashu moaned.

"Go lower!" the older Princess shouted.

"And crash?" he roared back. He pulled through another vertiginous swoop with a groan of his own. "Stupid clear air storm – stop thrashing me this instant!"

The airstream summarily failed to behave like normal air and shoved his tail, body, head and wings in an infeasible combination of directions all at once. A sharp, rising shriek made him try to retract his wings but, to his horror, the left wingtip wuthered and then both ripped and folded around the outer margin, ruining about a quarter of his entire wing surface.

Freak-gnarr-WHAT? His swearing struck a deafening

pitch of indignation. Supportive struts were not supposed to turn into a porcupine-like bundle at the end of one's wing.

With that, the turbulence ended.

Dragon coasted through clear, cool mountain air, wondering what in all of Solixambria had just hit him.

A thousand-tonne velvet hammer?

A literal bolt from the blue?

Whatever it was, no Dragon appreciated being treated like a strip of cloth dangling from a Human clothesline as hurricane force winds ripped through.

On the ground, Azania's lack of certain Princess skills extolled by the ballads came out in full force as her younger sister coached her through making running repairs to Thundersong's wingtip. The point was to ensure that nothing ripped completely free on the way to Juggernaut's lair, where a proper repair could be effected by hands both skilled and untainted by Terror Clan nastiness.

"No, I did not excel at fancy needlework," Azania growled, plying her needle with care.

"Did I say otherwise?" Dragon purred.

"You thought it."

"This time it's you projecting, Princess. I also heard you listing your least favourite adjectives for your hair."

A tiny muscle twitched in her jaw. "You heard that?"

"Complex topic, a black woman's hair," he noted, at a deliberately mild temperature. "One could almost relate it to draconic attitudes toward scales."

"How could this tangle possibly be compared to lovely smooth scales?" she hissed, stabbing the needle with increasing force.

Inzashu hissed, "Be careful, Az –"

"I am being careful!" After a moment, she bit her lip

and groaned, "Obviously, you've touched on the reason Azerim was so upset with me. Can't wait to sieve through that sand for scorpions with him all over again."

Thundersong exchanged sidelong glances with Inzashu, who shrugged, clearly no closer to the meaning of this cryptic comment than he was.

He said, "What reason, Azania?"

"Well, if you must know, it's … it's my marvellous Azania quality of being the kind of Princess nobody wants to accept, if you follow my meaning."

He shook his muzzle. "I don't."

"Thundersong – really? Now's when you choose to be obtuse?"

"I apologise." Touching her shoulder gently, he said, "Sharpen this obtuse fire-breathing reptile into a more acute creature, please. It's all about finding the right angles …"

"Mathematical puns are a bad idea right now," she warned, stitching assiduously down one of his wing struts. "Look, while it's all fun and games flouting the norms as a Dragon-Riding Princess and all that, there are times when I fear it would be easier just to fit in. Be … normal. Sorry. I do remember that word has some history between us but now the paw's in the other shoe and –"

Ha-haa-harrggh!

She pulled up at his chortle, bristling visibly.

"Oh, come on. That was funny, you have to admit," he said.

With a visible effort at pulling herself together, she said, "It was. I was about to say something about spending too much time with Dragons but that's about as ridiculous a thing to say as – I don't know what I want to say."

Inzashu said, "Is this fear speaking?"

"Yes. No. Maybe," Azania muttered, covering all the options with style.

Impressive talent. Almost Blitz-like in its comprehensive avoidance of a straight answer. However, since this massive quadruped had recently discovered considerable personal growth in the sensitivity department, he executed a dint of comprehensive avoidance of his own.

He said, "I smell a buck upwind of us. Anyone fancy chargrilled rump steak à la Thundersong?"

"For breakfast?" Azania protested.

Inzashu grinned, "We wicked scions of Skartun, accustomed to supping upon the entrails of our enemies, will eat meat anytime. Bring it on, Dragon."

"Why, you wicked little Dragoness," he purred.

She showed two rows of woefully undersized teeth in return. Deficient in the dentistry, like all Humans. Pathetic display – apart from the colour.

"Princess, your teeth have turned green," he said.

"*Green?*"

"Grass green."

The girl yelled, "Do you think it's this illness? Terror green? How can my teeth be green? Azania? How can this mist permeate tooth enamel? That's scientifically – Dragon!"

"Aye, I am scien – *OUCH!*"

As if hurled forth by her fury, the green mist poured out of the girl's mouth.

A white paw plucked Azania off her feet, mid-denial, as Thundersong fled. His aggrieved bellow and her squeal of shock spooked a small spiral-horn bushbuck out of hiding nearby. Instinct awakened his inner hunter. With a low, throbbing roar directed at a pair of quivering haunches flashing away through the bushes, and along with them his hopes of a decent breakfast, he pursed his lips and summoned his fire.

Skiss-KABOOM!

The buck flew fifty feet through the air and landed in a smoking heap on a patch of light green grass.

Ooh, one of his fireworks! "Nice," he growled.

"Nice?" Azania spluttered.

A brutally charred tree toppled to his left paw.

Thundersong ignored the tree with enormous hubris as he stalked past. "Clean kill, slain and cooked in one breath!" he declared, double-checking over his shoulder in case the green mist might be sneaking up in ambush. Being a predictably behaved ghastly artefact of Terror Clan magic, it had either dissipated or returned to Inzashu. Great. He growled, "Crispy on the edges and tender on the inside."

He was quite certain he could hear the Princess' eye fluids swilling about in their sockets at the eye roll she produced.

"It'll be a new fashion in cooking – flash fried!" he insisted, scooping up his bounty. "No, lightning grilled! Oh, where's the …"

"Missing hind leg?" the Princess cooed. "Right here."

He rumbled in great satisfaction. Took a real Dragon to blow a buck to smithereens.

Azania tossed the portion into his paw and stalked off, blowing on her fingers as if the heat had hurt her. He was about to inquire solicitously after his prized captive when she threw over her shoulder, "Well, don't dilly-dally, Mister Pitter-Patter Paws. Shake your tail and at least one scale."

He growled, "Pitter-Patter Paws? Is that an insult?"

"Only if you take it that way, fancy scales."

Grrr.

"Gargling an oversized gnat, my ornate, highly polished carriage?"

He snarled, "Whoever thought to distil pure vexation, give it a tongue and call it 'woman,' I ask you?"

Inzashu burst into peals of laughter.

"What?" he and Azania asked at the same time.

"You are too funny, the two of you," the younger Princess giggled, wiping her eyes. "You're like an old married couple."

"We are not," Thundersong protested.

"You're not my sister, you're a beast."

"With green teeth," he put in, over the girl's continued chuckling.

On that note of blatant falsity, having checked for further signs of green smoke, they broke their fast with slivers of succulent pink venison carved by a Dragon's talon blade for the ladies and a few tasty morsels for the Dragon. They chatted about topics ranging from the fundamental nature of magic to the crimson fires of an Ignis-ascendant dawn and from scale care to ladies' underwear. Too much information, Thundersong mused privately to himself.

Hope the green teeth were not a permanent fixture.

He caught Azania whistling a ditty as they climbed steadily into the skies an hour later.

"Happy to see Azerim again?" he inquired.

She reflected upon this for a minute. "Perhaps happier to be heading north than south. Matters are complicated with him for certain, but the south …"

Her admission trailed off as she gazed over the mountain peaks at the wonderful scenery that unfolded before them like a scenic carpet slowly unrolled by the talons of invisible, godlike Dragons. Thundersong examined the mettle of his own hearts and came to a surprising admission of his own.

"It will be a fearful thing to stare into the eyes of the Skartunese horde," he said slowly, "to know that those we love most might suffer or be lost in such a conflict. Oddly, this Dragon fears this more than the ravages of Terror Clan magic or, indeed, the tortures of those Dragon-subjugating scum and cowards! Aye. My fears used to be many. Now, they revolve simply around the matter of –" he chuckled gruffly "– those with whom I allegedly bicker like an old married male."

"Allegedly?" Inzashu smiled.

"Oh hush, you chattering child," he snorted.

She replied, "For my part, I fear my mother's tender

mercies most. I believe it is a … a twisted kind of love, I suppose, that drives her ambitions for me. She sees some kind of grand, dominant future together, but unfortunately that's all in her head. It has nothing to do with what I might want. In fact, I'm not even sure she acknowledges I have wants."

The youngster wrung her hands in her lap, staring unseeing over the vast array of sharp, snowbound peaks that lay ahead and around them.

Thundersong wondered what it was about beauty that opened a creature's hearts to an awareness of the deeper, oftentimes unspoken realms of the heart. Somehow it surfaced matters like a slow, churning ocean current, like what the Sea Dragons had taught him upwellings did, bringing nutrients and microscopic animals toward the surface for consumption by the great food networks of the ocean. Was that what beauty did to the heart? Was it a nutrient-rich current for the soul?

Softly, the younger Princess added, "Perhaps Nahritu-N'shula cannot bring herself to admit that I ever left the womb? She still sees us as connected, as if by an umbilical cord. I have no rights that I might call my own. I barely have personhood, in her eyes."

"That's such a shame," Azania returned.

"It's her way. A strange form of motherhood, perhaps."

"She's a sick woman," Thundersong stated.

Azania hissed at him, but Inzashu nodded. "I've long suspected her of being a psychopath. She exhibits all the classic signs – high intelligence, lack of empathy or capacity for love, a complete lack of remorse for manipulating and ruining lives and she's the utter centre of her own universe in which she is queen and all others are subjects. Slaves, even."

Azania pursed her lips and puffed out her breath. "In a word, delightful."

"Quite," her sister chuckled.

THUNDER O DRAGON

To Thundersong's surprise, the simple comment appeared to shiver the dark, depressed colours of her emotions – that was the best word he had to describe it – and rainbows suddenly surfaced in multiple places through the morass. In a moment, her whole psyche stabilised.

Tough girl.

Gladness transferred into his being, causing him to spread his wings upon the light breeze and forge upward with strength that seemed limitless. They soared up into the lightest of azure skies but only to a height that was not uncomfortable for his Riders. Desert Princesses were not best accustomed to the vagaries of mountains weather but a downward glance assured him that Inzashu had donned her finery of thick gloves, padded jacket, scarf and woollen hat and now she wriggled deeper into a blanket. Azania similarly resembled a small, padded sack –

Thanks for that image, she said dryly.
Most beautiful sack in the seventeen realms, he replied.
I'll sack you, Dragon.
Oh no, I've been sacked!

Given a long pause for Inzashu-N'shula's sake, as her sickness morphed into a bowel disorder, signalled by her frantic aerial fertilisation of a hitherto innocent rocky mountain slope, Dragon and his two Riders winged into Juggernaut's lair midmorning of the following day. Cheerful draconic bugles and Human style hand waving and cheers greeted their arrival. Aria raced up to greet him with a dazzling wing-ripple about his muzzle that almost made him sneeze the instant she snuck her muzzle out of hiding behind that cobalt wing-edge blur to caress his cheek intimately with hers.

Shaping fire with his tongue, he drew a white-fire heart in the air between them as she backed away a few dozen feet to gauge his reaction.

Aria's eyes whirled with bright approval. *Thundersong!*

My Aria, he replied, stressing the possessive.

The Dragoness rumbled and arched her back with feline limberness. *I missed you – you picked up a wing injury?*

Not for good reason, he purred. *Too long apart, beauty. Far too long.*

Alright, Mister Suave, Azania giggled privately. *Oh look, here comes Azerim.*

The tall King shielded his face as Thundersong's wingbeat caused dust to billow up from Juggernaut's training sands. Observing how he landed Inzashu carefully aside, the Dragon saw him turn aside to instruct Sankir Farizam. His keen eye inventoried signs of readiness about the place, from neat rows of Ranger packs laid out ready to go, to the stacks of lances, Dragon bows and saddles stacked up against the cliff face beside Juggernaut's personal lair.

He almost expected the powerful Orange Dragon to pop up from where he would be beating up a few trainees to growl, 'About time you deigned to turn up. Debriefing. Now.' The place seemed emptier without him.

It was Everdeep who greeted him with a low rumble, as Sirensong rushed to see to her new patient, and suggested they speak.

Meantime, he deposited Azania on ground level. She hesitated slightly, but seeing Azerim's open arms and broad grin, her reservations fled. The Princess rushed into his arms; he held her tenderly, then swung her off her feet to deliver a passionate kiss. *Blergh.* Saliva. Simply no end to Human nastiness. The King patted her and delivered a comment that slipped into Thundersong's attentive ear canals like a playful barb:

"Sneaky desert Princess! I shall have to watch you more closely in the future."

"Oh?" She pretended innocence.

"Vanrace," said he.

"I overthrow kingdoms with the mere breath of my lips," the Princess flirted, making it more than clear that she meant kings, too. Lowering her eyelashes demurely, she added, "I was *wholly* obedient to your word, Azerim. I trust this result does not merit disapproval?"

Oh, how well she played the game! Thundersong had no need of his emotional sense to detect the steam rising out of the young King's ears.

Recovering, he said cheerily, "Far from it!"

Liar.

For a moment, their gazes sparred and sparked. The jut of his chin proclaimed his annoyance at being bested. The flash of her dark eyes proclaimed she was proud and that, if he thought he could treat her so high-handedly again, he had better think not merely twice, but thrice. It caused a Dragon to wonder if fire in a relationship was as desirable to Humans as it was to his kind. Both were proud creatures in their own way. Yearning ran like molten metal between them. Would this strengthen or further damage their relationship?

Bending close to her ear, Azerim whispered a few words.

Thundersong blinked. Had he just heard that simple apology through Azania's *mind?* He also sensed the sudden, sharp prick of moisture in her eyes and a hot tightness in her throat as she thanked him in a hoarse whisper and said she would endeavour to be less difficult in the future.

Had he misjudged the man, thinking an apology beneath him?

One sentence had restored so much between them. Just look at how shyly he laced his fingers into hers now and conducted her gallantly into a larger storage cavern which must have been emptied during preparations for the flight south. Here, Juggernaut had set aside a space for meetings – Everdeep was already present and several of the Tamarine Dragons elders from different Clans.

Thundersong courteously preceded Aria into the

cavern, making her snort in consternation until he explained that it was the male's duty to ensure that any danger within was dealt with rather than allow his smaller mate to be put in any danger.

I am the paramount danger around here, she protested, nipping at his flank.

Predictably dangerous, yet dangerously predictable, he said and earned himself a nip for real this time.

He cracked open his jaw to give her a dangerous flash of his white fangs, complete with controlled fire backlighting the ranks of slatted draconic ceramic-metallic dentistry. The Cobalt Dragoness bristled instinctively, wings flaring and fires rumbling deep in her chest and belly as she stiffened; then, with a low, throaty laugh each, they rubbed flanks and she chucked him beneath the chin with a coy wingtip.

Oh, go get a roost, you two, Azania chuckled merrily.

Fires are great for a relationship, my Rider.

Her dark eyes widened in realisation. *Oh, is that so?*

Thundersong's philosophy of the day, delivered with all humbleness and self-deprecation.

Ha ha.

Everdeep called the small meeting to order. The Humans – Azania, Farizam, Azerim and several of Azerim's lead Rangers – sat upon three-legged wooden stools at a long trestle table. A parchment map of southern Solixambria covered its surface, held down in a few locations by gold ingots probably sourced from the warrior Dragon's personal hoard. Excellent quality. The Dragons huddled around, bringing massive muzzles and burning eyes closer to the centre. Everdeep had to curl up his massive body to fit between the cavern's edge and the trestle but this gave the Humans a warm place against which to lean their backs. Azania did so with aplomb, her promised much more charily.

The Sea Dragon said, "We've received the first reports from Juggernaut regarding the T'nagrun situation. In general, the state of war readiness is gathering pace. The most concerning detail is that there have been attacks on several of the citadels by marauding Terror Clan Dragons – testing the state of their defences, he says." Reaching out a talon, he indicated four of the most southerly and easterly Human citadels. "These are the locations. A further three Dragons have become infected but it is clear that the Terrors have chosen to withhold several talons of their paw at this point."

Azerim said, "Ah, that is – oh, I get it. Aye, Everdeep. The attacks and patrols have been predictable up to this point. No strange magic, no swapping aerial positions as you reported, Thundersong, and no undue influences – none they were able to detect, anyhow."

"The Skartunese?" Azania put in.

"No change in deployment or movement," Everdeep said.

"Desert season?"

"Unchanged as yet," he replied. Baring his fangs, he added, "Daytime temperatures averaging around 144 Fangheat. Frankly, I'd rather swim through boiling lava."

Several of the Dragons chuckled at his complaining tone.

"That's the deep desert for you," Azania said.

Gale the Windchaser, a great Red elder of his Clan, said, "Brother, don't you go evaporating in a cloud of steam now."

"By the waves, that's what we Sea Dragons all fear," he guffawed massively, almost shaking Azerim off his stool. "The detail of the tidings from the south is all of lesser consequence but we hear that the Human armies are finally on the move through Vanrace thanks to a paw and a hand of intervention. Thundersong, Azania, tell us everything we need to know. What's new under the suns?"

CHAPTER 19

INTO THE FIRE

AZERIM GAPED AT AZANIA, clearly unsure whether his response ought to be admiring, censorious or utterly disbelieving. "You talked them into overthrowing King Tyloric?"

Azania smiled, "More …"

"A scam?" Thundersong suggested.

"Aye, 'scam's' a good word," the Princess agreed. The King made a strangled sound deep in his throat. "We scammed them – a few fake tears, a touch of draconic bluster, and the noble Vanracians did the rest. Considering what we're capable of, aren't you glad we gave you back your kingdom the other day, darling?"

"You … you!" he spluttered, turning crimson.

"Me and Thundersong, aye. Three kingdoms saved, if one counts Amboraine."

Thundersong rumbled, "Four, Princess, if you count T'nagru last time around. I believe we're in the kingdom business."

"You're as crazy as … as your hair," the King spluttered at last.

"My hair is not a character trait," the Princess said acidly.

Thundersong, Azerim and several of the Rangers made

identically surprised grunts.

"I'm so, so *tired* of all this!" she burst out. "It's exhausting. Azerim – and you, Thundersong –"

"Me? What did I do?" he growled, flaring his wings in shock.

"How can you not understand? Does no one here understand? For the ten thousandth ruddy time, you at least should know better – darn it!" She touched the corner of her eye. "I'm not crazy, nor unruly … that's not … me."

Her voice cracked.

"Whatever I said, I'm sorry," Azerim put in.

"And me," Thundersong put in, stung by her obvious disappointment as his mind served up the remarks she had mentioned with painful clarity. Had he not meant to compliment her? Why should she react as if he were the unreasonable one?

"Thank you both," she said, making a visible effort to regather her poise. "As I've told you before, hair has a painful history. Much is assumed about a black woman and oftentimes inferred by remarks about her hair. If it is straightened, she is biddable, accepted in society and well-behaved – whitewashed into some ideology of what conventional appearance and behaviour should be and that is wrong! If her hair is worn natural or curly, then she is wild, unmanageable, unruly, somehow … dangerous or *other?* My hair is not a character trait, as I said. It does not describe who I am inside. Do I suggest you're devious just because you have wavy hair, Azerim?"

"No," he said.

"Do reptilian scales make a Dragon cold-blooded, untrustworthy and repulsively snake-like?"

"No!" Thundersong replied, ruffling his wings to re-settle them. Fury churned within his Dragon hearts. For a creature who presumed to call himself this Princess' best friend, how could he never have stood in her paws nor seen the world in her way? Ah, his jokes about her hair being contrary had been nothing more than a talon in her side each time!

The Princess pressed, "Or shall commentary regarding Aria's beautiful frilly wings imply she is fickle and frivolous?"

The Cobalt Dragoness snapped her jaw shut as she inadvertently exhaled flame.

Clarifying flame touched his thoughts, bringing perspective. Just when a Dragon winged comfortably through his world, he realised how different it could be for females. So much rode upon appearances and the many-layered assumptions people made about others based on myriad cues – behaviour, form and deeds. So many judgements or misjudgements, to be frank. He himself had been bullied for being brown. He should understand, shouldn't he? Yet this was subtly different. With his brownness, there was no sense of agonising history, of creatures under enormous unspoken societal pressure damaging and even mutilating themselves, in some cases. Some of Azania's people had even been kept as slaves, prized for their dark skin, both by the Skartun and other kingdoms.

How could one even begin to right injustices on such a scale?

One scale at a time.

He shared his joke – amusing and serious as it was – with the others, who laughed a little too loudly, declared their commitment to defeating the scourge of racism just as much as the Skartunese horde and … the conversation moved on.

Thundersong worried at a sore spot on his gum with his tongue. That easy? *Blergh* – his favourite expression for moments such as these.

Azania's thoughts intruded delicately. *Thank you, Thundersong.*

For that timeless expression of linguistic precision and clarity?

The Princess' delighted inner laughter burst upon his

mind in a floral bouquet of pearl, teal and white notes. She said, *Not quite, but for that unforgettable expression, I will forgive you almost anything. I meant that I know you understand because I see it in your mind.*

He said, *For my part, Princess, I am sorry for all the times I spoke thoughtlessly or when intending to jest, caused hurt instead.*

Her answer was a mental sunbeam.

Prepared and determined to set out the following day for the south, Thundersong woke during the night to a restless prickling of the scales. Danger? No. Merely the arrival of a Tamarine storm that shortly shook the sinkhole and then settled in with the air of an unwelcome lair guest making himself very much at home. Any hints at moving on in a timely fashion most certainly ignored.

The squally winds and driving rains lashed the increasingly irritable war party for three days before finally deciding that scales were clean enough, hair mussed enough and frustrations piqued enough to consider it a job well done. The storm bustled off to annoy someone else.

"Quite enough of thunder's song, right?" the Princess cheeked him pertly in passing.

He mimed a snap toward her haunches. "Behave."

Aria took advantage of his momentary lapse of concentration to swipe his forepaw out from beneath him, breaking his headlock upon her. Down he went. *Ker-thump!* Mud splatter, Sea Dragon-sized.

Azania wiped a splodge off her cheek. "Thundersong!"

Chuckling, he flicked Aria up with his hind paw, anticipating her counter-manoeuvre as he corralled her movement with his tail. She landed up atop his chest, wriggling madly but unable to prevent him from hugging her in place with all four paws.

He nuzzled her neck and breathed, "Mmm, feisty

Dragoness. What do you mean by accosting me like this in public?"

"Death by flirtation?" she purred, holding his throat to ransom with her unsheathed talons.

"Ah, the cutting edge of Isles romance," said he.

Aria chuckled sweetly. "Actually, that twisting escape did hurt my neck. Mercy, o mighty adversary."

"Mercy?"

"You've never heard that word before?"

"Never from your lips," he admitted, setting her carefully upon her paws. "Trip to the healers?"

"I fear as much," the Dragoness conceded.

As she walked a touch gingerly toward the healers' cavern, from which King Azerim had just emerged to test his new boot insert with a short walk, Thundersong turned to the Princess and said, "I noticed your new, asymmetrical hairstyle with the flower-like patterning above your left ear. If I did wish to compliment your appearance without causing offence … might I say something like, 'I love the versatility of your hair?' "

"Versatility?" she giggled.

"Ahem. Sorry." Poking out his forked tongue, he pretended to check it for defects. "Ridiculous tongue. I am quite certain I had a different adjective lined up for use just a second ago."

Azania considered this head askance. "Did you?"

"Aye. Aria and I were discussing the matter last night while you were asleep – you know, how diversity is a form of beauty, so if I might say, 'I love your hair because it is so different' … would you see that as positive?" She nodded. "Or might I add something related to the striking design? Or express appreciation for how lustrous your curls look tumbling past your shoulder to this side, despite the greyness of the overcast sky above?"

"All of those," she smiled and put her arms about his muzzle. "I know I prickled at you the other day but I was just so frustrated. Do I truly have to explain to a friend how certain words can be deeply discriminatory?"

He said slowly, "Unruly, unmanageable, flyaway, complicated …"

"A prize selection of verbal fungi," she agreed. "You're forgiven."

"I'll do my best to think before speaking from now on," he promised.

"I told you to be 'normal.' "

"Forgotten. *Blergh!* That's a lie. Forgiven, aye. I shall have to work on the forgetting part."

"We'd say that's only Human," said she.

He clutched his chest. "Oh no. Mortal insult."

She smacked his flank. "As if."

"Highly discriminatory against all creatures of scale and fire."

"Are you making fun – you had better not be," she warned. "Or … fine. Do I detect a roundabout Thundersong apology?"

He grumbled, "Not all that roundabout if you read me that easily. Now, with the benefit of my own telepathic skills, allow me to accompany you over to where your gallant swain is trying out his upgraded boot."

"To where Aria Seaspray is being treated with heat packs?"

"Would I possibly be so shallow?"

"Never," she fibbed, leading the way to their injured partners.

Thundersong regarded his own wingtip unhappily. Despite Chanize's best stitching, his damage would take weeks to heal. Tricky business, wingtips. A great deal of wind shear force during flight was exerted by the outer third of the wing, especially during manoeuvring. Not a great injury to carry into any kind of battle, as Aria had made clear.

Tipping up his boot, Azerim extracted a soft leather insert and showed it to them. "The material was Farizam's idea, actually – a shaped wooden core, padded and then sewn into a pouch of soft kidskin leather. Super comfortable. Best of all, it fits into this nice gap in my foot here. See?"

"Lord Gazaram's blade removed your bones?" Thundersong asked curiously.

Azerim said, "Aye. Because of the boot, they said, it struck more like a blunt axe blade than a clean cut. Three-quarters of an inch of bone – these bones that form the arch of the foot – was pulverised and had to be removed or I would not be walking today."

"I'm sorry," Azania said.

"I'm not, because you're alive, dear one," the King said firmly. "Talk about putting my foot in it, literally … one day when I'm old and grey, there'll be a good tale to tell the grandchildren."

She arched an eyebrow. "Planning much, are we?"

"At least seventeen," he grinned.

"Best start polishing up your speech for my brother then, Azerim, and this time, please don't put your foot in it."

"Deal. Now, let me show you how I can walk without a cane."

Early the following morning, a huge Dragonflight lifted off, beating hard into a sky clearing from the north. The air was fresh and chill, the high mountains season already hinting at cooling toward the autumn. Very soon the desert season should change as well, from absolutely fatal to mostly fatal, Azania quipped cheerfully as they cleared the sinkhole's rim and welcomed a light tailwind.

Thundersong wondered if such an army had ever graced Solixambria's skies – Rangers and warrior Dragonesses of the Archipelago, powerful Sea Dragons and burly Tamarine Dragons, flying by Clan, many of whom had lost relatives to the Skartunese all those years ago. Their fires burned hot for revenge. In all, the Dragons numbered over two hundred and fifty beasts and their combined wingbeat made a rushing sound like a squall tossing a forest's treetops.

Surely, such a formidable sight must make even the Skartunese horde and their twenty-nine Jabiz take stock?

The army took the passes and rest stops with excellent discipline. The following day, they coasted down out of the mountains and rested at the edge, perhaps twenty miles short of Thundersong's favourite dell. Chanize checked over his wing stitching, while Sirensong and Inzashu worked relentlessly at the younger Princess' infection. It showed no signs of budging. Evidently, her sister was too congenial a hostess, Azania teased but, not so secretly, worried about her every moment of every day. Each night, she and Azerim made a cosy space for two and behaved themselves with almost indecent decorum. Honestly. He needed to teach them both to have a little less integrity – the royal example could take a *small* rest when they were hidden beneath his wing for the night.

Midmorning of their third day on the wing, the great flight of Dragons swept into Vanrace and set off a mass panic. Thankfully, it was more of a stampede indoors than a dangerous affair but, from the air, Humans had never looked more like a flock of frightened fowl, in a certain Dragon's jaded estimation.

His thunderclap of greeting had the salubrious effect of clearing the last stragglers off the streets with unseemly haste.

"Ah, my favourite tower is being rebuilt," Dragon reminisced dreamily as they spiralled down toward a castle with which he was well acquainted.

"Favourite?"

"Of course. It had you in it, Princess. Situation, rather less of a favourite – however, that has now been considerably improved due to your being my captive instead, has it not?"

She propped her hands upon her hips. "I knew you'd bring that up."

"We do need to settle upon your price."

"Every woman longs to be mere chattels in a transaction, Thundersong!"

"A lesser price would be frightfully dishonourable," he disagreed sourly. "How dare you consider my demanding less than you're worth? Out of the question."

Azania appeared to command a vast array of adjectives, some pithy and some rather less so, to lend fresh perspective to his thoughts. Unfortunately for her, there were few creatures under the suns as stubborn as a Dragon, especially one named Thundersong, and so they were still arguing by the time King Azerim had alighted to extend his formal greetings and congratulations to the newly crowned King Harikic and Queen Immiriza, now the rulers of Vanrace. Thundersong even approved of their body odour. Truly, they were like a fresh spring breeze about the place …

Behave, you cranky croc-face, Azania hissed in annoyance.

At the same time, she executed her usual trick of charming the very stones of the old castle to sit up and take notice of her presence, never mind the welcoming party. That suggested a twenty percent increase to her ransom price, he informed her as she bowed and greeted the royals with faultless poise even as she lambasted him mind-to-mind.

Ah, the desert-born. Gifted in so many sneaky ways.

Since the ground-bound armies had marched through Vanracian territory and should already be well on their way to T'nagru, this visit was more of a courtesy, a promise of far more cordial relations in the future. Due to potential instability in his realm, the new King intended to stay in place for a couple of months but he had promised to make himself a focal point of the supply lines that would shortly serve the war front.

Another location to protect, he told the Princess privately.

Good thinking, she agreed.

He said the same aside to Aria, who growled and confessed that they might have missed that detail off the strategic plan. Advantages of a detail-oriented mind, he told her.

Finicky-fantastic, she purred back.

What strength of character I possess. Had to be useful for something, right?

Aye, such as not having Terror Clan raiding parties wrecking our supply lines? she growled, as they prepared to take off once more.

King Harikic bowed over Azania's hand with dapper grace. Dragon eyed him balefully but it appeared that the man was only expressing gratitude for the precipitous removal of King Tyloric's crown – pity it was not everything above the shoulders – and hasty transferral to his own head. Good man. Predictable but, in a Dragon's opinion, a touch of gratitude did ease a great many problems beneath the suns.

He had noticed the Sea Dragons looking about curiously at this place of Human habitation and smelling the air with puzzled expressions. Ah, the unique local fragrance of Vanrace, that would be. As the flight of Dragons stirred the air over the town for a second time, Azania explained the deficiencies in their open sewer system to the increasingly mystified Dragons.

His relative Eversong gasped, *They basically live in their own sewage?*

Sweetsong bugled, *Surely the currents carry the waste away?*

Rain, aye – when it arrives, Azania said.

Not recently! Jainrielle, a light green Isles Dragoness, who was openly courting Eversong, bugled. *This is foulness beyond compare. Humans ... I shudder.*

Many of the Dragons gave their vocal opinions.

When Azerim asked what the kerfuffle was about, his Rangers became involved in the discussion, heatedly defending their system of sealed cesspits which captured waste, which was then pumped out, composted and transported to the fields to be used in the Archipelago's fertilisation programme. Azerim admitted that there had been issues as a result, such as the spread of a type of parasitic worm amongst the population. The Dragons almost exploded with disgust, until Everdeep gravely reminded his kin of a few of the more delightful oceanic parasites upon the Dragonkind.

One way to drag a conversation to its nadir.

The King grinned, "Maybe, when this war is done, we could share our Isles knowledge with the Vanracians without danger of the relationship tanking or turning septic."

Pinching her nose delicately, Azania cried, "Shovelling through this type of gutter diplomacy must surely be a man's job, right?"

"So I've turd," Thundersong put in.

The Princess gave him a swift kick. "I wish you'd grow up and act more manure!"

On that note of cesspit-worthy humour, they winged south with much guffawing, exchanges of uncouth jokes and even a couple of Dragons who were willing to demonstrate the art of aerial fertilisation over unpopulated areas. Truly a seminal moment in cross-species relations.

Yet Dragon and Rider knew that there was unlikely to be a single creature amongst their number whose thoughts did not creep ahead to the impending war. Every last one feared in their marrow what the morrow might bring – that first sight of the Skartunese war host, the prospect of shedding silver Dragon blood or crimson Human blood upon unforgiving, bleak sands. That was why they jested, scrapped and guffawed more robustly than was called for.

One way to push away that creeping sense of mortality.

Thus, they flew day-long and late into the evening, reaching Chakkix Camp well after the suns had set. Here, unlike their previous arrival, all was well – not calm in the slightest, but rather than fighting off a Dragon attack, productive insanity appeared to be the order of the day. Tarangis Lionbaiter viewed the size of their Dragon army with visible relief and very drily informed them that those who lacked the stomach for the forthcoming war had already made themselves scarce.

Such was the way when cowards faced reality.

Blergh, to put it mildly.

Thundersong greeted Garan and Yardi with good cheer and returned Tixyti's greeting with a grave paw-slap. The forges had not yet been banked for the night, he saw, and the mounds of weaponry and armour had sprouted in all sorts of encouraging directions since he had seen them last. Garan told him that his forge operation was only just achieving full efficiency, however, and he was already short of crucial raw materials Tarangis was trying to source for him. Time to rejig Aria's logistical plans.

Better still, speak to Azania and have *her* address the problem. A Dragon treasured marital bliss in his lair. Was he therefore faint-hearted or prudent?

After sitting down with the team for three hours that evening for a war planning session, Thundersong checked in with his dam and Inzashu in the cavern system used by the healers. Inzashu lay abed, propped up on several large cushions, looking far greener around the gills than a black girl should ever look.

"Alright there, Princess? Rid of your unwelcome visitation yet?"

"No," she scowled, "and don't you smile like that. It isn't nice. I demand sympathy."

"Did you just turn into Azania – *gnarr!*"

She jumped; he jumped too as the smaller Princess landed atop his tail, boots digging in as best she could. "My sister turned into me?" she inquired sweetly. "How kind of you to compare."

"Demanding is your middle name," he growled.

"We desert folk don't have middle names."

"Only appellations, such as 'Bristly Black Briar of the Desert?'" said he, with a chortle aimed to aggravate.

"Ouch, your humour's so prickle-ish," Azania replied, stalking past him like an ambulant thornbush toward her sister's bedside. An upraised hand halted her in her tracks. "Oh. Sorry. Talking about being demanding, I require a sisterly hug."

They mimed air-hugs at one another before she sat on a bedside ten feet from her sister.

"I hate this isolation!" Inzashu griped.

"Me too. So, how's the green-eyed monster?"

"Which of you is that?" Thundersong inquired, with his most helpful air.

Sirensong flicked her tail to smack him beneath the chin. "Speak respectfully to your Rider, son. Now, let us brief you on our progress. We have discovered and are busy fine-tuning the use of three disparate herbal concoctions generally aimed at the eradication of fungal infections of the bowels. However, since this infection also roots itself in the bloodstream, we're attempting to distil tinctures from those that can be administered via the eyes, tongue or –"

"Other places," Inzashu said, making a face.

Thundersong sneezed fire inadvertently. "You don't mean …"

"My ears, of course," she said, so blandly that he did a double-take before detecting a slight but definitively mischievous quirk to her lips.

"Why, you wicked little girl," he sneered.

"And you're a slug-ugly, snaggletoothed, lumbering old fossil on paws," she shot back.

He blinked several times.

"Too strong on the adjectives?"

"A touch!" Azania spluttered. "Thundersong –"

"Oh, just placing that gem in the petrified pathways of my reptilian brain, where the insult shall not be forgotten for a thousand years," he blathered balefully. "Meantime, that was rather amusing … for an incessantly whinging, snotty-nosed desert brat."

"People have odd ways of expressing affection," Inzashu commented.

He said, "People, aye. Good young Dragons listen to their honoured dams, however."

"About time," Sirensong growled lightly and proceeded to describe the different avenues of investigation currently underway. While much advancement had been made regarding understanding the phenomenon, the ultimate goal of healing or removal remained elusive. Azania joked about the need for an exorcism, earning herself tandem growls from Sirensong and her sister, while Thundersong dazedly wondered what it was about a Dragon-Rider bond that had just turned a Princess into … well, him.

Didn't he hold a monopoly on tasteless jokes?

However, just as he was about to assert his mastery of this particular talent, a swirl in the colours of Inzashu's emotional response caught him flat-pawed. Anger. Aye! That was the emotion which had threatened to dislodge the contagion before.

He said, "Sirensong, from what you've told us, if the magic does begin to emerge from a creature, it then becomes vulnerable, does it not?"

She stared at him, eyes half-lidded. "We've caught it *once*."

"Hmm."

"Why, what are you thinking?" his dam continued, still giving him the stingray stare, as his kin called it. "Nothing dangerous or foolish, I hope?"

Inzashu said, "If you're thinking of angering me – don't. I've been through a great deal, let me –"

"You mean, you don't handle anger well?" he interrupted.

"No, I handle it better than most people my age."

"Just like your mother?"

Azania squalled, "Dragon! How could you?"

Inzashu flushed in fury. "How dare –"

"Exactly. Like. Your. Mother," he ticked off on his talons, observing her outrage grow with every syllable.

Thundersong had never imagined the kind of rage that leaped into her visage just then. It was more than a murderous rage, it was despairing, as if his lie had touched a core of self-held truth she had never admitted to herself. A terrible shriek ripped from her throat. So fast did the green mist exit her mouth, it flashed across the space between them before he could duck. A fearful cold speared into his muzzle, but his reflexive mental swat somehow pinged the horror past him before it could enter or take root.

"AZANIA!" he roared.

The green mist rebounded off the cavern wall as no mist was ever meant to move and swerved back toward him with clear intent.

Everyone leaped at once.

CHAPTER 20

SNOOZING OFF TO WAR

IN THE ENSUING CHAOS, Thundersong thumped into his dam's flank, Sirensong curved her body to dodge Inzashu as the Dragoness sprang to save her reckless progeny and the younger Princess leaped to rescue the older as she hurled herself into the path of danger.

Thankfully, nobody except Azania had a clue what they were doing.

The two Dragons landed in a panting, squirming heap across the wreckage of the infirmary bed upon which Azania had been perched a moment before. Inzashu rolled beneath Sirensong's upraised tail and used Thundersong's left hind paw as leverage to pop herself back upright. All three of them gaped in surprise as Azania flicked a thick blanket over the mist. Quick as a wink, she twisted her wrists and flung the package aside with a violent shudder.

Thundersong queried, "Surely, that won't –"

At the same time, Sirensong bugled, "Will that – get *back!* Everyone!"

Grabbing a Princess in either paw, he promptly discovered how difficult it was for a quadruped to flee when two of his paws were occupied with treasures that were not to be spilled, thumped against the cavern ceiling or accidentally smeared beneath his paws. Thundersong ended up wriggling ignominiously out of the cavern on his hind paws and front elbows while Princess Azania yelled at him from the front and his dam from the rear.

Still, it worked.

By the time the mist managed to percolate through several layers of thick blanket, they had made good their escape. Sirensong monitored the mist as it made an increasingly weak attempt to move into an adjoining cavern. Finally, it dissipated into nothingness.

Turning to Inzashu, he said, "You're rid of it?"

Her eyes brimmed with moisture.

"You're despicable!" Azania hissed, punching his shoulder for emphasis. "I could wring your stupidly thick neck! How do you even begin to justify that – that –"

"Outrageous lie?" he said.

"A lie? Is that what you call hurting someone so deeply?"

"I had to lie – for her sake!" he growled. "I thought of the worst, most flagrant untruth I could imagine, don't you understand?"

"No!"

"Inzashu, you know that was a horrible falsehood, don't you?"

"No, but I am ... grateful," she said softly, falling into Azania's arms where she began to weep softly.

The older Princess glared at him over her sister's shoulder.

Another Thundersong – a Blitz of old, perhaps – would have curled up inside and fled as far as his wings could carry him. This Dragon stilled his twitching paws with an effort. He stood his ground. It was all he could do in the face of her ire. Vaguely, he wondered how any creature could make a Dragon feel this way.

After a moment, however, his Princess' face did some

kind of Human squishy-emotional thing – technical term, there – which promptly introduced a great deal of squish to his five Dragon hearts. Bizarre, but true.

To him alone, Azania said, *You might be a little rough around the edges, Thundersong, and far too hasty, but I know you meant well. Thank you for rescuing my sister from her high tower.*

Now his squishy hearts swelled with pride, quite the oddest sensation for a Dragon. Trying not to sound tediously self-satisfied, he said, *I'm glad my lies served some purpose. When I see a solution with such clarity, I find it very hard not to act, Princess.*

I understand. It's just hard to see my sister hurt.

Aye. Strange how blood was always blood. His own sire's treachery could not mask or erase the fiery love Thundersong felt in his hearts for him but the unreserved regard of his youth had changed to different, more complex shades, he realised. No love was perfect. Perhaps that was an illusion of youth – but it could remain true, stronger for having been tested and refined in the crucible of adversity. A Dragon must choose and choose again not to allow darker fires of bitterness to burn in his hearts, for nothing good could come of that. Just look at his brothers – his Tamarine brothers, he corrected himself, regarding the number of Sea Dragon family who, responding to the commotion, winged or ran closer with calls for clarification. Sirensong set their minds at ease.

Then there might be non-blood, creatures like an Isles Dragoness or a Desert Princess who, by some miracle beyond all magic, might come to mean more to a Dragon than life itself.

And a Dragon might learn afresh the magic of hugs. Just now, Inzashu's tiny arms curved about the base of his neck as she gave him a huge hug and told him – naturally – that he was the most awesome being on four paws under the suns. Only the slightest exaggeration. Completely forgivable character flaw.

That girl had been very sick.

While Aria, Azania and Azerim reorganised all the logistics to provide Dragon support for more urgent needs and to ensure any speculative Terror Clan attacks would be dealt with as they deserved – with lethal efficiency – he took the younger Princess aside and told her that, while he admired her bravery and spirit, salting in a touch more truth upon occasion was the flight path of wisdom. Inzashu promised to do better next time. After that, they discussed tactics against her mother until the girl grew visibly sleepy. By this time, Azerim sat back from the map table and declared with open admiration:

"Azania, you're good! Does any detail pass you by?"

She gave him an uncertain look. "That's just the way my mind works." *Thanks for your suggestions, Thundersong. Always, Princess.*

The King said, "I'll admit, I feel a bit like the spare cart wheel over here when you two get into your stride. Impressive."

"I'm sure we can find a suitable role for you, darling."

Azerim eyed the Princess speculatively. "What's that?"

"Well, someone has to stand at the front and look pretty." He gasped. A wicked smile curved her lips as she added, "I firmly believe that's your talent … you know, motivating the troops, leading the charge, all aided by this irresistibly handsome stubble …"

Reaching out, he trapped her against her chair with his arms. "So, sweet Princess, you'd taunt a wicked pirate from the Archipelago, would you?"

"Azerim? *Azeriii … mmm!*"

Predictably, kissing ensued. Enthusiastic, piratical kissing involving an unsociable raid upon the desert kingdom's finest treasure.

Even a Dragon must approve of such misbehaviour.

At the stroke of dawn, following a sweltering night, Dragons rose from the hills behind Chakkix Camp like the unfurling of a flower, heading for every point of the compass. They were mixed groups of Sea Dragons, warrior

Dragonesses and Rangers in the main. By far the majority headed directly for N'ginta Citadel, the capital city of the Desert Kingdom, with a second substantial group headed back to Vanrace to pick up and rush back with essential supplies. The balance, smaller scouting groups, spread out high and far, seeking sight or sign of Terror Clan activities. No-one expected an attack across the badlands of northern T'nagru, but the flank needed to be secured against any surprises. If they could disrupt Terror Clan movements, so much the better.

As Thundersong climbed away from the ridgeline, scenting the terribly dry, already overheated airstream pressing against their faces, Azania took a deep inhalation and quivered.

"What's that?" he asked immediately.

"It's the changing of the desert season – isn't it, Inza?"

The younger Princess shook her head slowly. "This heat? It's meant to be cooler – oh, I see."

"Well, I don't," Thundersong grumbled playfully.

"That's because you *smell* it," Azania teased on cue. "Let us educate our allies, sister. Lesson number one, meteorology. In this season, cooler air moves across Skartun from the south, bringing what *some* people have the nerve to call winter."

"Maybe even a spot of rain," Inzashu agreed. "Most of our water comes from aquifers beneath the desert, supplied by mountain ranges far to the south and west. Geography being lesson number two, sister."

Thundersong said, "And then?"

"Lesson three, physics," said Azania. "The cold, moister air pushes across the desert, lifting the hot air, which creates turbulent atmospheric conditions that often give rise to violent electrical storms and, rather less often, rain. Given temperatures around thirty degrees cooler on the Fangheat scale, a desert crossing is possible."

"So, can we hope that the Skartunese will be tastefully fried by the time they arrive in T'nagru?" Azerim called over, with a lilt in his voice.

Inzashu said, "Lesson number four, sociology. Skartunese do not fry easily."

"Darned shame," the King grumbled.

"That's my people you're talking about."

"You're far too nice to be lumped in as one of them," Thundersong said, earning himself a whole cartload of favourable points.

Azania said, "Anyways, it means that we have a week or two, at most, before the enemy arrives together with the cooler weather. If we can already feel the air movement here, that means they're on their way. Possibly up to a week ago already."

On that less-than-encouraging note, the Dragonflight bored steadily southward, crossing the cactus-strewn wastelands that separated the less official part of T'nagru from the desert proper. Flat, monotonous tan terrain spotted with the khaki stands of cacti slowly gave way to dark flowing sands and aeons-scoured patches of bedrock that Thundersong remembered all too well. Despite their altitude, the daytime temperature marched steadily from stultifying to broiling and onward to utterly unbearable, the suns blazing from a cloudless sky. Yet the worst offender by far was the searing wind, as dry as bones left in the desert for a thousand years.

When Azerim's Rangers began to complain of feeling faint from the heat, the Princess snapped her fingers and exclaimed, "How could I be so stupid?"

"You, Princess?" Dragon rumbled.

"Sarcasm not appreciated," she said crisply. "Thundersong, call everyone to attention, please."

ATTENTION, EVERYONE!!

Azania removed her fingers from her ears. "Thank you."

"Ouch," said Inzashu.

Ignoring the complaint, the Princess of T'nagru climbed her Dragon's back as if a mile drop was a mere step up onto her throne, and proceeded to teach all of Azerim's troops how to dress for the desert. The Archipelago Islanders did not much appreciate face veils and headscarves, but she smiled and told them that they were soldiers and invited them to do as they were told. Only Azania could get away with a trick like that.

On and on they winged into the white-hot heart of a forge.

An hour before noon, Everdeep crooked his neck to regard Azania and Thundersong, flying wing-second just off the larger Sea Dragon's right flank. He growled, "How can you stand this heat? My wings are wilting and I'm sure my left nostril just cracked inside."

"I'm sorry, but it's still early and quite cool," the Princess informed him. Sirensong's bright azure eye colour dampened visibly at the news. "We might need to consider resting until mid-afternoon and flying the second leg of our journey later tonight when it's cooler, although, that won't be saying much. This weather is famously brutal."

"Orders, Princess?" the huge Dragon panted, pleading with his expression.

Her eyes flicked to Azerim, who bowed over Everdeep's neck and made a courtly gesture. She called in a landing in the lee of a small ridge, where she knew of a tiny spring hidden in a gully. A couple of the Sea Dragons rushed toward the scent of water, scrapping and thundering, and had to be roared into order by Everdeep. By then, it was too late for one male Ranger – broken ankle, caught in the crush.

Everdeep told them what he thought of their behaviour in tones that rolled across the wastelands like thunder.

After that, he ordered the Rangers to transfer gourds and skeins of water to the roasting Dragons and to take some water themselves. Farizam taught Chanize how to splint an ankle so that the man could be transported to a surgeon. The Dragons lay in the suns with the smaller Dragonesses and Rangers sheltered beneath their wings and sweltered until late afternoon when it was time to rouse their roasted selves and fly on. Azania was right. As crimson tongues of fire licked upward from the horizon in a magnificent desert suns-set, the heat level barely changed. Incredible scenery.

"I thought clear skies were good for radiating heat back into the atmosphere?" Thundersong said.

"Not everything about desert physics is logical," Azania admitted. "I guess we'll make that another lesson, shall we? A lesson in the illogical mysteries that still plague science."

"I think the heat's frazzled your tiny brain, Princess."

"At least I have one, eh?"

"I've five hearts. Need a spare?"

Laughing, she said, "Why don't we put our Isles Dragonesses to sleep?"

Just off Thundersong's right flank, Aria bristled visibly. "What are you saying? I am not tired. Don't even think about it."

"Sleep flying," he returned briskly. "Remember how I told you that Sea Dragons can sleep while flying through water? Turns out, air's no different."

The Cobalt Dragoness gave him the fiery eyeball. "I am not –"

"Bedtime, sweet fires?" he crooned.

"Phew," said Azania, pretending to fan her face. "Not just the desert that's hot around here, is it? Come on, Aria. Better that we all arrive fresh in T'nagru, isn't it? You'd be doing the Sea Dragons a favour as well – they could do with the respite to grow accustomed to the heat."

The fierce copper and sea-green tones of Aria's gaze suggested that she knew exactly what her companions intended. "Very well," she agreed, flicking her eye membranes pertly at a certain someone, who perked up immediately. Fiery flirtation had to beat straight forgiveness every time.

His mate – ah, what a beautiful word – called, *All Isles Dragonesses, pair up with your Sea Dragons as we practised and get some sleep. I want you all as fresh as spring daisies come the morn!*

Shortly, after the expected round of snarling and displeased commentary, Everdeep struck up a Sea Dragon lullaby and every creature settled down. Even the Humans appeared to be lulled by the soft, rippling melody.

Spreading his wings upon the light breeze, Thundersong took a deep breath and gazed down at the undulating obsidian desert beneath its canopy of night. The sky above was gloriously starry, each source of light a perfect pinprick, the spiral galaxies seen through his spectacles crawling like radiant snails across the arch of the sky, achingly pure.

Time to snooze his way off to war.

A Dragon blinked and he was in T'nagru. Neat.

Stretching languorously on the wing, Thundersong peered ahead through his spectacles and spied the jagged silhouette of T'nagru Citadel etched stark against the pre-dawn sky. There it was, not smoking like the previous time he had arrived here. He hoped that King N'chala's major repair and fortification works had been completed. They would see soon enough.

Checking the skies, he noted the light-yellow form of Chalice circling very high above the citadel in her familiar role as sentry. Nothing passed her by. Mind, now that he was paying proper attention, he could identify at least four silhouettes of Dragons up at the citadel – not oddly shaped rooftops. Dragons. Excellent. He would have expected no less of Juggernaut the Grinder.

Satisfied that matters were as tight as the lay of a Dragon's scales, if said Dragon were not moulting – wince, ouch – Thundersong curved his neck to regard his passengers. Azania slept curled up on his neck with Inzashu-N'shula breathing lightly against her sister's nape.

Aww. Cute as a pair of turtledoves. Ariamyrielle Seaspray slept upon his mounded back, her slender muzzle curved aside so that he was able to discern the slight crack between her eyelids but, behind, her eye fires rested in the deep umber and copper-green tones of sleep. Usually, she was such a skittish beast, restless even at rest. It was unlike her to slumber so deeply, unless – could this tranquillity be ascribed to him? His influence?

His hearts swelled with pride, his belly fires gurgled with good cheer. Thundersong regarded the reaction with mild embarrassment and muttered to himself, *Alright, alright, keep it down in there. A little hubris is draconic. Too much turns one into … Brand or Brawl. Blergh.*

Nice alliteration. Brand, Brawl, *blergh.*

Perfect way to start his morning.

Crooking his neck once more, he scanned the great V of Dragons coasting toward the city. Even the Tamarine Dragons amenable to his idea, about a third of their number, had slept. The balance would be five or six hours behind by now, facing another gruelling flight through an overheated morning. His gaze drifted from Everdeep to Sirensong. Upon her neck, a pair of green eyes glinted beneath the desert headscarf. Aha. King Azerim was awake and alert, perhaps considering the importance of his impending meeting with King N'chala. Good man.

He nodded slightly, Azerim blinked in acknowledgement.

So serene, the desert. No birdsong disturbed the perfect silence, while the city ahead lay like an animal slumbering in the dawn. He wondered idly if it rested upon sand or bedrock since, in this region, dunes spread for endless miles – yet, if one knew the terrain, there were oases scattered like jewels across the sands, caves where a person or Dragon might take shelter and even the famous gold mines of the desert folk, their location a secret guarded since time immemorial from all invaders and spies.

THUNDER O DRAGON

No roaring this morning. Instead, in a whisper that slipped from his throat like the first stirring of a desert breeze, Thundersong began to sing the awakening song he had learned from his great namesake. Strange how elemental this Sea Dragon singing was, moving his soul in ways that defied description.

Even before he reached the second stanza, his kin began to stir and, with them, their passengers. Chalice's flight path dipped and swerved to let him know they had been recognised. The watch Dragons did not deign to disturb the silence as their kin flew up to the mighty curtain walls, an army of scales and magic such as this city had never seen and its populace had never imagined. Wings whispered through the balmy dawn air as the Tamarine Dragons split off from the main flight to greet their kin guarding the walls and the Isles Dragonesses spread out with martial eagerness to scout and evaluate the terrain.

Taking the lead, Thundersong and Azania led Everdeep and Sirensong to a careful landing in the gardens of the palace building. Aria alighted upon the topmost spire of a round tower as if to declare her dominance over the city but her gaze for him was mingled amusement and admiration.

Good flight, beloved fires of my soul, she said. *I haven't slept like that since I can remember.*

Thank you.

You're a creature of unexpected depths, Thundersong, complementing me in ways I had not anticipated.

Reading the nuances of her speech, he said, *Is the unexpected good or bad, Aria?*

Her laughter trilled forth for a second before she stilled the reaction. *You read me so well,* she purred, flicking her wings to indicate delight. Mesmerising colours. *Should a Dragoness' warrior hearts not thrill to the mysteries of her mate's song?*

His lower jaw plonked upon the grass at his paws.

Aria made a wriggle of patent satisfaction and turned her attention to the varying flights of her Dragonesses, seeking anything unusual, any sign of danger.

Azania stroked his neck. "That was an excellent flight, Thundersong. Thank you. I believe I hear the servants all in a kerfuffle inside. Shall we go –"

"Annoy them?"

Her tiny dark eyes smiled at him. "I'd choose a different adjective, but you have the idea. It's good to keep one's King hopping."

"Like a frog?" he snorted. "How inelegant."

Even as he spoke, a man he recognised came charging out of the palace building with a servant running behind trying to get him into some kind of robe. "Azania!" he yelled. "Azania! Sands alive, sister – how many Dragons? White Dragons?"

"N'chala!"

Crying, "You rascal! You little rascal!" he swept her up into his arms and spun her about.

Thundersong scratched an itchy spot beneath his chin. Apparently, he concluded, inelegance could also be strangely beautiful.

"How's Yuali?" she asked.

"Arrived yesterday. Wonderful," he spluttered. "She's … sleeping, I believe. You saved her kingdom, I heard?"

Princess Azania said, "Fairly minor. We slapped down an attempted insurrection."

"Not as I heard it. But, where's your Dragon – the Dragon, sister?" he asked, glancing about in confusion before his eyes lit upon Thundersong and recognition dawned. "You … changed colour?"

"I moulted to my true colouration," he rumbled, bowing his muzzle politely. "Well met once more, King N'chala."

"Well met indeed!" he said, finally succeeding in tying his robe over his sleeping shorts and shirt. "And this … aha! I know you too – Azerim, unless I'm sorely mistaken?

King Azerim? Welcome to T'nagru, my friend and brother-to-be, I understand?"

They exchanged an Isles bow and a fluid desert genuflection, before embracing and exchanging manly backslaps. Thundersong grinned. Dragons and Humans could be so alike at times. Just look at how chary these males were of a public display of affection, despite that Azerim clearly could not be happier at this manner of greeting and N'chala appeared to be on the verge of taking wing to soar with the dawn. Was this the scent of hope filling this young King's heart? Most gratifying.

Azania took over, introducing Everdeep and Sirensong, before beckoning to Aria to flit down and meet her older brother. N'chala declared his admiration of her beauty as much as the size and heft of the swords she carried; Aria promptly promised to perform nasty culinary operations upon their mutual enemies. Thundersong concluded that the relationship would work out agreeably.

War made for the unlikeliest friendships.

N'chala invited everyone inside for breakfast and a touch of catching up on the news, not without a wary glance at Everdeep's immense heft. However, as it turned out, light and airy desert architecture left enough space for the Sea Dragon to enter even these halls and so, the King of T'nagru hosted perhaps the strangest meal imaginable, attended by three different types of Dragons, the Princess of a faraway kingdom, the King of the even more distant Vaylarn Archipelago and N'chala's two openly discomfited brothers, the Princes Yadaxu and Aragu.

Gnarr.

Thundersong made sure to give them an extra-toothy smile of greeting. Certain Humans behaved far better when reminded of their edible properties by the apex predator of Solixambria.

For Princess Yuali, risen from her royal slumber looking infeasibly vibrant and un-mussed, he had greetings of a far more affable nature. Last she had heard, her father was back on his feet, walking with difficulty but improving daily. Seemed being royal was a risky business nowadays, he noted, causing Azerim to cough and splutter into his goblet of pomegranate juice. Azania clapped him upon the back and told the Dragon that he might attempt to take a more positive tack in the future.

Grrr, he disagreed. *I'm a realist.*

You're a pessimist.

If I wished him ill, then aye, Thundersong growled. *I'll admit, I've once or twice imagined clapping him upon the back a touch harder than you just did.*

Me too, she giggled inwardly. *Or, about the earhole.*

Good thing Azerim did not know how they joked together in private.

As N'chala's request for a rendition of their epic journey to the Archipelago perked Azania up, Thundersong's attention drifted to Juggernaut, participating patiently in the meeting. The Orange Dragon met his eye and shook his head slightly. So, no sign of the Skartunese yet? That made a Dragon's scales itch, a thought that promptly introduced a literal itch to his left wing-pit. Still, the desert was very wide and the weather had kept the patrols relatively close to home. Even Dragons were limited in terms of what they could withstand of the fullest brunt of the desert weather.

He clenched his left forepaw purposefully before checking the state of his personal cutlery. His talons needed sharpening after all this flying about lugging cargo.

Juggernaut's jaw cracked open into a slight grin. He said, *Keen for battle?*

Aye. I've a few Jabiz I'd like to introduce to their own entrails.

The other Dragon's grin widened. "King N'chala, would you excuse us Dragons? I'd like to show Thundersong progress on the fortifications, settle in the new arrivals and set patrol, communication and defensive assignments. I haven't received reports from the farther citadels since last night. I'm sure Princess Azania's reputation for running a thorough briefing precedes her."

When Azerim chuckled dryly, Azania mimed tossing her fruit juice at him.

On that note, the Dragons departed, with a promise to return later once N'chala had caught up on his sister's news.

As they winged easily down over the city toward the main gates, Thundersong said, *So, tell me why I'm so excited about a review of the fortifications?*

Everdeep chortled massively, *Indeed, why?*

Sirensong said, *I'm eager to meet those Dragons you rescued before, Thundersong. I'm sure they'll need my healing capabilities.*

Juggernaut replied, *Basic tactics. Azerim and Azania need to declare their intentions before King N'chala, who will duly consider the matter and come around to the issue of his sister's ransom. Without Dragons present, the Humans will be encouraged to speak freely. I believe you shall shortly receive a proposal that may well hint at hidden resources in the Kingdom of T'nagru.*

Resources? he echoed curiously.

Juggernaut rubbed his paws together. *Gold, my fine young Dragon. The best gold comes from the desert. What you need to consider is how you might broker Azania's future, given Azerim's keen but – shall I say – monetarily constrained proposal, the relative riches of T'nagru and the power you hold in your right paw.*

I don't care greatly for hoard or gold, he mused. *Ahem. Do you, Aria?*

No, she said.

No?

Do you count riches in ingots, Thundersong?

Not me, said he, mocking a playful nip toward her wingtip as they circled, seeking a landing space on the battlements beside the main gates. *My concern is for Azania's honour and for her future.*

Aria said, *Given your artistic skills, I doubt we shall ever want for ingots. Perhaps the greater question will be to work out how to navigate this issue, keeping both Azania and Azerim's respective honour intact. He is a proud young man, often stubborn, and in many ways a good match for her.*

I see that. Do you think he'd accept a loan from me?

The Cobalt Dragoness shook her head slowly. *I doubt it.*

Thundersong dipped his head. How could this ever work? If T'nagru paid her ransom price, that would effectively place her in N'chala's hand. He trusted the King of T'nagru but distrusted his brothers fiercely. Azerim could never afford her price – not an honourable price anyways. Nor could Thundersong pretend to lose her to Azerim. That would simply not wash. There must be a way, perhaps a solution of suitably draconic cunning …

Turning to regard the impressive gatehouses, he said heartily, *Very good, Juggernaut. Tell me all about these nice, shiny new gates and the additional defensive fortifications. My wings quiver in anticipation, my very paws ache to hear every salient detail–*

One more word and I'll turn your tail into my personal chew toy, the other growled.

Always subtle, Juggernaut. Right there in the name.

CHAPTER 21

BENEATH THE DESERT

KING N'CHALA HAD MADE considerable progress on the repairs and additional features of his fortifications, in addition to changes to his other major citadels in the south of his kingdom. The gatehouses had been massively reinforced, with granite quarried in the deep desert, and fitted with oil spigots to give approaching troops a roasting welcome. He had added nine feet in height to the outer walls, additional archer slits and reshaped the merlons and crenels atop the battlement to make it harder for grapnels to find purchase. An overhang had been added to offer a decent obstacle to anyone assaulting the citadel by ladder or rope.

Modern siege warfare demanded modern methods.

A detail that did interest Thundersong was that this citadel had been constructed directly upon a layer of bedrock some thirty-five feet beneath the desert sands – an immense undertaking back in the day – which meant that the enemy could not easily tunnel beneath. This was not true for all the citadels. Some stood upon deep sand. That would pose unique challenges for the defenders should the

Skartunese indeed possess the ability to create tunnels.

Maybe, if that were the case, there might be a unique manner in which Sea Dragons could take the attack to the enemy – his mental pathways burned with new ideas – maybe those seismic sounds Everdeep in particular excelled at?

When he put his thoughts to Juggernaut, his mentor stared at him as if he had turned into a Bloodworm. "Thundersong!"

"That's my name?"

The other Dragon clouted him so hard upon the shoulder that Thundersong stumbled into Aria, which promptly fetched him a sharp clout from the other direction, too. He ruffled his wings with an air of feigned outrage.

"That's what we'll call it," the warrior growled. "The Thundersong."

"What, by my wings, is a *Thundersong?*" he snorted in bafflement.

Juggernaut shook his muzzle sadly. "Here I was just about to compliment you on your intellect, young Dragon, and you immediately do your best to disprove my claim."

Aria burst out laughing, the traitoress.

Perhaps a Dragon had never managed to look quite as woolly as he was capable of.

"A Thundersong, apart from being a kingdom-wrecker of mythic proportions," the Orange Dragon explained with a sly air, "and being a brash, upstart young fire-breather whose snout I've ground in the dirt more times than I can count –"

GNARRR!! he felt obliged to protest.

"You're excused," Everdeep put in promptly, causing all of the Dragons to burst out laughing. The Humans nearby glanced about in surprise.

What? Of course Dragons had a sense of humour.

He'd eat anyone who suggested otherwise.

Juggernaut said, "A Thundersong is a means of hunting

the Skartunese. You see, I believe we've hit upon a new method – King N'chala's scouts are convinced, for a variety of reasons, that they must be tunnelling and travelling beneath the desert, perhaps using ancient underground watercourses, cavern systems or other magical means. We should go flush them out with a salutary Thundersong."

"Ooh, a Thundersong," his dam teased.

"What, pick him up by his tail and aim him in the right direction?" Everdeep put in, gripping Thundersong's tail in his massive right paw. "I could see that working."

"Get off!"

Pulling his hindquarters up by his tail, a most undignified and unwelcome experience for the large male Dragon who was the object of the joke, the huge Sea Dragon rumbled, "Ready, aim …"

Thundersong grumbled. "Careful, you comedian, or this joke may *backfire* quite badly."

Aria gasped, "Thundersong! That's terrible."

"Do I detect a cultural gaffe?"

"On the Isles? Worse than terrible – please don't tell me you Tamarine Dragons …" When Juggernaut guffawed loudly, she said, "Toilet humour is so juvenile."

"We aren't all as serious and focussed as some Dragons," he shot back, buffeting her playfully upon the shoulder. A blur of martial arts moves later, Thundersong learned that he still knew very little about paw-to-paw combat.

Good to understand the extent of one's ignorance. Clearly Aria had been holding back when training with him, which also explained how he was still alive to enjoy this realisation.

Marvellous.

Feeling rather disgruntled about his mate's abilities, and even more disgruntled by the fact that he felt disgruntled, Thundersong tucked his tail back where it belonged and decided that having a war method named after him really ought to be written down in their journal. Most gratifying.

If it worked.

The following morning dawned even hotter than the one before, if that was possible. Azania was right. The desert heat followed no laws of physics he could discern. Hotter and hottest blurred in meaning at this end of the Fangheat scale.

That was why, by the time dawn actually dawned, Ignis and Taramis might have been rather startled to discover a line of Sea Dragons trying to blow up the desert.

Following King N'achla's advice, they had set out two hours before dawn to reconnoitre in the region south of the capital city. While Thundersong could not detect any signs of tunnelling, along the way, the King's desert scouts told him of scraping noises they had heard below ground in the deep desert, the occasional muffled clink of what they took to be chisels and more frequently, minor earth tremors. Now, the Sea Dragons worked in a steady line across the terrain, essentially fishing for a bite, as they put it – much to the amusement of the desert folk looking on.

Fishing? In over two hundred feet of sand?

The Sea Dragons sniggered and told the desert folk that a mere two hundred feet was ridiculously shallow.

King N'chala clearly enjoyed his first flight aboard a Dragon. He had been teamed with Juggernaut, an unlikely but effective pairing. Thundersong took Azania and Azerim together on his neck. Occasional grotesque mammalian smacking and slurping sounds – just a touch of hyperbole there – emanating from a short ways behind his skull assured him that their relationship was now very much on track. It seemed that Azerim must have learned a hard but valuable lesson about the Princess of T'nagru, one not many of her enemies had survived to reflect upon.

THUNDER O DRAGON

As he well knew, Azania had a knack for arranging matters to her satisfaction, nowadays, with a draconic talon further stirring the cauldron from time to time.

The other thing N'chala vocally appreciated was the opportunity to see his kingdom from above for the first time. Even Juggernaut's eyes glazed over by the time he had found a dozen ways of describing how wonderful the sand dunes were. Thundersong appreciated his enthusiasm. Juggernaut visibly tuned out, his mind clearly churning through matters military.

With progress made only in the area of sore throats, N'chala called the flight in around mid-morning, as the temperatures soared. Time to hit the maps again.

Back at the Palace, the Sea Dragons tried out the newly enlarged entryway to an underground reservoir set aside for their use. Very popular. Thundersong, denying his inner urge to jump in as well, joined a betting game as he, Azerim, N'chala, Azania, Farizam, Juggernaut and Aria placed bets on the likeliest places they might dig up the Skartunese war host.

After that, everyone tried to find the coolest possible place to escape the noonday heat.

Thundersong wandered down to the cistern and wandered out again. No, he had not needed to know that Everdeep and Sirensong's relationship was on a healthy footing too. Not in that way!

Thankfully, no Humans would be drinking from *that* water.

Ahem. Hopefully.

He found Azerim and Azania relaxing beneath a gazebo in the cool – relatively speaking – outer portico of the palace building, nibbling grapes and cherries from a tastefully arranged golden platter while they tried not to expire from the heat.

Indeed, the temperature of the day was very shortly eclipsed by Princess Azania.

"So, I have been priced!" she said snippily.

"Priced?" Thundersong echoed.

"Aye, the *men* agreed on my ransom price – can you imagine such a thing? I might as well be put on display by some local shopkeeper!"

"How much?" he inquired.

"Four thousand T'nagrun ingots," she hissed.

"Four *thousand?*" Even a Dragon's eyes could grow round.

"Four! It's ridiculous!" the Princess huffed.

"Too little?" he inquired.

"There isn't that much gold in all of Solixambria!" Azerim groaned. "Well, let's just say it would take more than my lifetime to collect. Apparently, Vanrace was prepared to pay most handsomely for the Black Rose of the Desert. I'm a poor Archipelago Islander. What am I supposed to do, Thundersong?"

"A roguishly handsome poor Archipelago Islander," Azania said, in not a terrible attempt at being supportive. Thundersong felt that fell rather flat, but she did feed him a grape from her own lips.

Blergh! Honestly?

Things no creature needed to know about Human courtship behaviours.

Azerim explained, "Apparently, the grape feeding ... activity, is cultural in desert courtship rituals. I just view it as an excuse for more kissing."

Gnarr. Necessary lies. Was he not discomfited?

"Moving swiftly on?" the King suggested.

"Quite," he growled. "So, tell me, how much have we extorted from Vanrace so far, given as they started this whole mess?"

They both stared at him.

"Was it the word, 'extort?' " he asked, with a curl of his lip. "After all, the whole experience was terribly distressing for the Princess – being held in a stinking dungeon, threatened with forced marriage to Floric the indescribably festering and flatulent –"

Azerim spluttered, "You devious … Dragon!"

Thundersong said, "Are Dragons known to be any other way?"

The young King said, "That … could help. N'chala does seek the best for his sister, but her price is a matter of honour, as you rightly pointed out, Dragon. This tactic could get us partway to the most expensive bride in history, I – *ouch*."

Having punched his shoulder, Azania said, "I protest."

"Rightly so," Azerim agreed. "Where did you learn to punch like that?"

"Juggernaut."

"Figures. Still, I remain an impoverished royal from a faraway Isle with zero prospects of purchasing – ransoming, whatever –" he protected his shoulder, only to receive a punch on the leg "– ouch times two, my future bride."

Thundersong began to scratch his chin and then roared in delight, *MWAA-HARR-HAARRGGH!!* "I have it!"

Azerim clutched his chest. "Aargh!"

"Frightened, little king? You should be, for I am a renowned re-arranger of kingdom affairs –"

"Thundersong. Behave," Azania snorted.

"Princess, what will your dowry from the Kingdom of T'nagru be?"

"I don't –"

"One thousand ingots," Azerim said promptly.

This time, it was his turn to receive a filthy glare. "You men! You went behind my back?"

"We were trying to close the gap," her fiancé objected. "Everyone wants the best for you – for us, even."

"Oh, it's best I be sold off like a piece of jewellery?"

"Crown jewels, at the very least!" Azerim protested. Not a bad effort. The Princess favoured this with a frustrated glare.

"So, here's my deal," Thundersong purred. "Vanrace pays me for the emotional damage incurred by Azania.

T'nagru pays you the dowry, Azerim. We put those two amounts together –"

"Making you a stupidly rich Dragon, because I then have to pay you for her?" he snapped. "Sorry, but … aye!"

Thundersong, that's just silly and it can't possibly work, Azania said privately to him. *You couldn't fit all that gold into any Dragon lair in all of Solixambria.*

Good thing I don't mean to then, isn't it, Princess?

What do you mean?

Switching to Human, he said, "What under the suns do you two think I'd do with all that gold? Four thousand ingots? Do you not know me at all?" Lowering his voice, he plucked up two grapes and popped one each into their mouths. "Chew and listen. With said gold, I intend to make a range of rather large and well-chosen investments. No, I am not buying any kingdoms. How frivolous do you think I am? Rather, I believe I shall invest heavily in the future of the Vaylarn Archipelago, as I happen to know a certain royal family of the very finest character. You, Azerim, need a fleet. I think we should buy you one. No, by my wings, we'll buy up every fleet on the coastline of Solixambria. We'll monopolise the trade."

Azania's eyes widened, as well they might.

"In exchange for my largesse, I expect a handsome return on my investment. In order to secure that return, I shall loan you someone I trust implicitly, who has quite extraordinary skills to bring to bear on the matter – namely, Princess Azania."

"Now I'm being loaned out?" she snorted, but not without admiration.

He rubbed his paws together. "You are mine to do with as I please. What I please is to give you the happiest future imaginable with a man who I believe will treat you as the irreplaceable jewel you are. However, I reserve the right call upon you in the future to overthrow the odd kingdom, that sort of thing. I expect the man in question to be unreservedly grateful."

Azerim almost nodded his head off his neck. "Oh, I would be for … ahem!" He chuckled softly. "Thundersong, would you truly do all this for us?"

"Baubles hold no interest for me," he said, "unless they come in the form of a –"

"Don't you dare!" Azania said, but her smile had never been more radiant.

"– dusky desert Princess with a ridiculously feisty attitude," he finished loftily. "So, my friends, how does this sound to you? Acceptable? Oh, before I forget, one condition. You shall grant me a lifetime's supply of art equipment and a home for yourselves which I shall personally decorate. Those two things are essential codicils to any deal."

This 'essentials' list is bound to grow, isn't it? the Princess teased.

Silence, waif. I am busy selling you off to the highest bidder.

Oh, I must have missed that bit.

Pay attention – oh!

To his surprise, he collected his very first manly hug from Azerim. It was even tearful, which he understood was a highly significant emotional behaviour in the Human male. He hugged him back cautiously. Perhaps this behaviour was infectious? After a moment, he collected Azania into a hug as well and shortly, felt compelled to explain:

"Well, it was providential that I discovered you in the high tower that day, Azania, and so a Dragon might consider it somewhat ridiculous to become the recipient of some four thousand T'nagrun ingots by dint of having been the one to spring you out of captivity, a mere few seconds' work."

"You lovely nitwit, it's all that came after that counts," Azania corrected. "Besides, I can hardly say I'm a mere few seconds' work."

"Indeed not," he coughed.

"Quick, ink that on a scroll and seal it!" Azerim cried.

THUNDER O DRAGON

That was why, when Aria approached, she found King Azerim being chased by a wicked Princess around a Dragon's tail.

Early to lair, early to rise, made a Dragon healthy, wealthy and wise.

Thundersong stirred at Aria's insistent paw-touch. *Whasssup … dawn already, dearest fires?*

Dawn hasn't dared to light the skies, she said.

How's about a few more hours then?

Eh. Early to rise, made him sound like a rusty hinge.

Time to warm up your throat, Thundersong. Come. Or were yesterday's exploits too much for you, you brutally brilliant bad Dragon?

The way she said it made his fires blush. *Whomp!* Ahem. Very well, an oath-bound Dragon could most certainly think such things about his mate, even knowing that she meant the success of his devious, dastardly, delicious scheming. Missives had been sent, deals clinched and crystal wine goblets clinked in celebration.

Now, if his undeniable brilliance could only convince the Skartunese to shove off and bury themselves beneath the desert sands for a thousand years …

Wrapped up in that pleasant daydream, he turned to wake Azania up and received a bop on the nose.

"I'm awake."

"Do roses not sleep?" he grumbled.

"Lightly," said she, already strapping on her sword and checking her braids.

"You look perfect, Princess."

"Whoever imagined you'd turn out to be such a nice Dragon?" she teased, with a pert flick of her fingers beneath his chin.

Gnarr.

THUNDER O DRAGON

"Ooh, I quiver in fear."

An hour later, they arrived on Juggernaut's patch of the desert, which as far as patches went, was not a great deal different to most other patches. Sickle-shaped obsidian dunes, sculpted over aeons by the desert winds, lay pristine in the moonlight. Even at this hour, his outspread wings warmed at the heat radiating off the surface. Everdeep landed a few hundred paces away, further along the base of the dune. They glanced at one another.

Ready.

At their signal, the scouts placed cone-shaped listening devices against the ground and bent their ears to the task.

Three … two … one … GRABOOM!!

After a few moments, the scouts raised their heads and waved a negative.

Nothing. Just like the day before.

Twenty minutes later, the thirty-four Sea Dragons helping to quarter the area lifted off, headed for Aria's patch.

Nothing, once again.

On the way over to Azerim's patch, he told King N'chala that his desert was a big old place. The fellow had the cheek to comment that even a Dragon might need to learn patience here in the deep desert. A Dragon! Patience? The nerve of the man.

Suddenly, an idea fired up his brain, so much so, that Azania flinched on his neck. *Ouch! Thundersong, what was that?*

A moment, Princess.

Turning to Everdeep, he called, ≈*Do you remember how you taught me to find Sea Serpent eggs? Remember? You tracked and traced the echoes.*≈

The huge Sea Dragon rumbled, ≈*Of course, but how's that applicable out here?*≈

≈*This is an ocean —*≈

Several of his Sea Dragon kin began to josh him but Everdeep quieted them with a sharp word.

Flushed in his fires, Thundersong said, ≈*Imagine this is like the ocean. The rock below the sand is the ocean floor, while the sand itself is like water. What we need is not a map of what lies above, but what lies below, unseen. Right? Peaks. Troughs. Watercourses. Caverns …*≈

≈*AYE!!*≈

The great Dragon's thunder boomed across the desert with enormous power, causing many of his kin, never mind the Rangers and N'chala's scouts, to cry out in shock.

Everdeep said, ≈*You're right. We just weren't … listening right.*≈

Landing, he and Everdeep briefed the scouting party about his idea, which they grasped at once. However, their deployment to test and identify the under-sand structures took time and it was several hours before they worked out that they stood right in the middle of a vast inland sea of sand, in places, up to three miles deep. Surely, no living creature, save a Bloodworm, could move through here and any tunnelling would be impossible to shore up and keep safe for passage?

However, twenty-five miles away to the west, the Sea Dragon soundings had identified a kind of hidden plateaux that, in just a few places, stood exposed, according to N'chala's scouts, and it was to this that their thoughts turned.

"Azerim's patch," Thundersong noted, pointing to the area on the map with his foreclaw.

"Right on the fringe," Juggernaut observed.

"I'll still take the plaudits," Azerim grinned, "even if they're only marginally deserved. What do you say, Farizam?"

"I say my patch is right next door. Let's see the Vaylarn Archipelago take this one."

They exchanged hand slaps.

"We still haven't found anything," N'chala challenged.

"Do we want to?"

THUNDER O DRAGON

At Princess Azania's sobering reminder, they flew westward in silence.

The soaring suns turned the dark desert into an oven. No creature could have walked through this and lived, Thundersong knew, not even with the help of coldstones. In the heat shimmering and shifting slowly from the south, there was no hint of respite.

As they had done numerous times already, the Sea Dragons spread out across the sands, taking positions every few hundred Dragon paces to both parallel and cover the area of the hidden rock formation. The sand was mere ripples several feet tall here, hardly even worth the moniker of dunes. Thundersong adjusted his spectacles as he peered about, checking the Dragons and Riders as they deployed over an area of perhaps a square mile. His scales prickled with that awareness he sometimes experienced. Could this be the place?

He was on the cusp of speaking a warning when the Sea Dragons began to make their deep, sonic blasts, directing them down into the sands beneath their paws, while others listened with their ear canals pressed to the sand, interpreting the echoes that returned.

Once more, their fishing expedition had failed to land a catch.

Everdeep, however, had other plans. He commanded the group to take up positions another half-mile to the west where he said he sensed a difference in the lay of the hidden plateau, perhaps a weakness or a fault line. After flitting over one more time, the Dragons arranged themselves in a now-familiar routine to quarter the ground and ensure that no effort went to waste. Numbers of the Isles Dragonesses landed as well in order to rest their wings and the Rangers stood aside from the Sea Dragons as the booming sonic effects were hard on the eardrums, despite that they wore protection.

Thundersong watched and listened. He was starting to get the hang of the echoes. Definitely something down there, more jagged than before. He murmured to Azania, *I wonder how many secrets these dunes cover?*

She kicked the stippled black surface with her boot. *Very many, I suspect.*

BOOM! BOOM! came down the line, low cracks of thunder echoing across the stark, empty desert. N'chala jotted notes busily on a scroll as Juggernaut drifted along above, relaying the Sea Dragons' soundings to him.

Our turn in a moment, Azania noted, before her voice rose in shock. *What was that?*

Thundersong stared at his paws. *Earth tremor? I don't like –*

Without warning, a whole section of desert quivered and dropped a pawful of feet. A low, hissing sound began to rise from beneath paws and boots.

He snatched Princess Azania off her feet. She clung to his wrist, shouting in alarm.

Juggernaut thundered, TAKE OFF! GET ON THE WING!

Everdeep boomed, ≈*AWAY!*≈

The tremor hit a second time, much harder than before. Sea Dragons, scattered across the sands like white gulls, whirled to seek their Riders, plucking them up, spreading their wings as they suddenly fought for footing in sand that had turned to soup. Thundersong saw at least three or four Rangers drop out of sight as if they stood upon water. Quicksand? All along a long, narrow depression that had appeared in the sand about a hundred paces off to his left wing, Dragons and people sank with terrible speed, some up to their knees or their necks, some writhing to free wings or tails.

Sand poured down into that depression as if an hourglass had suddenly been tipped over and begun to flow.

The cacophony was awful, the effect more terrible still. As if the previously solid ground had developed a maw attached to a vast appetite, it sucked everything away. From both sides of the depression, Dragons bellowed and thrashed as the heavy sands pulled them inexorably into the centre, where they were rolled under, crushed and buried as the avalanche gathered pace.

Snagging Azania in his paw as he too, began to slide with the sand already clasping his knees with hot fingers, Thundersong whirled and stamped his way free. *Dragons, with me!*

Catching Aria beneath the belly, he steadied her and then flung her into the air with a massive heave. She shook violently, spraying sand about as she gathered height. The treacherous, sliding slope pitched further and further as the sands sucked away but this also gave the powerful Sea Dragons a chance to swim out of danger – many did, instinctively treating the sand as if it were water, pulling free with companions clutched in paw or clinging to necks. Thundersong could no longer hear himself think. Untold millions of tonnes of sand poured like a waterfall into that depression, with a roar so loud that it shook his bones. His kin thundered but could no longer be heard. He saw Lovesong shake free and pause, despite being in mortal danger, to help Eversong shake a buried wing free and take to the air. White paws scrabbled in the slope, pulling out several more Rangers, including Sankir Farizam.

Azerim? Safe!

Eversong dived for the narrowest part of the gap, where a sand maelstrom churned as the phenomenon gathered pace.

Thundersong gasped. *Oh no!*

What's he doing? Azania screeched.

Jainrielle! I just saw her wing disappear down there!

The Sea Dragon dived for the Dragoness he had been courting without thought for his own safety, landing headfirst where twin waterfalls of sand ground away, pouring into an unknowable space below. His paws reached deep, cupping, driving beneath his quarry. Thundersong saw Everdeep. Mouth agape in a bellow of horror, he clapped his wings together with a surge of power and began to sprint over, but the sole of a boot sliding in the sand caught his attention. He swooped, catching a foot in his hind paw. A shake and a wriggle, and he carefully hauled out a young female scout, one of N'chala's crew.

One must be careful not to tear a Human in half.

Azania called, *Good job! Give her to me.*

Thundersong transferred the unconscious young female into his forepaws, gazing over at Everdeep as he flapped above Eversong, now buried up to his haunches in shifting sand. Eversong undulated his body like a fish, his tail end sinking deeper and his wings buried beneath the sand avalanche, while his front half curved upward with immense power and eventually, Jainrielle's muzzle popped out. Her eyes were wide, dark with terror; she coughed weakly and spat to clear her mouth.

Eversong shovelled her to the surface, where Aria and Everdeep caught her up, but the movement drove him deeper.

GET UP, BROTHER! Thundersong bellowed.

Sand poured over the Sea Dragon, inexorably dragging him downward. He had learned how heavy water could be. Sand must be many times worse. All that could be seen of the young white Dragon now was his upraised forepaw, gripped in Everdeep's left paw.

≈*HELP ME!*≈ the great Sea Dragon roared.

Thundersong found himself there, somehow fighting to keep his wings free and his paws digging in deeper as the sand sifted relentlessly away beneath him. His half-brother roared in anguish from below. His body – what he could reach – felt as if it were stuck in stone. Not even Everdeep's great strength could shift him. The two would-be rescuers were in danger of being sucked in as well. Everdeep raged and bugled in distress as another sudden lurch sucked Eversong completely under. With the landslide gathering pace, Everdeep's forelimb disappeared up to his shoulder in a matter of seconds. At Azania's urging, Thundersong himself only just managed to claw his way to safety from the insidious pull.

Everdeep lost his grip. He came up spitting sand and thundering, ≈*NO! EVERSONG! NOOOO!*≈

≈*You have to get out!*≈ Thundersong roared at him. ≈*Brother, o brother …*≈

When Everdeep did not respond, perhaps overcome by grief, he cracked open his jaw and hit his left flank and then the half-buried hindquarters area with sonic blasts, both shocking his dam's mate and providing enough vibration to shake him free.

He and Everdeep took off heavily from the gushing sand slope, sharing a single, aghast glance.

How many had they lost?

What was down there beneath the desert?

CHAPTER 22

SANDS ARISE

WHEN ALL THE SHOUTING, gnashing of fangs, weeping, roaring, self-recriminations and fury were spent, King N'chala gathered his advisors, as the suns set on a blisteringly hot late afternoon, on the open portico overlooking the Palace gardens.

Thundersong rubbed his breastbone. Had the Skartunese quarried out his hearts and left him hollow, this sense of despondency would be far less acute. Thirty-one souls buried alive. Seventeen Dragons and fourteen Humans. Seven of his Sea Dragon family, including one of his five siblings, all of whom had chosen to fly south with them. Unreal numbers. King N'chala received a late report from his scouts, his dark face never graver. A king – well, this king – wore his losses in the lines of his face. Did the burden of rulership fall so heavy, ageing a man a dozen years in as many hours?

He said to Azania, "What grates me the most is that we lost so many without chance even to raise paw or hand in battle. It just … it feels –"

"As if their lives were cheated from us, not even stolen or honourably spent," she said.

"Aye."

"We will avenge them and bring honour to the memory

of their souls," the Princess added. She flushed slightly as she realised her words had rung into silence.

King N'chala nodded. "Well spoken, sister. I have just received report of a sinkhole developing out to the West, almost in a direct line with that –" he paused, searching for the right word "– that sand slide we triggered earlier. My scouts and Aria's Dragonesses concur. They think the Skartunese are digging their way out."

Farizam ground his teeth audibly.

"I need to go check this place," Juggernaut growled, leaping to his paws and spreading his wings.

"A moment, Juggernaut," N'chala said.

He snapped, "If they are about to emerge, we should seize the advantage!"

"Agreed," Everdeep rumbled.

"We all agree," N'chala said. "However, I am not in the mood for any further surprises. I need ten minutes of your time. Collapsing their digging might be an excellent tactic, but we still have no idea what may lie below. We should be prepared, at the very least, for Bloodworms and Talon Clan magic – who knows what else? Thoughts?"

Sirensong said, "We attack their diggings with care and aerial cover."

"I'm with her," Everdeep said.

"Go in loaded for Bloodworm," Thundersong said. "That oversized crossbow you carry, Everdeep, should be just the perfect talon against those beasts."

"No-one goes in on foot or paw," Juggernaut added. "Not yet."

"Good point," N'chala approved.

Princess Yuali said, "I've relayed the reports to the other citadels as you requested, my King, and received all confirmations."

"Thank you – Chanize?"

The woman paused her whispering to Sankir Farizam, who had leaned over her wheelchair to hear. They whispered briefly, before he suggested she make her point.

The seamstress did not appear comfortable with speaking in front of the group, but she cleared her throat and said:

"I'm not very experienced, but I was just suggesting to my husband that we should check for similar activity around the other Citadels and –" her face formed into a desperate, apologetic grimace "– I was thinking, I'm sorry, especially those that rest upon sand. Their walls could be collapsed in minutes if they were undermined … in the same way. So, evacuation plans should be made ready, see? I'm sorry!"

Thundersong swallowed back a string of swear words. "Good thinking, Chanize!"

Her high colour said, 'Good? This is terrible!'

"Thank you, Chanize," N'chala said, plucking several hairs out of his beard and then glancing at them as if surprised by their appearance in his hand. "Juggernaut, Aria, can you arrange the patrols? We need to know if anything's coming up underneath or near our other southerly Citadels – G'nandu to the west and easterly, V'antu, J'zabur, N'gurma, but skip Tha'gunli and Z'bora. Since they were razed last year, we put all rebuilding works on hold and deployed our labourers to other locations."

Azania said, "There's no Watch, brother? No men at all –"

The King sighed. "Missed that. *Don't* skip those. Princess Yuali, would you draft and send missives to this effect, please?" She nodded. "Include the need to be ready for evacuation and for Tha'gunli and Z'bora, order immediate evacuation. I'll sign and seal them as soon as you're ready."

"My King."

"N'chala, please," he said.

"Not before we are married," the Princess of Amboraine said, stroking her blonde hair nervously. "It is not proper."

N'chala smiled at his fiancée. "Huh, and I thought I was the old-fashioned one. Since when should a King of the Desert teach anyone modernity? Anon, my sweet – ahem."

"I've a monopoly on sweet around here," said Azerim, grinning at Azania.

"Your sweet little desert dagger?" said she, drawing chuckles from the group.

On this note, they quickly made ready to fly out. Yuali had been assigned a small team of scribes, so she dictated and wrote one message scroll herself while their quill pens scratched assiduously, rapidly copying the missive. They sanded the wet ink more out of habit than need, for the days' heat sucked the ink dry before their eyes, then rolled up and sealed the scrolls and passed them to the falconers.

Aria touched Thundersong's shoulder gently. *Have Sirensong or Everdeep arrange to have one of the Sea Dragons listen below this citadel, alright?*

Do you think – he began.

No surprises, she and Azania chorused. The females shared the type of glance no sane Dragon would ever walk between. Danger of losing a body part.

He said, *Then, let's privately let Azerim and N'chala know what we're doing. No need to alarm the populace, but we should inform our leaders as they consider the worst.*

Poor Chanize, the Princess said thoughtfully. *Thinking the worst doesn't mean you* want *the worst. I suspect she thinks herself the most awful person in all T'nagru for raising that particular point.*

Speaking of which, where's your sister been? Thundersong asked her.

Azania gaped at him.

Since we were thinking of the worst …

His version of the worst turned out to be that Inzashu-N'shula had become absorbed in working with the Tamarine Dragons they had previously rescued from the

Skartun army under Jabiz Urdoo. They complimented the young Princess on her knowledge and tenacity. Thundersong exchanged wing-slaps with them and briefly retold the story of how he had ended up being mostly white, by which time Juggernaut was champing fire between his fangs to get moving.

As it turned out, gazing at a large, inverted cone of sand was less than exciting.

Seen by the dying rays of Taramis in the early evening, the hundred-and-fifty-foot deep cone grew steadily, perhaps by a couple of feet an hour, in diameter, they estimated, the sand slowly sucking away into realms unknown.

Everdeep and two Songs popped down to take measurements. He returned shortly to say, "It's not even deep here. Only two hundred and twenty feet. What's down below that is anyone's guess. It sounds like rock strata but if these Skartunese know how to drill through stone …"

Azania said, "It looks like an antlion's nest."

"What's that?" Azerim asked.

"It's a small insect that makes cones much like this. Usually, the creature's smaller than the size of my fingernail. The cone's about two inches across. It's basically there to trap crawling insects. They fall in, exhaust themselves trying to climb out and eventually fall toward the middle where the creature snaps them up for lunch."

N'chala said, "You're saying there's a creature down there?"

"It wouldn't surprise me."

"Something large enough to swallow a corner of a city?" he asked, not mocking in the slightest.

Several of his scouts gasped aloud.

Inzashu said, "Your Aunt Ignita taught us, Thundersong, that dark magic practitioners are obsessed with creature magic – essentially, they believe that living structures hold magic more efficiently than inanimate ones and larger structures, more efficiently than small ones."

He shrugged with his wings. "Which means?"

"They try to augment animal growth with dark magic."

"Ooh. I see. Big scary spiders?"

Inzashu said, "I can see why he needs a good kick every now and again, sister. No, Thundersong – to be honest, I don't really know. That kind of magic was always a rumour when I was growing up and I wasn't much one for monsters in the dark. I had my mother and, trust me, her meddling with everyone's minds was plenty to deal with."

He said, "I'm sorry." Azania echoed the same.

The airborne Dragons circled the cone uneasily, exchanging glances as much as they gazed across the desert, each thinking different thoughts.

"Thundersong?"

He glanced back at Inzashu-N'shula. "Aye?"

"I'm not sure there's anything down there – nothing living anyways. I'm trying to penetrate the sand but it's very difficult. Like chewing a mouthful of horrid stodge."

They tried together, but she was right. A Dragon might better attempt to fly through a mountain of sludge. However, he too could neither detect anything living down there nor find sign of dark magic. They agreed that no-one would believe that for a second. Everdeep tried a few sonic effects, which accomplished nothing at all, and then Juggernaut set up a watch schedule and they returned to N'ginta Citadel to chew the fat, as Dragons would say.

Nothing to it but to run a few drills and then turn in for the night, with all the sentries – on the wall, drifting above and around the city on the overheated air and down at the bedrock level – on high alert.

Three days passed.

Silence and heat. Heat and silence.

"They're out there," Thundersong growled, far too early one morning to be thinking about lying in the garden with his eyes open, contemplating the gorgeous, starry desert sky. "Not a flea is moving on those sands, but I can feel them, Aria."

"Go to sleep."

"I can't."

"Need some distraction?" she purred.

He cracked an eye open a slit to ogle – ahem, regard with respect, that was – his gorgeous mate. Azania had slipped inside in the early hours to be with her sister, who had experienced a terrible nightmare. Her mother's doing? Maybe that was why he could not sleep either.

"Distraction sounds … wonderful but there are sentries everywhere. Literally, everywhere."

She said, "Aye. Shall we take a swim in the Sea Dragon cistern?"

"Am I not clean enough, Aria?"

Her heated laugh whispered into his ear canals as she leaned close. Very close. "Sea Dragons say that water is very … invigorating."

He gave her his quietest evil Dragon laugh yet, *Mwaa-haa-harrrggh.*

Most invigorating!

Afterward, they lay upon the stone steps as the ripples slowly settled in the cistern, lit by but one oil lamp at this hour. Thundersong caressed his mate and told her that even though he thought she was the most amazing creature in existence, he still feared losing her. She told him she'd look after his pretty paws. No problem.

A few minutes later, she said, *Are you angry with me, Thundersong? Stop twitching your tail.*

Huh? he grunted, hitting the high notes. *I'm not.*

Is this a Thundersong fib?

Cracking open his eye again, he frowned down at his sleek mate. *I'm not sure what you mean?*

It's obvious. Your tail's rippling the water.

My tail's on this side of you, he protested, tickling her flank with the tip, an intimacy no Dragon would dare except with his beloved. *I do try to tell the truth upon occasion, you know.*

Minor squabble it might be, but he felt unreasonably hurt by her accusation. He always did his best. He might not be some perfect-paws Isles male but Aria had known that about him from the very first moment she had tried to scare him right out of his scales. It had even worked, in retrospect.

He glared at the water, watching the ripples coursing across the dark, oily surface. If he and Aria had finished making ripples and he was not flicking his tail idly in the water, then what exactly …

ARIA! RAISE THE ALARM!

Aria leaped twenty feet into the air and landed in a befuddled heap next to him, snarling, *Thundersong! Don't you ever – what did you say? Why?*

Those ripples, Aria – what's making them?

She took one look at him and raced out of the cistern as fast as she could, bellowing at the top of her lungs. Given his relative size, he was a great deal slower than his dainty mate through the narrow tunnels, but then only one of them could shake N'ginta Citadel with his thundering.

The question was, what else could shake an entire Human city?

Thundersong emerged into a lower city thrown into chaos by the alarm. People rushed about helter-skelter in the pre-dawn gloom, all memory of drills apparently erased from their minds. However, he also saw signs of sensible organisation, especially up on the battlements where squads of soldiers moved with purpose and in the air above, where a Dragonwing raced westward to check up on something he could not yet see.

Rather than add to the confusion, he sprang into the air with a powerful vertical leap and twirled to face the direction that appeared to have attracted the most excitement.

No spectacles.

Marvellous example of an obsidian blur below with a lighter sapphire blue streak above as dawn began to peel back the arching vault of stars, never more perfect out in the desert – when one could see it. Well, one did not need spectacles for what he and Aria had been up to, which might be the last time, if things went sour. He thrust that thought away with an irritable snarl. This was no time to bring out the old, inwardly hostile Blitz.

Away, Blitz! Arise, Thundersong!

Tilting his wings, he hurtled down to the Palace gardens, where Everdeep thundered at the Rangers to get his treble Dragon bow strapped in place.

Azania stood at the ready, taut and – hmm. No Dragon was supposed to admire those leather trousers. Nevertheless, she looked perfectly martial in her light armour, saddle and bows stacked neatly on the grass beside her, despite that it could barely have been a pawful of minutes since Aria had raised the alarm.

As he rushed into his landing, she asked, *What kept you?*

I'd say, but it'd make you blush, he said, so smugly that she could not fail to miss his meaning.

With an exasperated snort, she threw the saddle at his neck. *You!*

Wasn't just me. News?

Disturbance out to the west. Not far below the surface. Bloodworm is my first thought. Shall we go and see?

Yours to command, Princess.

Hmm, that's an improvement in your attitude, she chuckled, buckling the neck saddle with an experienced hand. *Inza should be here any second. Says she has some ideas for us to try. She'll ride second with me.*

Good.

Inzashu arrived, wheeling a hand cart that held four oddly shaped metal barrels. Four Rangers helped her fit a temporary harness behind the secondary saddle upon his back. They were not too heavy, but liquid sloshed inside and Thundersong wrinkled his nose as a whiff of the contents escaped.

"What's that?"

"Magical-chemical bombs," she grinned.

"Widespread destruction?"

"That's the idea."

"Ooh, you are my new favourite Princess."

"Silence, you wicked turncoat," said Azania. "Mount up, Miss Usurper. Second seat, in case you're wondering about your station in life."

Thundersong pretended to whisper past Azania, "*Psst.* She'll be a Queen soon. Then you'll definitely be my favourite Princess, alright?"

A pair of diminutive boots kicked his neck. "Gee up, horsie!"

"I say, that is quite out of order," he snorted, fixing Azania with a baleful glare.

"Aye, horses don't exactly talk back," she said blithely. "Do spread your wings and do what you do best, Thundersong. The day grows no younger."

"As you wish, my chattering little neck ornament."

"Fighting talk," said she.

A true Dragon let his deeds do the talking. Executing a fast takeoff that snatched the breath from his Princess' lungs, he set his muzzle to the west, away from the sky turning pink behind his tail. Out there, Juggernaut's scouts reported disturbances beneath the sand – three parallel tracks of disturbance, in fact. His first sight of the moving mounds suggested Bloodworms. The mounds of dark black sand were fifty feet tall and well over a thousand feet long, burrowing at a Dragon's walking pace on a direct bearing for N'ginta Citadel.

He murmured, "About your little beasties, Inzashu?"

"Bloodworms, maybe," she said, scanning the phenomenon intently.

"Very hot Bloodworms then," he put in.

"Aye, and over twice as long as that one we destroyed before," Azania said. "Inza –"

The girl said, "Can't detect any trace of my mother down there. I'll bet you anything you like this is the war host – some kind of war host. We should go discuss the matter with a few of Everdeep's bolts. You and I will try to stop one in its tracks, Dragon … ah, Thundersong. Let's get above it – no, before that, a quick consult with Everdeep."

After checking in with Everdeep to help his team pinpoint the likely vulnerable locations, they left him hammering the moving sand with those massive quarrels, while he climbed again to about half a mile in height. On the way, Juggernaut dropped by for a briefing about what they had learned. Inzashu fixed fins and a point to one of her bombs. She explained that the idea was for her to drop the load into the Bloodworm's body from high enough to penetrate the sand and its thick hide. Thundersong would hit it with one of his fireworks at just the right moment – on impact – to hopefully blow the creature sky-high or, at least, blast a hole large enough to stop it in its tracks.

"I don't think the quarrels are working," Azania noted.

"Could be armoured; might not be a Bloodworm at all," Inza snapped. "Sorry. Just … focussed."

"Line us up, Azania," Thundersong said.

"Everdeep's reloading; still no sign of any impact," the older Princess observed. "Juggernaut's suggesting a few shots further back."

Inzashu said, "Good. Ready?"

"Ready!" Dragon and Rider growled as one.

"Bomb overboard!"

Thundersong watched the silver barrel drop away, the fins keeping it on a good track – mostly. Something in the build could not have been right because it veered steadily away from the hidden enemy. At what he judged to be the right moment, he unleashed one of his fireworks. It arced downward, homing in on the barrel as he touched it with his mind. And …

GRRAABOOM!!

"Nice shot. Hope that wakes them up," Azania said.

A great plume of dark smoke, laced with sapphire blue flames, rose from the impact site. Briefly, they saw segments of a Bloodworm shifting beneath the displaced sand, and perhaps a smear of green ichor, but the damage they had done was insufficient. It continued to press onward.

"Again," Thundersong said.

"Those fins were poorly designed," Inzashu said. "I'll drop this one without. A little lower, please."

In a minute, their second shot was underway. The Dragon watched with narrowed eyes, counting down his shot. Everdeep, having spent another round of quarrels, appeared to be landing alongside that second beast's path, along with ten other Sea Dragons, while a heavy force of Tamarine and Isles Dragons lurked above in support. Sonics? Excellent idea. Maybe that would force the beast to surface and they could work out what they were dealing with.

"Let's show them how it's done," he murmured.

Pursing his lips, he fired another brilliant white fireball into the pre-dawn sky. Down, down it shot, somehow seeming to slow in his perception although he knew it must be travelling at a tremendous speed. Inzashu's mind linked lightly with his as they observed, physically and magically, the intersection of bomb and pure Sea Dragon fire.

Half a second after the barrel vanished into the sand, his firework burrowed in behind.

GRRAABOOM!!

This time, the fountain of flesh was visible even from afar. The creature shuddered and ground to a halt.

"Shot!" Azania shouted.

Thundersong furled his wings. "Let's go take a look –

carefully."

His stomach lurched up into his throat as the gravitational forces of his quick descent made their effects felt. He eyeballed Aria, the beautiful creature hovering two hundred feet above Everdeep's back. She raised her paw in a signal. *THUD-THUD – THA-BOOM!!* Dull detonations reached their ears as the Sea Dragons worked their particular magic.

Suddenly, the sand fountained as the Bloodworm, perhaps reacting by instinct to the threat, surged up to the surface with a cunning sideways roll toward the attack. A wall of sand rushed toward the Sea Dragons, who were caught flat-pawed in surprise.

"No!" Thundersong gasped.

≈*MOVE!!*≈ Everdeep hustled his team out of harm's way in the nick of time. They floundered in the fine, flying sand but backed up, somehow evading the rolling wall of flaming Bloodworm flesh as it squirmed over the area where they had stood a moment before, crushing everything bar a set of fast-departing white tails.

Flaming? That was new.

Plus, it wore some kind of metal armour over the vulnerable brain node area, which was why the quarrels had not penetrated deeply enough to do real damage.

Azania cried, "Look! It creates a kind of crusty tunnel in the sand and it's towing something."

A very long grey-green – well, it must be a kind of organic pod – could be seen three-quarters buried in the sand behind that Bloodworm. A massively thick hawser anchored it to some harness arrangement apparently bolted into the Bloodworm's tail. Their own victim must have been dragging something similar but that was wholly buried – only, not for long. Already, he saw movement beneath the sand. Something was shifting, breaking open, the sand pouring away down the sides.

Thundersong frowned. "That substance …"

"It's the same as what we saw wrapping up that Sea

THUNDER O DRAGON

Dragon fledgling!" Azania cried.

"That's it! Terror Clan magic!" he boomed.

They watched in growing trepidation as a host of feelers and legs broke the surface, digging busily. Dozens of massive insects, beetles and cockroaches in the main, he thought, squirmed to the surface, closely followed by silver-armoured Skartunese warriors. The pod behind Everdeep's victim split open along its length like a pea pod, revealing an army standing ready in its belly, several thousand strong. The soldiers were mounted upon insects. They saw shiny black millipedes the size of Tamarine Dragons with huge, jagged mandibles projecting from their mouthparts, outsized orange beetles dragging siege weaponry and crimson scorpions, the size of houses, with stingers curved up above their backs.

"What the *freak* is all that?" Azania hissed.

"Bad news," said her sister.

With a mighty roar, Juggernaut unleashed his forces. *DESTROY THEM ALL!!*

CHAPTER 23

SIEGE

IT STRUCK THUNDERSONG IN that first second of comprehension, which cramped his gut and electrified his Dragon hearts, that this was nothing like the army which he had expected. Where were the foot soldiers, the static siege weapons and the Dragon thralls?

Then, he realised that an army of insects of that size might just run up and over the walls in three seconds flat. Took any siege out of the equation.

Brutally brilliant, if one looked at it from their perspective.

Gnarr-blergh evil genius! he snarled.

Princess Azania scrambled up onto his neck, manning – silly word; could it rather be 'womanning' – the Dragon bow mount. Meantime, Inzashu-N'shula worked through her limited knowledge of beetles, trying to work out what types these might be. As the insect-borne army found their thousands of legs, they skittered away across the sand, racing for N'ginta Citadel in the distance. Thundersong recalled what he had learned about 'First Mover' advantage in the Skartunese mindset. What might seem to be a reckless or even suicidal attack in his mindset, was brave and honourable in theirs. Just a difference of viewpoint.

The insects spread out, trying to thin and confuse the

pursuit. Juggernaut's Dragons swooped, the first volley of crossbow quarrels scything in with brutal effectiveness. All those hours of drills. He reckoned that over seventy percent of that first wave struck targets, smashing into the carapaces of beetles and scorpions, stopping them dead in their tracks. Their riders ate desert sand.

The next wave roared through, mostly Tamarine and Isles Dragons who favoured close combat. Suddenly, powerful spouts of white steam shot from a number of the beetles. The Dragons who were hit screamed in pain and slewed or fell immediately.

"Bombardier beetles!" Inzashu cried.

"Steam attack?"

"Chemical heat," she said, shuddering. "That's … brutal."

"Alright, Inza. Stay with us," Azania urged.

The Dragons were somewhat protected by their scales, but the steam was so hot that he saw a four-foot hole stripped through a Tamarine Dragon's left wing in seconds. Their Riders fared worse. Juggernaut roared at his team to target the beetles with crossbow bolts, while the Isles Dragonesses hit the millipedes and disabled the scorpions. Everdeep's massive quarrels skewered enemies like kebab sticks. A single hit was enough to take out any of the giant insects and he had three skilled Rangers on his back, each working a Dragon crossbow.

Azania's first shot punched into a millipede's midsection, knocking it over.

Passing just overhead at high speed, Juggernaut thundered, "What the blazes do you two heroes think you're doing? Go stop that other Bloodworm!"

The Princess muttered something rude, as did her Dragon.

They were just in time to see the famous Juggernaut battle-roll. King N'chala must have been transferred to another Dragon, because his back was bare. Curling up, the Orange Dragon suddenly spun himself sideways on his longitudinal axis and smashed into a group of millipedes with a crunch that echoed across the dunes.

"Ooh!" Inzashu gasped.

"Mashed insect stew," Azania whistled. "Watch out, here comes the cavalry!"

"More horsey jokes?" Thundersong complained as he surged out of the way of eight Isles Dragonesses shooting diagonally across his flight path. They mowed through what Juggernaut had left, finishing everything in sight – one was Aria, he saw, her *kaniaxi* blades reaping Skartunese soldiers like wheat.

"What's not to love about that, eh?" Azania sang out as half a leg whistled past her nose.

Her sister suddenly retched and decorated the sands with aplomb.

"Sonics ahead!" his Rider yelled.

Thundersong reacted instantly, not having seen six scorpions scuttling behind the low brow of a dune ahead, a touch to his right paw. Pursing his lips and stretching out his neck, he built the sound, as the Sea Dragons had taught him in a refinement of his first, instinctual attempts.

III – AMM – DEAATHH!! he bellowed.

The blast of his throat hit them like a windstorm. Plucked off their claws as the wind curled beneath them, the scorpions whipped up into the air, their riders screaming or slumping unconscious over their backs.

"Watch this," Azania hissed in the same moment, sliding a quarrel into the fray. It punched right through the head of a crimson scorpion, pinning it to the thorax of a second.

"Not bad, but I can do better," he said, puffing out a stream of hot white fire. "I call this technique '*toast*fully chargrilled.'"

"Oh dear," Azania groaned. "Gives a new meaning to fresh, in-flight Dragon snacks."

It was Inzashu's turn to groan.

Leaving the charcoaled remnants of their victims to

drop into the sand, they vaulted into the sky, on the hunt for that third Bloodworm. Vanished? Not for long. With the aid of two Songs that Everdeep had dispatched to help, they located the underground disturbance, still headed directly for N'ginta Citadel. It was too deep for Inzashu's remaining two bombs.

"Let's sing them aloft," said the younger Princess, rubbing her hands.

"What do you mean, sister?" Azania asked.

"Who's got the biggest Thundersong in this desert, I ask you?" she said. Guffaws! "You and I are going to do a big, bad seismic boom – otherwise, I'm afraid I'll be left feeling like the spare Princess around here."

He said, "Spare? Aye, there's an idea."

Azania stamped her foot on his back. "Murder's too good for you."

"Just evaluating my options," he grinned.

"I am not some random, spare *option!* Seriously, Dragon, how many times –"

"Will I wind you up?"

"Aargh!"

"Like a spring," he said, with maximum annoyance factor. "Right, so that's … Sweetsong and Lovesong, right? Just the ticket. Let's go sing that Bloodworm a sweet love song, shall we?"

Landing on the hot desert sands beside his two kin, Thundersong observed his dam flying out with a strong force to go see to the wounded farther from the city than their current position. Taking no chances, a strong escort flew alongside, dark shadows steadily gaining texture and definition as a gorgeous desert sunrise of pinks, oranges and reds brightened the horizon behind them.

No time for beauty. He and his kin quickly exchanged notes. The Bloodworm travelled over one hundred feet deep, slowly grinding its way along toward the rock shelf on which the Citadel stood. They assumed it would be forced to surface there. Given the run-around the warrior-carrying insects were still giving Juggernaut's numerically much smaller force, allowing this army to reach that position – perhaps half a mile from N'ginta – struck them as a poor idea.

"To work," he said. "Let's listen to Inzashu."

Her ladyship the allegedly spare Princess, had a number of ideas which they tried in quick succession – penetrative sounds, deep earthquake-like sounds, sonic detonations and dissonances that set the Sea Dragons' fangs jangling in their gums, they complained. Nothing. Azania joked sourly, 'Deaf Bloodworm?' Guess it had to be a possibility. They tried any number of different frequencies and effects, without success, glancing up more and more frequently as the great insect chase rolled past them and on toward the citadel, not so far distant now.

"Alright, this is ridiculous. Now I feel like the spare chump Dragon," Thundersong snapped at last. "Which part of me was supposed to be Sea Dragon again? Or, actually useful for anything?"

Just then, Chalice raced past in pursuit of Juggernaut. She called down, "Another Skartunese army is approaching N'ginta from the East on foot!"

"How do they hide whole armies in an empty desert?" Lovesong snorted.

Sweetsong, meantime, fixed him with a long, appraising look and murmured, "Thundersong …"

"Allegedly," he said. "Also known as Thunderminnow, Thundertiddler and he who paddles in the shallows of oceanic experience. How may I serve you?"

"Thunder … song," she mused.

Wonderful creatures, Dragonesses, but about as opaque as his scales at times.

"Oh, are you thinking what I'm thinking?" Azania said.

Gnarr. Inscrutability being a transmissible disease among the female kind! "Do please enlighten the rather blunter talon in the paw over here," he said, simultaneously sarcastic and pleading. Now there was a tonal nuance he had not ever imagined.

Sweetsong said, ≈*My song is sweet. Yours is thunder.*≈

≈*Which means …*≈

≈*The Name of your wave was always prophetic, Thundersong,*≈ she said. ≈*What if it is? What if your song … is thunder?*≈

≈*Real thunder?*≈ he spluttered.

≈*Just as your dam has a magical ability to sing creatures to sleep,*≈ she added.

≈*OH, YOU GENIUS!!*≈ he roared. Ahem. Sort of knocked her to her knees there. ≈*Sorry. Very sorry, Sweetsong, but you've just given me two keys to the castle –*≈ she stared at him without comprehension ≈*– erm, let's just say you've shown me a new wave, dear kin-sister. Two new waves!*≈

Turning to his Riders, he quickly translated the gist of their conversation. "So, I think I could make real thunder! Maybe. And Sirensong, she could sing Skartunese soldiers to sleep, given the right opportunity. Those are two techniques we haven't even begun to consider!"

"Sing them to sleep?" Azania asked. "And us? We'll be nodding off just in time to let the Skartunese horde make merry –"

"We'll work it out," he grumbled.

"Thunder first," said Inzashu. "Let's work *that* out of your system, Dragon."

Amazing how two sisters could have grown up hundreds if not thousands of miles apart, yet clearly shared the same aptitude for snark. He, Azania and Inzashu quickly worked through a set of mental techniques for the amplification of his sound waves – a bit like shaping a sonic firework, he thought, holding that concept lightly in his mind as they rapidly sketched out the details. It was not a Dragon's usual full-throated roar. In fact, he realised belatedly, the only way he could move the air fast enough to create the effect of thunder would be to cause it to vibrate far faster or perhaps to shoot a firework of a completely different kind – one based on Sea Dragon lightning …

Down into sand?
Blergh.
"No, let's work with that idea," Inzashu enthused.
Oh, alright. Anything for the keen young ones, he complained to Azania, who chortled briefly before her concern returned full force to his awareness. *Aye, I know,* he said. *Treat the jokes as a kind of self-defence mechanism against the fear, will you?*

A tiny hand patted his neck. *You're the best. Let's do this.*
GRR-BOOM!
Not really effective.
DA-DA-DA … BOOM!! DA-DA-DA BOOM!!

Now he just sounded as if he wanted to start a Sea Dragon dance. To his surprise, his kin walked up to press against him in the Sea Dragon way, Lovesong to his left flank and Sweetsong to the right.

≈*Together,*≈ said Lovesong.

≈*This is your wave, Thundersong,*≈ Sweetsong put in. She smelled salty, like the ocean.

≈*Lean on us. Lean on our magic,*≈ they chorused.

≈*Pardon me,*≈ he said politely. Leaning over, he took a deep, long whiff of that salty scent, a friendly gesture between Sea Dragons of the same pod. ≈*I see … ocean combers slowly rolling across the deeps, the restless power of tides, the majestic thunder of breakers upon the … argh! This isn't working.*≈

≈*Oceanic lightning storms!*≈ said Lovesong, a tempestuous picture of jagged violet lightning forking across black clouds standing clearly in her mind. He had never seen anything like it.

≈*Awesome!*≈ he growled.

With that, power suddenly waxed in that space he remembered behind his keel bone, the place he had once been forced to tear open to find his whitest, most beautiful fires. Azania had helped him that day. Now, he must be her strength, her bulwark against these invaders. He was very far from being able to do it all himself, but this bit, he could do. He knew it in his every Dragon heart.

Summoning up his rather paltry stores of self-belief, he fortified himself with the memory of that day. The way he had reacted when he feared Jabiz Urdoo might well have killed her. That incredible sensation of his white fires rising. The blazing-sweet pleasure of draconic revenge.

His long throat worked as if he had a great hunk of meat stuck down there. The deep pain became exquisite, an inner conflagration that, quite suddenly, lit even the brightening dunes around him with the light his kin were capable of. For a millisecond, because of Sweetsong and Lovesong, perhaps, he thought he touched that mystical quality of *y'liss-al-horyam,* the extraordinary characteristic of Sea Dragon magic that gave the Lumis Ocean its very radiance.

Holding back as long as he could, he forced the power to build, to feel and rebel against the constraints.

He was sure he'd end up looking like a bug-eyed toad. Or, constipated.

With that, his intended explosion of mirth turned into an explosion of a very real sort. *KER-AAA-KABOOM!!*

Thundersong pitched forward rather indelicately, right on his nose, and wondered why the whole desert had just turned black …

"Knocking yourself out is absolutely not the idea!" Aria roared, spitting with rage. "Thundersong! Azania! Whatever were you two thinking? Inzashu? What do you have to say for yourself? How do you feel, Thundersong?"

"Like I've a hammer whanging the inside of my head every time someone speaks. What … hit me?"

"Your own stupid paw!" his mate growled.

"Half the desert!" Juggernaut snapped.

"My stupid – half of what? Why does everyone sound so far away? I'm fine – my head hurts a little, but I … I can fly."

Squirming up to his paws, Thundersong promptly toppled over onto his side.

Guess that went well.

Aria said, "Fine, was it?"

"Oh … alright, own up, you lot. Who or what walloped me; why's my head swimming off my shoulders and why's … oh. Oh! Someone tell me that Bloodworm's feeling a whole lot worse than me?"

"Nothing moving down there," Inzashu said.

Squeezing his eyes shut against dawn's dazzling gaze, he heard a touch of smugness in her voice and more so, the glares that Aria and Juggernaut turned upon her. Sizzling glares.

The younger Princess said meekly, "Well, it worked. Nothing left alive down below, as best I can detect. We just didn't expect the auditory backlash to be violent enough to knock him out. I've a headache the size of Solixambria too, if it matters."

"Nobody cares," Aria purred.

Thundersong appreciated both the tone of rebuke and his mate's evident relief that he had not done himself worse damage than – this. Judging by the state of his sense of balance, he was about to take a long walk back to the citadel, for he felt as if he had detonated that thunderclap right inside his own head. Probably had, actually. Either that, or the sand right in front of his nose had done the trick. Maybe there was a reason thunder preferred clear air miles away from something that could bounce it right back again?

Cracking open an eye, he found himself lying on a sheet of obsidian glass.

The Dragon reflected back looked in worse shape than he felt, to be honest. Golden Dragon blood had leaked out of the corner of his mouth and pooled around his muzzle. His eyes had a glazed, unhealthy cloudiness within the usually vibrant fire orbs.

THUNDER O DRAGON

Snuff his mortal fires, this thunder power was nothing to play with.

"What's with the glass mirror?" he asked.

"Your lightning power did that," Azania said.

"Lightning?"

"*Kerzap,*" she clarified, which thankfully, was as much science as his brain could contemplate just now.

Wobbling up onto his paws, Thundersong discovered the joys of trying to walk while absolutely drunk. Thunder-drunk? Whatever the case, the horizon would not stand still, his four paws kept trying to amble off in different directions despite his best efforts to make them behave and his speech emerged noticeably slurred. A suggestion that this was just the type of Dragon Ariamyrielle Seaspray might love best, earned him a firm nip on his tail. Point made, pointedly.

Given that Skartunese armies kept popping out of nowhere, he needed to return quickly to N'ginta Citadel. An attempt to lean on an Isles Dragoness ended in an embarrassing squashing episode. After that, Everdeep called in his family. Echosong and Ripplesong, both younger than him but ten feet longer and tonnes heavier, took charge of their errant half-brother with a combination of encouragement and nursing of the biting sort. A firm shoulder upon either side kept him on track. That left only the pitching forward onto his nose, which he did with frustrating regularity.

Ripplesong sang her Sea Dragon healing magic gently over him and they soon joined with a second group of wounded walking in with Sirensong.

≈*Overdid it there, son?*≈ she inquired smokily.

≈*A touch,*≈ he admitted.

≈*Good oftentimes does not come without struggle,*≈ she said wisely, causing his scales to tingle as she checked him over with her magic.

Thundersong nodded slowly. Perhaps so. He was one of the fortunate ones, in truth. Some of the other injuries in this group were far worse than his. Four Dragons could not walk at all and were being stretchered in on smooth pallets that slid along the sand. One Grinder had a foreleg burned to the bone – he had no idea how a Dragon even recovered from an injury like that. Another Isles Dragoness had heavy wrappings over her face. She must have been hit full in the face. A soft inquiry had his dam shaking her muzzle. How did a blind warrior continue in their culture? How might she be valued?

Worse were the bodies covered in cloth wrappings. Dragons who would never roar again, Humans who would never laugh again. War never discriminated. It took without ever giving back. A Dragon wondered what it was that drove creatures to war and moved some to the love of war. Was there any more terrible endeavour of man or Dragon under the suns?

Unfortunately, he had more than enough time to reflect upon this over the following days. While his brain state improved – a brain fog, Inzashu had called it – his sense of balance did not. He could not even take a drink without threatening to fall over.

N'chala and Azania put a ferociously grumpy Dragon to work on administration. His favourite. Never mind that he wanted to be out there chewing up enemies, testing out his thunder and winging Azania to the stars. Never mind that his pedantic penchant for particularity lent him real strengths in this area. Never mind that he and Princess Yuali formed an excellent team, honing a system for communication and logistics between the citadels that King N'chala assured him would save lives. He badly needed to wreak havoc and destruction.

For a Dragon once laughed at for his inability to raze a single grass blade, never mind an actual village, this was a novel contemplation. Most invigorating. His mood improved immediately.

For four days, this or that Jabiz turned up at the gates to threaten them with a range of horrible torments leading to the ultimate death. Not one specified a single condition for surrender. Not a word generally found in Skartunese vocabulary. On the third morning, Azerim's best archer used a crossbow especially developed by Garan and Yardi to place a bolt perfectly through Jabiz Maradoo's throat at a distance of over two hundred paces. The following day, Aria told him gleefully, the next Jabiz stood considerably further back. The Ranger still scored his shoulder with a bolt. This Jabiz did not flinch. Instead, he spent the rest of the day having his army lob wicker baskets filled with killer wasps up into the city. The Dragons rushed hither and thither, trying to flame the baskets before impact.

Seventy-three people died from wasp stings alone.

Three armies came up against the other citadels, while six assaulted the capital. That fourth day was also the moment they learned that N'gurma Citadel, under command of N'chala's brother Prince Aragu, had fallen, its walls undermined by creatures burrowing beneath. Forewarned, the citadel was evacuated in good order by a massive, day-long airlift of Dragons to the nearby fortress city of J'zabur. For good measure, the Dragons airdropped stones, debris and even cacti from the wastelands on the enemies' heads while travelling in both directions.

As it turned out, even Skartunese warriors did not enjoy becoming the targets of accurate Dragon fire.

The other armies camped around N'ginta and busied themselves with the matter of putting the fortress city under siege. Azerim or Azania came to brief them at regular intervals. These armies, under separate leadership, were conventional in structure and composition. Each morning, as if triggered by sand running out of an hourglass, they charged up to the walls with a roar and beating of war drums fit to wake the dead, never mind the living, raised their ladders, threw their grapnels and tried to scale the battlements in great, seething masses of men.

The defenders' job was to make their lives as miserable as possible. Arrows, spears, stones, burning oil – whatever it took. The carnage mounted up daily, but under this kind of assault, there was relatively little danger to the defenders even though the pressure was intense at times. With the support of Dragons, they dealt efficiently with wall breaches but a couple of times the remaining insects scaled the battlements in the dead of night.

To Thundersong, it felt as if something must be waiting to happen. This assault was of relatively little consequence, perhaps only a softening-up process. At the strategic meeting that evening, he put this viewpoint to his friends, who all agreed. A greater danger by far lurked out there.

Nahritu-N'shula the Psyromantic Mage and the Terror Clan Dragons. Where were they? Where was the dark magic?

CHAPTER 24

NIGHT TERRORS

THE DAY AFTER A palace wall and Thundersong's nose became better acquainted than he would have preferred, he woke two hours before dawn to a whiff of cool air – correction, cooler air – greeting his nostrils. Even a briny tang of moisture. Rising with great care, so as not to disturb his mate or Princess Azania, both sound asleep after flying innumerable sorties the previous day, he stretched languorously and discovered that the treacherous ground – for once – neglected to attempt to swap places with the sky. Oh! All well again? Balance good?

Testing his reflexes, he padded in a quick circle on the palace lawn. Perfect. He could even catch his own tail, a game that Dragon hatchlings loved to play.

After another experimental wing check, warming up his shoulders, he raised his wings and coiled upon his hind legs. He adjusted his spectacles. Ah! Drawing his silencing magic about him, he whispered aloft as if silently shot from a catapult. Pleasing.

Barely disturbed a grass blade.

Stealth Dragon.

Chuckling at his inane ideas, he shot into the still-dark cathedral of sky, working on maximising his stealth technique, which he shortly decided ought to be called draconic stealth mode. A way in which a largely white Dragon could steal about a black night sky without standing out like one of those fireflies he had seen the previous evening, as the starlight gleamed off his fetching white scales.

Ah, the perils of outrageous handsomeness. How he suffered.

Circling wider, he peered down at the deployment of Skartunese forces across the moonlit dunes, spectacularly stark as their brows stood outlined by the faint, diffuse light. Was it his imagination or was that a great many more soldiers than Azerim's scouts had tallied and reported the previous evening? Having not seen himself, he could not judge – but a slow prickle of awareness spread along his spine from the base of his skull right down his tail. Something was not right here. He clipped his wings, rising higher. In fact, something stank like rotten fish.

Literally.

As if he had passed through some opaque atmospheric layer, Thundersong suddenly barrelled up into the midst of a flight of Green Dragons. More Greens than he had ever seen in his life. They were as startled to see him as he was to see them.

What the – almost mewling in the grip of icy talons of fear, he spun in place, finding Dragons hemming him in from every direction. Snuff his mortal fires! Where had these fishy – these foreign – these Terror Clan Dragons come from?

Terror Clan!

He stared at them, all five hearts thumping away in his throat as if they had lumped together to make a bid to escape his body. Hundreds of flaming crimson and yellow eyes stared back, but among them was one white Dragon. He wore a metal cage upon his head, but from behind their barred confinement, Thundersong could clearly make out his eyes, almost black with pain.

For the first time in his life, he gazed into the eyes of a

Dragon in mortal fear of his life.

Eversong! he gasped.

He had mourned his half-brother's death. How had he escaped?

The woman seated upon his back spread her arms in a welcoming, mocking gesture. "Thundersong! How nice of you to join us. Your brother has told me all about you and your … unique capabilities."

"Nahritu-N'shula!" he rasped.

Every barrier he had or knew, slammed up in anticipation of her mental attack. The woman simply laughed, loudly and long, even removing her battle helm that he might better appreciate the scorn writ upon her handsome features. Every bone in his body froze. He could not process Eversong's capture, his total submission to her power, the number – the sheer *multitude* – of Terror Clan Dragons filling the night sky right above N'ginta Citadel.

His mind cried out for Princess Azania.

She guffawed again. In a heavy Skartunese accent, she said, "You're pathetic, wailing for the Princess who twisted you into who you've become – a pitiable, artistic Dragon given a fresh coat of scales, but nothing can disguise the yellow-bellied, shrinking coward you've always been inside. You are nothing but a flying worm."

The Terror Dragons chortled cruelly at her insults. For a second, all he saw was an old Blitz being jeered at by his brothers, scorned by the younger females – that poor, gawky Brown Dragon of old.

"Aye, her mastery over you is complete. You see, women will always rule. They are born for it and you poor males will always remain our lackeys, servants and bootlickers. The Princess Azania is a worthy enemy. I shall snap her tiny neck beneath my boot."

He spat, "It's a shame you only have courage behind an army of thousands."

"Is that so? Would you challenge me?"

THUNDER O DRAGON

Drawing a great breath, Thundersong made to thunder his special challenge, but the Psyromantic Mage was faster. With a dismissive flick of her hand, she smote him out of the sky. Not a single Dragon of those surrounding him was touched. Only him. It was like being hit by a sledgehammer a hundred feet long, weighing multiple tonnes. He saw more stars than there could possibly be in the heavens.

As he fell away, he saw a cruel smile touch her lips.

She cried in a mighty voice, "After him, my Dragons! Rip off his wings and let him fall into the streets as my first warning to these craven fools!"

With a massed snarl that reverberated the heavens, hundreds of Terror Clan Dragons gave chase.

When every bone in his body begged to turn tail and flee in ignominious defeat, a Dragon should perhaps be moved to listen. When his wings refused to respond, his hearts should turn to ice. He should be Blitz the Fritz, panicked, helpless and alone.

Instead, he saw everything in fractured shards like the purest crystal.

He fell backward, his wings flapping uselessly, without volition. The Terrors winged after, a great wedge of green Dragon flesh pouring from the pristine heavens above the citadel he had sworn to protect at all costs. Above them, Nahritu-N'shula winged high, alone, supremely confident in her victory. Such hubris! Such ironclad self-assurance. Thundersong knew he must warn his kin. He must ensure that the city woke to the present danger – but if his wings failed him, he also knew that he must take as many of these creatures of dark magic with him as possible. Make his death count. A fall from this height, over a mile and a half above the rooftops, could only be fatal – unless his

THUNDER O DRAGON

Dragon kin caught him in time.

Where was the watch? Where was Chalice?

That was the detail he had missed – how could he have been so foolish?

He knew one thing. He must not give these Terrors a chance to suspect what he was up to. Aye, if he was Azania's lackey, as the Mage claimed, then he would do what he did best. Mindless imitation. Maybe he would just summon up his inner Princess, an idea which previously had incensed him, but now struck him as the most apt response possible to Nahritu-N'shula's claims.

He should be stronger, but her words *hurt*.

Allowing his wings to remain flaccid despite the speed of his fall, he summoned the power that had most recently knocked him unconscious.

Plummeting belly-up was a surefire way of inciting chasing Dragons to a killing rage. Thundersong saw the fires behind their fangs as the dark and medium green Terror Clan drew closer in pursuit, their body orientations far more streamlined than his, eyes ablaze with hatred, their talons already clenching in anticipation of rending him limb from limb and decorating the city with his leftover bits. The pain behind his keel bone speared deep, filling his chest with white-hot agony, but greater still was his fear of slamming down in a great splatter of blood and bone.

What a waste that would be.

Shortest song of thunder in history.

Therefore, he planned to give them a bravura performance. Truly, a Thundersong to remember.

As he heard a Tamarine Dragon down below bellow the alarm, he cracked open his jaw into the evillest smirk a pitiable, artistic Dragon could manage and let rip with everything he had.

KER-AAA-KABOOM!!

Thunder ripped from a clear sky. At the same time, Thundersong tried to protect himself with everything he had, but the air sucked away from his nostrils only to return in a fraction of a second like a gigantic buffet about the muzzle. Even though he had his ear canals firmly closed, the sound still detonated inside his skull, scrambling all his senses for long, long seconds until he was able to shake some sense into his head – just in time to hear a Dragoness screaming at him from somewhere that he realised must still be distant, but nonetheless set his brain matter alight.

Thundersong! Pull up!

He spread his wings and promptly had them smashed out of shape by a rain of Green Dragons. Grunting with impacts against his head, his shoulders and his tail as he tumbled muzzle over paws mid-air, Thundersong fought for clear airspace like the mad Dragon he most certainly was. He clawed, clambered, punched and bit his way through, despite realising that most of the Dragons around him were unconscious. Others, higher up, flew in dazed circles or strange, jinking patterns, clearly stunned out of their wits and bleeding from their mouths and ear canals.

Wings out, you –

Good thing he did not hear that last bit. Snapping open his wings at the very last instant, so late that he actually touched the Palace rooftop with his left wingtip, he cupped the air to arrest his tonnage into a landing that pounded paw prints ten inches deep into King N'chala's lovely, manicured lawn – right in front of Aria and Azania.

They gaped at him identically.

No-one said a word as Green Dragons plopped, thumped and *whomped* down throughout the city, caving in flat-roofed buildings or hammering down onto walls and cobbled roadways with horribly wet-sounding, fatal impacts. He had no idea how many. Dozens. Hundreds, perhaps?

"I found the Terror Clan," he said politely.

Aria tried to speak, but apparently, she was shaking too hard to actually form a coherent word. Thundersong had never seen that reaction in her before. Shock, disbelief and … horror, perhaps?

His head swung up. "That – that *was* Nahritu-N'shula."

Nothing about this made sense. Had she just abandoned her allies after his solo masterstroke? Or unleashed the remainder upon N'ginta Citadel? Juggernaut already led a flight heavenward to cut off the remainder of the Terror Greens. They appeared bent upon making a single, overwhelming assault on the city and were still hundreds strong. How did they field such numbers? His scattershot thoughts decided that they must be twice or three times as fertile as the Tamarine Dragons.

A small body landed upon his neck. *Shake a wing, Dragon!*

Warn the defenders! Aria cried.

DEFENDERS! he bellowed, at top volume. *TO ARMS!*

Azerim appeared at the run on the outside portico, armed and sword in hand. Azania yelled at him, "Terror Dragon attack! Get the populace under cover! We need support from the walls …"

Her voice trailed off as a barbaric cacophony of trumpets, horns and drums struck up on the sands outside the city.

This would be a co-ordinated attack.

Thundersong snapped, "Every Dragon! Get everyone aloft – they're targeting the walls."

"On it," said Azerim.

"With me, my King!" Sirensong landed deftly in the space beside Thundersong, somehow already saddled up and armed with a Dragon bow. The King's Rangers? Ah, Farizam flew aloft on Everdeep's back. Excellent readiness.

Quickly, they swung aloft. Green Dragons rampaged through the city in multiple locations, flaming anything that moved as they closed in on the catapult and ballista emplacements located on the outer and secondary walls.

THUNDER O DRAGON

The defenders, caught between the attack starting without and the Dragons within, were slow to respond, confused as to which way to point their weapons. Orange flame flickered over the flat stone rooftops as several caught alight, burning fiercely. He saw squads of knights from Vanrace, Garome and the kingdoms farther north drawing together to attack and slay the downed Dragons, hoofbeats and wild cries echoing through the cobbled streets.

Above, Juggernaut rallied the defence, bellowing orders in his best battleground voice. Quarrels spat at the marauders. Soldiers ran along the battlements, only to be plucked off and smashed to the ground or torn apart by the Terrors.

Follow me, Aria called quickly.

Teams of Isles Dragonesses flitted lightly through the rising smoke, falling upon Terrors only to have their *kaniaxi* blades slice through clean air as their dark magic caused them to flicker here and there. Isles Dragonesses and Tamarine Dragons began to fall as the wily Terrors ganged up on them, striking from unexpected angles.

Inzashu. Where's Inzashu? Azania cried.

Thundersong cursed. In the chaos and confusion, they had missed the younger Princess. She must be somewhere about but he could not sense her anymore. Had the mother executed another cunning kidnapping from beneath their very noses? As he observed the way the Terrors used the smoke and darkness as a cloak for their cunning, he became aware of an idea form in his Rider's subconscious. Clean air. Purity. Light. Aye, Azania was on the right flight path, as usual. Was there not a way to burn through their dark magic, to his dismay, a capability that mirrored the camouflage magic Sea Dragons were so adept at?

Guess his peculiar skills might come in useful for something after all.

Pretty fireworks, he said, crooking his neck. Up and up his ball of light arced.

THUNDER O DRAGON

What the — Azania spluttered.

Your idea.

Ah, incoherence in a Princess. How wonderful. She kicked his neck smartly, but her concentration did not falter for a second as she pinged a quarrel straight up the nose of a Terror Green trying to backstab Aria. The Dragon dropped away with a howl of agony that Aria cut off with a lightning-fast thrust of her right paw blade.

Shot! he growled. *NICE, ARIA!!*

The Cobalt Dragoness gave him a glare that made him realise that she did not need a cheerleader during battle. Maybe a wing-second or someone to tidy up the mess she inevitably left behind her.

With a muffled detonation, a shower of pinprick white sparks flowered over the city in great, shimmering petals of light.

Ooh, pretty, Azania gurgled, cranking her Dragon bow expertly.

Pretty sparkles for a pretty Princess, he cooed back, just as vacuously, and whirled to tail-slam a Terror who had snuck up behind them. He sank his fangs into the other Dragon's throat, snarling, *Sneaky, ugly brutes, aren't they?*

With a violent headshake, he snapped the other Dragon's neck.

The Princess slid sideways, yelping, *Thunder —*

Got you. Sorry.

Azania re-seated herself on his neck. *Guess saddles are useful for something after all. Let's go help Aria. Ready to prettify the place again?*

I'd bring down the very stars for you, Azania.

Her little heart did a flip-flop that he sensed through their connection.

The sparkling white fire-dust that emanated from his fireworks had its uses, somehow crumbling the dark magic protections the Terrors enjoyed. His third shot revealed an additional flight of Greens above the city, co-ordinating the attacks and providing magical cover and confusion.

Everdeep hurtled upward at the head of a team of hulking Sea Dragons to encourage them to find gainful employment elsewhere, which was not a concept Dragons intent on war tended to understand. They exchanged bitter, terrible blows, bites and mighty gouts of white and orange Dragon fire.

A bitter battle developed in the skies over the citadel, soon matched by a mad scramble for the walls as the Skartunese attacked at five different locations. Thundersong and Azania screamed around a full circuit of the walls several times, helping to stem the tide. He spurted his fire so many times, his throat glowed white-hot and became too dry. He had to pause to take on water. During that space, Dragon and Rider observed that the Terror Clan attack had finally broken and the remaining Greens had fled out into the desert. Everdeep, Aria and Juggernaut led Dragon counterattacks against the hottest points of conflict on the walls, dealing with the places where the professional Skartunese troops had established footholds, giving King N'chala's beleaguered defenders some measure of relief.

Over the course of several hours, as Ignis and Taramis made their combined heat felt once more, the defenders slowly regained full control of the city. Clean-up crews of Tamarine Dragons and soldiers rushed around dealing with downed Terror Clan Dragons, while the rest flew sorties against the attackers, quickly collecting dozens of minor arrow, spear and quarrel wounds. At one stage, Azania cried out; Thundersong glanced back to find her wearing a barbed Skartunese arrow in her hair braids on the upper left side of her skull. Blood trickled down around her ear.

"Nothing serious," she assured him quickly. "Only a flesh wound. Guess a helmet might have been a good idea, eh?"

"Could be," he agreed.

Quick as they were, the Dragons also made for large,

readily identifiable targets. As the Skartunese host pressed forward, their siege engines came into play, lobbing boulders up against the battlements and firing projectiles at the defending Dragons. The Terrors had done their job all too well. Over half of N'chala's static emplacements had been burned out. However, two attacks on the gates fell foul of his new oil spigots. Spray and burn. Dark smoke rolled up from the conflagration, smudging an otherwise perfect morning sky.

Thundersong decided he really did not enjoy the stench of barbecued Human meat. It was sickly sweet but without the savoury tang of wild pork.

"Stop that," Azania ordered.

"Stop what?"

"Thinking about the qualities of Human meat. It's disgusting," she said. "Look, Aria's calling us in."

Dragons gathered from all over the city. Most wore at least a few arrows in their hide; some had tattered wings or more substantial wounds from Skartunese axes and swords. The panting Sea Dragons took on water at Everdeep's gruff orders, while Sirensong and her healers checked them over, withdrawing two vocally frustrated Isles Dragonesses for urgent, life-saving treatment.

Calling them to attention, Aria said, "I, for one, am tired of being used for target practice. I'm calling for a sweep around the back of that force, like we planned – we go in hard and heavy, a ground and air assault which will take out every one of their siege weapons. Load up. Tamarine Dragons, get your armour on. There's going to be a great deal of paw-to-paw combat. Sirensong, I want you to ready a team to take on those captive Dragons we saw to the south."

"Consider it done," his dam said.

"How many?" Thundersong asked.

"Four dozen, at least," Aria replied. "None of the electrical machines, so far."

Thundersong scratched his unmentionables unhappily.

An arrow had penetrated a rather painful location. Azania hissed at him.

He mused, "My scales itch …"

"What now?" Everdeep growled angrily. "We've fifty problems to solve and you're –"

"Everdeep," Aria said. "This is Thundersong's 'ideas face.' Listen to him."

"Oh, I mistook that for indigestion," he rumbled, amused at her defence of her mate. The Cobalt Dragoness bared her fangs at him. "Speak, Thundersong – but quietly, lest you slay hundreds more of the enemy with a mere word."

To his surprise, the Dragons standing or hovering all around gave a great roar of approval. The Tamarine Dragons rumbled compliments, the Sea Dragons fluted excitedly and the Isles Dragonesses saluted him with drawn blades and their scale-shivering war cry, *HAAI-ARR!!*

A lesser beast might have admitted to a slightly goofy grin at their praise.

Sidling up to him, Aria tickled him beneath the chin with a fluttering wingtip and cooed, "That gives me an idea. Thundersong, since you're so very … *distracting* –" his fires blushed furiously as the Isles Dragonesses hooted with laughter at her flirtatious compliment "– and so devastatingly handsome, I do believe you should be the one to create a diversion while we make our assault."

"Uh … um," he just about managed.

Beautiful butterfly wings being the cause of an intellect snafu on his part.

Even Juggernaut chuckled at his bemusement.

Azerim and Yuali came dashing up. "Urgent message," he panted. Azania gave his hobbling a pointed look. He admitted, "Just about fell down the stairs. Sorry, my love. Yuali?"

The pale Princess flushed beneath the scrutiny of several hundred Dragons. "I … well, received a message from V'antu Citadel in the east. The Watch Dragons, including Chalice, turned up there about an hour ago, very confused but otherwise safe." Juggernaut puffed out his cheeks. "Long-range scouts to the east have seen no sign of Skartunese. The northerly routes and Chakkix Camp are safe. Garan Blacksmith is sending some more fancy weaponry down here. Says here … he has some ideas for bug spray?"

With a wry grin, Azerim put in, "Inzashu is missing. It seems this morning's raid might have been all about stealing her back. Or – sorry, sweetheart – she might have gone willingly. I don't –"

"Azerim!" the Princess wailed.

"I don't believe that, I was about to say," he said.

"I don't, either," Thundersong put in. "Azerim, why are you wearing full armour?"

"Because I am tired of limping about on this bad foot, that's why!" he growled. "I'll be better use to everyone on a Dragon's back – Yuali will tell you. Grumpy as a –" he chuckled and deadpanned "– as a Grinder Dragon who's been robbed of his favourite bone."

Azania gave him a measuring glare. Azerim turned on his most charming smile.

The Princess said, "One condition. No fancy clothing that proclaims you a King. Take off that rubbish and put on something plain."

"This is my favourite green surcoat!"

Juggernaut growled, "She's right. Why don't you just paint a target on your forehead?"

"Women!" Azerim grumbled and had to jump as Juggernaut made his annoyance at that comment plain. "I didn't mean you, Dragon – never mind. Sankir!"

"At once, Sire."

The Grinder added, "And you, Thundersong. No thunder. It tends to knock you silly – sillier than usual – in case you hadn't noticed. Stick to your usual mild egotism: 'I am Dragon!' 'I am so handsome!' 'I love my own reflection!' You get the idea."

That would be the notorious teacher cutting his student down to size with his equally notorious subtlety.

Thundersong asked, "Any other orders?"

"Aye. Pick a place the sand is softest and try out that other idea you had."

"Southeast quadrant," Princess Yuali said promptly. "We already had the Sea Dragons measure the sand quality and depth all the way around the city."

"Very good," said Juggernaut. "When we're ready, you'll go tease them in the southeast quadrant. Meantime, I'll have Strongfist the Crusher, a few Grinders … Destructa and Overkill, aye, and Flinryielle of the Isles, you four mix up those guerrilla hit squads we talked about. Go annoy the enemy with fast, incisive hits until we're ready."

They growled acknowledgement.

"Sirensong, healer squads?"

"Prepared," she said.

"Good. Azimyrelle, find King N'chala and brief him."

"At once," the light-yellow warrior Dragoness saluted. "Princess –"

"Main gates," Princess Yuali said.

Reaching out, Juggernaut patted her back in approval. "Does anything slip by you?"

The girl turned as pink as a desert suns-set.

As the preparations turned to a more belligerent, counterattacking mode, Azania and Thundersong discussed the matter of Inzashu in low, troubled voices. Nobody in N'chala's palace security team had any idea what had happened to her or how she might have been kidnapped. One obvious conclusion was the one that had upset the Princess so much she was leaking around the eyes and he could not blame her. The girl might have abetted her own escape. Worse, she might have been in cahoots with her mother the whole time and been playing them all along. Given her considerable mental gifts, it had to be a possibility. More than.

The tiny noises intensified into outright sobbing.

"Hug?" he offered gently.

"Dragon …"

"Allow me," said Azerim, doing the needful.

She breathed against his chest, "Tell me everything will be fine."

"Everything will be fine," he said, telling a big lie through his little teeth. "You'll see. It's actually a cunning plot on her part whereby she'll sneak into mommy's good graces and at the perfect instant, slip in the dagger sinister."

"Perfect," said Azania, adjusting his armour buckles. "Ready to fly?"

"Never more ready."

"Stay safe, alright?" she murmured, rising onto her tiptoes to steal his breath away.

Two minutes later, that tiny chin rose and with it, a certain Dragon's spirits, which hitherto had been languishing somewhere near paw level. The Princess gave him a look he knew very well indeed.

"Buckle up and double up on the ear protection," he said.

"Can't hear you," she grinned, swinging onboard. "Quarrels and oil bombs loaded. Spectacles?"

"Thank you, Your Highness."

"Only when I'm aboard you. Otherwise, I'm generally known as Your Tininess."

"They say the smallest packages are the most explosive."

He watched as Overkill the Grinder roared overhead with his squad of eight Dragons – four Tamarine, two Isles and two Sea Dragons – on their last pass along the northerly battlement where the fighting had been particularly arduous.

Juggernaut nodded at them. "It's time. Go sing our enemies a lullaby."

He and Azania nodded as one.

"Join us as we swing up from the west. Until then, you'll be the only Dragons on the northerly battlement, hear me?"

As the warrior Dragon turned away, Thundersong whispered to his Rider, *Hear that? You've been promoted.*

I know, she chuckled. *Princess Dragon Breath, at your service.*

He said, *Correction. That would be, 'Dragon Heart.'*

Perhaps a touch squishier than some, but a Dragon heart nonetheless.

CHAPTER 25

QUICKSAND

AT THE HOUR OF noon, Thundersong assumed a proud, majestic stance upon the northern battlement. Below him, a force of some four or five thousand silver-armoured Skartunese warriors seethed across the dark, powdery sands like waves rippling against the seashore – only, this shore was the towering battlements of N'ginta Citadel. The sound of their roaring was like great combers rushing in to pound rocks, but it came interspersed with sharper cries from some warriors, the ringing clash of weapons and the deeper-throated booming of rocks striking the battlements with monotonous regularity. The foot soldiers attacked with flurries of grapnels, arrows and the support of squads of archers on the ground and up in three hide-covered siege towers. The larger siege engines, some towering over seventy feet tall, stood at the back under light guard – stone throwing and projectile weapons in the main.

He knew that they would instantly become a target for every enemy but a true artist did not rush his moment upon the stage. Oh ... *blergh!* Whatever. Pretending he was indeed preening in front of a mirror, Thundersong struck a splendid, chest-popping pose, flatly ignoring some immature guppy's giggling behind his ears.

He thundered, *III – AM – DRAAAGOONN!!*

Sand exploded at the force of his shattering roar. Men fell over. Ladders toppled. One of the siege towers swayed, but to his intense disappointment, failed to tip over or summarily collapse in a heap of splinters. Most disappointing. Meantime, four dust devils danced off into the near distance, knocking over numbers of soldiers who had not been impressed enough by his initial blast. Unbelievers. Troglodytes!

Aye, the dictionary words will certainly impress them, Azania noted. *Quick strut to your left!*

He sidestepped rather nattily, as seen in retrospect, as a four-foot, rust-red sandstone boulder hurtled past his left shoulder. Without her timely warning, that would have been a mighty short performance. He spread his wings.

No. We promised Juggernaut!

That … that needs an answer! he roared.

Most certainly, which is why we're going to give them one. How's about you drop a firework on that nice mangonel?

Mangonel?

The trebuchet with the sling arrangement for hurling big, nasty boulders at our nice city over here.

Ah, a mangonel mangles things. I see. Sounds like my kind of equipment, he said dreamily. *That's quite a shot, Princess.*

Who's a devastatingly handsome Dragon then?

Me, me, pick me! he chortled, dancing along the battlement to the bemusement of attackers and defenders alike. In truth, the idea was to throw off their aim in case they had another go at splattering his brains halfway across the city. *You're such a nice Princess. Have I told you recently what a nice Princess you are?*

Totally, she agreed, popping a vector graphic of an arced shot into his mind. *How's this?*

Teensy adjustment … away we go!

The Princess of T'nagru provided a soft whistle of approval. *Sweet shot!*

The firework overshot its target by a matter of several

feet, but it struck something behind the mangonel – barrels of tar, perhaps? A few of those had been lobbed at the city, but since everything was made of stone, there was little to burn. Something began to burn fiercely back there; the little ant-figures, seen from this distance, dashed about trying to put the flames out. Thundersong assumed that they must have been saving the barrels for the excitingly flammable buildings of Vanrace. Either that, or they could set the local gas production facility alight, namely, Prince Floric's –

Dragon! You're despicable, Azania snorted. *Please don't put that in our memoirs, alright?*

Very good, Princess.

They gave a grunt of satisfaction as one of those barrels went up with a grand explosion and with it, the mangonel and half of its crew. Oily black smoke billowed from the site of destruction. Perfect.

You always were a Devastator, Azania noted.

Ooh, what was not to like about this Princess?

Taking aim, he fired a speculative shot at a second pile of barrels. One really should not leave one's rubbish lying about. Beautiful shooting, Azania approved. All thanks to her mathematical brain, he congratulated her. Raising the Dragon bow, she sighted along the wall and hammered a bolt through a Skartunese crew trying to fight their way over the top. The defenders cheered and jeered as the ladder toppled sideways. She cranked the Dragon bow immediately, ready for the next shot.

"Oil bomb?" Azania suggested.

"Fire away, Princess."

"Watch this," she said, deftly fitting one to the shaft of her next Dragon bow quarrel. Mournfully, she added, "Inzashu's design."

"Hold!" He danced another sideways step. Three four-foot quarrels whipped by. Those Skartunese were decent shots. "That area, right at the base of the ladder?"

Azania lit the fuse and let fly.

Burning oil exploded above the soldiers.

"The story ended, 'And they were fricasseed happily ever after,' " he noted, as the screams began. "You're a wicked Princess."

"Should've considered that before you had those manacles removed," she replied tartly. "I am a wicked Princess, unleashed – now, Juggernaut's on his way. As our next order of business, I propose you demonstrate your evil-dictator-Dragon laugh for your adoring audience."

That would be the audience firing volleys of arrows at his hide, aye. Fancy that? Some people clearly had no idea how to express gratitude. Where were his plaudits?

"Is this where I laugh maniacally and threaten to destroy all of Solixambria just because I don't like the colour of the grass?"

"Ah … whatever suits?"

"Doesn't the evil character always do that in the stories?"

"Together with repeated episodes of pointless, maniacal evil laughter," she agreed. "Alright, but only because someone has to conform to the stereotypes around here. Distract them."

Down below, his audience had men wielding whips to drive their soldiers against the walls. He had read about this. Many of the Skartunese infantry were slaves, men of other races forced into the army and used, not to put too fine a point on it, as fodder. Expendable front-line troops. Did that mean the real trouble was brewing somewhere else?

MMWWAA-HHAA-HAARRGH!! he thundered.

"Your best yet! Again!" the Princess yelled.

HA-HA-HARR AAARRRGHH!!

"Music! Poetry! So sublime!"

GNARR BRAA-DA-GNARRR!!

"I quiver in ecstasy."

"Don't let Azerim hear you say that. He'd faint on the spot."

Chuckling as they dodged another boulder whistling by that the Skartunese must fervently have hoped would send a desert Princess hurtling past the moons, he summoned his memory of what they had practised together. Thundersong had tried the ultra-deep seismic vibrations but he had never been excellent at it, unlike Everdeep. This matter of sand was trickier – the theory was that they should discover the precise frequency which would cause the sand to vibrate in just the right way to create a phenomenon called dry quicksand, rather than the wet type which was caused by sand particles in suspension.

Sea Dragons understood such things. Thundersong had wondered where they had travelled on their migrations and what they might have seen, to know about such fascinating scientific idiosyncrasies.

Azania had confirmed that desert folklore referenced, in numerous places, travellers and entire caravans of goods vanishing into the desert sands, never to be seen again. She also said that the fine sand from the obsidian desert had some strange, perhaps magical, properties, not always settling immediately as if inert, but sometimes … flowing. Flowing how, he had inquired? Oddly, was the answer. He loved oddities. Best part of life.

Time to find out what this sand did.

"Ears tuned?" he asked.

"Let me just pop these earplugs out … aye, ready," she said. A Dragon was supposed to have sensitive hearing. He knew one thing. Azania's ears were better than his, certainly regarding fine-tuning.

Maybe all this thundering did damage?

Starting with a plaintive bugle, he let the sound of his cry flow through and out of him before lowering the frequency, lower and lower, almost into the subsonic range. Now, it became a vibration that Azania's mind told him set her teeth on edge. Lovely. They experimented for ten or fifteen minutes, enough time for the Skartunese troops to stop glancing about as if they feared some dark magic was being cast over them and to resume the assault. A Ranger came to inquire if they could perhaps add more firepower to the defence since the enemy had massed for a larger assault. Azania thanked him and told Thundersong that she saw a messenger racing around to the back of this army, hopefully conveying the news that the counterattack was doing brutal, unforgettable things to their rearguard.

It was now or never.

Louder? she suggested. *A touch higher. Louder – no, softer. Much softer.* She listened intently. *I can almost see the sand shifting down there. We're so close! No, don't stop. More of the same …*

That was me needing to breathe, he snorted.

Breathe less.

As if in reply to her wry statement, the army charged with a mighty cry. Ladders bristled from the mass before him, angled to be wedged against the wall. Azania cried out as a grapnel struck her knee, but kept her concentration. Her mind tweaked and fine-tuned the sound, softer still, now more plangent, until the sound rang like eerily beautiful horns above the strangely muted clamour of battle. Dragon and Rider were together. One creature, one sound, one purpose.

Suddenly, the sand beneath their boots appeared to ripple. The middle ranks sank away as if sucked downward by invisible mouths. The whole area before the walls, maybe as much as ten thousand square feet in extent, turned into a thrashing black bathtub. Hampered by the weight of their armour and weapons, the Skartunese soldiers sank rapidly out of sight – so rapidly and so completely, only the tops of a few ladders remained to show where they had stood but seconds before.

Hard-bitten soldiers they might be, but the Skartunese teams working the siege weapons paused, clearly aghast.

Thundersong bit off his soft song.

"Here come the others," the Princess said in a choked-off voice.

THUNDER O DRAGON

For the first time in his life, he understood tears. He understood by the reaction that prickled in his throat and made his five Dragon hearts feel as if they were filled with sand as hot and heavy as that in which they had buried those men. He understood by the silence that hammered at his ears and a strange dark fire that filled his eyes, like a mist that momentarily obscured his Dragon soul.

"Let's go join them," he rasped.

He could not bear to look at their allies on the battlements. Nor could Azania.

She said, "I hate war."

"Aye, Princess. So do I. Never more so than right now."

Juggernaut's force rolled in like a wave. From above came the mighty Sea Dragons, heavily armed and armoured and bearing squads of archers and crossbow engineers that targeted the Skartunese with deadly volleys of arrows. A second after they pinned down the soldiers, the Isles Dragonesses plummeted from above, with one job. Find and finish the defenders. Since most of the siege weaponry was so massive that sword blows could do little damage, Tamarine Dragons walked up behind, setting fire to everything in sight. Scorched earth. Already, a semicircle of dark smoke marked their progress around the city.

Everdeep paused to bellow, "What happened here?"

"We buried them," Thundersong called back.

"Buried alive?"

He waved his paw. "You see what's left."

Times were even a Dragon felt as small as a mouse and this was one of them. That was how he felt beneath Everdeep's hard-eyed stare. Seated upon his neck, Azerim's expression appeared to show only bewilderment. After a moment, the huge Dragon nodded and said:

"Please will you check on Sirensong for us and ensure that the liberated Dragons are taken safely to the city? We've rescued over fifty so far."

"Fifty? Great numbers," he said, but every Dragon could tell his hearts were nowhere in it.

How could a resounding victory feel so hollow?

As they departed, he saw from the corner of his eye, King Azerim raise his hand in acknowledgement. Ah, so he did understand now. He and Azania winged on to help Sirensong and her teams bring in the Dragon thralls. As before, their initial responses demonstrated nothing but response to pain. Once the commands to remain docile were given, teams of Smiths and Rangers went to work around their heads, using metal saws to cut apart the cages until the most delicate stage of the operation could take place, the removal of the terrible ear probes. As these Dragons stood no chance of flying after all the atrophy caused by decades of static captivity and drudgery, the desert folk flung open the main gates to let them in. Some even cheered.

An hour later, the Dragon Rider team accompanied his dam on another sortie to recover eight more Dragons.

Good work. Honest work.

By the day's end, the Skartunese forces were scattered far and wide. Working in shifts, Aria and Juggernaut's teams hunted them relentlessly, backtracking two groups to cunningly hidden tunnels – created by Bloodworms, they thought. The Sea Dragons went in and collapsed the tunnels as far as they could track them, which took all night and well into the following day.

Once Thundersong had been freshly plucked of arrowheads and spear points and all the assorted nastiness the Skartunese had flung his way, he thanked Chanize gravely and bade her get some rest.

"No end of patients," she said.

"When last did you eat?"

"Ah …"

"I'll organise something for you. Thanks, again, for stitching me up."

He left the young woman sorting busily through her threads and supplies, tallying up a list of additional requests that would shortly make its way up to Chakkix Camp, no doubt. He tracked down Sankir Farizam and ordered him rather bluntly – talons sheathed as opposed to talons extended, in Dragon parlance – to go take care of his wife. Farizam suggested he do the same for his mate, since she happened to be dripping blood everywhere she stopped.

Off he went to risk his neck.

Double jeopardy, as it turned out. Rolling over to show one's belly, in Isles culture, was the ultimate sign of cowardice. He thought Aria might just break out in a cold sweat at his request. For a creature with no sweat glands, this was rather impressive.

Once he had argued her down, he found a piece of barbed nastiness embedded in her belly. With Chanize's and Sirensong's help, they extracted a wide, flanged arrowhead from her lower belly. In a jewel-like setting at the base of the arrowhead, it held one of the characteristic green verdelite gemstones.

Thundersong held it up for Aria to see.

"I don't even want to know," she hissed. "Tracker? Something to infect me? Get it out of my sight!"

Chanize said, "Sirensong, your team should check it, right?"

"We will," she said. "Then, we need to check every other Dragon who's been hit or worked on … those we've liberated … this could all be part of some cunning plot, couldn't it?"

"I wouldn't put anything past Nahritu-N'shula," Thundersong said. "I'll go brief our royals."

"I'm coming with you," Aria said immediately.

"No."

"Thundersong!"

He rounded upon her. "You will stay here and get yourself fixed up! When you aren't bleeding all over the place, you may return to your duties!"

Her fangs clacked against his lip but when he snarled back at her, ten times louder, he saw her take pause for the first time. He did not feel good about his reaction, which caused Chanize to gasp in shock, but thought it best to swagger stiff-legged out of the infirmary. On his way out, he murmured – deliberately loud enough to be heard:

"Phew, Azania! Quite the Dragoness, eh?"

She elbowed his flank firmly. "Face it, my friend. You're in love."

Aria called after, "I appreciate the sentiment, but you two are utterly transparent."

"Time to make good our escape," he chortled, speeding up.

Aria promptly threatened him with marital dismemberment. Mmm, sweet and smoky fires! All part of a healthy Dragon relationship.

Night crept up on a strangely quiet desert citadel and settled over the flat-roofed houses like a stealthy blanket. With Aria away campaigning in the eastern reaches of T'nagru, Thundersong slept, as he always did, out in the garden with Azania curled up in the crook of his neck, resting wholly upon his forepaw, as had become her habit of late. Due to the lingering warmth of the evening, he did not fully shield her with his wing. A girl needed to breathe.

After a long while, his eyes lidded.

A Brown Dragon walked in a summertime meadow, high in the Tamarine Mountains. Wildflowers tickled his ankles, their bright floral scents entering his mind as vibrant blots of colour. He smiled. With such colours, a Dragon could paint a masterwork. Maybe he could work incense or fragrances into his paints in such a way that his art would have a lasting scent, an additional layer of complexity for the discerning patron? Perhaps by bonding the scents into the paints with a complex magical structure …

A while later, in that slightly misty dream space, he found himself jogging along, following a new, enticing scent. What was this? How intoxicating! A hint of saltiness, a zesty flick of tropical flowers and the sharp underlying tang of … of weapons oil …

He knew this scent!

Lighter and lighter his paws trod upon the ground, dancing now, touching down with ethereal ease. Who was this fantastically sought-after male who pursued the object of his desire?

Thundersong, he murmured. *I am the voice of thunder. I slay my enemies with a word!*

The Cobalt Dragoness smiled coyly at him.

He chased after her for the longest time. She led him by devious ways to an exquisite little waterfall that sprinkled from five separate flows into a sparkling mountain pool, as clear as crystal.

Ariamyrielle Seaspray, I love you, he declared.

Oh, how she preened before the regard of this mighty Dragon, this dashing wrecker of kingdoms and bold kidnapper of beautiful Princesses! He was the one and only Thundersong, the fire of her eye and the song of her Dragoness hearts.

Aria crooked her fore-talon at him. *You are so … overwhelming, Thundersong. What a great Dragon you are. I slaver over your majestic haunches.*

He wriggled with pleasure, aware in some dim, faraway corner of the oddity of this un-Aria-like statement. What did it matter? He pranced to her, chest outthrust and wings held high in an attitude of dominance and reached out to caress the finely detailed patterns of her cheek scales.

"We meet again, worm!"

"You!"

Nahritu-N'shula's dark, beautiful features did not lose an iota of their composure.

"What have you done with my Aria?"

"Nothing."

Completing the sweep of his paw, he gripped her about the lower torso and legs and squeezed. "Tell me where she is!"

She chuckled scornfully. "Your brothers called you a brown slug. I can see why. Your dreams are so pathetic – majestic haunches, was it?" His paw tightened upon her. "You risible piece of filth, who do you think you're fooling? Blitz the Fritz. What a perfect name for you!"

"I am not Blitz the Fritz!"

"Aren't you? You wreck everything you touch."

"You be quiet!"

"You can't even stop me. Weakling. Is this your strong right paw?"

Her swelling laughter incensed him. She found him funny, did she? She dared to mock him as he had been teased and mocked and put down countless times over the years? Rage swelled in his breast, uncontainable.

"Thunderfool, was it? Thunderubbish?"

Roaring, "I'LL KILL YOU, YOU DESPICABLE WOMAN!" he shook her violently. A bone snapped sharply beneath the pressure of his powerful talons.

"Aww, you poor, sweet little thing. Look at what you've done now. Look closely …"

Thundersong's blink seemed to take forever.

Look? Look at what?

As if by magic, Nahritu's face rippled and changed into a well-loved one, wracked with pain.

"Azania!" he gasped.

"Thundersong, you're … killing …"

His gasp threatened to tear his hearts clear from his chest. With a convulsion of horror, he unclenched his paw. Azania tried to step backward but her ankle folded at an impossible angle beneath her. She fell with a sharp cry.

"Azania! *Azania!* I didn't mean – it was a dream –"

"Thundersong!" His dam landed heavily beside him, panting from the exertion. "You roared – what have you done?"

"Nothing. I dreamed ill, that's all!"

Sirensong wailed, "You hurt her! What did you do?"

He stared at his paw, unexpectedly returned to white. "I … don't know. Azania –"

"Don't touch me!" She gaped at her twisted leg. "Oh dear, that's not good. Same leg, you – just leave me alone! It hurts, oh, it hurts so … you, you stupid –"

"Lie down, Princess Azania," Sirensong urged. "I'll get healers and splints, plus something to dull the pain."

Thundersong shuffled forward. "Don't say it. Please. I can't believe – Azania – it was her, don't you see? That – that wasn't me. You have to trust me."

He bit his tongue in an agony of fury. How could he do this to her?

She sank back, wan with pain. Her little chest moved up and down with her laboured breathing. She touched her flank, exploring something else that clearly pained her. A Dragon remembered his contemplations regarding turning Humans blue and hung his head. This was worse.

Azania said, "Thundersong?"

"Aye? I am so, so sorry, Azania. I don't know what came over me."

"I think we both do." Holding up her right hand, she said, "Don't you dare go anywhere. I am not losing you again. Come here."

He glared at his forepaws. Traitors! All he could think was that he had almost crushed his best friend in all of Solixambria with his own forepaw. This was beyond any kind of fritz he had ever imagined. This was … horrific.

"Come here, I said. Or shall I whistle you in like a hound?"

Had he tried to smile, his lips might have cracked right

off his face. "No need." Approaching upon the softest of paws, he touched her outstretched hand ever so carefully with his talon. "Here, I'll take your pain. Give it to me – *aah!*" He stumbled to one knee upon the grass. "That's bad."

"Better for me, thank you. Might have broken a rib, too. Thundersong, before you beat yourself up too badly – I remember now, while you were dreaming, you called me Nahritu. You were dreaming, right?"

"Aye." He met her dark eyes at last.

They crinkled a touch at the corners. "Now, ready for a jaw-dropper?"

"Hit me with your best – ah," he grinned awkwardly.

"Was it a *normal* dream?"

Thankfully he did stand a little aside from her, because his jaw clunked down on the grass. "Are you thinking what I'm –"

"– thinking? Sometimes, I wonder if we're still two creatures, Thundersong. Or, one brain with two feet, four paws, two arms and two wings? It was an attack, a personal attack on us, and it so nearly succeeded."

"I broke your leg."

"You're monstrously strong when you're angry, Thundersong," she said quietly, as a bevy of healers came charging out of the palace building, led by a distraught King Azerim, "but even I know when you're not angry with me. Have them search the palace. Turn over every stone and tile. I'm convinced something isn't right here."

In the end, he turned over no tiles and no stones because the two Kings met him with stony-faced expressions and informed him that one, Azania was now sleeping, two, the structure of the Palace was not to be disturbed, which most certainly included not removing stones from their foundations, and three, there was simply no point as N'chala's teams had already been over the building no less than three times and found nothing larger than a few mouse holes.

The mice had been exterminated.

Azerim's expression suggested a certain temptation to suggest doing the same to large white Dragons who had the nerve to attempt to squeeze the juice out of his fiancée. Since the hour was by now extremely late and, by and large, Thundersong agreed with their assessment of the situation, he promised that no nocturnal stonemasonry would be undertaken by himself. Instead, he took himself off to his patch of grass to snatch some rest.

Sleep? What sleep?

Instead, he stared upward as the desert skies, improbably, began to cloud over. The timing and tenor of the attack was bothersome, he decided eventually. Did it somehow lack the brutal edge, the killer instinct he associated with Nahritu-N'shula? Could it be that the daughter had attacked them? Could she still be somewhere inside the city, plotting their downfall? Might Nahritu-N'shula yet have a secret passage into the palace itself or somewhere nearby, since she had made herself very much at home during the deceased King N'gala N'gala's reign?

Three hours of sleepless staring later, the clouds had moved on, doing everything normal clouds did except that they neglected to shed a single drop of rain. Just about as contrary as a large white Dragon he could prod with a very short talon just now.

Thundersong narrowed his eyes. He had promised not to touch a stone. What about the gardens? He had promised nothing about those. Maybe he'd just take a good sniff around this building, starting with the gardens and flowerbeds right beneath the open porch of Azania's old chambers, the place where they had once ambushed her younger sister …

CHAPTER 26

WATER SNIFFER

COME MORNING, A CERTAIN dreamy Dragon found himself firmly ensconced in what Humans called the doghouse. This was not so much a place as a state of great penitence, he understood, wherein it was the job of one creature to wander about looking very repentant for one's misdeeds while all the other creatures glared at him and shook their heads. Only, hounds were tiny in comparison. Therefore, his problem was that his was not a small doghouse, but a most indubitably Dragon-sized dragon-house.

Bad, bad Dragon, he grumbled to himself. *Nasty Dragon. Fancy trying to hug a Human to death?*

Hugs must be unexpectedly dangerous.

Either that or he had the worst wing-pit odour in history. Even Aria had acted put out this morning, giving him a parting sniff that made him wonder if he might not be growing personal fungus farms somewhere. Off he went to bathe. Alone.

Miserable creature.

True to form, he had not missed his chance to make just any blunder. This Dragon did not settle for anything less than the most gargantuan clangers in history. Steal a Princess in her bed? Aye, following which, he had nearly brained them both against the castle wall. Or what about his epic struggle to fly through an ocean storm, only to discover he was half Sea Dragon and could have taken a much easier, far more scenic route? Or his nice little night flight that had catapulted him into the middle of several hundred Terror Clan Dragons? Well, at least trouble usually knew when he was around because he was the one flying smack into it at high speed.

Bobbing about in the cistern for Sea Dragons, he reflected upon his utter failure to find anything of use the previous evening. Nothing in the Palace building, nothing in the manicured gardens – admittedly, the grass had not appreciated his tromping about. Nor did the gardeners. Their expressions had been especially mournful this morning.

Twenty tonnes of Dragon tended not to mix well with one's lawn management.

Funny thing about water was how different it could smell. This cistern's scent was quite clean, just the slightest tang of minerals. Seawater was fresh, with that invigorating nasal slap of salt. Whatever a nasal slap was – his chortling echoed in the dim chamber. Drinking deeply, he recalled the very special reek of Great-Aunt Ignita's swamp.

Young Dragon, you should follow your nose, said the image in his mind.

Ignita never suffered fools gladly. Azerim and N'chala were not fools but neither were they right about preventing him from sniffing about the Palace.

Immediately, along with this thought, another scent memory intruded. He was good with scents. Plenty of practice smelling out peoples' emotions. Had the gardens smelled slightly … different? More brackish, stronger on the mineral tangs, as if it had come from an underground water source. Azania had told him about aquifers, like great rivers of water that ran beneath the desert in some places and surfaced as oases. The theory was that this water came all the way from the swamps of southern

Skartun.

The water for the gardens smelled … odd. Like it had leached through rocks for a thousand miles and come out rather different to any other water he had ever smelled – not that he understood the science of aquifers in the slightest but big underground rivers implied space, perhaps space an army could somehow navigate …

The water in the cistern slopped violently as he thrashed about, changing direction and charging up the steps.

Slow down, Dragon. Think before he built himself a bigger, smellier dragon-house.

In a few minutes, he had returned to the Palace compound through the main gates. Trying to keep his paws mostly on the stone pathways, he wandered through the gardens, searching out one of the few hapless gardeners left making sure that the King's roses did not suffer the ravages of neglect, let alone war. Aha. Here was a suitably gormless one.

"You! Tell me, my good man – oh."

He eyed the prone body. Not dead, thankfully. Just a fainter.

"Are you from Amboriane, perchance?" Snigger.

Wandering around the back, he sensed the Princess' mind come alive to his presence. *Erm, alright there, Azania?*

Very much better and very much bored out of my –

– very much little? he put in deftly, merely for the pleasure of collecting her mental kick about the cerebral cortex.

– brain! she finished crossly. *Thundersong, you sneaky old reprobate. What are you doing beneath my window?*

Merely smelling your flowerbeds, Your Highness.

Oh?

He loved how her mind came alight. It was as if gears whirred, switches clicked and everything suddenly fell into a dazzling pattern. Effortlessly, she read the scents out of his brain and then her mind went haring off to various conclusions.

THUNDER O DRAGON

I shall consult my brother who shall summon a servant who shall rush to find some septuagenarian architect who shall remember a tale from his youth ... she chuckled. *Crutches. Anon, mighty Dragon!*

Ha. Thought that sort of nonsense would fly with him, did she?

Riding roughshod over the protests of several servants, who had clearly been primed to keep her exactly where she no longer wished to be, his Dragon Rider swung her way down a marble-floored, gorgeously appointed hallway to the main conference room, alias the King's boudoir – a name never mentioned before two particular royal males of the kingly persuasion – and swept inside with her usual inability to fail to draw absolutely everyone's attention to herself instantly.

So Azania.

Thundersong chuckled to himself as she kept a running internal commentary on her progress. Wrangle the brother. *Twist him around my little finger.* Dispatch the servant. *Looks like he's just seen a Dragoness.* Wholly unapologetic snuggle for Azerim. *Mmm, the manly stubble.* Really? Humans liked their chin fungus? What an odd species they were. After checking in with Princess Yuali and suggesting four points her peers had neglected to adjust on their strategic map, she winkled out of N'chala that he really had no clue where the water came from.

"Why do you want to know?" he asked for the fifth time.

"It's whiffy," Azania informed him.

"What; you're concerned about the smell outside your bedroom window?" he coughed, his voice squeaky with disbelief.

"Not Azania," her betrothed said stoutly. "She's up to something, trust me."

"My obedient, submissive little sister? Surely not."

Azerim chortled, "Them's fighting words, mister! On the high seas, you'd be thrown to the sharks for that kind of talk."

"Ooh, you're a *nice* king," Azania purred.

"And you are one distracting Princess! Off! I will have the truth out of you, wench – *ouch!*"

"Wench me one more time and I will wrench something you don't want wrenched … my dearest darling turtledove."

"Turtledove?"

Yuali chuckled, "I like that one."

Lurking not very far off, Thundersong made a face. Honestly? The royal kissing thing was like some nasty infectious disease. Close the ears and avert the eyes, every Dragon! Although, a jaded old matchmaker like himself did have to admit that Princess Yuali's combination of gentleness and steel did appear to be doing N'chala a world of good. Less so, the brothers. He had done well to ship them off to command other citadels where they were creating the usual amount of trouble and headache.

One could not choose family, as he very well knew. Maybe one could consider selling them into slavery for a profit? An image of a Dragon's agony in a Skartunese head cage interrupted his pleasant reverie. No. Not even them.

The nose, you chattering fool! Follow the nose!

Ooh, the presence of Great-Aunt Ignita was strong with him this morning. Even as a figment of his imagination, she proved impossible to ignore. Like a hound he had once seen on the scent in northern Vanrace, he snuffled his way about the garden in search of the scent of fresh water. No gardeners died of apoplexy as he pushed a gorgeous climbing rose over – oops – when Azania popped into his mind to inform him that the suitably elderly architect was now scrabbling about in the Royal Archives with rather un-elderly haste, his report having failed to satisfy the Black Thornbush of the Desert.

Meantime, the Dragon had prowled his way to the tall, white back wall of the Palace compound. The freshest scent of water led right here. He took a sounding with an Everdeep-ish flair about it and promptly – but rather gingerly – scaled the wall with a gentle bound. Desert walls were built five feet thick, the better to withstand the ferocious heat. That said, it was a gorgeous day but those clouds were building up again. Did he scent a storm?

Mind on the job, young –

Ignita! Do you have to? Giggle. *Azania! You pest.*

On the hunt, my Dragon?

Powerful predator in his prime, said he, peering down over the wall. He overlooked a narrow alleyway at the back of the Palace which must have been built atop a rocky outcropping, he realised. Many houses abutted the rock face, over a hundred feet below. Five children wearing cream desert robes played a game of ball right beneath him, totally unaware of the doom on paws snooping on their doings.

Behave yourself, the Princess said. *Blast. My brothers! Back in a bit.*

Flipping open his wings, he dropped down on the rooftops, very careful to place his paws in places that would not cave in any of the stone buildings.

Leaning over, he bunted the ball along with his nose. "Good shot."

Squeals, shrieks and gasps accompanied what he thought was not a terrible effort at nose ball. Or paw ball? Either way, he was quite certain he saw a future in this game for Dragons, if they could avoid flaming the ball or stepping on it.

"It's the big noisy Dragon!" cried one of the girls.

"He's the Princess' Dragon," said another. "He's nice … I think."

"Don't eat our ball, sir," said one of the older boys, with a worried frown.

"Wouldn't dream of it, young man," he reassured them.

Another boy, rather younger than the first, squealed, "I knows you! You's … your name is … Thunderpants!"

Quashing his anger, he grinned, "Be careful, or I'll thunder your pants right over the moons! Say, can any of you children help me? I'm on the hunt for your water supply."

One way to confuse them.

"Do any of the houses here have a deep well or someplace where water comes from the ground?" he pressed.

The oldest girl, a petite little sparrow just like Azania, said, "You do come from very far away, don't you, Mister Dragon? This is a desert. Water doesn't just spout from the ground."

"Does too," said another girl. "It's called a quiffer – I learned it in school."

"That's 'aquifer,' " said the boy, with great scorn. Thundersong eyeballed him intently. "Um … sorry, Mister Dragon. I can't think of any – hold on, I know. I've got an idea!"

" 'Cause you're a know-it-all," scowled the girl.

"Children, this is important," Thundersong said, prodding them each with a sheathed talon. "Princess Azania and I need your help. Will you be my royal helpers?"

Phew, one way to raise screams far louder than before!

"What's your idea, young man?"

The slender young fellow, perhaps ten or eleven years of age, said, "Well, just down here is a house – you see, each one has a sign on it? That one there's called the Water House and that next neighbour, which is my Uncle Hafari's place, is called the Pumphouse."

He brightened. "Excellent! Lead on, please."

Since he could not possibly fit into the alleyway, he stepped from roof corner to roof corner, having to detour to avoid someone's washing line, a few shade-covered rooftop vegetable gardens and another rooftop covered in mats, upon which someone had spread out spices for drying. Ooh! He'd love to cook with some of these. What rich, exotic smells! Saffron, cardamom, red and yellow chilli peppers, turmeric, black and red pepper kernels, cumin ... ah, and here were jasmine and lemony sumac, to which Azania had introduced him, fenugreek and ...

Hurrying along before Ignita harassed him again.

Perching on the rooftop of the pumphouse, he sneezed energetically. Spicy! Right, one paw in front of the next, Dragon. Perching atop the house, he leaned over to peer inside, whilst taking a massive inhalation which almost sucked Uncle Hafari out of his front door.

The man gathered his robes about his spare frame in shock. "Dragon!"

How perceptive. Politely, he said, "I am on a mission for King N'chala. Can you help?" A fluid desert bow was his answer. "I am searching for the source of the Palace's water. My scent tells me it is nearby, perhaps behind or beneath this house. Are you aware of any access to a well or source hereabouts?"

"I'm sorry, but no," he said, "but I do know who will know – my mother-in-law, who lives next door. It is a rule in desert society that one's mother-in-law knows everything and she is always right."

"Goes for Dragons, too," he agreed, thinking about how much little Charielle Seaspray enjoyed being wrong about anything. One did not lightly point out her faults.

His mother-in-law Tanzahri was a bent-over old woman who was also blind. She greeted him cordially and listened to his question with her head tilted aside to present her better ear, she said, to his voice. At once, she replied:

"Well, young Dragon, my grandfather used to say that there was a well behind this house, but I don't rightly remember if anyone has seen it ... well, in decades. Funny thing is, there was a nice lady here just the other day asking about it –" his scales prickled as if someone had poured strong acid down his neck "– no, no, it must have been last week? Maybe last year. I don't remember very well anymore, you know. Very nice lady. Just the sweetest voice, she had. Why anyone would want to know about the water, I don't rightly know, but you are very welcome to come inside and take a look for yourself, as long as you don't leave a mess. Since I can't see anymore, I do like everything left just so."

"We'll leave it just so," Thundersong promised. "However, it won't be me, I'm afraid. I'm a little too large to squeeze inside your house. May I bring Princess Azania to take a look?"

"The little Princess? I remember her," mused the old lady. "Terrible thing when the Vanracians kidnapped her, it was. Do I look alright? How's my hair? Not every day one has royal visitors, I daresay. Are you the Dragon who saved her?"

"I am."

"You're a good one. I do love the sound of your thunder. Gives an old lady the most wonderful shivers, it does."

"Mother," Hafari spluttered.

"Well, it's true! Now, run along and fetch the Princess, if you must."

A hop, a skip and a flip of the wingtip later, Thundersong returned with a Princess and a bonus King in tow. N'chala had promised to send additional workmen to help. At least fifty neighbours had gathered by now, drawn by the kerfuffle. They stood about, energetically swapping notes about the history of the two houses, which turned out to be a great deal of information which, for the purposes of the investigation, was intriguing but rather useless.

Azania and Azerim spent a while searching the back rooms of the house, tapping here and pressing there, to no avail. Thundersong took a few soundings and sniff tests as best he could, confirming that he definitely scented water back there and that there must also be a hollow space. Aria, returned from a scouting sortie, joined him, together with five of her warriors and next, Sirensong winged down to add her own voice to the others, along with several of his siblings. Everyone had an opinion of what ought to be done. After two hours of fruitless searching, it was clear that only the neighbours were gaining any entertainment out of this affair.

Standing atop the old woman's house and the neighbouring rooftops, Thundersong, Aria, Sirensong, Azania and Azerim put their heads together. What had they missed? It was clear to everyone that they were on the right track – the hollow echo-soundings behind the house, the dank scent of water, the reference to the nice woman, which might very well be Nahritu-N'shula …

He ignored the several hundred people who had now climbed onto their rooftops, the better to goggle at goings-on. Humans. Pack hunters at the best of times.

Eventually, Azerim said, "Could we just be searching in the wrong place?"

"As in, the answer's right behind Thundersong's tail?" Azania grinned, pointing with her crutch at the rock wall abutting the rear of the house.

"Exactly!" he crowed. "Genius!"

The Princess puffed out her cheeks. "You were being literal?"

Thundersong put in, "Of course I'm a genius; all you need to do is explain how and how much."

"Flaming," said Azerim, clearly in good spirits despite the disappointment so far. "All I was thinking was, how come we're only searching inside the house? The roof is just as easy to access via this outside stairway and probably less trouble if you were trying to … uh …"

Azania took her foot off his – the good one, Thundersong noticed, and chuckled, "Don't you dare finish that sentence."

He winked at her. "I have plans for you, Princess. Wicked, devious plans."

"Thundersong?" She clicked her fingers. "Sort him out."

"Don't be rude," he snorted.

N'chala's scouts swarmed over the wall, peering closely at every detail of the grey granite across the width of the house, before fanning out to check the neighbours' as well.

Thundersong said, "It's probably hidden by magic."

"That's true," said Sirensong. "Allow me through, please."

Singing softly to herself, she hissed in annoyance as he pushed her paws to safer locations. Working methodically up to a height she checked visually against Azerim's height, she moved from right to left, checking every detail with her Dragon sight and deep Sea Dragoness magic.

≈*There's something here! Thundersong …*≈

He helped her poke, prod and probe at the small crack, to no avail. Was it a keyhole? Could it need a magical code or passphrase?

A crutch tapped him on the wrist. "Perhaps it takes a Human touch?"

"Obviously," he sniffed, steadying her with care as she snagged her splinted, bandaged foot on Sirensong's paw.

Azania had barely touched the spot when there was a loud *click* and a broad section of rockface hinged away into a dark, clammy – well, not a tunnel. A vertical shaft.

She exchanged a paw-hand slap with him. *Nice one, Thundersong.*

Takes a woman's touch, I believe.

And a Dragon's cunning and instinct. This, I believe, will be of great interest to King N'chala.

Sirensong peered within. Her voice echoed hollowly as she said, "That's deep." Listening to the sound of her voice, she added, "Very deep and it leads to open water. Clearly. I can tell by the way the water's dripping."

Azerim said, "May I take a look?"

"Light?" Thundersong offered.

"Please do set him alight," Azania said, then giggled at her own joke. "Oops, sorry. That came out wrong."

"I wonder what mechanism brings water from the bottom to the top."

Azania jumped. "Azerim! Not in public."

"I like bottoms and tops," he said, patting her bottom and kissing her lips at the same time. Good co-ordination there, Thundersong approved, as his Princess told him off for unbecoming behaviour that would set the entire neighbourhood's tongues wagging. Indeed, this renewed kissing business drew a few scattered cheers.

"Kiss him again, Your Highness!" someone shouted, to much laughter.

"Avast! This barbaric pirate of the Vaylarn Archipelago does all the kissing around here," Azerim declaimed in a loud voice, seizing his intended prize.

Oh, and now there was, 'Unhand me, thou fiend!' and 'Kiss me, o beauty of the desert!' which proved very popular with the ladies. It seemed that the King had gathered himself a bevy of new admirers. Azania did not miss her chance to add to the drama, prodding Azerim in the ribs with her crutch to fend him off. 'Scoundrel! Is this any way to treat a lady?'

Once those shenanigans died down, Thundersong curled his talons about Azerim and Azania before the three leaned over together to gaze down that shaft. It was wider than he had expected, about twenty feet by fifteen. Sirensong squeezed her muzzle in above Azania. With that, he carefully tipped a fireball off the end of his tongue. What a wonderful sensation! It dropped away, gathering speed as it hurtled into the void, eventually fizzling in what appeared to be a lake far, far below.

"Again, please," Azerim asked.

This time, Thundersong noted that a hawser depended from the wall to his left paw, anchored in a perfectly massive eye bolt – but, all the way down, there was nothing attached to it. No easy way to investigate then. For a quarter-mile drop, the space was too narrow for a Dragon to spread his wings but that hawser had to be eight inches through its diameter, the most substantial rope he had ever seen. After that, the perfectly carved shaft appeared to widen out, until they could no longer see the sides. The dark water had to be at least three-quarters of a mile below the city's lowest foundations, they estimated.

"An underground lake," Azania said at last. "That's worth knowing about, isn't it, Thundersong? Quite the strategic advantage." She peered at him. "No."

"No what?" Azerim asked.

"No flying down there to take a look. We've no idea what we'd find."

He showed her a very fine set of fangs.

"No, Thundersong."

"I can fly vertically," Aria put in. "Plenty of room for us smaller Dragons."

"No," he said at once.

With her signature 'look at lethal little me' look, the Cobalt Dragoness said, "I say ten warriors, you, Thundersong – you're the smallest of your brethren and the only one likely to fit – and Azania, Azerim and a good number of Rangers. Not investigating this place means placing every life in this city at risk."

She was right.

"Let's saddle up and arm ourselves," he said. "Time to break open these desert vaults."

CHAPTER 27

WHAT A PLOT

WITH ARIA LEADING THE way, Thundersong followed on, clambering paw over paw down the light-tan hawser. As always, Azania took first position upon his neck. Azerim rode with Aria, strapped on with a harness, that the Rangers had finally worked out, which did not impede the Isles Dragoness' flying or fighting style. Aria did not say so, but he suspected she must be proud to carry a Dragon Rider like him, a King and a man of noble character.

Given his strength and tough paws, climbing or even sliding down the thick hawser was no trouble at all. Along the first, narrow section it was anchored every hundred feet or so but, after that, he suspected it must dangle freely all the way down to the water. Azania pointed out fresh scrape marks on the walls that suggested the use of some kind of platform.

Suddenly, the light vanished.

"Guess we forgot to check how to open the door from this side," Azania's voice said in the darkness.

Aria's muzzle appeared nearby, her fangs backlit by flame. "How's this?"

"There's daylight and there's fang-light," Thundersong quipped, cheerfully noticing how his natural Sea Dragon glow strengthened with the surge of his feelings toward her. "Very tasteful, my lovely mate. Of course, my hearts shine for you alone."

"You are our guiding light, Thundersong," Princess Azania put in.

"What a bright comment, Princess."

"I merely illuminate your dazzling prose, Dragon."

Never missed a beat, did she?

On that note and with a few grins even from the stern warrior Dragonesses, they continued the descent and someone above reopened the door. Slowly, at first, the speckled grey stone drew away to reveal that they descended into a conical cavern, like a great tall hat that branched off this ancient watercourse. Whereas it was clear that the upper thousand feet or more must have been hand-chiselled through stone, this lower part appeared completely natural. Azania noted that the geologists had told her aquifers were usually porous rock, but plenty of stories – usually taken for fables – suggested the presence of underground rivers beneath the desert.

As they descended to the water level, the Princess voiced what had been bothering him, subconsciously at least. "It runs east-west."

"Indeed," he purred.

The dark, perfectly still black water pooled out in this section to about three hundred feet wide. The cavern roof quickly narrowed down in both directions, leaving a narrow but navigable watercourse. The northern side even had a sandy bank, the same obsidian colour as the desert sand above. Water stains at different levels created striated patterns on the arched walls. Water dripped in the distance but the surface here was mirror calm, making it impossible to tell in which direction the water flowed. Aria's Dragonesses spread out, keeping guard with their usual vigilance.

≈*Thundersong,*≈ his dam called. ≈*Don't forget to take vertical and longitudinal soundings.*≈

Completely overlooked. ≈*At once, mother.*≈

What a good egg he was!

He also loved to crack a few side-splitting yolks from time to time –

Oh, stop it, you're killing me, Azania groaned.

Just egging you on, Princess.

"Would you take us to that bank, please?" Azerim asked Aria meantime.

In a moment, the Vaylarn Islander alighted once more with a slight, but discernible wobble on that bad foot. Sirensong had suggested that he ought to wear a brace in his boot but Azerim happened to be rather stubborn on a few issues and this was one of them. He said he needed to strengthen the ankle, not weaken it with a brace. Either way, he winced a second time as he knelt to check several faint marks in the sand.

"Definitely been some kind of vessel or raft here," he said.

Azania sighed.

"Aha! Didn't you give your sister this type of hair clip?"

He plucked a tiny, diamond-studded hair ornament from the sand. Aye. Thundersong had definitely seen both Princesses wearing those, one of Azania's less necessary purchases in Chakkix Camp. Could Inzashu have meant to leave them a sign? Azania kicked his neck and then groaned between her teeth as she realised she had used the wrong foot. When she was in pain or deeply worried about her sister might not be the best time to tease her, he thought, gazing from left to right and then surveying the water very carefully before landing for a depth check.

"Thirty-two feet," he reported.

Plenty of water. If it was potable, that would be enough to ensure that N'ginta Citadel would never, ever run out, even during the longest imaginable siege. Next, he took soundings in either direction. The river must bend, because the sound returned to his ear scrambled, but what he did hear suggested this was no mere lake. Meantime,

Azerim walked along the shore and around a natural bend in the bank. He called back that he had found the pump mechanism, a very long tube that worked silently and under no form of power he could see.

"You know, given the direction this river runs, it could connect all the southerly citadels," the King began to say.

Flinryielle cut him off with a sharp warning, "Ripples in the water! Alert!"

The Isles Dragonesses, as one, flitted toward Azerim, but by unspoken agreement, left Aria to snatch him up in her paws. Thundersong rose powerfully with them, putting a goodly two hundred feet between himself and the surface before everyone paused, watching a white glow rapidly approaching along the watercourse. A low roar of displaced water rapidly rose to deafening proportions, echoing around the cavern. Within seconds, the water level surged and a massive, flattish white monster charged out into the open – strangely, having run along the *roof* of the tunnel. Upside down?

Thundersong had no more than half a second to appreciate the fact that it was some kind of white monster millipede with no apparent eyes, when it smoothly changed direction to race up the side of the cavern toward them. Its mouth cracked open. He saw brilliant white within …

STOP!!

His sharp sonic attack smashed it off the rock wall. The creature splashed down heavily, the wave it created swamping the beach where Azerim had stood moments before. Dazed, the pretty-winged Isles warriors swarmed toward him.

GET OUT OF HERE! GO!

This time, the thunder did not shake them as severely. Accustomed to taking orders, the Dragonesses flitted upward over a hundred feet before Aria began to turn, realising that her mate hovered protectively below them. That monster was at least the size of one of the granddaddy Sea Serpents, if not larger still. Squirming upright, its many feet waving in synchronisation just like a millipede, it oriented itself upon the intruders and let rip with a bolt of lightning.

KERACK!!

Thundersong tried to throw himself in between, into harm's way. His eyes felt seared; every nerve jangled as the tremendous current played through his body but this was his second experience of being hit like this. The Skartunese machine had seemed more painful but he knew what to do this time. He absorbed the power straight into his body, into that deep chamber used for the Sea Dragon electrolysis processes. It ignited immediately, sending the lightning shooting back to where it came from.

Searing white exploded in the cavern. There came a tremendous crashing and thrashing as the creature, clearly hurt, beat a hasty retreat. The sounds quickly faded toward the east.

Jainrielle! someone cried.

He gave chase to the falling Dragoness but was too late to prevent her from landing with a violent smack in the water. This light-green Isles Dragoness was his half-brother's romantic interest, he recalled briefly, as he air-braked hard, submerging beside her. Ah! How he mourned Eversong's capture, his fate! Then his paws curved beneath her limp body, bringing her muzzle to the surface.

Breathe, come on, please, he urged.

Jainrielle coughed very weakly, then vomited up water. *Oh, oh … I wished to die …*

Azania burst out, *You must not! Do not despair. We will move these very deserts to see Eversong restored to you, Jainrielle – that, I promise you.*

Is the creature gone? another Dragoness called.

I think so, Aria said. *Everyone alright?*

A chorus of assent rose from the teams, including Azania.

Jainrielle said, *I think my Rider's gone.*

She was. Sadly, Thundersong and Azania checked the

body, but the woman – Varina, he recalled – had not survived the massive electrical jolt. Three other Dragonesses had been burned by secondary branches of lightning, one so badly that he took her upon his back to bear her up into the bright daylight.

Another failure.

Over the following couple of days, they learned that no less than eight citadels sat above this ancient watercourse. How it had been discovered and exploited in the past, was unclear. The stonework was immaculate, the source of power for the water, unidentifiable, and the fate of Nahritu-N'shula and her daughter, unknown. Everyone assumed she knew how to tame the blind millipede – the assumption was that she might even have placed it inside the watercourse as a guardian of her secret.

Did the main Skartunese armies know of this route? Or only her?

Secrets within conundrums within mysteries.

King N'chala tore out a few more beard hairs coming to terms with the idea that every one of his strong fortresses had a back door that his worst enemy, the slayer of his father, had used with impunity for years and likely could again.

No mind.

For a week, absolutely nothing happened. It really was strange how absolutely nothing could drive everyone absolutely stir-crazy. The Dragons patrolled ceaselessly. Work on additional fortifications reached a fever pitch. The Sea Dragons checked the sands every day.

Endless heaps of nothing.

Azerim and Azania had another of their spirited rows that ended with him holding his head in his hands and calling himself crabby. Azania, giving him a conciliatory hug, made a face at Thundersong behind her fiancé's back. He had to remove himself forthwith, before a great bray of laughter overtook him. He tried to disguise it as a thunderclap, really he did, but Azerim tracked him down later and had a few words for him. Wise words, plus a few vexed truths. Being engaged to such a spirited soul as Azania was definitely a challenge, he said, his eyes sparkling.

Good man.

In the early hours, Thundersong snuck Princess Azania out of her bedchamber – ah, sweet déjà vu – and absconded into the restless, breezy desert night with everyone's permission except for King N'chala. North they flew, all the way up to Chakkix Camp in a single very full day on the wing, courtesy of a nice Sea Dragon snoozefest midway to enliven matters, where Azania's arrival, once again upon crutches with a broken leg, caused a sensation.

"You poor girl!" cried Yardi, wrapping her up in a huge hug.

"Ribs. Ribs!" Azania gasped.

Garan twirled his hammer in his fist. "Who do I brain and where are they to be found?"

Thundersong decided that he might not answer until everyone calmed down.

Tarangis Lionbaiter turned pale. "I hope I'm not in trouble again?"

The Princess dropped a decorous kiss upon his cheek and told him that if he did not find himself a wife soon, he would indeed be in trouble.

"Where exactly am I supposed to purchase one?" he inquired.

"Tarangis!" she snorted.

"I'm a businessman," he explained. "I'm just not good with relationships that don't involve mutual profit. Plus, it does happen to be wartime."

"You perfect barbarian," she sniffed. "Even you aren't that mercenary."

"Takes a special woman to love someone like me."

"Someone with a mind as sharp as a tack –" he brightened visibly at her compliment "– and morals like an open sewer."

"Ouch. I'm wounded."

Thundersong wondered if he meant to refer to his foreshortened legs. Azania, having ignored that inference as perhaps it deserved – he could only imagine how complex and fragile a creature's feelings about the loss of a limb must be –gave him her patented devious-and-despicable-plans glare. Tarangis Lionbaiter met this with his usual urbane business face. That face challenged, 'So, what are you going to do about it, Princess?"

Thundersong chortled and whispered in his Rider's mind, *Do it. I dare you.*

She said, "Tarangis, my brother King N'chala requests your presence at N'ginta Citadel. That is why we have come north."

"Requests?"

"In desert speak, that means 'requires.' I don't know what has gone wrong but, last I saw him, he had papers from you turned over on his desk with a dagger for a paperweight." She smiled thinly. "I'm quite certain you know what that means as well as I do."

"I have not cheated him! That's a ridiculous accusation."

He could never get over how good this girl was at playing the game. Azania met his gaze levelly, daring Tarangis to call her bluff.

After at least a minute, he threw up his hands. "I'd rather roll about in the cactus wastelands for a year but, so be it. I planned to go meet with him but this blasted little war got in the way. Thanks for dropping this delightful snippet of news on my desk, Princess. I'll go pack, shall I?"

She touched his arm. "It … may not be *your* doing, Tarangis."

"I see."

"Be ready to fly at dawn."

"*Fly?*"

"That's what Dragon Riders like to do with their friends," she said, lightly stressing the last word.

Take your bows now, Thundersong applauded her privately.

They passed the evening having a merry time with Yardi and Garan in the forge, learning all about his new weapons – explosive crossbow bolts and a burning oil sprayer machine that created a gout of flame twenty-five feet long. Not quite up to Sea Dragon standards but even Thundersong appreciated how having burning oil sprayed from a height might discourage even the most zealous attacker.

When they had a chance to be alone, he inquired from Azania what her cryptic comments about it perhaps not being Tarangis' doing were all about. After all, this false conflict was most certainly not his doing. It was all a fine, fat lie concocted by Azania on the spur of the moment.

A necessary fabrication, she suggested delicately.

Gnarr, he said, threatening her with a set of fangs each as long as her forearm.

She pushed him off. *Don't interrupt me when I'm lying, plotting, swindling and matchmaking. It just isn't done – now, can you guess who I have in mind?*

He thought for a long moment. *Tazshuria, the King's most feared right-hand woman?*

One and the same.

Interesting choice. He did not know what she actually did or what her title was, but what she was not in charge of around N'ginta Citadel was not worth the mention. She was younger than he had expected for a woman in such a powerful position, perhaps in her forties, but – aye, universally feared was one way of putting it. Fearsomely astute, too. Tazshuria and Tarangis?

They'll hear the explosion all the way up in the Archipelago, he said feelingly.

The Princess rubbed her hands together gleefully. *I know! Isn't it just wonderful?*

Maybe, but he could also think of five thousand ways it could all go horribly wrong. No mind; that was a problem for another day. Right now, he clasped Azania very gently in his right forepaw and said:

"Let's go stargaze."

"What? Thundersong, I'm so tired. I just want to sleep for a year."

"Then, you shall fall asleep watching the stars. You need a chance to relax. Dragon's orders … and besides, before you know it, it'll be husband's orders and then … everything will be very different."

Quite unexpectedly, she placed her hand on the sensitive scales beneath his left eye, gazed deep within and said, "Dragon, you are my best friend in all of Solixambria and that will never change, not even if Azerim and I have all eleven children we're planning on. Of course things will change, but this friendship is forever. Now, stargazing with you is something I wouldn't ever pass up on. Shake a wing. Top of the ridge?"

"Sounds perfect."

What was it about stars that sang to the souls of every Dragon and every Human who ever paused to take in their ethereal beauty?

In the morning, Tarangis tried to play fifty questions with the Princess, clearly wanting to winkle out of her what exactly the trouble might be. She assigned him to fly on a different Dragon, a young Sea Dragoness called Riptide, one of the Tide pod.

Gazing south as they lifted into the air, heavily loaded with Garan's creations, she said, "The southerly horizon's a little hazy, wouldn't you say?"

"I saw a few lights flashing down there last night – lightning, I thought," he said.

"Most likely. This time, when the seasons change, can be unsettled," she agreed. "I wouldn't be surprised. The lightning storms can be pretty spectacular, especially if the winds pick up. All that friction, the scientists say."

"I wouldn't be surprised if the long-range scouts haven't picked up sign of a Skartunese war host marching across the desert."

"Cheerful. Thanks."

"I do try, Princess. They counted five or six Jabiz', at best, amongst the armies that came against us. That leaves a good number out there, unaccounted for."

"As someone I know would say –" she chuckled, *Blergh!*

"Exactly!" *Blergh.* "And on that note, hasn't our Tarangis Lionbaiter turned a lovely colour? What do you call that, nauseating nettle-green?"

"Vomitous violet?"

"Whatever it is, I'm not sure it goes very well with the Human complexion. Or the beard."

"We should go encourage – ah, too late."

"Isn't the saying, 'Better out than in?' "

Azania chuckled, "For whom?"

On that bilious note, they flew on into the morning.

As ever, the desert day was hot and dry but the heat had clearly lost its lethal edge. They stopped twice on account of the less hardy riders in their crew, overnighting in a small cave system now frequented by Dragon transport teams flying in either direction. Tarangis was his usual charming self, telling amusing tales of life in Chakkix Camp, but Thundersong had to wonder if his laughter was just a little too bright, perhaps a touch forced?

Had it been fair to force a man in his situation to fly into the battle zone?

Hmm, he mused. Did he also think less of those Dragons who, now liberated from the Skartunese, had wings so damaged or even amputated, in two cases, that they could no longer fly?

Maybe his views needed adjusting.

As the neat V of Sea Dragons bored southward the following morning on a direct heading for N'ginta Citadel, he began to see and scent signs of the unsettled weather Azania had referred to. A fresh, metallic tang of ozone carried on the breeze, along with a hint of moisture – a strange combination of desert dryness and humidity that confused the senses. Being heavily loaded, the flight took longer than he had reckoned upon. They arrived at N'ginta in the late afternoon as the skies threatened to cloud over once more. Enormous thunderheads piled high into the sky but, once again, he doubted it would actually rain.

This weather was all growl and no bite, as Dragons would say.

Thankfully, the horizon and the sands remained stubbornly clear of what he had fully anticipated, a vast Skartunese war host. Still that echoing silence, that barrenness, that visceral sense of expectation. They were out there somewhere. Nothing could be more certain.

To Tarangis' clear surprise, Chanize rolled out to greet them as they landed in the Palace gardens. Thundersong was convinced that they must have met back at Chakkix Camp but he could not recall just now. He introduced them politely, just in case, and tolerated the healer's fussing over how he popped Tarangis into his wheelchair. They rolled off together so that she could show him the facilities modified by King N'chala for her needs.

Sankir Farizam gave Tarangis a very eloquent glare, one that promised the most exquisite torture to anyone who dared to lay so much as an inappropriate eyeball upon his wife – however that worked.

Azania grinned, "Let the plot begin."

Chanize called over her shoulder, "You are to go see Sirensong at once to check that leg, Princess. And you, Thundersong. The last stitching is due to come out of your wingtip any day now."

Dragon and Rider glanced at one another.

"Someone's getting cheeky," Azania said at last. "So, who shall we go annoy first?"

"The tall, bearded man in the shadows ogling your legs?"

"Ooh, I do adore a good old-fashioned ogle," she chirped, sort of crutch-hop-dashing over to collect herself a welcoming kiss.

Hopeless case.

Since King N'chala had declared that a light dinner should be served for his new arrivals, Thundersong and Azania walked up to the main dining hall, nineteen-twentieths occupied by large Dragons and one-twentieth by the Humans. Not that any nit-picking Dragon happened to be measuring merely for the purposes of drawing an amusing comparison. Not him. Everyone spent the meal being very cordial to Tarangis, seated opposite the formidable Tazshuria, which left him a visible bundle of nerves by the end of the evening.

Later on, as he lay and chatted with Aria in the gardens, he heard muffled shouting down in Tazshuria's office. Azania peeked over the balcony and had a huge grin for him. Oh, how she loved her shenanigans!

That was, until Tarangis visited her chambers later. He had his suspicions but had not yet made the potential romantic link. Azania managed to confuse him enough that he went away believing that King N'chala was really seeking to drive a hard bargain and reshape the relationship with his father's long-time business partner, but she assured him that this was just cloak-and-dagger desert negotiation technique. Thundersong saw him wheeling down to his chamber stroking his neat beard, thinking so hard an emotionally sensitive beast like him – *hargh hargh hargh* – could practically smell the smoke rising from the man's mental processes.

He almost went to Tarangis Lionbaiter to appraise him of the plot. Almost, but a deep-seated old fear withheld his paw – that old fear of being scorned and rejected, he realised late in the evening.

Hush your fires, mighty one, his mate whispered into his ear canals.

Or, did she?

His mind snapped into high-flame alert, thinking a million questions, only one aspect of which he could articulate. Was this the touch of Nahritu-N'shula somewhere nearby? Or merely the fear of her?

He went to check in with the sentries guarding the old well, but they had seen and heard nothing – and were clearly on the alert for dark magic. Excellent. Now that he had disturbed Aria, he tried to get back to sleep and failed miserably. Marvellous.

His day improved even more when, at the crack of dawn, he heard the crunching of wheelchair wheels on the garden path and Tazshuria appeared, helping Tarangis along. Thundersong cracked open his eye. To say they looked steamed was an understatement. Tarangis, usually so dapper and perfectly presented, had dark circles beneath his eyes. Tazshuria had a couple of hairs out of place. Her sable curls had a reputation for always being perfectly coiffed. Some even whispered that she used glue to achieve that never-changing look.

"Morning," Tarangis said tightly. "The Princess is –"

"Present," said Azania, emerging from beneath his wing with her usual infeasible morning cheer. Her smile faded slightly as she took in their expressions.

"How could you?" said Tazshuria.

"I'm hurt, Princess, and deeply disappointed," Tarangis added, in deeply embittered tones.

"A … about what?" Azania asked. "Has something happened?"

"Aye, it has, and that something is you," the Lionbaiter continued. "I simply cannot fathom why you, of all people, Azania, would do this to us. What do you stand to gain? I thought … I even dared to imagine … that after all we've been through, we were more than merely business partners. Friends, even. How mistaken I was!"

Frowning down at the Princess, Tazshuria drew her dark desert robes about her spare frame with a pernickety gesture Thundersong warmed to instinctually. The older women was a handsome creature, with high T'nagrun cheekbones and eyes of a startling blue, similar to the waters around the Archipelago. With her dark complexion and hair, the eyes became arresting. Right now, they pierced Azania through and through.

Azania began, "Ah –"

Openly angered, the woman said, "Princess, I have known you since you were born. This is the last thing I would ever have expected from you. Tarangis and I stayed up the entire night trying to work out what you mean by this plot, what you stand to gain from it –" again, Azania made to speak, but the woman cried, "– and why you would seek to ruin us, and the Kingdom of T'nagru, in this way!"

"Ruin you?" Azania spluttered. "I hardly –"

"What is it? Angling for the throne?" Tarangis spat.

"No!"

"The Dragon put you up to this base treachery?" Tazshuria hissed. "Seeking to wreck vital business partnerships and cut T'nagru off from the northern kingdoms?"

"Treachery? Whatever are you two talking about?"

To him, Azania said, *Thundersong, help! This is all going to a pile of crock and I don't know what to do.*

What I will not say is, 'I told you so.' Let's just ... hmm. I have an idea. Aloud, to the group, Thundersong said, "Well, it is a plot of course – you two are very astute to have sniffed it out – but I am afraid you have, how do you Humans put it, entirely the wrong end of the tail?"

"Stick," Tarangis growled. "I should have known. Dragon, did you put Azania up to this?"

"Aye, in a manner of speaking. Tarangis, as you know,

I have a penchant for emotional magic and Azania is a bit of a fixer. When you told us you were in the market to acquire a suitable woman to wife, I am afraid … well, this is awkward to admit but, things got a little out of paw, shall we say?"

The man shook his head slowly. "A … wife? What?"

Tazshuria spluttered, "This is nothing to do with thrones or kingdoms or wars?"

Azania shook her sable curls contritely.

"Princess Azania, you were expecting me to – to find a *wife* – for Tarangis? Young lady, that is terribly old-fashioned and … well! Rather unexpected, I'd say. Quite the ambush."

"Not … exactly," she said.

The pair stared at her, clearly beyond befuddled – relieved and speechless, but no less clued-in to the plot than before. Time for a Dragon's delicate touch to dig his best friend out of this pit she had dug for herself.

Thundersong cleared his throat. "The lady we felt most suited to Tarangis Lionbaiter's particular brand of genius, lady Tazshuria, happens to be you." Gasps! "A most apposite arrangement, I believe," he added. "Tarangis is in the market and you, I must say, are a most excellent and worthy catch. Do tell me, what is your price?"

"Dragon!" Azania squealed, halfway caught between hilarity and horror.

Tarangis flushed mightily. So did Tazshuria – but an astute Dragon caught a whiff between them, even though they neither touched nor made any other outward signal and he knew that, against all the odds, Azania's instinct was once more bang on the mark. How did she do it?

The Lionbaiter said, "If I was 'in the market,' you two rotten meddlers, I would not put it in such a way. Fancy … are you matchmaking for me? You dare?"

Thundersong said, "Well, Princess Azania has a price. Do you not?"

"Me?" he howled. "*I* have a … what is this?"

He spread his paws. "A man of your immodest gifts must be fearfully expensive. Can the Kingdom of T'nagru even afford you? However, I am an immodestly wealthy Dragon as a result of my mighty and noble deeds. May I negotiate on your behalf, Tarangis Lionbaiter? I assure you, the terms shall be favourable."

Tarangis folded his arms. "Most certainly not!"

Azania's laughter pealed in his mind as she realised for herself what he had sensed.

"Are you defying a Dragon?" Thundersong threatened, looming over him. "Tazshuria, now that we have this notorious reprobate in our talons, what say you, we find him our most comfortable accommodations down in the dungeons? I am sure that after a few years of mouldering away down there on a diet of mouldy palm dates and daily sips of brackish water, he will be amenable to anything we ask."

"Thundersong, you are despicable!" Tarangis frowned.

To everyone's surprise, Tazshuria burst into laughter. "Oh, enough! Tarangis, I do believe we have been hoodwinked, double-crossed and entirely found out."

Visibly trembling, her hand slipped over to his bearded cheek. After a second, he sighed and returned the pressure. The yearning that dwelled between them lifted all five of his hearts as one.

Azania sighed.

Tarangis said, "What I want to know, is how you two knew? What gave us away? Look, there's a bit of history. King N'gala forbade me from ever stepping foot – ahem," he chuckled awkwardly, "or running my wheels, that is, about his kingdom due to an unfortunate mistake I made some years back. Notoriously, N'gala was not a forgiving man. I'm not certain where the new King stands on the matter, but since I am not currently languishing in said dungeon, I did dare to entertain some hope that this regime might be … more amenable."

Tazshuria said, "Tarangis and I have been writing to

each other privately for years. N'gala knew and forbade me from leaving the borders of this kingdom. When you intimated that N'chala felt he had been cheated by Tarangis, we feared the worst."

"I'm so sorry," Azania said. "That was complete fiction. I'm a compulsive meddler and I had no right … I'm sorry, Tazshuria. I've treated you terribly."

The woman held out her arms; the Princess fell into them with a muffled sob.

Tarangis gave a gruff chuckle and did his beard-stroking routine. "I guess it didn't work out too badly after all, Tazshuria. Now, Princess Azania, one thing you could do for us …"

"Anything."

"Could you speak to your brother in the strictest confidence?"

"Nothing would please me more."

"Because I have a certain business acquisition I wish to make."

"Best think again. You're on my home territory, Tarangis," Tazshuria threatened. "I'll be the one doing the acquiring. And, if you think you're the Lionbaiter, remember, I'm the lioness around here. Ready to do business?"

"Roaring to go," said he.

Thundersong said, "One piece of relationship advice for you two lions?" The three Humans turned to stare at him in surprise. "Take it in bite-sized pieces."

CHAPTER 28

WAR HOST

LATE ONE AFTERNOON, A week after he and Azania had, by sheer misadventure, rescued that relationship from the savage jaws of misunderstanding and strife, the whole of the already smudged, southerly horizon turned dark. This was not the dark of the growling, prowling thunderstorms of late, which had left the air feeling supercharged with electricity. This was a wholly different phenomenon. The black clouds slowly boiled upward, like a living thing.

Mighty horns of war began to sound a range of doleful, echoing notes, causing the air to shake and the Humans to complain of the hairs on their arms standing upright. Made a Dragon shudder to think upon it. *Blergh!*

Thundersong winged skyward with all the other Dragons and Riders to take stock. In the distance, the dunes turned silver as ranks of Skartunese foot soldiers poured over them in a living wave, changing the colour of the desert. On and on they came in their measured, disciplined ranks, in numbers beyond counting or belief. Above the sea of silver helms and tall spears, flocks of giant crows turned the dawn sky dark, birds such as Solixambria had never seen. These black-feathered birds were eight feet in wingspan and as tall as a man. Even from this distance, the chorus of their baleful cawing chilled his bones.

"A murder of crows," Azania said quietly.

From his new position above Aria's shoulders, Azerim said, "I don't even know how to count that many."

"That's not all," said the Cobalt Dragoness, pointing.

Across the farthest dunes came an array of creatures Inzashu had described to them, creatures out of T'nagrun legend or simply, their nightmares. The six-legged armadon was a living battering ram measuring forty feet long and standing eighteen feet tall at the shoulder. Few city gates in the world would fancy a visit from such a beast. This army had a dozen. Behind them appeared a shaggy mass of giant heads belonging to towering, sallow-skinned ogres. Thundersong estimated that any of the one-eyed creatures would be able to stare at the defenders on the battlements eye to eye, such was their height, and the musculature of their girth – as much as their sheer unsightliness – was breathtaking. Any Dragon would think twice before taking on one of those. He noticed, narrowing his eyes, that each had two handlers standing in cages either side of the ogre's head. More electricity? He would not be surprised.

Loudly, Thundersong said, "Well, they'll definitely beat us on the ugly front."

Dragons and Humans laughed nervously.

Another insect-borne army made up the eastern flank, creating an iridescent ripple as they swept across the dunes. From the west came thousands of soldiers mounted upon the backs of coal-black Skartunese warhorses and a troop of several hundred mounted upon white unicorns – again, to his horror, captives in the same manner as the Dragon thralls had been. It had always been that some creatures thrived upon inventing new ways to degrade, enslave, torture and kill others. To him, this was incomprehensible.

Great columns of slaves trailed into the distance,

dragging the siege weapons and supply carts necessary to keep this massive army on the march.

No-one could fail to look upon this war host and quail. This was more than an army, it was a sea, a full-scale invasion of the north of the continent. Inzashu had described her peoples' empire-building ambitions. Here it was. This was no friendly visit, no bracing, chivalrous war undertaken upon agreeable terms. This was a little light genocide before teatime, a snack to whet the appetite before they marched on to annihilate anyone else who dared to stand in their way.

There would be no negotiations and no quarter given.

Acid spread in the pit of his stomach. How could so few even hope to fight this army? They would be swatted aside like bugs.

The dark, dense formations of crows swirled as if reacting to a command. In a moment, the cause became clear – Nahritu N'shula emerged from their midst, flying aboard Eversong. In her right hand, she gripped a staff that looked fit to split mountains. It held a large green gemstone at its tip, from which an unholy light blazed, that turned her golden armour a rather less appealing colour. Everything about her appearance screamed, 'evil sorceress!' in case anyone was not paying sufficient attention.

Severe lack of fashion sense, he said to Azania.

Would you look at that, she said, pointing. *My baby sister, flying right behind mommy on her way to world domination. I don't think I've ever hated anyone so much in my life.*

Azania, we don't know for certain –

Look. Just look at them!

It does look bad, he admitted. *Not exactly kicking and screaming, is she?*

No.

Inzashu-N'shula was dressed like her mother, in ceremonial golden armour – an exact copy, just on a smaller scale. Her tiny hands clasped the Psyromantic

Mage's waist. Thundersong steeled his mind against intrusion. That child was more than dangerous.

Juggernaut discussed assault options with King N'chala. Even he looked openly troubled, not his usual gruff, professional self.

The army spread out as they marched on, step by sand-churning step. Nahritu was clearly yelling orders, although they could not hear her voice above the tremendous hubbub. The army now covered the dunes all the way to the horizon and there was still no end in sight. He had not known that there were this many Humans on the entire continent of Solixambria. Could have done with ten thousand of his relatives around about now, right? Instead, they were off on some mystical migration that promised to tidy up the world and its errant magic – while right here, at this moment, he saw the end of his world.

How was this fair?

They could never have imagined such a day, he said quietly to himself and Azania. *Won't this change the equilibrium of everything? Won't this eventually affect the Sea Dragons as well?*

Talk about the long-term view. Her tone communicated reluctant agreement.

Ah, and a few old friends fly high, he added, pointing out how the Terror Clan Dragons, previously hidden, flew among the crows. Magic had shielded this entire war host and brought it undetected across the desert. He sensed the birds' desire for blood, their glossy black eyes communicating intelligence and hostility in equal measure.

It doesn't feel right, does it? Azania said. *They look …*

Exhausted, he realised aloud. *I wonder if it was dark magic that brought them across the desert so fast, perhaps pushing them beyond the endurance of normal bone and blood?*

Even those mighty ogres, mouths agape in what he had taken for bestial bloodlust, had sat down now and refused to move, no matter what their handlers did. One of the armadons collapsed onto its side with an impact they heard from half a mile off, and did not move again. Nahritu-

N'shula's frustration reached an apparent peak – then her eyes turned to measure the deployment and paltry numbers of Dragons above N'ginta Citadel and she smiled a smile of rampant wickedness. Whirling the mighty staff about her head as if it weighed no more than a twig, she cried out in a mighty voice.

The entire army sat down as one. All the way to the horizon. Even the crows folded their wings and landed wherever they could, turning the sands silver and feathered black.

In the silence, King N'chala's expletive rang clear.

"That's one way of putting it," Azania said, as the Mage turned Eversong about and winged away. "Nothing like a little psychological warfare to spread fear and discord, is there?"

Juggernaut glanced over at her. "No discord here, Princess, only determination. Let's go talk somewhere they can't overhear, lipread or whatever."

"That's the spirit," said Azerim, the first words he had spoken since he saw the Skartunese.

By the scent sense of his emotions, Thundersong realised what he must be thinking. Aye, this enemy was as innumerable as the fish in the ocean. Could they find a way to introduce a few sharks into the equation? Try to do something, anything at all, that might make a difference in the face of such overwhelming numbers?

That Azerim continued to prove himself as a man of mettle and honour. Could he ever, ever bring himself to give Azania over to him?

What would Thundersong the Elder do?

If you're listening, great-grandsire, he said quietly within himself, *we really could do with some inspiration today. Otherwise, what does it even mean to belong to such a family as mine?*

The consensus was to hit the enemy and hit them hard. There were knights from the northern Kingdoms who were raring to have a good, old-fashioned cavalry charge and had been denied so far. Coupled with Dragon cover, they ought to hit and disengage cleanly enough that even Juggernaut admitted it should not pose a great risk to the forces. The timing would be crucial.

"You disengage when I say," he warned. "We'll flank you with a rolling assault that will also need to break off at the right moment, when we're starting to get bogged down."

"Sheer numbers," Azerim said tightly.

"Should we go for the ogres or the armadons?" Thundersong asked, before answering his own question. "No. We shouldn't strike that deep. Not yet."

Juggernaut eyeballed him. "One of your feelings?"

He had never appreciated lack of inflection in a voice more.

"Nothing specific, but aye."

"If you sniff out the slightest thing more than one of those ogres' backsides," the Orange Dragon growled, "you sing out, alright? That goes for everyone here. I want support waves. No getting so drawn in that we lose our heads. These brutes have been full of surprises. Clear?"

"Sir!" the Humans roared.

The Dragons growled in assent.

"Azerim?" Juggernaut put in.

"I reckon Everdeep's crew could hit those one-eyed ogres in a pinch. The distance looks about right and they make flipping massive targets," he stated blandly. "In the mix, why don't we slip Everdeep over to the edge or above your rolling assault and see if they can't pick off a few?"

"Nice," he agreed. "Let's do this!"

HAAI-ARR!! the Isles Dragonesses yelled.

Thundersong resettled his wings crossly. Gave him the shivers every time they did that. He caught Aria grinning at him and realised he had been read like an open scroll.

He said, "May your blades run red with the enemy's blood, o Ariamyrielle Seaspray."

She nodded, a fierce light glinting in her eyes. "Thank you, Thundersong. May your strength ever prevail."

To his frustration, Thundersong found himself assigned to one of the uppermost roles in the 'attack stack,' as Juggernaut had dubbed this strategy. His mentor explained in brief terms. His job would be to bomb the enemy at just the right moment and in just the right places, for example, if the fighting became too hot in one location or, most importantly, when the time came to disengage. A great many lives could be spared by a well-timed withdrawal, coupled with the right amount of distraction. No fireworks or sonic booms for the sake of the horses, he added – this time.

With that, the main gates of N'ginta Citadel parted to allow the ground forces egress. No less than four hundred heavy mounted knights and one thousand light horse rumbled out into the warm evening. Forming up in magnificent array, they swept forward at an easy trot. Barely a quarter-mile separated the vanguard of the Skartunese host from the gates.

A full battalion of Garome longbow archers was next out of the gates, rushing to take positions in support of the cavalry. Their longbows had a much greater range than the more accurate desert weapons. A minute passed before the waiting Dragons heard the chilling sound of a thousand arrows taking flight at once – like a disturbed hornets' nest, only much louder. A second time, the wuthering, buzzing sound rose and faded into the distance. Thrice, each time within five to six seconds. He had seen them practising this fast reload but to see the way that thickets of arrows darkened the sky, was another matter altogether.

Juggernaut roared, "Let's fly!"

As Thundersong launched up above the level of the battlements, the volleys of arrows continued to soar, arch lazily over the Skartunese forces and fall like a deceptively soft rain. The result was carnage. With men sitting or lying down shoulder to shoulder, unprotected by shields, the long shafts had plenty of targets to hit and they continued to fall until the ground resembled a wheat field. As the horses thundered into the charge, the command came to extend the range. Again and again, the arrows shot forth, the next volley rising before the one before had time to fall.

Ascending steadily, he had plenty of time to see the Dragonwings forming either side of the charging horses. Black sand churned up in great sprays behind their hooves. The Skartunese warriors reacted belatedly, as if dazed; many were still in the process of clambering to their feet when the heavy knights smashed into them with a crash that echoed off the battlements like thunder – where the men and Dragons manning the defence raised a great cheer. The flashing hooves smashed armour and kicked men aside, while the knights struck left and right with their longswords and battle axes.

The Amboraine contingent hasn't even fainted yet, the Princess noted accurately.

Quite, he agreed.

This was a type of warfare that knights understood. So did the squads of light horses that cut in behind them, tidying up. Less so, the two Dragonwings that peeled off left and right in the now-familiar pattern of raiders and runners, as the Dragons called their assignments. A mighty thunder rose from the belligerent, keyed-up Dragons as they swept in, flaming the Skartunese to broaden the wedge the cavalry had already speared toward the heart of their force. The Tamarine Dragons flew in low, landing amongst the enemy soldiers to wreak havoc with whirling tail strikes and flashing talons – some even simply rolled over the enemy, a Grinder favourite – while tight knots of Isles Dragonesses swirled about them, appearing to dance like butterflies through the swirling flame. Their blades winked and whirled, cutting holes, as if by magic, into the tapestry of battle. He briefly saw Aria swirling through smoke and flame before her swords cross cut sharply, decapitating three soldiers in a single stroke.

He and Azania saw now why Juggernaut had issued the warnings he had been so keen on. The sheer numbers acted like sand sopping up a tide. The knights and supporting cavalry slowed and came to a standstill. Despite that he was busy flaming soldiers left and right, Juggernaut bellowed his orders.

That's our cue, Azania said.

The two arms of Dragons began to curve toward the centre, carving through the Skartunese forces like so many living knives. This created a pincer shape that would relieve the better-organised squads of enemy soldiers coming into contact with the knights now.

Hold, hold … he said. *Go!*

Bombs away.

The more massive explosions engulfed men in walls of flame but also acted to rouse the enemy force at last – again, as if they responded to an inaudible command. The crows took to the air with a sound like a storm wind rising. Suddenly, hundreds of Skartunese warriors whipped to their feet and deployed devices that shot nets a hundred feet or more, snarling up the smaller Isles Dragonesses most especially. The flurry was far too thick to be avoided. Everdeep ordered his Sea Dragons into a low sweep to support and free those entangled, while Thundersong and Azania unleashed a second round of the chemical bombs.

I still have two dozen of those nice explosive quarrels, she said tightly.

Shame to waste such a nice invention, he said.

Swinging perhaps a touch wider than Juggernaut had authorised, Dragon and Rider eyed up the first of the ogres sitting nearly four hundred yards away.

Dragon shot, she said, lowering the Dragon bow into his palm. *I'll supply the visuals.*

Nocking a six-foot quarrel to the string, he sighted high

and far. The touch of her mind brought him down six feet or so. Too high, last time. This time would be perfect.

Tzoing!

His quarrel hissed like an angry snake with the force of his shot as it raced away into the deepening cobalt of the gathering evening. He narrowed his eyes. "Looking good."

"Oh no!"

"What?"

In the distance, an ogre's nose exploded as if he had suddenly grown a crimson flower on his face. Thundersong spared a thought for the poor beast. At least it was a quick death.

"Under the sand," the Princess said. "Something's moving down there … call them out, now!"

Thundersong's swift scan took in dozens upon dozens of large mounds moving rapidly beneath the sand, closing in on the Dragons and knights. His warning bellow seemed to stick in his throat for an eternity before belling out, easily loud enough for Juggernaut and the others to hear. He and Azania took a shot and a bomb each at the nearest mounds, blowing something plant-like – khaki green leaves and tendrils – sky-high.

Juggernaut's force had not disengaged yet.

The Princess called, *He's protecting the knights – it's going to be tight! Help them –*

GET OUT OF THERE!! Thundersong roared.

Good. Another shot!

In the crucible of his dread, nothing happened quickly enough. The light horse and knights streamed off toward the gates now, but many stopped to help lift comrades or chop snarled-up Dragons free. As they had been trained, the Dragons worked in teams to help one another avoid capture. Juggernaut barrel-rolled over an enemy troop to give Aria, unfortunately entangled by at least two if not three metal-reinforced nets, a chance to struggle to her paws. While the Dragons took off and flamed their way to freedom, the mounds closed in at an infeasible speed.

Everdeep swooped for Aria, his crossbow team firing in concert to pierce several of the mounds right through, but the buried creatures did not even slow down.

Blast their orders! Folding his wings, Thundersong had just begun to plummet to help his mate when the sands beneath and around the Dragons exploded with green plant tendrils and great, snapping green mouths. Fire burst out of dozens of jaws, crisping the plants, but they lashed out at the Dragons and knights, entwining their limbs and wings, spitting the grey-green immobilising ooze over them as he and Azania had seen with that young Sea Dragoness. It was tough stuff, difficult even for Dragons to saw through, clearly a creation of Terror Clan design. The mottled green tendrils wound around them, pinioning or snarling up the Dragons just long enough for them to become targets – even those already in the air. In seconds, over a hundred of their force lay on the ground, squirming, flaming and ripping at the plants.

A plant mouth gaped wide to swallow Aria whole.

NOOO!! Thundersong raged, stretching his wings to his utmost. *No, Aria!*

No! Azania's scream echoed his.

Where's Azerim?

Up on Everdeep – they're going in …

They were still far from within range as he saw Aria, holding one of her *kaniaxi* blades, still hacking away furiously despite that she must have been blinded, disappear beneath the sands. Two plants had a hold of Juggernaut, another tried to wrestle Everdeep down by his right paw. White fire hosed around him, crisping the plant enough that he could tear free. He lunged for Aria, but the plant whisked her away at that same high speed. Other Dragons, knights and their horses vanished in the same way, like a magic trick played on an unbelievable scale.

I'll have to hit them! Thundersong gasped.

Let's do it, even if it hurts our own. We have to get Aria back – and Juggernaut!

Two of the plant mouths appeared to be battling over Juggernaut. The tough exudate covered his wings and upper torso but he still fought in a fury, giving back more than he received. Half of his body had vanished beneath the sand, the plants throwing more tendrils about his body now to lasso him and make his life miserable. A few Skartunese warriors tried to pierce him with swords. Juggernaut made them pay for their temerity.

Ears!

Twisting his body in the dive, Thundersong aimed his sound away from the citadel and the longbow archers, still working with great discipline to cover the cavalry's return. His chest swelled.

Ready!

LET THEM GOOO!! he thundered.

Not quite the words he had been looking for, but the soundwave rolled over the Skartunese in a visible surge, smashing crows out of the air and flattening their troops for a quarter-mile radius. In the distance, he saw the ogres blink as if surprised. Clutching their heads and bellowing in pain, four of them scrambled to their feet and charged blindly through the throng, heedlessly trampling their own forces underfoot.

Above them, he saw a speck of white.

Nahritu-N'shula applauded their effort sarcastically.

Shaking his head to try to clear the ringing from his ears, Thundersong glanced down to see the last plants retreating as rapidly as they had arrived, apparently unmoved by his blast. Mounds beneath the soil. A mile away, the movement vanished as if they had burrowed deep. All the Dragons who had been captured, were gone.

ARIA! I WILL COME FOR YOU! he roared.

In one stroke, their enemy had decimated their Dragon force. Halved their numbers – more than.

The Psyromantic Mage waved her hands.

With a mighty cry, her army rose to their feet and paws and began to march toward N'ginta Citadel. Apparently, all they had done had only served to warm them up.

That was his best, his greatest roar yet, and it had achieved nothing. What could a Dragon do now? Where did he go from here?

Nahritu-N'shula had drawn them in for the sucker punch. No need to raise an actual sweat. Just a simple, wholly effective battle plan based on their likelihood to attack first, as they must – or, as she had calculated proud Dragons would do. She had studied her enemy, divined his weaknesses and acted with devastating precision.

His hearts sat like five lumps of lead in his chest as he considered Aria's loss for the umpteenth time. Guilt and grief darkened his fires. Knowing that they could not have done more, even knowing that she did not expect to survive this war, did not help in the slightest. The only solace, perhaps, a sliver of hope, was that the actions of those plants suggested capture rather than killing – which most likely led to horrible torture at the hands of the Skartunese, but alive was better than dead and being digested by nasty carnivorous plant juices, right?

He clenched his paws into fists, all four of them. If they touched just one scale upon her back, just one …

Here come the crows, the Princess whispered. *Thundersong, I'm so sorry about Aria and … everything. This is about as spectacular a mess as we've ever been in. What will we do?*

We'll pull up our big Princess trousers, he said darkly, *and go rescue them. Nothing to it. Just go knock off a few million crows and mind the armadons don't batter down our gates first. Do you think the Skartunese are into bad jokes? Maybe helpless laughter will stop their army in its tracks?*

She chuckled miserably. *Obviously. Perfect plan.*

Right, plans. Get N'chala to open that pit in front of the gate. Nobody's going out that way anymore. Next, get all the Dragons down, landing them —

Down? Thundersong, you'll be chopped to pieces!

Down, he insisted. *It's our only chance to concentrate enough firepower to make those birds think twice. Remember Garan's bug spray? Well, those are feathered creatures. Can't imagine they like burning oil any more than you do …*

Nice! she smacked his neck.

Half an idea.

That's half more than we had before. Next, we arm everyone in this city and get them to barricade the rooftops. Anyone who can draw a bow, twirl a slingshot or swing a saucepan needs to be out there to help — the whole city.

Mmm, beauty and *brains. Always knew you had it in you.*

Charmer, she grinned.

Aye, if we can survive being overwhelmed by the crows, we might just be able to put up a fight against the rest. That's my most positive assessment of the situation here.

Now, she gave him a neck hug with her legs. *Don't despair, my friend. Aria is not going anywhere. If I know that Dragoness … there's N'chala, on the walls. Go to him, please.*

I just hate that woman. She laughed at us.

Let's just say, you're more than a loudmouth, the Princess noted. *I know you're going to come up with a brilliant idea, Thundersong.*

Snap of the ol' talons. No problem.

The question was, how?

Shortly, they put the matter to N'chala and Azerim. They immediately issued the orders, while Thundersong and Everdeep had a quick argument before coming up with an idea whereby squads of Dragons on the ground would cover one another from multiple angles. They hoped it worked, because out there, a murder of crows was planning its revenge on all of Humankind — and a few Dragons who happened to be caught in the way — for giving them that particular collective noun.

Azania chuckled, *You're ridiculous, do you know that? Nobody ever asked the crows their opinion?*

Linguistic fact, said he.

With that, they both glanced skyward as the incoming flock of heavy, slow-flapping crows blackened out the setting suns, winging toward the city like an airborne plague. Their cries grated upon the ear. Around the walls, a mighty war host gathered, clamouring to spill the blood of every creature inside this desert city. Here it was. This was the –

"*Not* the end," Azania snorted. "Honestly, Thundersong, I simply haven't had time to finish our writings or to record all of your terrible jokes. For that reason alone, I believe we are not fated to die today."

He guffawed, "Princess, I do believe that we're both quite mad."

"That, we can agree upon."

CHAPTER 29

ZAPPED

ALL AROUND THE CITY, the Dragons congregated against the outer and inner battlements, using the stone as additional protection for their backs or flanks. No Dragon liked to feel cornered, nor to cower from an enemy – but this was not just any enemy. Everdeep made his orders as plain as Sea Dragon flame. Survival first. Heroism and honour later, and no place for false pride.

Therefore, Tamarine Dragons stood shoulder to shoulder with Isles Dragonesses, Sea Dragons and their long-lost kin from the mountains. Each knot of eight to ten Dragons faced in different directions and to the vertical, covering one another as best they were able. N'chala's runners brought skeins of water to the thirsty Sea Dragons. No creature wanted to run out of flame. Above, on the battlements, the soldiers hunkered down beneath shields and warmed up Garan's oil sprayers.

Thundersong and Azania stood together with his three sisters, Echosong, Farsong and Ripplesong, three Grinder Dragons and two Isles warriors near the main outer gate. From his position, he could gaze down a straight road, now fortified and barricaded, to where Sirensong took her stance against the main gate of the inner battlement, together with her assigned squad. Everywhere else he looked, Humans strung up ropes and nets, moved furniture to use as barricades and hunkered down. The knights and cavalry who had survived that charge, formed up into troops to scour the roads, while dense packs of longbow archers spread out along the battlements. They would be busy enough, soon enough, for he reckoned there had to be fifty crows for every person or Dragon in this citadel.

Sure, the odds were ridiculous.

He cudgelled his brains for any hint of that useful madness Azania had accused him of. Supposed to be the creative sort, right?

Was creativity the other face of a coin called insanity?

Aria, he whispered. *Stay strong.*

They were out of time. With a ragged chorus of grating cries, the first crows bombarded the battlements with their talons outstretched and their beaks agape. Arrows smacked into the black avian bodies, sending them tumbling end over end. Swords flashed as the first flurry of birds thickened and became a rushing storm. A preternatural twilight spread over the citadel. Suddenly, there were bodies and feathers everywhere one looked, a furious mêlée experienced in bursts of clacking fangs, blasts of fire, battering wings and hooked avian talons. Thundersong roared as a flurry of beaks and claws stabbed around his eyes; he instinctively swatted away a bird that tried to lift Azania off his back. Her dagger clinked off bone as she fought back grimly.

On and on they fought, for many minutes and then, for a time that seemed to stretch into hours.

He and the Dragons in his group became separated from the rest of the world, it seemed, caged by a blizzard of birds. His white fires slashed out again and again, a billowing beacon that conversely, drew in the enemy like moths to a pyre. He lost count of the number of bodies that caught alight, still cawing their hatred and struggling as they went down in flames. Switching weapons, Azania spent all her arrows within a few minutes. No need to aim. She could fire literally anywhere and hit an enemy.

This was real madness!

Just like that, he had an odd idea – not so much a sonic punch, as a sonic reverberation. Between flares of flame aiming to keep his group safe, he tried a few sound effects.

Not quite the thing? Azania inquired.

No.

Can I help? What are you trying to achieve?

He showed her a mental picture, meantime, enjoying a moment's respite that allowed him to see desperate fights taking place on every rooftop, outside of windows, around his dam … nearby, a small family fought with a fire poker, two kitchen knives, an iron skillet and half a chair! His hearts swelled with admiration for their courage.

Azania burst out laughing at his idea, but then stilled. *Call your dam. Bounce the sound back and forth. You Sea Dragons are built for it after all.*

Ah, a concerto! Perfect.

The Dragons around him startled as he roared for Sirensong. Rather than query his idea, she immediately cried out in Dragoceanic, calling for all the Sea Dragons to help. Thundersong turned to his half-sisters, explaining his idea quickly.

≈*What's it supposed to do? Confuse them?*≈ Farsong asked. She snapped up a crow and spat out a mouthful of feathers. ≈*Anything's better than dealing with more of these feathered pests.*≈

Sirensong led out with a deep, sonorous note that reverberated off the city gates. *WHABOOM!*

Thundersong's scales prickled. Awesome mother! *WHOMP-WHABOOM!* he responded, pitching the sound back as if they were playing a game.

WHABOOM!

≈*I get it now,*≈ Ripplesong grinned.

"Here comes the next flurry!" Azania shouted.

WHOMP-WHABOOM! he and his sisters responded.

THUNDER O DRAGON

WHOMP! came back from Sirensong, faster, louder and higher-pitched.

The team by this gate responded by imitating her, returning the resonant beat with interest. Faster and faster, they bounced the sounds back and forth. As the black crows attacked again in thick numbers, their feathers thumped back and forth beneath the percussive beat.

Everdeep came charging down the street, crying, ≈*What are you doing?*≈

≈*Echo chamber!*≈ Sirensong called. He stared blankly at her. ≈*Help us. You'll see.*≈

WHOMP ... WHOMP-WHABOOM!

The beat picked up, forcing the crows to flap wildly against the powerful reverberation, only to be shoved back in the opposite direction immediately. With the vocal power of Everdeep added to the mix, the incoming flights of crows began to mill about in confusion, baffled by the immense sound and where it was coming from.

≈*Faster!*≈ Thundersong yelled.

You are completely potty! Azania cried. He had no idea what this meant, but it sounded rude and complimentary at the same time. Perfect.

The two teams of Sea Dragons redoubled the speed, thankful now for the great city gates that acted like mighty sound boards, amplifying their efforts.

Then, what he had hoped for, but could never have put a talon upon, happened. The sound mingled and merged, hitting a height of amplitude so powerful, a massive soundwave shovelled the crows bodily away from Sirensong and Everdeep, as if they flew into a headwind. The birds shrieked in fury. Aye! Feeling a bit rattled by all the thunder and storm, right?

Just wait until the true perfidy of his plans came to light!

Together now! Azania screamed, even though no-one else could have heard her.

Thundersong and his sisters slammed back the beat, so

powerfully that they ended up plastered against the gates, but the intersecting soundwaves smashed all the crows between them. Feathers exploded into the air, ripped off their bodies by the sheer excess of auditory violence.

Then, avian bodies plummeted to the ground, leaving great cloudbanks of black feathers behind, floating in the breeze. Thousands of them. *Splat! Splot! Blat!*

By his wings, he had never seen anything uglier under the suns than giant, freshly plucked fowl.

Azania gave a wicked giggle. *How much naked poultry did you want, Thundersong?*

I know! he crowed in delight. *Truly, we stoned these crows.*

The birds looked ridiculous, stripped of their feathers. Hardly a threat at all. Over on that rooftop, an elderly desert matron slew a struggling crow with an expert flick of her knife, unmindful of the spray of blood. Everywhere, people dashed into the streets to take up the slaughter as the stunned crows began to twitch or stagger to their feet.

Everdeep stared across at him, a slow grin spreading across his huge face. ≈*Thundertiddler, eh? That's only because you choose to paddle in the biggest oceans.*≈

≈*Go spread the news, my hearts' song,*≈ Sirensong said, her eyes gleaming across at him.

≈*That I surely will!*≈

Azania chortled, *That's my talented Dragon. Come on, let's go help everyone around us.*

Break out the barbecue, he snorted. *No shortage of drumsticks today.*

It took until well after nightfall for the defenders to deal with the crow attack, with many losses of their own, but by the time the city was covered in freshly air-plucked fowl – truly a foul sight, Azania quipped, making Azerim groan in despair, to which Thundersong added that the streets were only covered in a paltry amount of poultry, which made a muscle in the King's left cheek twitch – they learned the reason for the delay to Nahritu-N'shula's attack plans.

As it turned out, a creature of armoured muscle the size of an armadon was about as clever and compliant as the armour it wore. No amount of mental meddling could change the fact that there was very little brain to actually meddle with.

By the time they had lined up an attack on the main gates, the overcast night approached the midnight hour. The enormous mound of tiny-brained creature charged at the gates, making the entire city shake, and promptly toppled headfirst into the disguised pit King N'chala had prepared right outside, not for such a moment as this, because no-one had ever imagined such a beast, but it worked nonetheless. With a tremendous crash twenty feet short, it failed to do any damage whatsoever to the gates. N'chala performed a wholly inappropriate, out-of-character dance.

His defenders pitched a couple of barrels of oil into the creature trying in vain to wriggle its way out of the pit and set it alight. Sheets of flame roared upward, bathing the battlements in orange light.

"How's about that barbecue I mentioned?" Thundersong suggested.

More than a few Dragons growled their agreement. Most had lost so many scales they looked somewhat henpecked, besides having suffered innumerable injuries to the wings and several severe wounds to the eyes.

Nahritu-N'shula responded by waving in the full attack.

There followed a night of bitter, attritional battle in which neither side gained a measurable advantage. Each time the attackers found a foothold upon the walls, the defenders pushed them back with Dragon fire, wedges of knights or withering flurries of poisoned desert arrows. Three times, they attempted to send ogres to scale the walls, only to discover the power of Garan's explosive quarrels. The third ogre collapsed across the battlements. Everdeep shoved the creature away.

"Foul," was all he said.

After that, conventional warfare came into play. Heavily armoured and shielded formations of men trooped up to the gate pit and began to fill it with sand and stones. The army dragged up their siege weapons and began to bombard the city with everything they had. The rain of rock and shrapnel became brutal. By the occasional light of the moons gleaming between the scudding clouds, they saw Nahritu-N'shula taking counsel with a group of men they took for the Jabiz or ruling council of Skartun atop a faraway dune. They were meant to be seen, of that no-one had any doubt. But what was her scheme this time?

In the early hours, the Skartunese army wrestled the biggest machine anyone had yet seen toward the gates. A grey tarpaulin covered the massive bulk of the machine, perhaps fifty feet high and treble that in length, lying over lumps and jutting objects for which he could discern no purpose. A large, dome-shaped mound stood near the back, the dents in the tarpaulin suggesting a birdcage-like structure.

N'chala, Azerim, Azania, Thundersong and Everdeep gathered to view what was coming against the city. It could be nothing good. The fighting was still fierce on the walls but, for the time being, the defenders held their own. To Thundersong, it looked like a supersized version of what Jabiz Urdoo had used to jangle him silly and which had led to his moulting before – not an experience he cared to repeat, even if it had ended well.

The machine rolled along upon dozens of wheels each as tall as a Dragon. Two ogres pushed it from behind, while dozens of Dragon thralls pulled it by thick hawsers from the front. Their handlers drove them so hard, he saw flashes of electricity lighting up their ear canals and their pained bellowing was terrible to hear. Many Dragons and those of his kin lined up on the battlements above and around them, waited to see what this thing might be.

Another lightning thrower? Azania guessed.

Aye, that's what I'm thinking, he said.

With an inordinate amount of effort over the course of several hours, they dragged it all the way up to a distance of two hundred Dragon paces from the gate, where the defenders could have fired upon the Dragon thralls, if they wished. N'chala ordered his teams not to. Instead, they aimed for the ogres, but this time the great explosive quarrels vanished in tiny puffs of green smoke not ten feet from the oblivious faces, not even disturbing their straggling, greasy black hair. Seemed the enemy had learned from their mistakes.

The other thing they had learned was patience.

The machine sat there all day doing precisely nothing. Meantime, the immense armies of the Skartunese threw themselves four, five or six at a time at the walls of N'ginta Citadel. A certain rhythm developed. First, a Jabiz would announce himself at a thunderous, magically enhanced volume:

"I am Jabiz Tankandoo! I will throttle you with your own entrails! Prepare to die!"

"My name is Jabiz Bardoo!" Smashing his fists upon his copper breastplate, the man screamed, "I will rend you limb from limb and scatter your parts from here to the Vaylarn Archipelago! Fight me, you cowards!"

"I am Jabiz Angdoo! I will butcher your children like rats and set their heads upon pikes for the vultures to devour!"

"Oh dear, that one was predictable," Azania groaned.

Next, each Jabiz retreated to the rear of his army, where he whipped up his troops with a great speech – all the usual elements of slaughter, bloodshed and undying glory – and then, they charged the walls with admittedly impressive ferocity. Absolute berserkers. There simply were not enough defenders to go around. Thundersong kicked far more ladders off the walls than he could count.

He roared and thundered himself hoarse, breaking through dangerous incursions into the lower city. The Dragons all wore spears and javelins and arrows by the dozen in their hides and still the massive armies rolled on.

One army retired. A new Jabiz announced himself:

"I am Jabiz Murderoo!"

"Did he just say, 'Murder you?' " Azania asked, lining him up with their last explosive quarrel. "Thundersong?"

"Absolutely!"

GRAABOOM!! Azania blew on her fingertips as if to cool them off. "There, we just gave him the fate his parents always wished for him."

Hurgh-hurgh-harrr! "Three hundred paces if it was an inch and you made him eat that quarrel!"

He caught Azerim staring at the Princess, probably wondering what under the suns had become of his delicate little Black Rose of the Desert. Better he learned a few details now rather than later, right?

By the ninth Jabiz, they worked out what was going on. This was a proving ground, a kind of competition run by Nahritu-N'shula, aiming to work out which Jabiz was most fervent and unstinting in his loyalties. Meantime, sharp eyes noticed activity beneath that tarpaulin on the machine. Something was brewing, but anything they shot at it crashed into an invisible barrier and failed to do any damage whatsoever.

Meantime, the defenders suffered. They had been fighting non-stop for a day and a night now. Exhaustion began to take its toll. Injuries and casualties mounted up. The defence grew thinner and thinner, while enemy fighters commanded the top of the outer battlement in dozens of locations now, almost unopposed. King N'chala kept putting off the decision to abandon the lower city. 'Not yet,' he would say. 'We'll rally again.'

Rally they did, but at what cost? Thundersong lost count of the number of comrades and friends he saw fall or have to drag themselves away from the front line.

He himself grew hoarse; Azania had to drag him away to refill on water when his flame guttered. The great Skartunese armies came on in wave after wave, with the insects proving the most tenacious and troublesome. Garan's oil sprayers ran out of fuel. The archers ran out of arrows. They drew swords or borrowed them from fallen comrades and joined the battle in their droves. Late in the afternoon, four flights of Dragons came screaming in from the other cities and from Chakkix Camp, bringing vital supplies and reinforcements. With their help, they cleared the lower city of enemies – for the first time, he saw the two Princes of T'nagru distinguish themselves in battle, fighting at the forefront of cohorts of desert warriors. Slingers took up where the archers had left off, soon having to tear up and break rubble to gain themselves enough ammunition.

As the suns fell, five armies streamed away from the walls and four new Jabiz introduced themselves. Very polite of them, until their armies charged with wild screams and battle cries. These were green-skinned men from the far south and west of Skartun, men able to climb the walls using the soft, tacky skin of their hands and feet, even though it appeared bark-like in composition.

On and on they fought, deep into the night.

Azania and he were there when Everdeep fell. He took a quarrel to the flank which penetrated his lungs and was forced to land so heavily that they heard the bones of his left hind paw crack. No mind. He had the presence of mind to swat down a couple of Skartunese warriors hiding in the shadows before he slumped to the ground.

"What – can't he walk?" Azania cried.

"Collapsed lung, I think," Thundersong spat. "I wish we had Juggernaut or Aria here. They'd know what to do."

"Would they?" she said softly. "My friend, if we don't make it –"

"Don't say it, Azania. We will turn this battle."

She squeezed his neck with her legs and arms,

communicating what he saw so clearly in her heart, which was so little compared to his, yet mighty.

Weak-kneed with emotion, he whispered back, "I feel the same way."

Suddenly, out in the desert, the great horns of war began to sound. The Skartunese withdrew from the walls and the inner city, which they had commanded almost in its entirety. Mystified, Dragon and Rider watched them go.

"That's odd," he said, scratching at a spear wound.

"I know what it'll be," Azania said. "Nahritu-N'shula. Didn't Inza … didn't she say something about the mythical power of the perfect revenge?"

"Aye," he said slowly, spreading his weary wings to bring them swooping over to the Palace building. "She believed her mother's ambition was to become the Jaraa-Jabiz, the ultimate unifier of all the Skartunese tribes – basically, the Empress of Skartun. That required this perfect revenge business, which most likely means –"

He paused to grit his fangs.

"Us," she finished for him. "Us and this city. I can't imagine a simple death will be on the cards. She has something more subtle in mind. Something vile."

The word 'vile' had barely left her lips when they heard a Dragon scream.

It was not just a cry of pain. It was a paean of horrific eloquence, a long, lingering expression of mortal agony that chilled the soul, never mind turning the stomach. Worse, it was amplified to a deafening pitch. That first cry rumbled over the city at a volume even a Thundersong would have been proud of. It trailed off into a low whimpering, before a sharp – *kerack!* – made everyone nearly jump out of their hides and skin and the cry sounded again.

"It's a Sea Dragon!" Thundersong gasped.

"Eversong?" Azania guessed.

Immediately, in his hearts, he knew she was right – and he knew who would be perpetrating the torture. There could be only one.

White rage sheeted over his vision.

Nahritu!

He winged aloft, finding himself atop the battlements before he knew where he was. Princess Azania had to scream in his mind to bring him to his senses or he would have flown straight out there and attacked in a frenzy without even being aware of what he faced. Thundersong immediately bellowed a warning, bringing the other Dragons aloft back to the wall.

The first thing he saw was Everdeep trapped inside a dome-shaped cage atop that great machine. It hummed and sparked with huge power. No Dragon would escape from that place without being frazzled, he realised. Around the cage, on the cart and even below his paws, Thundersong saw now, stood the great power coils. They shimmered not with pure white this time, but with a corrupt, Terror Clan green taint. It cast a glow far and wide, over the dunes and the waiting armies, to bathe the city in its eerie light. In addition to his captivity, however, Eversong wore another of the devices clamped around his head. Large metal probes jutted from the region of his ear canals. This head cage, made of a highly polished silver metal he did not recognise, was affixed to great cables that ran out to the stacked coils either side of his cage.

The whole arrangement struck him as some nightmarish attempt to suck the magic clean out of a Dragon or to pour corrupt energies into them.

The machine hummed at a low frequency that set his scales itching.

Farther back, he saw another three of his Sea Dragon kin wearing the head cages, fighting their handlers. It was not going well for those Dragons. They too had been affixed to thick cables that ran from the back of the machine. He squinted out there, thinking it a miracle that he still wore his spectacles. Why Sea Dragons? What could they provide that others could not?

THUNDER O DRAGON

Azania said, *I just put them on you ... there she is!*

Nahritu-N'shula approached from a half-mile back. She sat on a great throne borne by hundreds of slaves. They sweated and staggered as they carried her over the uneven sands, their backs bent beneath six great carrying poles that supported the structure. She wore robes of pure gold and a crown upon her head that had to be two feet tall. He was surprised that her neck did not snap beneath the weight. Behind her, in massive array, came the Terror Clan Dragons. They were still at least two hundred and fifty strong. Their malevolent orange eyes bobbed along like a sea of burning lanterns.

Every inch the barbaric empress with her retinue, Thundersong hissed.

It's when the show stops that we need to worry, the Princess said, making her mount catch his breath. *Aye, Dragon. This is all calculated to the finest degree. Do you trust me?*

With my life, Azania.

A great congregation stood now upon N'ginta Citadel's outer and inner battlements, even up on the Palace roof, he saw. This was King N'chala's new favourite lookout as he tried to manage battles on six fronts simultaneously. Thundersong was a little startled to see quite so many Dragons still on their feet. He had thought that the injuries and deaths had been worse than this. Even Sirensong appeared briefly, before leaving, perhaps to attend to another patient.

It took ten or fifteen minutes for Nahritu-N'shula to reach her destination, the machine. All this time, the defenders waited in silence. The usual nightly storms prowled around the dark horizon, flashing lightning constantly. He scented the air, testing the tangs of ozone and moisture. A storm was definitely on its way.

Any help would do.

At last, the Psyromantic Mage's procession wound to a halt. She stood. Without apparent amplification, her voice rolled out to the entire city.

THUNDER O DRAGON

"Greetings, citizens of N'ginta Citadel. I have fond memories of visiting your quaint hovel in recent times. Today, I wish to announce that I am about to return you all to your wretched ancestors and raze this fortress until one stone does not stand upon another – but first, a small demonstration of my undeniable power."

He snarled, *Gets right to the point, doesn't she?*

"Witness the power of my lightning thrower. Attend."

Raising her hands in a grand gesture, the Mage smiled as the machine beside her came alive. A spear-like point of silvery metal extended from among the coils at its front, aiming directly at N'ginta's main gates, massively armoured and reinforced. The low hum rose rapidly into a piercing whine, before a thick bolt of lightning spat forth.

KERACK!!

Everyone on the battlements staggered.

As the beam continued to play against the gate, Thundersong saw the metal on the inside rapidly begin to glow red, orange and then white-hot in a ring about four feet wide. A second later, the beam broke through, spraying molten metal into the street. Many of the defenders cried out in horror.

"Ah, what a nice little peep-hole," she chuckled. "With this weapon, I will cut your city into pieces like a block of that smelly Vanracian cheese – but this is only the beginning. 'Why the Dragon?' you ask." The woman gestured toward the cage. "Well, this special part of the demonstration is in your honour, Princess Azania, and that pathetic Dragon you ride – what was his name again?"

THUNDERSONG! he bellowed.

"Can't hear you," she mocked at double his volume. "The two of you have been a thorn in my flesh once too often. That stops tonight. I have here your half-brother, I believe, a Sea Dragon by the name of Eversong. Thanks to your foolishness, I have captured dozens of your kin-Dragons. I discovered Sea Dragons have certain unique properties that I have never encountered in your kind before. Shall I reveal this secret? I call upon my special assistant for the evening, Eversong. Will you help us my good Dragon?"

At her dramatic gesture, the green light intensified around his cage. Pulses of green light speared into his head. The Dragon screamed again, that terrible, unending cry – and quite abruptly, Thundersong and every Dragon in the city who could still fly, found themselves up in the air. Even Everdeep, badly injured as he was, hovered up high!

Dragons bellowed and snarled in shock.

"Aye, I know!" the Psyromantic Mage cried. "As it turns out, I won't even have to cage you all, much as I would relish the challenge. All I have to do is to cut through the protections of your minds using this special technique my daughter and I developed. You can try to resist, Thundersong, but I'm afraid that a future as my mindless slave beckons. Up, Dragons. Up – Eversong, do summon them, please?"

Her beautiful voice contrasted jarringly with his unending wail of pain and terror. Hot sparks poured down his ear canals, setting his brain alight – perhaps boiling the water within, Thundersong feared. Eversong thrashed and juddered like meat frying in a pan.

Behind and below, he sensed even the previous Dragon thralls who could not fly, climbing up onto walls and houses to peer over at the Psyromantic Mage. Chuckling in her massively amplified voice, she encouraged them on. Thundersong tried to fight it, to find Azania amidst his confusion at this most unexpected and apparently irresistible mode of attack, but he could not.

What had she done to their minds?

Raising her great staff above her head now, Nahritu-N'shula cried out in a great voice, "BEHOLD, MY REVENGE!"

Every Dragon was compelled to gaze at her.

A flash of light, so brilliant it outshone lightning itself, burst from the machine.

Thundersong clapped a paw over his eyes, but it was too late. He saw nothing. Only whiteness.

The Mage's laughter screeched over them, triumphant. "So, Thundersong and Azania and all your scaly stooges – how does it feel to be completely blind?"

CHAPTER 30

TOGETHER, WE RISE

THE MEETING THAT GATHERED in King N'chala's hall half an hour later reeked of fear and despair, Thundersong thought. Outside the gates, Nahritu-N'shula was still laughing without apparently pausing to take a breath, an impressive feat in its own right. He wondered what it was about blindness that she considered it her ultimate revenge – or was it experiencing the shock and fear of her enemies that she enjoyed most?

The chase or the kill?

Lingering over the demise of her foes?

Against a city now over sixty percent blind, including every Dragon who had dragged themselves to the battlements or taken flight, victory was more than assured. Her final word had been to promise that Azania and he would be tortured for as long as her master torturers could keep them alive – likely decades, if the Dragon thralls were anything to judge by.

Thundersong decided that he did not really want anyone teasing his intestines with red-hot irons for a few minutes, let alone years. Ouch.

Azania's hand touched his neck. *I can still see — through the sunspots. I will be our eyes.*

I appreciate it, but I fear this blindness is permanent, Azania.

It'll come back.

I'm worse than useless now, he said, clenching his paws. *How did you escape the flash?*

I was looking at the back of your neck the moment it erupted. My eyes aren't great, but I can see enough, she replied. Aloud, for all to hear, the Princess said, "We will fight."

Prince Aragu scoffed, "Oh, is that the truth, sister? You and your blind Dragon?"

"Let her speak," N'chala said. "We need some hope, anything at all —"

"Hope, brother? Don't be ridiculous," Aragu argued. "We have to open the gates and surrender. What other choice do we have?"

"Need I remind you what the Skartunese do to those they regard as cowards?" King N'chala grated. "We need to fight. It would … it would end easier that way. Who of us can still see? I cannot."

A couple of 'aye's sounded, but not many. Azerim had peripheral vision in one eye but none in the other. Between him and Azania they might have one working set of eyes, a certain Dragon thought sourly. Marvellous. The blindness angle still puzzled him. If she wanted to gloat, Nahritu-N'shula must know that she would have all the time in the world. Could it be that there was something she did not wish to be seen? A woman of her cunning and high intelligence did nothing without purpose.

Where was Inzashu-N'shula? What was she plotting?

Prince Yadaxu said, "We should hand Azania and Thundersong over to the Skartunese in exchange for peace. It's those two she wants most, right?"

"Thanks, brother!" Azania growled.

"It's a valid strategy," he protested.

Thundersong clacked his fangs toward the sound of his voice. "Brilliant. My strategy will be to bite off your idiotic head!"

"Thundersong," Azania said.

"Thundersong, wrecker of kingdoms," Yadaxu mimicked. "Can't imagine where we'd be without your help – oh, maybe alive to see the morrow?"

"Maybe, little princeling –"

"Enough foolish talk!" Everdeep snapped.

Breaking the ensuing silence, N'chala said, "The Skartunese don't believe in peace. Meantime, that woman's poking holes in our gate with her super weapon and etching her name on the walls! Also, that Dragon – that Dragon's wailing … it's driving me *insane*."

So it was. More than anything, that convinced him and Azania that their nemesis must have a different motive, something that they had not begun to suspect. Revenge? Power? Domination? Why should she be waiting – for Azania had said it best; this was all for show, but when the show stopped, that was the moment to beware. Under indescribable torture, Eversong must have given up many of their secrets. How could he not? He must have spoken of Sea Dragon powers, of the migration … which meant that all his family could be in danger! Did Nahritu-N'shula's ambitions extend to them and to their unique powers – could she want him for experimentation – what about their cleansing, light-shining oceanic magic – the restless power of the tides – the strength of song, of togetherness … his mind raced, aflame once more, yet his scattershot thoughts kept coming back to one truth.

That machine was too powerful. Nothing and no creature stood a chance against it.

As the others argued bitterly amongst themselves, berating and blaming the Dragons for their failure, his awareness swirled inward. Deliberately invoking the sense of exclusion from the world he enjoyed during his best painting episodes, Thundersong thought as he had never thought before.

Lightning lived inside Sea Dragons in the same way

that pure fire lived inside Tamarine and Isles Dragons. He had taken Jabiz Urdoo's shots before. That charge had nearly killed him. This was an order of magnitude greater, minimum. Maybe two or three.

It could not be done.

He must conclude that Inzashu-N'shula, with her special knowledge of Dragons through the bond they shared, must have helped her mother to plan and execute this masterstroke. Since she had not been present, that meant she was still elsewhere, plotting and planning. What had become of the Dragons the Skartunese had captured with their alien plants? They had not reappeared in head cages.

Nothing he could change there. Focus on the present.

What if she wanted unconditional surrender? Could Nahritu want as many Dragonkind as possible … for their magic? What had made the Terrors so fertile, so numerous? Why did they hate Sea Dragons with such a passion and seek to steal their young during the migration?

≈*Keep thinking, son,*≈ said his dam, drawing close to his left flank. He knew her by touch, by scent and the timbre of her voice.

≈*We believe in you,*≈ Everdeep rumbled.

Family.

His scales itched as if responding to the rising tide of his thoughts. Sea Dragons flew through the oceans as one great family. Imamate the Whisperer had taught him a special Sea Dragon word to describe that, which his fevered mind only remembered as a complex burble, but his throat served up as a low croak:

≈*Serendipity-of-togetherness.*≈

≈*What did you say, son?*≈ Sirensong asked.

He was many mental miles away – leagues, as Sea Dragons measured their migration – and accelerating fast. What he had been before and what he had learned though Azania stormed through his memory like a wild crashing wave, seeming to tumble him from all directions at once. A

Dragon could change his scales. He could learn to love a Human and be loved in return and that love could teach him to love himself, thereby becoming a better, nobler beast altogether. He could nurture the strangest family in Aria, Azania and Azerim, one of great differences but enormous strength.

He could find his true fires.

"Why's Thundersong glowing?" Azerim asked. "Is now the time to be happy?"

Aye! A rough chortle moved in his throat as if he gargled these new insights and prepared to spit them out.

"That's Sea Dragon magic, not simply a sign of happiness," Azania explained. "This is what Sea Dragons do when they migrate together or act in harmony –"

"HARMONY!" Thundersong boomed.

Everyone cried out at once.

"Sorry. Too loud, I know," he apologised. "Azania, help me. What was that – that thing – I don't remember …"

"What Thundersong the Elder taught us?" she supplied immediately.

"Aye, that –"

"Lesson on why the Sea Dragons chose to swim against their old nemesis, despite the inevitable losses?"

"Exactly!" he boomed. "And then, there was that … ah … useless brain! I can't ever –"

Shh, Dragon. To the others, she said, "He called it a sacred duty."

Awash with exhilaration, he spluttered, "And then he said that other thing! Tell them! I can't speak – but if I can't, you always have the words –"

"You're telling me," Azerim put in feelingly.

He heard Azania's hand smack the King's arm. "Behave. Thundersong the Elder, my Thundersong's great-grandsire, taught us a mighty truth about Solixambria and indeed, about our entire world. We all depend on one another."

Aragu snapped, "Harmony? Family? Have you gone completely suns-crazy, sister?"

She said, "He told us to never stop standing up for what is right."

"This is utter garbage," Yadaxu spluttered. "Why are we even listening to this Dragon and his little Princess?"

"Because they're the only ones who know what they're talking about," Azerim shot back.

"Clichés!" Prince Aragu spat. "Clichés and idiocy! We're about to be gutted slowly over a fire and she's gabbling on about working together as a team. Forgive me if I tend a little more to the practical side, sister, but I simply must intervene before you toss us all off a cliff yourself. See what's happened – see what you've allowed, N'chala? You let our sister run off with a Dragon and now her head's filled with all these crazy, un-Human thoughts! You should have put her in her place immediately. She's not only mad, she's this Dragon's pet to do with and think what *he* pleases. After all, it's this vixen's fault these Skartunese – *unh!*"

Blam! A body fell nearby.

By the sounds of the movement, that had been Princess Azania's strike.

"Nice right hand, sister," King N'chala said softly. "I've been waiting for that for years. Somebody drag this fool away. Meantime, I want to hear your ideas, fast – or that madwoman will have her way."

"We'll go out there together," Azania said.

"That's the last thing we should do!" Thundersong gasped. "We'll be roasted, grilled and spat out as charcoal dust!"

"Exactly," Everdeep agreed.

A tiny hand patted Thundersong's neck. "My dear Dragon, allow me to explain your idea to you. All it needs is a little straightening out of this muddle in your head and in your hearts and you'll soon see that I'm right."

"I had an actual idea?"

"Beggars belief, doesn't it?"

He rasped, "Princess, with all respect, speak or I really will be tempted to eat you this time."

"Remember, I'm the rose. My thorns will only get stuck in your tongue. Now, listen closely as I explain what my Dragon meant to say."

Twenty minutes later, the holey gates of N'ginta Citadel swung open with an unholy groan to disgorge a close-moving phalanx of white Sea Dragons and one small, dark person of the royal persuasion. Not even Azerim had been able to persuade her to remain behind.

"This is my job. Someone has to be their eyes," she had insisted. When he protested, she said, "Family sticks together, Azerim. You must stay here and rally the defence – that's your duty. This is mine."

They embraced, kissed and said a few things he might have considered unbearably soppy not too long ago. Now, he could only yearn to be able to tell Aria how much he loved her one more time. He did not care how maudlin it might sound. War, grief and loss taught a Dragon to reevaluate what was important in life; the little things, like the person seated upon his neck. He must hope against hope that this foolish idea she had unscrambled for him would not be the end of her.

He could not imagine any future without Azania.

I asked if you trust me, she said.

Scent sensing her hurt, he replied, *With my life, I said, and I meant it. Here I am literally giving you my blind faith. Don't mistake my inner fears for distrust, Princess. You are worth far more than that.*

Oh. Oh, Thundersong.

They shared a mental embrace.

Chuckling self-consciously, she said, *Inzashu did teach me something. Look.*

After a moment, he purred in surprise as a picture blurred into being in his mind. After a few seconds, as he concentrated upon it, the image stabilised. He saw the now-familiar dark, slightly rolling desert landscape outside of N'ginta Citadel and had the disconcerting experience of someone blinking – not himself – as if darkness had smudged across his vision.

By my wings, I'm seeing through your eyes? he gasped.

Spottily, she said.

Better than a kick in the fangs, he said.

True enough. As the image stabilised, looking oddly narrow, he realised that a Human's field of vision was very different to his own; much more restricted. Curious. There was the great machine, replete with power, and the mad want-to-be Empress taking her ease on her ten-foot throne, enjoying a light snack, by the looks of things. His view of the gloomy scene, irradiated by that sickly greenish light, bobbed up and down with the movement of his walking, making him slightly sick to the stomach. No mind. Left and right, he saw as the Princess' gaze responded to his mental cue, came his Sea Dragon brethren, among whom he was the smallest by a fair margin.

But always the best, he read from his Rider.

Though a Dragon stood taller for such encouragement, he was still far smaller than Everdeep, leaning heavily upon Thundersong's left shoulder as he limped along, rasping horribly because of his lung injury. Ripplesong and Farsong walked on either side of them and, beyond and behind them, he saw more muzzles, shoulders and wings of those shuffling along in formation, all touching one another as much as possible.

It must look as if they were cuddling one another for moral support.

The more pertinent fact was that not one of them could see – except for him – a number could not stand without support and two, including his half-brother Lightsong, were physically being carried along but had refused to remain behind. That would be largely due to some thunder-mouthed fellow jawing on about family, right?

Who was that idiot?

Self-talk, Dragon, his Rider said pertly.

Her gaze returned to the fore. Nahritu-N'shula stood upon the steps of her throne, goggling in clear disbelief at this rather sorry-looking, shambling posse some thirty-two Dragons strong. Aye, he would not have been too impressed himself. Furthermore, megalomaniacs were notoriously tough to impress, unless it related to their sense of their own overweening brilliance. The Mage was one such creature. She simply stared at them as they approached along a lane that quickly developed between the Skartunese troops. The Terror Clan Dragons spread out behind her – keeping a respectful distance from the terrible machine, Azania's alert mind noted. He agreed.

Thundersong scented its terrible strength, the almighty glut of power collected in that machine, and firmed his posture – as if that gesture would translate instantly into real courage. Failing that, he might pretend his hearts out.

In her vast voice, Nahritu cried, "What is this pathetic display I see crawling toward me? Do you come to grovel at my throne, begging for mercy? For I will have none of it, I tell you!"

≈*Time for a song?*≈ Everdeep rumbled.

Sirensong said, ≈*We are Sea Dragons. We are family!*≈

As his soft, impossibly deep refrain began, Thundersong sensed the joining in spirit his kin were capable of. It was the strangest sensation, like a rubbing together of souls. Nahritu warned them to stop. The Dragons marched on. She ordered the lightning rod lowered to point at them – judging by the angles, directly at his own nose, to be precise – but they did not stop. The Psyromantic Mage struck out with her mind but the combined mass of Dragons withstood the blast. Shuddering, gasping, some groaning piteously, they threw off her attack and trudged on, one paw in front of the next.

"Before I blow you all into the Lumis Ocean," Nahritu-N'shula roared, "beware, for the city behind you lies unguarded and my daughter, the mighty Inzashu-N'shula, approaches with her new army of Dragons!" Cackling loudly, she raised her staff to point up into the city. "Poor Juggernaut, poor Aria, all those poor kin of yours you left to rot beneath the sands! I have rehabilitated them and made them mine forever! Aye, Thundersong, that is your mate you abandoned, isn't it?"

Stay together! the Princess commanded. The rattled Sea Dragons drew closer. *I'll look – oh my stars, no, she's right.*

Through her eyes, Thundersong saw a strong flight of Dragons rising above the inner city. They could only have come through that watercourse they had discovered. This had been her plan all along.

My sister's riding Juggernaut, his Rider lamented. *What do we do, Thundersong? What now?*

We do exactly as we planned, he said.

The Mage called, "Ah, you poor, lost little Dragons. Are we thinking of surrendering? Don't bother. I have my weapon aimed right at you."

Then, why not shoot? Why not wipe them out for good?

"I can't wait to see you destroyed by those you love. Oh, this is almost too precious and delicious to bear." In Azania's sight, Nahritu licked her lips. "What now, Thundersong? Will you sing another sweet song to entertain my troops?"

Not a terrible idea, the Princess said. *Now, Thundersong.*

Drawing breath, he said, "All the Jabiz know the stench of your cowardice, Nahritu-N'shula, which rises around you like this green mist. By my very wings, I cannot imagine why any true Skartunese warrior would choose to follow a creature like you, one who has lied, cheated and stolen all her life and continues to do so to this day. You have no honour."

As she screeched in anger and the Skartunese soldiers jeered, he added, "You don't even have the courage to finish this attack yourself."

"I will end you!" she thundered.

"Why don't you, then? I defy you. I call you a weakling, a charlatan and a liar. I call all these men you claim to lead, slithering worms and lickers of dogs' vomit."

At last, this insult drew their full attention. The soldiers snapped instantly from jeering to furious hissing, the sound rising from them like waves striking the seashore. Many spat beside their boots; in the desert, a gesture of ultimate contempt.

Need to be quick, the Princess said.

Not quite over the edge yet … he called, "Poor little Nahritu-N'shula. Everyone sees how your daughter is stronger than you. She's been using you all along. How does it feel to be deceived by your own whelp?"

"She is mine! Inzashu – attack!"

Too late.

Thundersong roared, "Sea Dragons, attack!"

They had barely taken two steps down the road when a shattering power sizzled into his chest, dead-centre. Thundersong knew he'd die. Maybe his hearts would stop. The heat was insane, the force driving him back into the wedge of Sea Dragons, who closed about him in support. He saw nothing but white for the longest time. It took every drop of courage he possessed not to fight the tremendous surge of power, but to welcome it in, to drive it through his body and immediately out into the bodies of his kin.

Alone, he would have been carbonised on the spot.

Thirty Sea Dragons barely rode it out. He sensed two of his severely wounded kin perish almost immediately but the others at the edges of their formation rotated and unleashed the weapon's power on the armies standing around them. Why not share? Together, they absorbed the strike and were able to fire back, exactly as they had hoped might happen. For several long seconds, the desert in the Princess' vision turned a blinding white, as if a blizzard had improbably struck. The clouds above looked like wisps, the city's walls like faint outlines etched in glaring white beach sand. The lightning itself, he imagined, gazed upon this new phenomenon in a jealous rage.

Everdeep aimed at the Mage but, of course, nothing touched her.

Not so much five of the Terror Clan Dragons standing nearest her. In his future lair, charred statues would definitely be a feature, Thundersong decided. No painting needed. Just that rough texture of charcoal …

Brace! Azania yelled.

How are you still –

KERZAAAPP!! The machine howled as Nahritu forced it to new heights of operation. Mingled into that sound was the dreadful song of Eversong's suffering. Their formation wavered under the brilliant, intense assault. Three more fell away and two collapsed but their brothers and sisters lifted them up.

Everdeep roared, ≈*March!*≈

The family stepped forward as one. Lightning spat in all directions from the formation, almost like one of his fireworks. The power mowed down huge swathes of Skartunese troops as the Psyromantic Mage refused to give quarter. She expended her power without ceasing or stinting, attacking their minds as much as their bodies but, in this, the lightning attack became their friend. When one's brain sizzled unhappily in its own juices, there was not much thought of anything else. He had no idea how Azania focussed through the pain, but he could not.

≈*Keep taking it in!*≈ Sirensong bellowed. ≈*Stay strong, Thundersong!*≈

Suddenly, the attack guttered.

"More power!" Nahritu-N'shula screamed.

The machine whined and flashed as it clearly struggled to meet her demands.

To everyone's shock, Eversong, still stuck in that cage, gave a great bellow of laughter. "What's the matter with your daughter, lady?"

Nahritu-N'shula's eyes snapped up. Thundersong's vision swung over to the city, where a girl in golden robes sat aboard Juggernaut, who suddenly had very much of a different gleam in his eye. He and the Dragons in their flight ripped off their headgear with triumphal cries and expressions of disgust. Aria whipped out her swords. The girl gave a rascally wave and thumbed her nose at her mother.

This was a moment Thundersong knew he would never forget, not as long as he lived.

Beautiful.

At the same time, however, he scented for the emotions of their quarry for the first time. He scented what she would do before the woman even acted. To her, this was the greatest betrayal yet. Using her great staff, she vaulted aboard the machine. The lightning rod began to swing upward.

Roaring, *I AM THUNDERSONG!!* he pelted into a full charge, leaving the others coughing in the dust he kicked up. He spread his wings, flapping his utmost to accelerate so hard, black spots stood in front of his new vision.

No! Azania shouted in his mind. *We have to stay together; that's the plan!*

Family protects, he gasped. *Family gives all.*

For a second, her horror and despair almost paralysed him.

Then, the Princess said, *We are family.*

His crashing roar blew their foe away from the machine for a second, but only for a sliver of time, for she threw out her staff and whirled about it in mid-air, reversing direction with a flare of her golden robes. Landing on the platform beside one of the coils, she cranked a lever to bring the machine in line with that faraway dot, the daughter she had dressed just like her. Princess Inzashu would never know what hit her. Juggernaut and his lethally beautiful muse must suspect the worst but they screamed down into the attack anyways.

Dragon and Rider sprang into the air.

They were one.

Together, they were more.

This time, they did not wait for Nahritu-N'shula to fire first. Instead, his mighty white fire lanced out with a sonic explosion to impel it two hundred feet in a mere breath. Fire enveloped the Mage but her form shimmered, as an egg-shaped area of protection developed instantly around her.

The machine hummed eagerly.

Call upon the storm! Azania shrieked in his mind.

Clarity speared into his mind. *This* was what Thundersong the Elder had meant – or if he had not meant it, he must have presciently sensed some iota of the future – for he was a creature of mountains fire and oceanic storm. Both powers ran in his blood. Moreover, he had a secret of his own, a dark, decidedly Princess-shaped weapon upon his neck, tucked in tight; she was his eyes and his focus, like the point of a spear. Her strength merged with his as his scales came alive to the presence of the storm above and a different storm below. His senses traced the forms guiding the torrents of power within the machine and, in a split second, he and his Rider made a joint decision.

They pulled all that power inward.

Twin bolts of lightning smashed into him from above and below. The coils crackled and sparked as the huge draw drained them too fast. His jaw gaped in agony at the forces he was – insane idea – trying to control. As he held fast, a relatively weak jolt from the lightning rod speared into his lower belly, jangling a very painful part of his anatomy.

GRROOOAAARRGHH!! he bellowed.

A monstrous fireball, laced with lightning, burst out of his throat.

BRAABOOM!!

The front section of the machine exploded in a ball of white flame. True to form, that entirely failed to destroy the Psyromantic Mage, who shot away to land in a smoking, yet very much alive, heap in the sand. Unfortunate.

Since his behind was still the target of the storm's wrath, Thundersong spat a series of fireballs at her, again and again, peppering the dunes with fireworks. She simply would not die. Repeatedly, the staff swung up at the last split second to knock his attacks awry. Nahritu launched numerous smashing attacks of her own but, with Azania's eyesight and accuracy, he picked them off with precision each time. Green fire and smoke exploded against his white-hot fireballs. Dimly, he became aware of the force under Juggernaut rolling toward them, while Everdeep, Sirensong and his kin charged past to his right flank, heading off a Terror Clan retaliation. He had no idea how the Sea Dragons knew where the enemy were until he heard their high-speed clicking and realised that they were hunting like bats or dolphins, using echo-location.

He and Azania hunted the Mage relentlessly. Several times, she tried to slip away, only for his emotional sense to pick up her location. The flurries and exchanges became more and more desperate, the stench of smoke, gasses and fire, overwhelming. His throat was raw, his chest burned with the effects of keeping up with all the fire and lightning.

Did he even have a drop of water left in his body?

Keep going, Azania panted. *One more.*

That was when Nahritu-N'shula went for Inzashu. They had not realised that she was so close. In a split second, the mother vanished and reappeared on Juggernaut's back, holding a dagger to her daughter's throat. For an instant, they all three locked gazes, as seen through his Rider's eyes.

Then, the girl blinked and he saw her intent.

"Thundersong, no!" Inzashu screamed. He fired straight at her. The girl shrieked, "Mother!"

Thundersong wanted to blink, but it was Azania's motion made on his behalf.

A slim dagger quivered in the older woman's throat.

The talon dagger!

Nahritu-N'shula tried to make a motion to jerk it out but her hands did not appear to respond. She stared across the narrow space separating them in the air, her bloodless lips framing a question she was physically unable to ask – perhaps, 'why?'

Azania shouted, "If you knew anything about me, lady, you'd know I protect my family."

Slowly, the Mage's eyes fluttered closed. She slipped off Juggernaut's back and fell to the desert sands below. Neither the Dragon nor Inzashu made any move to stop her fall but the young girl's tears followed her in falling, too.

A small hand touched his neck. *For the record, you are definitely a Thundersong and you are beyond awesome.*

For the record, you will always be the Princess of my five hearts, he whispered back, *and you're not too shabby yourself.*

Not too shabby? Dragon! I'll bottle you for jam!

Alright, Princess Awesome, just you keep those smoking hot trousers on – except for when you're around Az –

Dragon!

Call me Dragon. It's all in the name.

CHAPTER 31

EPILOGUE

THUNDERSONG FLICKED THROUGH A sheaf of scroll leaves, trying to gather his thoughts. Very difficult with such a busy lair in the making these days, with Ariamyrielle Seaspray brooding over a clutch of no less than seven eggs – cough, splutter and *don't* choke – *I'm going to be a sire! Seven hatchlings at once!*

There went his befuddled thoughts again, wafting straight out of the window and into the suns-set, and what a glorious suns-set it was, too. He'd always adored the cliffs of Hamirythe for their incredible view across the Lumis Ocean but, most especially, because that was where he expected his family to arrive from in exactly ninety four and one-quarter hours' time, given an exacting Dragon's most exacting calculations.

Ten thousand-strong family! Sure made for busy annual reunions these days.

Gnarr! He would never get these scrolls in order.

Visitors, Aria cooed from her prime position next to the hearth in their high sea cave in the famous white cliffs. She whirled her cool, blue-green eye fires coquettishly at him.

I ... er ... blast it!

I know. Blasting things is an hourly hazard for any beast with 'Thunder' in their name, isn't it?

THUNDER O DRAGON

He stared at the sleek, gorgeous Cobalt Dragoness with fake suspicion. *Did you just kidnap my sense of humour? Give it back. Are you alright? Comfortable?*

Aria chortled appreciatively. *Go welcome them in, you fusspot.*

"Any wicked beasts at home?" Azania called from the entryway. "Lightsong dropped us off a little early –"

MWAAA-HAA-HAARRGGHH!! he roared horribly.

Squeals and shrieks – happy ones – came from the entry hall. 'Dragon!' 'It's Thundersong, come on, you silly slowpoke.' 'I am so not slow, you meanie.' 'Yay! Oldest first!' 'Mom, he elbowed me!'

In a second three boys, ranging from six to four, surrounded him, gabbling nonstop about all their news. Gracious, and he had only seen them last week. Children certainly knew how to communicate at high speed. Now, if he could harness their ridiculous excess of juvenile energy to turn this scrollish heap into a finished book at that sort of breakneck pace …

"Finally get to have a break," Azerim said, kicking off his boots in the hallway. "So, Thundersong, a little birdie tells me you have some amazing news?"

The tall King of the Vaylarn Archipelago paused in striding into the main living space of the lair to check up on his wife. Twice married – once down in the Kingdom of T'nagru and once in the Vaylarn Archipelago – made one very married indeed.

Queen Azania pushed past him with a fond hand that lingered impolitely upon the royal behind. "I barely have a bump to show off, Azerim, and may I remind you, I have flown all over Solixambria in various states of pregnancy, so please do stop worrying. Now, will you show me the long-awaited eggs – oh, Thundersong, are you *still* working on our memoirs?"

"Since *someone* left them in such terrible shape …"

He must remember to note somewhere that Inzashu no longer had green teeth. All of the Dragons had eventually regained their sight, but for some the process had taken over six months. Aye, and Everdeep had recovered from his injuries – but Eversong and his own sire, Blaze the Devastator, had never been quite the same afterward. Inzashu-N'shula's colossal hubris had left so many scars in her wake.

"Now, now, no need for grouchiness when you're about to be a father," Aria cooed. "Come in and be welcome. Congratulations yourself, Azania – now that it's official. Although, where you hide your eggs – I mean, your babies – I'll never know. With this large a clutch, I've been waddling through my sword training for months. No more of that for a while."

While the females swapped notes on the mysteries of eggs and joined the children in admiring the very fine – if he did say so himself – clutch of eggs neatly nestled beneath his mate's trim belly, Thundersong clapped Azerim on the shoulder and plucked his crown off his head.

"I'll have none of that in my roost," he chuckled.

"Jolly official duties – they couldn't resist making this an official visit to Hamirythe," he complained. "Prince Zaran, those swords are not for playing with."

His oldest boy scowled at him. "Aw, come on, Dad."

"Aria will have your head, son, and I've no desire to sweep up any fingers you chop off."

The three boys were peas in a pod in terms of facial features. Zaran, the oldest, at six, had sprouted to the point where he was talking about overtaking his mother. No chance of that for a good few years but, judging by the paws – ahem, feet – on the lad, he would take after his father. He had short, very curly hair in the desert style. Farinz was five, a quieter soul altogether, with a head of curls his father privately lamented was the envy of any girl. Ahlzarim had just turned four – Thundersong quickly reminded himself to check on certain birthday preparations – and was the quick, live wire of the family and an inveterate joker.

Got that from Uncle Thundersong.

Privately, he thought to Azania, *You should rest.*

I will. Never been so sick with littles ones in my life. The midwives have threatened me with saying I'm having a girl. I feel like I'm – oh dear, the smell of your cooking …

She dashed to the bathroom.

Azerim followed her with his eyes. "There's been a great deal of that."

"I'll check on her. I know a few things about listening to stomachs and egg sacks these days. Sirensong taught me the basics," Thundersong admitted. "She's what, four months along?"

"Five."

"No signs of –"

"No, thankfully," Azerim sighed. "I wish she'd rest more, but you know the whirlwind that is my wife … boys! Traditional wrestling match over on the Dragon cushions?"

Two seconds later, a rambunctious wrestling match developed in the corner. Aria closed her limbs and wings over her clutch, beginning to growl warningly in the back of her throat, but stopped herself with a smile. Dragoness instincts? He caressed her fondly with a trailing wingtip as he walked into the kitchen to check up on his meal. Being a celebrated chef these days – Kings and Queens invited him to cater for their banquets – one had standards to keep up. This meal was crispy Dragon-fried strips of red snapper served with a piquant pomegranate sauce on a bed of pan-seared tubers, with a range of side dishes carefully chosen to enhance the flavours and delight the curious eater.

Azania might not keep any of it down.

Hmm. Now, he had a few herbs for just such situations which Inzashu had recommended to him just the other month …

With preparations seen to and a steaming mug of

herbal tea popped into his Rider's tiny hand, he plumped the couch cushions and settled her down.

She said, *Please don't fuss. The midwives say I'm doing well this time.*

Prin – o Queen, he grinned, *I'm sorry, but having three miscarriages so close together makes a friend worry, alright? Sirensong identified the issue?*

Azania made a face. *She has me eating kelp. Imagine a child of the desert eating dried seaweed for breakfast? Still, so far it's kept – kept my baby* … Tenderly, he embraced her mind. *Thanks, Thundersong. You're the best.* Wiping her eyes, she added, *I've also never been so leaky during a pregnancy. Quite odd. What a lovely cup of tea. You do spoil me.*

Inzashu's brew.

Oho!

You need to rest more, he pressed.

Azania made a face. *Since when did you become the pushy one in this relationship, eh?*

To everyone's considerable surprise, thanks to the tea the Queen of the Vaylarn Archipelago did indeed keep her dinner down and a copious quantity of it, too – considering her inconsiderable size, Thundersong teased. Excellent work by Inzashu. Aria could not bring herself to leave her eggs, not for one second and so, as a doting and loving mate, he fed her choice titbits from his own talons. Meantime, he took a quick peek at the seven eggs, only for about the thousandth time. Perhaps he needed to check that they were indeed not a figment of his imagination. Quite an unusual clutch, by all accounts – there were three pearly white eggs, easily double the size of the others, then one aqua-blue, one tiny sky-blue one, a pink egg and one as black as onyx. No-one knew what that meant. The last recorded Black Dragon had died over a hundred years before.

He grinned as Aria growled at him, warning of too much attention. Brooding Dragonesses were nothing if not hormonal.

THUNDER O DRAGON

Clearing a few dishes, Azerim elbowed him in passing. "So, zero to seven in one leap, Thundersong? That's quite the brood you'll have."

"I know," he said. "It's been eight years waiting. After that –"

"– after that terrible injury I took to my manly parts during the battle for T'nagru," his rascally Queen put in with perfect timing. She grinned impishly at him. "We've all heard a hundred times before. You did write that bit in our story, didn't you? Please don't tell me you used the words 'epic' or 'awesome' anywhere near that part?"

He scratched his chin thoughtfully. "I believe the line goes, 'Badly injured in a part of his anatomy the Skartunese could not possibly miss on account of its being so stonkingly humungous' –"

Everyone shouted at him at once.

'Daddy, what was stonker … mungous?" Prince Farinz inquired.

"Story time?" Azerim spluttered.

Thundersong said proudly, "Well, it did take a while, but would you look at what a wonderful clutch I have sired? Seven eggs, by my wings!"

Azania put in, "Aye, because the males do all the hard work, right?"

Aria chortled merrily, "I certainly know how to make him thunder and sing; what about you, Azania?"

Her mate clouted his head inadvertently against the wall. "Ouch!"

With a King turning every colour of overheated from hot pink to crimson, story time from Uncle Thundersong, bath time in the great Dragon tub and then bedtime did indeed take place. After that, the weary parents settled back down in the living area. Azerim propped himself on a cushion a foot or so from Aria, while Azania made to take over the couch before Thundersong bade her press her stomach to his left ear canal. He listened very, very carefully indeed.

Then, he listened a bit more.

Azerim said sleepily, "Oi, Dragon. Paws off my mate."

"Remind me, how many hearts are you Humans supposed to have?" he asked archly.

"Just the one," he replied, "plus one for the babe, of course. Two."

"Huh, only two? That's odd …"

It took a few long seconds for it to sink in. Azania gave a screech that had Azerim up on his feet in a shot, shouting, "What? What did he – who – how much?"

"Just asking," he purred, showing the couple a few fangs.

"As if, you great tease," Azania protested. "Are you … teasing?"

"Want to have a listen?"

Sitting back down again, the King protested mildly, "Not fair, you two and your telepathic link. What's that – darling – now you've made her cry. Thundersong! Did you have to?"

However, Azerim looked agog, as well he might.

"How's this my fault? Sirensong did warn you about the kelp treatment, right?"

"She did," Azania whispered, dabbing ineffectually at her eyes as she chuckled, sobbed and sniffed all at once. Humans and their leaking. This time, he understood perfectly.

To him alone, she said, *How can I ever thank you enough? Thundersong, my joy … it's …*

Oozing out of your pores? he suggested. *I do smell it, you know.*

My heart's just so full, I could burst – oh. Into tears, of course. Excuse a pregnant woman who is over the moons for joy!

Me too!

"Well, come on, man – woman, Dragon, whatever!" Azerim cried. "Spit it out."

By way of reply, his Queen curled up beside him and, after holding three fingers up in front of his nose – Azerim broke down on the spot – there was a very long, rather unsociable cuddle.

Glad beyond measure that his friends felt so very much at home, Thundersong bustled about the lair, lighting lamps, checking on the three little Princes, tidying up the kitchen and verifying that all his arrangements for their stay were just right. Meantime, his five Dragon hearts throbbed with joy uncontainable. Phew. Might have to get a bigger roost if he and Aria planned to host all of these younglings in the future!

In his huge studio, he popped the lids on a few of his paints and paused to eye up a full-length portrait of Azania and Azerim he had been working on.

Another time, he told himself. *Now's time for my family.*

Back in the roost, he found that Azerim and Aria had both fallen asleep. Her wing rested over his shoulders; his hand clasped her forepaw as if they were a couple courting. Truly, they had grown so close.

His family.

Azania smiled at him. "We really do need to arrange to have Aria kidnap him, don't we? Then we could have a story about a handsome King who is kidnapped from his high tower by a fierce warrior Dragoness."

"On his next birthday, as a surprise?"

"You are a wicked Dragon," she smiled.

"Always have been. We Dragons are not cuddly little lambs, you know."

"Huh. I have to say, I prefer Dragons a million times over. Sheep are stupid as a brick, smelly and have no sense of humour. I definitely outdid myself in picking you."

"You picked me? Who kidnapped whom, may I remind you?"

"I am a devious desert girl. You had no idea what you were getting into – don't nod like that, you rascal!"

"Oops, sorry. A touch too strong on the truth, there?" Chuckling at her expression, he said, "No, I did not, but I would not swap this adventure for the moons and all the stars above, Azania. Could a dismal Dragon and a prize Princess ever have imagined such a fate? I mean, you literally made me … Thundersong. All I am. You might have a tiny right foot, but you kicked me into shape like no force this world has ever imagined."

As they spoke, he sorted through the scrolls. One question … maybe two …

Aye! He never had never written down the part where Aria and Juggernaut had escaped being gobbled down by gigantic mutant dark magic-fuelled plants – had Princess Inzashu abetted their escape? How under the heavens had she kept *that* secret from her monstrous mind-bending mother?

She said, "Without you, I'd still be a scared Princess – well, Queen of Vanrace, or something worse."

"There's worse? I highly doubt that."

"You've a question?"

"Aye, I do. I was just writing this last chapter – which I called, 'Together, we Rise' – when it struck me that I didn't know what actually happened to Nahritu-N'shula at the denouement. I also haven't written about the part where the Skartunese stuck around for two years afterward, laying siege to N'ginta Citadel and dying like fleas on the sand … that plague of green, pustulent boils they all caught was particularly nasty, do you recall?"

"Traced to the Terror Clan," she said.

"Was it? I did not –" he boomed, then lowered his voice. "Sorry. So, it was Terror Clan work?"

Azania nodded. "Sirensong's healers traced its origins. I believe you may need to record that, maybe as a codicil to the main text? I understand that the Terror Clan was not best pleased by Nahritu-N'shula's first using them, then abandoning them to die. The plague was their revenge."

He shuddered. "Horrible."

"Don't remind me. Is there more tea – and, perhaps a smidge more dinner? I'm starving."

"Eating for four? Aye. You must be feeling better."

"I always seem to do better around you, Thundersong."

He grinned at her from the open kitchen area, rubbing his paws together. Was there ever any happier Dragon beneath the suns? "I'll rustle up a little snack and that tea, coming right up."

She said, "So, her death? It was simple, really. A fraction of a second before you fired at my sister, I hurled my dagger overhand. My sister ducked. I think the fireball and the blade must have struck her at exactly the same time. She stopped the fire, but the talon dagger somehow evaded her magic and lodged in her spinal cord. That's what they said. After that, the Terror taint entered her and that was the end of that."

"Nice. I'll have to write that down more poetically than you just put it."

"Thanks. Are you ever going to finish?"

"Well, I've a few more tasteless jokes to add but I should very shortly have the text finalised – which, I might add, you have largely approved? I know, I know, authors have this urge to tweak forever but even if there are a few omissions …"

He eyed her speculatively.

"I will not be drawn," she said. "Finish it properly, Thundersong."

"Me? I am never pedantic."

"Do you think people will want to read our story? Hard to imagine," Azania said. "Plus, your jokes are just the worst. I think I should definitely be your editor. I mean, how can we record his name in history as Floric the Flatulent, for example?"

"That one stays. I will not skimp on the truth. I insist."

"Oh, a Dragon insisting, is it? Well, I think you should call the scroll, 'Call me Dragon.' Wasn't that what you always used to say? 'Call me Dragon. It's the last thing you'll ever do.' "

He chuckled, "Did I? I don't remember that."

"Clearly, there's a reason I'm your editor. Pass those

scrolls over, you wicked, beastly beast. What's this, 'Dragon Fires Rising?' You aren't seriously considering that as a title, are you? Where's my quill and ink? I just need to make a few small changes …"

"Women," he snorted.

"Dragons," she snorted in the same tone.

"Oh, fine. I'll get the main title and you can have the subtitle. I am the bigger beast, after all."

"Want to fight me over it?"

"Oh no, not in your condition," he said. "Fine. You can have the main title as long as I get to say 'Call me Dragon' several times during the story. I … I don't sound too pompous saying that, do I?"

"Not in the slightest."

Liar.

Soon, her dark head bent over the scroll, the quill scribbling away busily.

He brought a couple of lamps closer and adjusted them, then curved his neck to snoop on what she was writing. After a moment, he purred, "I mean, 'Call me Princess' just doesn't have the same ring to it, does it?"

"Of course not. Only a Dragon would declare his awesomeness on every other page and think he could get away with it."

"Azania, don't you dare delete that – Azania!"

"What? Every good story needs an ending, so I was just writing 'the end.'"

"It's only the end when the Dragon says it is. Therefore, this is the end."

"Until our next adventure …"

"Azania!"

The End

I hope you had a rollicking good time with a Princess and her Dragon on this adventure. Or is that a Dragon and his Princess? I'll let you decide … either way, thank you!

THE END

ABOUT THE AUTHOR

Marc is the bestselling author of over thirty fantasy books and is published in five languages. Born in South Africa, he lives and works in Ethiopia with his wife and 4 children, 2 dogs, a rabbit, and a variable number of marabou storks that roost on the acacia trees out back. On a good night you can also hear hyenas prowling along the back fence.

When he's not writing about Africa or dragons, Marc can be found travelling to remote locations. He thinks there's nothing better than standing on a mountaintop wondering what lies over the next horizon.

If you enjoyed this story, please consider leaving a review on Amazon.com. Every review matters and I read them all!

Where you can find me:

Email: marcsecchia@gmail.com
Twitter: @authormarc
Facebook: www.facebook.com\authormarc
Website: www.marcsecchia.com

THUNDER O DRAGON

Newsletter Signup:
www.marcsecchia.com/p/contact.html
Amazon:
www.amazon.com/Marc-Secchia/e/B00BATIZTI
Goodreads: www.goodreads.com/marcsecchia

Other Books by Marc Secchia

Santaclaws: *Discover the true origins of Santaclaws in this seasonal Dragon tale.*

When a boy brings home a Christmas miracle to his suffering family, everything will change. Wishes are different when it comes to Dragons. Wishes take wing, and come true.

A Dragon For Christmas: Santaclaws #1
A Hatchling for Springtide: Santaclaws #2
A Fledgling for Summer's Rising: Santaclaws #3
A Talon for High Summertide: : Santaclaws #4
A Fang for Autumn's Richness: Santaclaws #5
A Dragoness for Winter's Storm: : Santaclaws #6

Call me Dragon: Spill-your-coffee hilarious!

Blitz the Devastator has never done a decent day's devastating in his life. Fireless, artistic and shunned by his Dragon Clan, he struggles to pillage even the meanest village. A future full of misery and failure beckons.

This much is true until the day the burly brown Dragon successfully – imagine that – kidnaps the Princess Azania. As a black Princess of T'nagru, this spirited beauty is by definition the most unforgettable woman in the seventeen realms. Knights errant, men-at-arms and sundry Princes expire at her feet in drivelling worship.

Unfortunately, they all want his scaly head on a platter shortly thereafter. Goes with the territory.

To Blitz's consternation, the royal nuisance refuses to behave herself and be a typical pampered Princess. With

humour, unconventional flair and the odd stomp of her diminutive slipper, she sets out to reform her Dragon.
One question remains. Who will save the Dragon from the Princess?

Call me Dragon: Dragon Fires Rising 1
I am Dragon: Dragon Fires Rising 2
Thunder o Dragon: Dragon Fires Rising 3

Shapeshifter Dragons: *Be the Dragon*
Five allied series of bestselling Dragon adventures. Prepare to wing away to a unique world of mighty Dragons and volcanic Islands above the deadly Cloudlands!

In chronological order (Island-World timeline):

Dragonfriend series: *Dragonfriend, Dragonlove, Dragonsoul,* and *Dragonstar*
Scrolls of Fire series: *The Dragon Librarian, The Dragon Loremaster*
Shapeshifter Dragon Legends series: *The Pygmy Dragon* and *The Onyx Dragon*
Shapeshifter Dragons series: *Aranya, Shadow Dragon, Song of the Storm Dragon* and *Beautiful Fury*
Standalone Books: *Dragon Thief, Chaos Shifter, Tytiana*

Set in the same world as the Shapeshifter Dragons series, join Zhialeiana in an oceanic adventure with Whales and Sea-Dragons:

IsleSong series: *The Girl who Sang with Whales, The Girl who Loved the Whales,* and *The Girl who Swam with Whales,* after which this series connects with *Shapeshifter Dragons* above in *Dragons of Sea and Sky,* coming soon.

Contemporary: *The power of dignity and redemption.*
Experience the restoration of Mister Drainpipe in this novel that explores the issues of homelessness and mental illness in the African context.

THUNDER O DRAGON

Mister Drainpipe

The Equinox Cycle *Amputee, survivor, heroine!*
Trapped in a car wreck, crushed by a train. In seconds, Zaranna's world is torn apart and she must start life anew, as a survivor. A double amputee. Yet why does this promising equestrienne remember a flash of sulphurous fire, and a crimson paw hurling her mother's car onto the train tracks? Why does a tide of beguiling butterflies flood her increasingly chaotic dreams?

As Zaranna Inglewood adjusts to life minus legs, plus gorgeous Alex, the paramedic who cut her body from the wreckage, she learns the terror of being hunted. Relentless and inimical, the enemy lures her to a world where dreams shape reality. Equinox. A world of equinoctial storms; lashed by titanic forces of magic, dominated by the Pegasi and their centuries-old enmity with Human Wizards and the Dragons. This is a world where a girl can Dream her destiny. Where her soul can fly, or be chained forever.

She is Zaranna, the Horse Dreamer. Survivor. Fighter. A girl who doesn't need legs to kick an evil fate in the teeth. All she needs is courage–the courage to Dream.

The Horse Dreamer (Equinox Cycle Book 1)

Whisper Series: *Enter the Canyon Maze*
Conjured by the sadistic Warlock Sanfuri, Whisper faces a stark choice. Run with his message, or die. Bound by the Warlock's unbreakable magical imperative, Whisper is forced to navigate the tortuous pathways of a labyrinth twenty miles deep, riven by Dragon-infested canyons and scorched by sunstrike. An extraordinary legend is born.
Whisper Alive

The Shioni of Sheba series: *Discover ancient Ethiopia!* A unique African historical fantasy adventures for middle grades readers set among the myths and legends of ancient Ethiopia.

Shioni of Sheba #1: The Enchanted Castle
Shioni of Sheba #2: The King's Horse
Shioni of Sheba #3: The Mad Giant
Shioni of Sheba #4: The Sacred Lake
Shioni of Sheba #5: The Fiuri Realms
Shioni of Sheba Box Set – Books 1-5
Shioni of Sheba #6: The Night of the Hyenas
Shioni of Sheba #7: The Secret of the Simiens
Shioni of Sheba #8: Storm over Sheba

Epic fantasy:
Epic length tales of unique worlds and powers.

Feynard
The Legend of El Shashi

Foreign language editions

Italian – *Dragonfriend, Il Drago Pigmeo, Aranya*
Spanish – *Dragonfriend, Aranya, Tytiana, The Pygmy Dragon, The Dragon Librarian*
Portuguese – *Aranya, Shadow Dragon, The Pygmy Dragon, The Onyx Dragon*
Chinese – *The Pygmy Dragon, Aranya*

Printed in Great Britain
by Amazon